Deadly Vows

Haley Stuart

PAGE PUBLISHING, INC.
Conneaut Lake, PA

First originally published by Page Publishing 2018

ISBN 978-1-64298-466-8 (pbk)
ISBN 978-1-64298-465-1 (digital)

Printed in the United States of America

Warning

Before you read this story, note that this is a very dark romance. There will be strong sexual content, violence, language, etc. If *any* of these things offend you, you need to stop reading now. This is not a traditional love story; this is very vulgar and disturbing in some areas. I don't want to hear any complaints later on. I have warned you. You have been warned.

Chapter 1

Elise

Sixteen. The age of becoming a woman. While normal girls were getting licenses, wearing makeup for the first time, and going on dates, when I turned sixteen, it was the day my life ended. I'll never forget the feeling I had once my father called me into his office.

I had a big smile on my face. It was my birthday, after all. And my father never wanted me for anything. So when his right-hand man told me he wanted to see me, I believed it was because he wanted to tell me "Happy birthday!" and finally acknowledge me.

When I was four, my mother died. She was taken by a rival Mob and killed to teach my father a lesson, which left him with a daughter as his successor. He had never been kind to me, and I believed it was because he wanted a son. But I was what he got. And he made sure to keep me busy. No sooner had I been able to walk than he made me take violin lessons, never caring when my hands would blister from all the practicing. He would step into the room, listen, and leave. He never complimented me, told me he was proud, or gave me any indication that he was pleased with me. Or something I did.

I'm practically running to my father's office, excitement bubbling up deep inside me. I stand in front of the massive white doors and knock lightly. My father's deep voice come from the other side of the door, giving me permission to enter.

He doesn't look up upon my entrance, which makes my heart sink a little, but I won't let it deter my mood. I take a seat in one of the chairs, waiting for him to speak. To tell me he loves me. Or

"Happy birthday." Or that he is proud of me. Something to indicate that he cares. After a few minutes pass, he finally looks up. But he isn't smiling. My smile falls off my face immediately. My heart sinking into my stomach at his expression

"As you know, relations with the North Mob have been all but nonexistent, and with the expansion of the Russians in our territory, we must band together to form a more stronger union. The head capo's son has been single for a while now and is getting older. It's time for him to marry."

I feel my stomach begin to clench in dread as I anticipate where this conversation is going.

"Since you are the only child I have been able to legitimately conceive to this point, it is only fitting that you be the first bride for Luca Pasquino."

My heart literally drops out of my chest, and It takes everything in me not to fall out of my seat right there. I'm no a fool. Luca is widely feared. Widely misunderstood. And if it weren't frowned upon in the world I was born in, I would call him clinically insane.

Luca was made a man at the tender age of ten. The normal age for our boys to become a man is at least sixteen to eighteen. Luca is what any man in our world wants their son to be. He is malicious, cruel, and emotions are the last thing on his mind. When Luca was seventeen, he had killed a man with his bare hands. And I don't mean he strangled him; no, he beat the man to a literal pulp, smashing his head in.

My father is rambling on about how this is a great opportunity for my family, for our clan, but I'm not listening. I feel as though my body has become numb. My father has never been a loving man. Hell, I have barely seen him in the sixteen years I have been alive. But this is something I can't believe he's doing to me. He is marrying me off to someone who is barely human.

I look up as silence envelopes the room, realizing my father is waiting for me to speak. I know the last thing he wants was for me is to express my disappointment. The last time that happened, it didn't end well for me.

"I ... uh, when are we to be wed, Father?"

"When you are eighteen."

I nod, keeping my eyes downcast.

"This will be good for us, Elise. All of us."

I could almost laugh at his blatant disregard for my feelings. This is beneficial for him and his cronies, yes, but it has nothing to do with me.

I stand from my seat in my father's office, ready to leave.

"If that is all, Father, may I be excused?"

His bright green eyes fall on me, and I can tell he's deciding whether or not to reprimand me for my blatant dislike of the situation. Finally, he nods to me, and I hurriedly leave the room. I finally reach my bedroom and flop onto my bed, tears flowing at an endless pace down my face. My life is over.

* * * * *

"It may not be all that bad. You never know, you might even grow to love this man. I know he won't be able to resist loving you." My cousin Arianna is smiling at me, trying to reassure me about the marriage.

She doesn't understand, though. She's one of the lucky ones. Her husband loves her. And he treats her like a queen. I came to her house to get some comfort, but what I'm receiving instead is far from it. I haven't yet told her who I've been chosen to marry.

"You don't understand, Ari. I have been given to Luca Pasquino." My voice catches on his name. I'm still not used to the thought of being married to that monster.

Ari's whole demeanor changes. Her face grows pale, and she tenses. She's no fool either. She knows as well as the rest of the women raised in our world what I have been subjected to.

Luca is cruel unconditionally. Gender doesn't matter to him. I remember, when I was eleven, I attended a gathering with my father, and Luca was there. I'll never forget the shriek of the unfortunate female as he snapped her wrist for touching him. Everyone stared in shock as he stalked from the room, not batting a lash at what he had done.

Ari is still rubbing my back, helping to distract me from the terrible direction of my thoughts.

"Well, you still have two more years until you are actually married to him. In that time, you are your own person." She tries offering me a comforting smile, but I see through it immediately.

We both know what my life will be like the moment I say "I do."

Chapter 2

Elise

Two Years Later

I sit in the practice room of my home, playing to my heart's content. The only thing that can drag me from this hell I call life and give me some peace is playing my violin. It gives me sanctuary. Two years have come and gone so quickly, and my wedding is less than a week away.

I still have yet to meet the man I am soon to marry. The only indication that he is aware of our union is the fact that he sends me gifts on birthdays and holidays and flowers before recitals. Other than that, he keeps his distance, never once looking to meet me. It makes me feel uneasy but a little happy at the same time. With him not being around, I can pretend I am destined for something greater.

The engagement party is being held this weekend at our home. I'm nervous, because this means I have to meet him now. No more hiding and pretending. I have secretly been hoping that he won't be so bad. I've also been wishing that his reputation would be different, but it has only gotten worse. Scarily worse. He doesn't just kill because he has to; he does for sport. And the fact that they believe he needs a wife is beyond me. But apparently, his father is close to retirement, so Luca will be next in line to be the head of the Northern Mafia, which means a wife and children aren't a bad idea, since a target will constantly be on his back.

I flip the page of my music sheet and let the melody I'm playing pour out of my fingers. I close my eyes, already having memorized the music, and play and play, feeling the rhythm and beat deep within me. I can't help the smile that creeps onto my face. When I play, I lose myself. I'm in a place that no one can ever find me and ruin. It's my sanctuary.

I finally finish the melody and set my violin on my lap. I'm startled by the clapping that echoes throughout the room from one person. I turn in my chair, and my heart drops. Luca Pasquino is standing in the doorway of the room. He is dressed in dark jeans and a dark dress shirt. I can't help but stare as I take in his features. The pictures don't do him justice. *Handsome* is an understatement. He is perfection at its finest.

His hair is a pitch-black that is a mass of big curls that fall gently on his face, barely touching his forehead. His face is cleanly shaven, and his jaw is sharply accentuated. His lips are nice and full, put on his face to commit all kinds of sinful acts. And those eyes. Bright steel-gray eyes watch me with such an intensity that I almost squirm. This is the man that will be my husband. And he is looking my body up and down without shame.

"So you are my future bride. You are quite the beauty."

I can feel the blush creeping up my neck, and I look away. At five foot four, I am no model. I am tiny. My hair is black and falls to my waist, and my eyes are a bright brown on my face.

"Thank you."

How could this be the man that all those stories came from? If I hadn't seen his true nature before, I wouldn't have believed it. Part of me is shaking in fear from him being so close. He reaches out, and I close my eyes in fear, but then I open them when nothing happens. He only pushes some stray hair back behind my ears.

"So you play." His voice sounds so hypnotic and entrancing it takes me a moment to realize he is speaking to me.

"Uh, yes." My voice comes out a small whisper.

He walks closer to me and touches my instrument lightly. "That was a beautiful melody you were playing."

I look up, and he is smiling at me. His teeth are perfectly straight and brilliantly white.

"Thank you," I say.

"What is it called?"

I gesture to the music sheet. "Yamagasumi."

He laughs, and the sound is earth-shattering. "Sounds very interesting. Do you have a recital coming up?"

"Yes. My last one, you know, before …" I trail off awkwardly, not knowing what to say or how to finish my sentence. We both know why. We know why he is even here in the first place.

He lightly traces the top of my hand in a small circular pattern.

"Boss, it's time." A man I have never seen before is standing in the doorway of the room.

Luca stands, and his whole demeanor changes. He is the cold and cruel man I have read so much about. He walks to the door and turns right before he reaches it, winking at me. Then he exits the room quietly.

* * * * *

Later that night, my maid, Sylvia, fixes me up for the engagement party. I'm wearing a nice sundress that shows off my legs and clings to my body. My heart is hammering against my chest, and I am terrified. I met my soon-to-be husband earlier today, and he has done nothing but intimidate me. Now I will have to go the whole night by his side and pretend that I am excited about marrying this monster when I am anything but.

I walk into the corridor that leads out to the party area. I am to wait for Luca there. I turn to look into the mirror that hangs delicately on the wall. My hair is curled into large rings that fall gently down my back, and the way my makeup is done makes me look innocent. But if you look into my eyes, you can see the blatant fear that resides there.

"Hello."

I jump and squeal in shock. Luca is standing right behind me with an unreadable expression on his face. I squirm under his glare, unable to move. His eyes roam shamelessly up and down my body, lingering on my most intimate parts. I can't help but look away, a heavy blush crawling its way up my neck.

He seems to enjoy my unease. He walks closer to me and pulls the hem of my dress so that I am forced to be flushed against him. A small noise escapes my lips, and I try to pull away, but he has a firm grip on my dress.

His hands roam around my body, and he holds me against himself. Even in my heels, I still come right below his chin. He leans close into my ear, and I can feel his smile as he speaks.

"I can't wait to bury myself in between your sweet little thighs."

I gasp, and he finally lets go of me as I stumble back, blushing furiously. The door to the party area opens, and my father and a man I have never seen before step into the hallway.

"Are you two ready?" he asks.

Luca only puts his elbow out for me to hold on to as we make our way into the crowd.

The night drags on for what seems like forever. People come up to us, expressing their congratulations. So many people. And smiles. I don't even remember any of their names. But Luca seems to have everything under control. He never falters as he expresses his thanks and "excitement." I just stand next to him and smile when the moment arises that I need to.

I feel numb. Everyone here knows this union is arranged. They know we feel nothing for each other. They know we are only getting married because our fathers have arranged for it. Yet they smile for us and tell us how happy they are and how we will make a fine couple. I could almost laugh. Everyone here knows who Luca Pasquino is. They aren't fools. Yet they act as though they are best friends with him. But we all know it is fear. Fear of the monster that lurks beneath that cruel exterior.

Luca finally lets me go when I see my cousin Arianna standing in the corner. She smiles at me once she sees me and embraces me in a big hug, squeezing me tight.

"You look beautiful, Elise."

She is smiling at me, but I can see the sadness that lurks deep in her eyes. She knows what this is signifying. My eyes travel across the room to the man I am soon to marry. He is watching me with such an intensity that I feel as though I am going to explode from his gaze. Someone is speaking to him, but he keeps his eyes trained on me.

I finally look back at Arianna, who is watching me worriedly. I take a deep breath.

"I'm scared, Ari," I say to her, finally revealing my inner thoughts. And I am scared. He barely knows me, and he is already expressing his sexual fantasies with me. The way he watches me and speaks to me, it is as if I am a possession of his.

"You're going to be fine, Elise. Once all the marriage hype is over, he'll be submerged into his work and may not even have the time to see you."

Deep down I'm hoping what she said is true. Deep down I hope he will find someone else to focus his attention on. Because deep down I know what type of man he is. He owns things. And I am no different than another possession.

Ari's eyes suddenly grow wide, and I feel his dark presence behind me.

"Excuse me, but may I steal my fiancée back?"

I turn to see Luca's face in an intoxicating smile. Ari frantically nods and hurriedly runs away, fear obvious in her demeanor. I can almost scream for her abandoning me so readily.

I feel a tug on my arm and realize that Luca is dragging me to the dance floor. He pulls me closer against his body, and we begin spinning across the floor. Luca's movements are graceful and calculated.

"What are you thinking about?" he asks me suddenly.

I look at his face and gasp. His intense gray eyes are focused on me. "I ... I'm just nervous. This is all so sudden."

I hear his deep laugh. "That is to be expected. Tell me, Elise, are you on birth control?" He asks the question so nonchalantly, as if he were asking my opinion on whether or not it will rain tomorrow.

My cheeks heat up in embarrassment. He doesn't waste any time, does he?

"No." My voice comes out in a hushed whisper.

"We'll have to remedy that. Don't worry, I'll have something sent for you to take."

I don't respond to him, but he doesn't notice or seem to care. He leans down and begins nuzzling my neck.

"I want to have you to myself for a while."

I still don't respond. I look around the room to see everyone's faces smiling at us with happy and dreamy expressions. The fools.

"So the violin?" His voice breaks through my thoughts, and I look at him, confused. "Why did you decide to play?" he clarifies.

I only shrug. "It was my father's choice, not mine."

"As was our union, I presume."

I don't respond.

We dance until the music finally ends, and I walk out of his grasp immediately, not daring to look back.

The rest of the night goes by in a blur, with people smiling and congratulating us. My cheeks are beginning to hurt from all the smiling I have to do. Luca never falters. Never lets on his true feelings. He is a hard book that I can't read. I don't know if he is just being polite to make me feel better or if he doesn't want this union as much as I don't want it.

I eventually end up alone and look around to see where Luca has disappeared to, but I don't see his face anywhere. I see my cousin Ari standing with her husband in the corner. She is laughing, and he is holding her close to him. It is obvious they are in love. The way he holds her and smiles at her. The way he watches her when she is doing something else.

My heart is aching. I honestly just wish that somewhere deep down, Luca will find it in himself to love me and be kind to me.

I walk toward the table that has champagne bottles on it and hear a sound that makes me want to run come from the hall near the table. I follow the sound of the whimper and almost gasp at what I see before me.

There is a blonde. A really pretty blonde. She is up against the wall, and Luca's hand is around her throat. The look on his face is terrifying.

"You can't just do this to me—"

Her voice is violently cut off. "I told you, we are finished. How dare you show up here to my engagement party!" His voice is coming out like venom, making me want to shiver in fear.

The girl doesn't make any more sounds barely, and there are tears falling down her face. Luca finally drops her, and she begins to gasp for air, coughing and moaning. Luca reaches in his behind him and pulls out a gun, aiming it at the top of her head. Hate is clear in his expression. My legs move before I do.

"Oh my god, Luca, stop!" I shout from the shadows.

He turns his emotionless expression my way, and when he sees it is me, he only gets angrier. If that is even possible. My steps immediately falter.

"Elise, go back to the party." His voice comes out like a whip, with no room for argument.

But I can't just leave a poor, defenseless girl here on her own to die.

"I ..." I start but cut myself off as soon as Luca glares at me. I don't know what to do. I can't let him kill her. "Luca, please don't kill her."

He glares at me for a long moment before sighing and putting his gun away. He stands over her body and squats, yanking her hair up so she can stare at him.

"Do not come near me or my wife again, or I will kill you." He lets go of her and walks from the hallway, snatching me as he walks away.

I try to keep up and open my mouth to say something, but he cuts me off by slamming me against the nearest wall.

"Interfere with my affairs ever again, and I will break your pretty little jaw. Understood?" His gray eyes pierce through me like a knife. I can only nod slightly, with a newfound fear for the man I am going to marry.

We walk out of the hallway as if nothing happened, and people are looking at us, smiling and continuing their excitement. Luca smiles back as if he hadn't just threatened me, and almost killed a woman. The question flashes in my brain like a warning bell, *What will the rest of my life with this man be like?*

Chapter 3

Elise

I stare at myself in the mirror. The dress is beautiful, the veil is beautiful, the ring is beautiful, and even the woman looking back at me is beautiful. But on the inside, I am screaming. This isn't what I want. This isn't what I've dreamed about all these years.

Luca's steel-gray eyes haunt me the whole night in my dreams. I'm terrified. If there is anything beyond terrified, that would be what I'm feeling right now. My wedding day is here. And it is with a man I barely know and greatly fear. I sit in the chair, looking down at my palms. I can feel the tears begin to swarm my vision, but I can't let them fall. If my makeup is smeared, they will know, and I will be insulting my father, Luca and his family, and everyone else from my family that has faith in me. This is their salvation. My marriage to Luca is a gold seal of my family's protection. They are practically untouchable. But not me. After today, I will belong to him.

A knock sounds on the door, which is opened to reveal my father. He steps in and stands in the doorway for a moment, looking at me in my wedding dress. After a few seconds of deafening silence, he finally speaks.

"You look beautiful, Elise."

My breath catches in my throat. My father has finally said something meaningful to me after all these years. And it is the day he is giving me away to a monster. All these years, all I've ever wanted from my father is some kind of recognition, some kind of proof that he loves me. And he tells me this the day he is to give me away, against my will. I can feel the hate boiling up inside me.

The music in the church sounds, and that is my signal. With my father by my side, I walk down the aisle, to be handed over to Luca Pasquino for the rest of my life.

Luca stands at the end of the trail, eyeing me, his gaze traveling up and down my body. He looks devastatingly handsome in his dark tux, with his hair pushed back. If I weren't so scared, I may have been able to appreciate my husband's good looks.

Once I reach the end of the aisle, my father lets go of me and Luca takes my hands in his. The preacher begins his sermon, but I can barely focus on what he is saying. Luca is staring me down, his gaze never faltering as I repeat my vows.

It is almost as if he's looking at me like I'm his new, shiny toy and he can't wait to play. I can see the danger lurking behind his eyes. I can feel it radiating off his every pore.

The church falls silent as the priest looks at me for my answer. All eyes within the church fall on me. I stare at Luca and can see the smirk pulling at his face.

"I do."

As soon as the words are spoken, Luca leans in and puts his lips against mine. They are soft and warm as he reaches around me to cup the back of my head, claiming me in front of everyone we know.

* * * * *

The reception is grand. There are fountains of chocolate, decorations, desserts—the whole building looks like something out of a movie or magazine. Luca hasn't said two words to me since we've arrived. We are both seated at the table for the bridal party. Everyone dances and rejoices at the expense of my misery.

The night drags on, and so do the events. The mic calls for Luca and me to make our way over to the massive cake that is on the table before us. We each have a slice in our hands, ready to feed each other. I slowly press my piece of cake into Luca's mouth, and he does the same. As soon as the sweet pastry touches my tongue, I feel a warm mouth envelop my fingers. I gasp in shock as he focus on me, with those steel eyes.

He looks as though he wants to devour me, not just the cake he has in his mouth. I feel numb, and terrified, the events of the night scaring me to the point of nothing.

The reception is finally over—meaning, the thing I have been dreading all night is drawing even nearer. I feel a tug on my hand and look up to see Luca watching me.

"Are you ready?"

Even though it's a question, it comes out as a statement. He is watching me with such intensity that I can only nod in response. A smile stretches across his face.

"Good." He stands from the table, and hand in hand, we exit the reception hall.

The guests follow us out the door, smiles on their faces, congratulating us. Our closest family stands at the end of the line. Luca's father pulls him aside and begins speaking to him. My father stands by me and begins talking.

"I'm proud of you, Elise. You have made me and your family proud," he says.

I can tell it is all rehearsed, though. There is no smile from him or anything. All these years, all I've wanted from him is recognition. Love. Affection. The bare minimum. And he shows me something the day he gives me away. *Bastard.* Now all I want from him is nothing. I finally realize my hatred for this man.

I don't say anything to him. I walk right past him, intent on seeing Ari, when he jerks my arm, pulling me back towards him roughly. I let out a small whimper from the tight hold he has on me.

"What the hell are you thinking disrespecting me like that, you ungrateful little b—"

My father is cut off as Luca comes to my side. He immediately lets go of my arm. Luca steps closer to my father, his tone dripping with malice.

"As of four hours ago, Elise is now mine. *My* wife. You have no control over her anymore. So if you handle my wife roughly again, I will sever your fingers. And I don't give a damn who you are."

I feel a chill rush up my spine at Luca's words, and when I look at his face, I grow even more fearful. He is dead serious. My father's face grows red, but he knows better than to mess with the future capo of the North Mob.

I give him one last look before making my way over to Ari. She envelops me in a tight hug.

"I'm so scared, Ari," I whisper in her ear.

She stiffens as she takes my words in. "You'll be fine. Everything will work out." She smiles at me. "I love you, Elise. Don't forget to come and visit me. It may not be all bad."

I feel a tug on my arm and look up. Luca is pulling me toward the waiting car. *And my future.*

The ride to the airport takes about twenty minutes, and the plane ride is about two hours. The whole time, I am a bundle of nerves. He lets me change out of my wedding dress within the privacy of the jet cabin. Once we reach Luca's home, he will be ready to consummate this wedding. And I am scared to death. He doesn't seem nervous in the least. Of course he doesn't—he has done this sort of thing several times. I know because I have seen the magazines and news articles that follow his luxurious lifestyle around, and the women he shows up with on his arm are too beautiful to not be messed with.

"Once we land, the drive is about forty-five minutes to your new home." His voice pulls me out of my thoughts, and I look up to see him watching me with that intense expression. I nod, too nervous to speak. His face seems to transform into an expression of amusement.

"Are you scared, Elise?"

I can only shake my head. I hear his deep laugh.

"Don't be nervous. I'll make your first time pleasurable." He smiles at me. "I've been thinking all night about being buried deep inside you." He continues to make me nervous.

The plane finally lands, and he ushers me into the car, riding to my new home. Just as he has said, the ride takes forty-five minutes. We pull up to the front gate, and it opens. Lights shine up the driveway to reveal my new home. It is huge. Actually, *huge* is an understatement. It is massive. It is a wonder how one person can live here by himself.

"I'll be sure to show you around your new home sometime this week." Luca's voice pulls me out of my admiration, and I nod, not knowing what to say.

We exit the car, and Luca opens the front door, revealing a beautiful foyer with a dark staircase. The lights are off everywhere else in the house, so I can't see the rest of the home, but if it looks anything like this, then it is beautiful.

Luca leads me up the stairs by the hand. He stops in front of the third door down and pushes it open to reveal a beautiful bedroom. A massive four-poster bed sits in the center of the room, dark colors illuminating it. The room is obviously occupied by a male. And expensive.

"Do you like it?" I jump from Luca's voice. I turn to see him watching me with that same intensity he's had since we've met.

I nod. "Can I use the shower?"

He is silent for a moment before finally relenting. He pours himself a glass of some gold liquid and takes a seat, loosening his tie. He points me to the door on the far side of the room, and I hurry over, stepping into the luxurious bathroom. I turn on the hot spray after making sure the door is closed. I step to the mirror and look at myself.

My hair is falling out of its tight curls, making it look wavy, and my eyes are wide and filled with fear. Luca probably feeds off it. I step under the hot spray, letting it soothe my nerves, and I close my eyes.

I am married. To Luca Pasquino. I am now Elise Pasquino. Married to the most notorious son of the North Mob's capo. I don't know what to do. What to think. I just know that when I am near him, danger radiates off him in waves. It is terrifying. He is intimidating. And with good reason. Especially after what happened with him and that woman at the engagement party.

He was ready to kill her without a second thought. I'm willing to bet everything she was one of his exes. A poor, brokenhearted girl who is now facing the repercussions of this arrangement. Judging from his actions, Luca isn't going to seek pleasure elsewhere especially since he was about to kill her for showing up to his engagement party.

I let out a loud scream when I suddenly I feel hands around my breasts. I am roughly jerked back into a solid wall of muscle as I try to move away from the impostor. Except it isn't an impostor. It is Luca. I hadn't even heard him enter the shower.

"Shhhhhh. Don't move." His voice comes out very low. My heart begins to beat erratically in my chest. I can feel his hot erection pressed against my lower back.

"Just relax, baby. I'll take care of you," he whispers in my ear.

His hands begin to move, caressing my breasts. He grabs my nipples in between his fingers and begins rolling them. I gasp, as pleasure I have never felt before emits from my body, shooting straight to my core, the steam from the shower making me even more aroused by the second. Luca's hands drift down, running over my stomach and in between my thighs.

"So smooth," his voice rumbles in my ear. It mixes with the shower. It is customary for everything to be waxed before your wedding so you can please your man.

I can feel myself getting drenched between my legs as he plays in between my folds. There is something building, but I don't know what. My cousin Ari told me what to expect when having sex. She said it will hurt the first time, and if your man cares about you like Angelo cares for her, he will give you an orgasm. She told me it was currently an amazing feeling you can only get with your husband. Maybe this is what she is talking about. This pressure that is building deep within my core.

I feel myself about to go over when Luca removes his hand, whipping me around and claiming my mouth with his. He pushes me into the wall, the hot spray of the shower drenching both of our bodies. His kiss now is much more passionate than the one we shared when we sealed our union. This is more of a possession, like he is claiming every fiber of me. He thrusts his hand back between my legs, causing me to gasp.

Upon my gasp, he shoves his tongue in my mouth, stroking every corner. He nips and bites at my bottom lip as he thrusts a finger inside of me. I cry out from the uncomfortable feeling it causes, but I don't have time to register it because he is back at my mouth. His free hand rubs my breast. He inserts another finger, and the pleasure is too much. I can feel myself reaching for something.

"That's it, Elise. Come for me, baby," he growls against my mouth. As soon as he speaks the words, my body explodes in pleasure. I can feel myself clenching around his fingers. Involuntary moans erupt from my mouth. Luca keeps on kissing me as I moan into his mouth. He is swallowing every bit of it.

As my waves subside, I can feel Luca remove his fingers. I feel weak, my body like putty. Luca lays me down on the shower floor, the ground beneath me warm from the hot water. The water is still cascading over us from above, creating a blanket of warmth. I feel his warm lips press against my collarbone, and he latches onto my neck, sucking hard. I gasp aloud from the pleasure, already feeling myself get aroused once more.

"You are so beautiful," I hear Luca murmur.

I open my eyes, and the sight before me takes my breath away. Luca is straddled over me, the water from above causing his hair to fall into his face and drip from the sides. Droplets are falling off his lean body, running down his face and falling from his lips. He is staring at me with those unusually gray eyes. The black within is dilated. He runs his hand up my stomach and leans in to suckle my breast. I moan.

I can feel him positioning himself at my entrance.

"It makes me so hard knowing you've never been with anyone but me. All mine. My woman. My wife. My Elise. *Mine*." I take in his words with little clarity, the sexual tension clouding my perception.

Before I can take in another breath, he pushes himself slowly into me. I can feel myself spasming around his thick length as he makes himself at home within my body. He does one quick thrust, and I gasp from the pain. I whimper aloud. The pain is unbearable. I can feel my stomach churning.

"You're so tight," I hear him groan.

I can't breathe from the pain. He begins to suck on my neck and reaches a hand between us, massaging my clit. Slowly pleasure begins to replace the pain. Luca must have sensed the change, because he begins thrusting inside of me. He reaches around me and cups the back of my head, pulling me to meet his lips. He thrusts his tongue in my mouth.

The pleasure becomes too much. I begin moaning out loud, crying out from the pleasure. Luca's thrusts become more urgent; he pushes into me harder and harder with each thrust, making me slide up against the shower floor. He threads his fingers through my hair and forces my head aside, latching on to my throat and sucking. Hard. That is all it takes for me to rocket over the edge and scream as my orgasm rips through me, a thousand times more intense with Luca's large length pounding in and out of me.

I can feel him getting larger inside of me, if that were even possible. He groans in my ear, uttering a string of curse words in Italian before I feel him release inside of me. We lie like that under the spray of the shower—for how long, I don't know. Luca rolls me over so that I am lying on my side, facing him, and pulls out of me. He leans in and kisses me long and hard.

* * * * *

I am lying in bed, staring at the ceiling. Luca is lying beside me, with his arms wrapped possessively around my waist. After he finished, he bathed me, dried me off, and laid me to bed with him. Like a loving person. But I am not stupid. There is no telling how long this will last. I am married. I am no longer Elise Trovoli, but Elise Pasquino. I am no longer a virgin, thanks to my new husband.

His deep breathing is soothing. I want to cry, but I have no tears left. I want to scream, but I have no courage to. My life has been planned out for me to a tee. I've never had a say. And now that I have fulfilled my usefulness to my father, I am forced to fulfill Luca's every desire. Because that is what a good wife does. That is what the women in this world have been trained to do.

I am scared. I am terrified. I don't know what the future holds for me. I don't know what Luca will do to me. I don't know how his personality will reflect on me. All I know is that I have to do whatever it takes to survive.

Chapter 4

Elise

One Week Later

I awake to the sound of the shower running. There's sunlight streaming in through the window, and the warmth of it is hitting my face. I roll over in the large bed and slowly open my eyes, beginning to stretch. My motions cause the blanket to fall revealing my naked form. I wince, a little sore from the night. Luca woke me up three times throughout the night to have sex, each time pleasurable for both of us. But my body has yet to accommodate itself to him.

The door to the bathroom suddenly opens, and Luca walks out in a pair of boxer briefs and no shirt on. He is rubbing a towel through his thick dark locks. It is crazy to me how he can look so normal doing something so simple. I can't help but admire his physique. His whole left arm is covered in tattoos. There are also some on his right arm, but it isn't completely covered. It looks really good on him.

As soon as he emerges, his eyes makes a beeline for the bed, finding me. He drops the towel on the floor and runs his fingers through his hair, pushing it out of his face.

"Good morning," I whisper.

I can feel the heat climbing up my neck as I remember those same hands on my body.

Luca doesn't speak as he steps closer and closer to the bed. I subconsciously pull the blanket over my naked body. Luca's eyes follow the movement, and he visibly darkens. He makes his way slowly over to the bed and crawls up the sheets to me. He hovers right in front of me, his body still warm from the shower. He reaches a hand behind my head and threads his fingers through my hair, pulling me in, and roughly begins to kiss me. My mind is spinning, and I feel out of breath by the time he pulls away.

His eyes are digging deep into my soul. After a moment of silence, he traces a finger around my now-exposed nipple. I hadn't even realized in that heated kiss that the blanket fell off me. I shiver from the feeling.

"Don't ever hide from me what's mine. Understand?" He isn't looking into my eyes, but at my naked breasts, as he speaks. I nod hurriedly as my heartbeat skyrockets from the frigid tone of his voice.

After a moment, Luca finally gets up from the bed and heads into the closet.

We are both sitting at breakfast, eating in silence. It is a nice two-seater table that sits by the window in one of the dining rooms. Luca insists that we eat here and not in the grand dining room until I get accommodated to my new home.

Luca is watching me closely as he speaks. As if he is looking at each of my reactions. Reading me. I look out the window and let out a long breath. The yard is beautiful. It is more like a few football fields. I honestly wonder how Luca has lived here all this time by himself. Why not in a nice little bachelor pad? But Luca seems like the type of guy that likes to show what he has.

The first week of my arrival here has been blissful and peaceful. I actually, for a moment, believed that Luca would love me and come to care for me. But he instantly changed, and now everything he does terrifies me. He watches me like I am his possession. He never lets me go anywhere without him, unless, of course, it is around the estate. Lately, his fuse is getting shorter and shorter, so I try to keep quiet and stay out of his way.

Eventually, he leaves the dining room, giving me a kiss on the cheek.

As soon as he leaves, I make my way over to the practice room Luca renovated just for me. I close the door behind me, pick up my instrument, and begin to play. I close my eyes and let the sanctuary I have built for myself build its wall around me. I spend the whole day in the practice room, only leaving for a quick lunch and coming back, not caring that my fingers are on fire. This helps me escape this marriage I have been handed into.

"Mrs. Pasquino." The voice pulls me from my inner peace, and I open my eyes to see one of Luca's men standing in the doorway. He is watching me with cold eyes and an emotionless expression. "Your husband has requested your presence."

I only nod and set my violin down, ready to make my way to his office, but the man stops me.

"He asked that you bring your violin."

I am a little unsure how to react to that, but I reach for my instrument and make my way to the office. Once I am at the massive door, I push it open gently to see Luca standing over a man. Two of his men are on either side of the man, holding his arms and keeping him in a kneeling position. My steps falter, as I fear what I have just walked into. At the sound of my entrance, Luca looks up, and my heart flutters.

The crazed look in his eye is the same look he held seconds before he pulled his gun on that girl that came to our engagement party.

"Ah, my beautiful wife has decided to grace us with her presence!" His loud voice echoes off the walls, and I don't know what to do. Luca makes his way over to me, grabbing my elbow and pulling me over toward the man on the floor. He puts the tip of his shoe on the man's chin and tilts his head up to look at us.

"Now, don't be rude, James. Say hello to my wife."

The man looks at us with a hate-filled gaze.

What the hell is Luca doing? Before I can think, Luca's leg shoots out, slamming into the side of the man's head, sending him sprawling on the floor. Luca leaves my side and grabs him by the shirt, thrusting him against the wall.

"Now, listen to me, you little shit. Don't you dare disrespect my wife!" He pulls a hand back and punches the man across the face. I look away when he shows no signs of stopping, the sound of his fists colliding with the man's head making me sick. "Now, fucking say hello!" I hear Luca's voice grit out.

There is heavy breathing, and I look up, having to stifle a gasp. The man's face looks awful. His once-hateful gaze meets mine. "Hello," he quietly says out loud. Luca finally drops him and walks over to me. He grabs a fistful of my hair, pulling me in for a long, hard kiss.

"She is a beauty, isn't she?" he says, holding my jaw in between his thumb and forefinger. After a moment of silence, Luca turns to the man on the floor. "Isn't she?" he repeats.

The man nods, and Luca is satisfied.

He leads me over to a chair in the corner and begins to speak. "Not only is she a beauty, she is talented as well. She plays the violin, very beautifully, I might add. Unlike anything I have ever heard." He sits me down in the corner, and my heart rate spikes because I don't know where the hell he is going with this.

He pulls out a gun, aiming for the man. I can't help the squeak that emits from my throat. All eyes turn on me, and I shrink back in fear as Luca's intense gaze glares me down in warning. I bite my cheek, remembering what he said the last time I interfered. *Interfere in my affairs again, and I will break your pretty little jaw.* I shudder from the memory.

Luca begins talking again, pulling me from my unwanted thoughts.

"I want you to hear how beautiful my wife plays, James. So we're going to play a little game. Elise is going to play a beautiful melody for us, and you're going to guess what the song is. You get three tries. Only three." He cocks the gun and looks my way, excitement sparking in his eyes.

"Okay, Elise, play me a tune. Any tune your heart desires." Luca looks at me with a sadistic smile on his face.

My fingers are shaking, and my heart is pounding out of my ears. He is going to kill this man in front of me. He says if the man guesses any tune I play, he'll go free. And I don't want him to die because of a complicated melody I'm playing. So I do what any Good Samaritan would do. I play "Mary Had a Little Lamb."

I have done some dumb things in my lifetime, but this is up there at the top. The look that Luca gives me is enough to make anyone shit their pants and run screaming into the night. But I am his docile, obedient wife. So I have nowhere to go. A shot rings out, and I scream. The man hunches over in pain, but he isn't dead. Before I can celebrate my good fortune, Luca comes storming at me with the intent to kill. He hauls me out of the chair and drags me out of the room.

Once we reach our bedroom, he turns on me, slapping me across the face. Hard. Stars dot my vision, and I fall to the ground from the force of his attack. Before I can even register the pain, I feel a rough tug on my scalp. Luca is literally lifting me off the ground by the hair. I scream in agony, and a hand closes around my throat, pushing me into the wall. My vision is blurry from tears streaming out of my eyes, and I take in Luca's rage-filled face. He looks ready to kill. My chest is burning from the lack of oxygen, and I reach up, clawing at his hand. He slaps my hands away with his free hand each time. I am a fool to think I can even fight back. This man has been raised to kill. My attacks are probably nothing to him.

Just when I think he is going to kill me, he lets go of my throat and I collapse onto the ground, coughing and gulping in as much air as possible. He crouches in front of me and places a finger underneath my chin, lifting my face to meet his. Tears are still falling out of my eyes like a waterfall.

"I am Luca Pasquino, future capo of the North." His grip on my chin tightens, and I wince in pain. But I know better than to pull away. "When I give orders, I expect them to be followed. If you *ever* try to outwit me again, you will not like the consequences, Elise. I swear to you, you won't."

I shiver from his cold tone.

Luca is a man not to be messed with, and I am the fool that has provoked him. I nod, choking on a sob.

Luca's hand travels down from my chin to my breast. He cups it, giving a light squeeze, and I cringe from the contact.

"I have to admit though, Elise, no one has ever thought to cross me the way you did tonight." His hand reaches underneath my shirt, caressing my bare skin. "I was shocked, to say the least, when I heard that silly song coming from you." His hand travels down, and he lifts the dress that I am wearing, yanking my underwear down. My heart slams into my chest, and fear shoots down my spine. *Oh, please don't let him do this to me. Especially after he just beat the hell out of me.*

I feel his hand thread through my hair as he grabs a fistful, jerking my head back at an uncomfortable angle. I can almost feel the smile he gives me as he leans into my ear.

"We'll have to focus on your playing from now on." He tosses my underwear aside and begins sucking on my neck.

"Luca, p-p-please don't," I whisper in fear. My voice comes out tiny and shaky. Filled with fear.

Luca suddenly stops, letting go of me and stepping back. A dangerous glint in his eyes.

"Fine. I will figure out a suitable punishment for you later."

He seems to be thinking for a moment before looking down at me.

"I'm going to kill that man. Slowly and painfully. And when he thinks I'm going to let him have the mercy of death, I'm going to play him a little song that was his ruin. And begin his torture all over again."

My eyes widen at his words, and I tremble from his choice of words.

"No, please, Luca! I'm sorry, it won't happen again. Just don't—ah!"

I am immediately cut off. Luca is holding my jaw in his hand; an uncomfortable pressure where the hinges meet is making me cry out in pain.

"What did I tell you would happen to your jaw if you interfered, Elise?" His voice is deadpan, making me want to piss myself right here. The pressure on my jaw increases. I cry out in agony.

"I really don't want to see it, as I need your mouth for … other tasks." A small smile worms its way onto his face. "So I'll let it slide this time."

He finally lets go and immediately grabs my face, trying to deter the pain. He was about to break my jaw. He really was going to do it. I hear rustling, and he leans down, giving me a kiss on top of my head.

"I'll see you after I finish with my business." He walks to the door, pausing to look at me before speaking again. "I really wish he had heard one of your beautiful melodies before I ended his life." He smiles at me, a wicked, cruel smile. "Too bad. Good night, my wife," he says, closing the door behind him.

I sit there on the ground, not knowing what to do. Too shocked and afraid to move. This is Luca Pasquino. The *real* Luca Pasquino. The man that is known for killing someone with his bare hands. This is the man that is feared by all. A sob rips from my throat as fear for my future enters my mind. Luca is crazy. A man not stopped by emotion or a conscience. A man ruled by pure desire. How can someone so cruel exist? I hold myself. I am petrified. I have no idea what my future with this sadist holds. And that is enough to scare anyone.

Chapter 5

Elise

I sit in the mirror, brushing my hair out, like I do every morning. It is a routine I put in place for myself to keep some form of normalcy in my life. Twenty-three strokes on each side. I look at my left cheek and see a bruise forming from Luca's attack the previous day. I touch it lightly and cringe from the pain. Luca didn't disturb me when he came to bed last night, and he hasn't said anything to me yet this morning. I look in the mirror and gasp when I see him standing right behind me, watching me with an unreadable expression on his face. It scares me. I have no idea what he is thinking or what he has in store for me.

I step out of the room, heading for the kitchen. Somehow, I remember how to get there. I step into the five-star-restaurant-looking kitchen to see a whole slew of people working hard to make some kind of course. Upon my entrance, they all freeze and stare before immediately bowing their heads in respect.

"Oh, please don't stop on my account," I say, hoping they'll go back to their work.

They slowly go back to what they have been doing. I slowly step around them, focusing on what each of them is doing. This is the first time I have seen any people outside of Luca's men since I've been here. They all look at me like they are terrified, trying to avoid all eye contact with me.

A woman that looks a little older than me walks up to me with her head down. "Are you lost, ma'am?" She is still avoiding eye contact with me.

"Uh, no, I was just passing through."

She still refuses to look at me. "Well, the kitchen is no place for you to be, ma'am," she says, kind of rudely.

I am a little taken aback.

"And tell me, why is the kitchen no place for her to be?"

I stiffen as I feel Luca's presence behind me. The whole kitchen falls silent, all eyes on Luca and me. He puts a possessive arm around my waist, staring the woman down.

"I … I … I'm sorry, sir, it was not my place," she responds. Her skin is burning red, and she looks about ready to pass out.

"You're right, it's not your place. This is my home, as it is my wife's home. She can be anywhere she pleases. And if you have a problem with that …" He laughs a little and walks away, tracing his finger over a knife lying harmlessly on the counter. "Well, I know you better not have a problem with that." His face is completely serious as he makes eye contact with the girl.

She nods vigorously. "Yes, sir. I'm sorry."

Luca doesn't wait for a response; he grabs me by the arm, leading me out of the room. We stop in the entryway, and Luca turns to speak to me.

"The day's barely even started, and you're already causing trouble." There is a light smirk playing on his face. I look away, slightly embarrassed. His mood has improved, making me feel a slight bit lighter.

"Go get your violin and meet me in my office."

As soon as the words leave his lips, my heart drops in my stomach. I hope he isn't going to make me play again with some man's life in my hands.

Luca reaches out and lightly traces my bruising cheek. His gray eyes meet mine head-on, piercing me to the center. "Do as you're told."

I can only nod with wide eyes; he has me captivated within his trance.

I hurry to the practice room and grab my instrument out of its case, making my way to Luca's office immediately after. I push open the heavy door, expecting to see a poor man about to face death, but am shocked to see Luca sitting behind his desk with his head down, his focus on some papers in front of him.

He looks up once I step into the room. He motions for me to sit in the chair in the corner of the room. I make my way slowly to the spot, feeling uncomfortable under Luca's watchful gaze. Once I am seated, he decides to finally speak.

"Play me a song," he says simply. I am a little shocked, to say the least. I wasn't expecting that.

"Uh … what song?" I ask, a little shaken.

"Any song. Preferably the one I heard when I came to your home." He puts his head back down and begins to look over the papers that sit at his desk, waiting for a tune.

I close my eyes and let the music pour from my fingers. For how long I sit there, I don't know. But once the music finally ceases, I look up to see Luca seated back in his chair, watching me with that intense expression.

"You couldn't play any of those songs the other night when I asked you?" he asks. There isn't a hint of emotion on his face, so I don't know if he is still in a good mood or if something bad is about to happen. He gets up from his desk, standing at his full, intimidating height as he walks over to me, leaning in my personal space.

"I asked you a question." His voice is deadpan, making me fearful. I honestly don't know how to respond to him.

"I … uh …" I trail off as the door to his office is opened, and my heart drops.

The girl from the engagement party steps in. She looks a hot mess, if I'm being honest. Her hair is kind of tangled, and her eyes look wild. She looks at the spot behind Luca's desk, and when she sees he is not there, her eyes find him across the room standing by me. Immediately, rage bloom behind her blue irises as she makes her way across the room.

Instead of stopping at Luca like I expect her to do, she lunges straight for me, shoving me out of the chair I am in. Hard. I fall to the ground with a hard thud, crying out from the shock and the pain. I look up to see Luca holding her back from me. What the hell did I do? This insane chick just barges into the room, trying to fight me.

Luca shoves her back into the desk, annoyance plastered across his face.

"Jessica! What the fuck are you doing?" he shouts at her, but she is still trying to get to me.

I stand up slowly and try to back out of the office. This is clearly a matter for him and his lady friend, whom he just tried to kill a few weeks ago for showing up to our engagement party.

"Stay right there!" Luca's voice whips across the room, rooting me to the spot. I am too scared to move, but I don't want to be in there if he decides to play another game with her life on the line.

"You fucking whore! He doesn't love you! He loves me! He's mine! He'll always be with me! He'll never love you!" The girl—Luca said her name is Jessica—is screaming all kinds of obscenities at me. I honestly don't care what she says to me; I just wish she would shut up, because Luca's face is getting darker by the second. The last time he saw her, he told her if he ever saw her again, he'd kill her. And currently, he is seeing her again.

"I will fucking slice your—"

She is cut off in the middle of her shouting as Luca spins her and grabs her by the neck, slamming her face-first into the desk. We both shout unexpectedly. Luca's face is filled with an emotion I have yet to see.

"What. Did. I. Tell. You." As he whispers each word, it seems as if his grip on her neck is getting tighter and tighter. And if it were even possible, her face is getting pushed deeper into the desk. I stand helplessly in my spot in the corner, terrified that Luca is about to kill this girl in front of me. I know that if he tries, I will step in, but I also know that I like my jaw attached.

Luca looks at me and turns the girl's sobbing neck so that she is facing me. Luca has his whole body pressed into her, keeping her immobile on the desk.

"Do you see that stunning creature standing in the corner of this room? She is not a whore. She is my wife. And you threatening to kill her does not sit well with me." His hand loosens from around her neck, and he threads it through her tangled locks. He grabs ahold tightly, lifting her head and smashing it back into the desk. I scream aloud from the sudden movement.

"I told you that if I ever saw you again, I would kill you. So why is it that you have shown up, uninvited, to my home?" His voice is coming out cold and calculated. Her whimpers echo throughout the room.

"This used to be our home," she whispers as tears run down her face.

I feel my heart breaking for this girl.

Luca's grip tightens on her hair, and he lifts her neck at an uncomfortable angle, whispering in her ear, "This was never *our* home. This has always been *my* home. You just happened to be a warm body that I liked to use from time to time." Luca speaks the words with amusement. Like he has never cared for this girl. And I don't think he ever did. Suddenly, he looks up to where I am standing.

"Elise, do you know who this is?" My stomach drops in dread. He is pulling me into his sick, twisted game, and I want very badly to not be a part of it. "Elise!"

I jump as Luca shouts my name, pulling me from my thoughts and doubts. I shake my head quickly. He laughs to himself, keeping his tight grip on the girl. Her eyes are squeezed shut, and tears are falling heavily down her face.

"This is Jessica. I met her a few years back and kept her around because I wanted to. Of course, she wasn't the only woman I was with, and by no means was I loyal to her. But along the way, she seemed to think we were more than what we are."

I nod, as if I were listening. I don't know why he is telling me these things, but I don't like it at all.

He pushes her head back down on the desk and lays his head against hers.

"She seems to think I would leave my lovely, pure, innocent wife to be with her. She believes I will go behind your back and fuck her still." He laughs out loud. A genuine laugh, showing that he is amused by the girl's thoughts.

In my head, I am screaming. I honestly wish that is what he would do so that he would leave me alone. But now he is laying all my hopes to rest.

That's when it hits me. That's why he is telling me all this. He's letting me know that he will never turn his attention from me. He must have read the look on my face, because a sadistic smile creeps on his face.

"Oh, baby, don't you know better than that? Once something is mine, it's only mine. You are my wife, so no one else matters. I take my vows very seriously." His smile falls from his face, and he looks at the whimpering blonde. His hand snakes around to the front of her throat, and he begins to squeeze. Her movements become frantic as she tries to fight his steel grip around her throat.

He looks up, making eye contact with me, as if daring me to say anything. I take a step toward her, a hand outstretched. I open my mouth to speak, but I don't get a word out. Luca moves so quickly I don't have time to register it. He picks up the blonde and smashes her face into the desk, causing us both to scream in agony. She falls to the floor, clutching her nose. There is a fountain of blood running down her face.

Luca walks over to me and grabs a fistful of my hair, forcing me to my knees. He reaches around him and pulls a gun out. A sound escapes my lips, and he looks at me, quickly silencing anything that may have come from me.

"Jessica." He is looking behind me, but I can't see anything because he is making me face him on my knees. "You are nothing to me. I would never let *anyone* touch me except for my wife. I will never fuck anyone except for my wife. And I sure as hell will not tolerate you coming into *our* home disturbing my peace. Me and you? We are finished," he says as he raises his gun, aiming it at the poor girl. He pulls back the hammer with his thumb, making the sickening *click* pop into place.

In the next moments, I don't think. As soon as I hear the noise, I jerk my hand up, reaching for the gun. As Luca pulls the trigger, my hand connects with his, pushing the gun and causing him to fire a shot into the ceiling. Jessica screams, and her eyes are shut. Luca still has the gun aimed toward the ceiling. He looks at me, and I have to swallow the bile threatening to come up.

His eyes are filled with pure rage. I interfered. I interfered with what he was doing. I've stopped him from killing her. I have gone against him. I did it without thinking of the consequences, but I know if I had sat here and let her get shot, I wouldn't have been able to live with myself.

Before I can utter an apology, a blinding pain shoots across the side of my face. I fall to the floor with a cry of pain.

Luca steps over my body, walking over to Jessica. I look at him through blurry vision and can see him holding her up by the throat.

"Marco!" Luca shouts, and a man comes in the room, waiting for orders.

"Take this bitch off my property. If she ever shows her face around here again, shoot her on fucking sight." Marco nods and drags Jessica out of the room.

Luca isn't done with me, though; he walks over to me and straddles my body on the floor, slapping me across the same cheek. I cry out. I open my mouth.

"Please don't." The words come out shaky and desperate, but Luca obviously doesn't give a damn. He wraps his hands around my throat and squeezes.

"How many *motherfucking* times must I tell you *not* to interfere?"

I can't respond due to his hand around my throat, but he isn't thinking. He picks me up and slams my head back into the floor. Black dots cross my vision, and my head begins throbbing in pain. But I can only moan. He finally gets up and threads his fingers through my hair, letting go of my throat. I don't even have the time to breathe in, as he takes me by the hair, dragging me from his office. I scream from the pain of being dragged by my hair, the sounds echoing off the walls of this massive house.

Once we reach the stairs, he picks me up and throws me over his shoulder as if I weigh nothing. I am kicking and screaming and begging because I am terrified he is about to take me and break my jaw.

Once we reach our bedroom, he throws me on the bed. As soon as I get my bearings, I hop out of the bed and make a run for the door but am tackled to the floor as soon as I try. Luca puts his foot on my chest, holding me down.

"Don't fucking move." He heads into the bathroom.

I sit up and sit there silently sobbing. I just had to interfere. Why did he have to drag me into this? No, why did that girl have to show up here? If she had just stayed put, I wouldn't have tried to save her life even after she tried to fight me.

Luca reemerges from the bathroom with a pair of scissors in his hands, and my eyes go wide. What the fuck is he about to do to me?

"I'm going to give you a choice. You can sit still, or you can try to run. But if you try to run from me again, you will not like what happens." He yanks me off the ground and sits me on the bed. He threads his fingers through my hair, not saying a word.

"You have a pattern, Elise. Every morning after you shower, you brush your hair. Twenty-three times on the left and twenty-three strokes on the right. Before you go to bed, you brush your hair. Fifteen strokes on the left and fifteen strokes on the right." He raises the scissors, and my brain finally connects the dots.

I stiffen. "Oh god, no, Luca, please—"

I am cut off as he roughly squeezes my mouth together.

"Don't you dare beg! It'll only make things worse." He goes back to stroking my hair.

"I love your hair. So thick and soft and long. But you know who else loves it? You do."

He brings the scissors up, and I don't hesitate. I jump up from the bed and sprint to the door, only to be jerked back by the very thing I am trying to save. Luca throws me down on the ground, and my face collides with the carpet. I can feel as he pulls on my strands, a giant wad, and as the echo of the scissors cutting sounds, the grip he has on my hair loosens. Strands fall on each side of my face. Long strands.

I open my mouth and scream. And scream. And scream. I am cut off as Luca reaches around me and clasps his hand around my mouth. He lifts my dress and yanks my underwear down. I am screaming and mumbling underneath his hand, but he doesn't listen in the slightest. He enters me roughly, and the tears continue to flow out of my eyes.

As he lies on top of me, fucking me roughly, his hand snakes down around my throat.

"The next time you decide to get into things that aren't your business, I suggest you think about the consequences," he groans out roughly into my ears.

I look at the piles of hair that has fallen around me and cry harder.

He continues to violate me, not caring what he has just done is completely awful. Not caring he is punishing me for saving a life. The innocent life of a woman whose heart *he* has broken.

He is evil. He is sick. And he is heartless. And I belong to him. *Till death do us part.*

Chapter 6

Elise

I sit in front of the mirror for what feels like the hundredth time this week. I keep running my fingers through my hair. My now-short hair. My long, waist-length tresses are now gone. I had never cut my hair my whole life. It is something I take care of, and the only time scissors are put to it is when my ends need to be cut. But Luca has taken that away from me in the span of sixty seconds.

We had to go to a salon to get it styled because he cut it so unevenly. So now my hair barely falls past my chin. I have to stifle a sob as I move my hand through the now-empty air that my hair used to be in.

"No matter how many times you pull on it, it won't grow back." Luca's voice pulls me from my brooding, and I look in the corner of the mirror to see him standing with his arms crossed, watching me. He always has that unreadable expression on his face. But now I know it is because he is watching me, calculating my moves, my likes and dislikes. Anything he can possibly use against me.

We have barely been married a month, and he has already gone overboard with me. I guess I just wish I could have been lucky like Ari. But fairy tales are for fools. This is the real world.

Luca is still watching me in the mirror, and I shove from the mirror, walking past him without a word. I haven't spoken to him since he chopped my hair off. He never even apologized. Not that I would accept it, but still, I want some kind of indication that he has some form of emotions.

"You can't keep ignoring me forever, Elise." Luca's voice carries behind me, and I still ignore him. At least now he can't jerk me by the hair.

"Elise!" His voice comes out from behind me, and I stop in my tracks.

I know that tone. That tone means he is fed up. And when he is fed up, it is time for me to swallow my pride. He's proven to me that he is capable of anything.

I turn slowly around, facing him.

"You're acting like a child, Elise. It's just hair, it will grow back. You're still beautiful without it." He pouts in annoyance. So the great and powerful Luca Pasquino doesn't like to be ignored, huh?

"I'm a child?" My voice comes out before I think about what I am going to say, the rage from the moment he did this to me bubbling to the surface after I've worked so hard to lock it away. "You … you cut my hair! *My hair!* You cut it off! Because I was saving a woman's life that *you* destroyed!"

I am beginning to grow hysterical, but Luca doesn't get angry like I expect him to; he only raises an eyebrow at me.

"She *loved* you! She was heartbroken, and you wanted to kill her for that, and because I stepped in to save her life, you took my hair from me? But I'm the child?" The tears are coming on hot now, and Luca is still looking at me with a curious expression plastered across his face.

He pushes himself off the door and walks closer to me. "You are making me so hot right now with all your yelling. I've never seen you feisty before." He smirks at me.

I can't help myself. I bring my hand up, ready to slap him right across his smug face, but he catches my hand before I can, the grin falling off his face. If I hadn't witnessed it earlier, I'd swear it was never even there.

"You wanna play rough, baby? I can play rough." He squeezes my wrist in warning, and I cringe from the pain. I try to jerk my hand from his grasp, but he holds on tightly. "Don't try that ever again. I don't want to have to break your wrist because you can't control your temper." He speaks it so calmly and relaxed I actually feel my stomach churn in fear. I can't believe to this day my father gave me away so easily to *this* man to marry, of all people.

"Get dressed. We have some business to attend to." He walks out of the room, leaving me there with my thoughts.

* * * * *

I am sitting in the passenger seat of Luca's sleek white Zenvo ST1. I have never been much of a car person. My father never allowed me to drive or get my permit, anyways. But this car is nice. And Luca drives it like a bat out of hell.

The ride is silent, and I look out the window, watching the scenery go by. I feel a hand on my thigh and look over to see Luca's hand.

"You know, when my father told me I had to marry, I was pissed off." His eyes are still focused on the road as he speaks to me. "I actually told him to go fuck himself." He laughs aloud to himself. "But eventually, I had to accept it. If we were to be stronger and be able to protect ourselves in a wider range, a union needed to be existent. And who better to marry than the son and daughter of capos of the North and South?" He smiles, more to himself than to anyone else.

"When I saw you in that practice room, I thought, damn, this is going to be my wife. I never had this feeling about a woman. This possession. This need. This constant want. But you are just walking perfection to me. Pure and innocent when I met you. Never been anyone's but mine. And that makes me a thousand times happier when I wake up each morning."

I swear the temperature in the car drops as soon as Luca begins his next sentence.

"If anyone or anything ever jeopardizes this marriage, I will end them. Without a question or a second thought. You are mine. And no one else's. I will kill anyone who gets in the way of that. Of me and you."

He doesn't say anything more. I don't know if he expects me to say anything; I don't even know if that is his version of a love ballad. But I do know that Luca is serious about this whole marriage thing.

The rest of the drive takes about twenty minutes, and we end up in some kind of warehouse. Luca pulls up and shuts the car off. There are men standing outside. I assume they are Luca's men. Why would he bring me here if he's taking care of business? I'm assuming, from the location chosen, this isn't a deal of any sort, but a get-rid-of-someone type of thing.

Luca steps out of the car, but I stay in, hoping he doesn't expect me to come along.

Luca walks around to my side of the car and opens the door.

"Come on, Elise. Be a good girl and remember what I said."

I nod slowly. My hands are already shaking, and I don't even know what is about to happen next. He leads me into the warehouse, and his men are following behind us silently. The door to the warehouse is opened, and a loud groan sounds from the door being opened. It is dark in here; the only source of light coming the garage door that is opened for our entrance. Once it is shut, the whole place is enveloped by darkness again.

"Luca." My frightened voice quickly comes out, and I reach for his arm in the dark, clinging to him for dear life. I can hear his deep chuckle as his hand closes over mine, and he begins to rub mine comfortingly back and forth. Even though I have no idea where I am or what is about to happen, Luca's warm body and small gesture make me feel slightly safer. But I don't know the hell he is about to drag me through.

The lights to the warehouse come on suddenly, and we are standing in a massive room with cemented floors and walls, a fluorescent light hanging from the ceiling. Luca slides my hand off his arm and clasps my hand in his, the warmth from his body seeping into mine. He walks me over to a chair and sits me down in it, kneeling in front of me so that we are eye level. He doesn't speak, only stares at me with those intense gray irises. He puts both his hands on either sides of my shoulders and smooths them down until he has my hands by my side.

Click.

My heart stops. He cuffed me. He cuffed me to the chair. A ghost of a smile plays across his lips as he watches my distress. I yank on the cuffs, but they won't break.

"Luca, what is th—"

I am cut off. "Shhhhhh, baby." He leans in and kisses me lightly on the cheek. He stands and walks away from me. One of his men walks over to him and hands him a large gun.

"Bring him in," he says in an authoritative voice.

Another door sounds, and in walks my father. He looks beaten up and bloodied. There are handcuffs around his wrists as well.

A gasp escapes from me. "Papa?" My tiny voice carries across the chamber, and my father looks up at me, no emotion entering his eyes. But when his eyes land on Luca, all the rage he can muster appears. The men are rough with him as they shove him to his knees. They take a massive metal rod and push it into the ground so that his handcuffs are straddling the pole. He can't move on his knees, and Luca is standing over him like a judge about to pass judgment.

"Luca, what's going on?" My voice comes out in a frantic whimper. Luca only ignores me and continues to stand over my father. Hate fills his deep-gray depths. He finally turns to me. No emotion plays out on his face, and I feel like I am about to piss my pants.

"Why did your father tell you we were to be married, Elise?"

I look at my father, but he refuses to make eye contact with me.

"H-he said to make relations stronger." I am barely able to muster the words out.

Luca bursts out in laughter, shaking me to the core. "That was what he told us too. That he wanted to have good relations with the strongest of the bunch. So imagine our surprise …"

Luca makes his way toward me slowly and pulls a knife out of his back holster. I am shaking in fear as he gets closer, and I begin to squirm in my seat, trying to break free, the clang of the metal making a loud sound that echoes off the walls.

"When we found out that you are a ploy in his plan to take us down and be the head himself of both the North and the South Mob."

Luca is sitting directly in front of me now. I can't speak. I can't breathe. A ploy? That is what I am?

Luca's hand shoots out and holds firmly against my shoulder, keeping me still. He makes eye contact with me.

"One … two … three …"

I scream in agony as his sharp knife collides with the soft skin of the underside of my forearm. I try to wriggle away but can't from his firm grip. He twists the blade deeper in my skin. All the while this is going on, I am screaming and crying and begging for him to stop, and that is when I realize something. I am the only one begging for him to stop. My father hasn't spoken a word.

Finally, Luca pulls his knife from my skin, and with it comes a small green chip. Luca holds it between his fingers.

"Well, I'll be damned." He tosses it on the ground and smashes it with his foot.

"Your father planned to use that tracker to find your location… *Our* location. He was going to have my father killed and use it to find me and kill me so there would be no successor. And I'm willing to bet he was going to use you also to die with me. Wouldn't want a widow standing in the way of power, would we?" Luca is looking at my father as he speaks.

I look at him through my tear-streaked vision.

"That's not true," I whimper.

Luca turns to look at me. Actually look. And for a split second, I see pity flash behind his eyes. But then it is gone. Just like that. If I weren't watching, I would have missed it.

"Tell her," Luca says to my father.

My father looks up, making eye contact with Luca, and spits at him. That is the perfect opening for Luca, because he kicks my father repeatedly in the face.

"Luca! Luca! Stop! Please!" I am shouting at him like my father should have been shouting for me when Luca was digging a blade into my arm.

Luca finally stops and holds a gun to his head.

"Fucking tell her the truth."

My father laughs lowly. "You kill me then what? I won't be able to tell her anything."

A shot goes off, and my father cries out in pain. I am screaming from my spot across the room. Luca shot him in the arm. Luca motions in my direction, and I feel the cool press of steel against my arm. I start to hyperventilate, and fresh tears spring forth. Not because the man is aiming a gun at my arm, but because my father makes no move to beg or ask or stop him from doing so. Not even a flinch.

Luca nods, and a shot goes off. I shut my eyes and scream, waiting for the pain. But nothing comes. I open my eyes, and my father still hasn't moved. The man that aimed the gun at my arm has shot it millimeters away from my skin. I assume it was to get some kind of reaction out of my father. But he gets none.

"You are a fool to give away something so precious for your own gain. And to give her to me, of all people. Just a damn fool. You are a careless bastard, and you deserve to die." Luca pauses. "But I must wait on my father's orders before I do anything."

Luca walks over to my trembling form and squats down in front of me. "Get me a medical kit," he says to someone, but I don't know who.

The pain in my arm is nothing compared to the pain I am feeling in my chest right now. My father. I've always known he doesn't like me, but I never thought for a second he didn't love me. His own flesh and blood. Even when he had given me away to someone as heartless as Luca. But now I know. All those years, I have just been a blind and naive fool. Wanting to believe in something that isn't real.

"You can patch her up all you want to, but as soon as you kill me, they'll be coming for her. She was a failed attempt at a master plan. She's nothing to us now. Just a waste of space. A pathetic woman, good for nothing but keeping your bed warm at night."

Time stops as my father's words echo across the room.

Luca's body immediately stiffens. Rage pools deep beneath his depths, and I can see the muscle twitch in his jaw. He stands up quickly and makes his way over to my father.

"Luca, wait! Luca, no, please no. Luca, Luca!" I shout and scream and kick, but the restraints on the chair are holding me back.

My father is looking at Luca with a malicious glint in his eye.

"Luca!" I scream, but he still ignores me.

Even though my father hates me, I don't want him dead. He is my father. And I especially don't want to see him killed in front of me.

"Luca! Please!" I scream so hard my throat is burning raw.

As soon as Luca reaches my father, he goes to town. He kicks him, punches him, beats him within an inch of his life. All the while I am screaming for him to stop. But he ignores me. It is as if a switch has been flipped.

Luca finally stops, and there is silence. The only sounds being made are my loud sobs and my father's heavy breathing. He breathes in and spits out blood, looking Luca directly in the eye.

"See if she'll love you now." That last sentence is enough to push Luca over the edge. He pulls out his gun and empties it into my father's body.

I sit there and watch as my husband murders my father.

Suddenly, without warning, vomit comes pouring out of my mouth from the gruesome violence I have just witnessed.

"Look what you fucking made her do." Luca is in front of my father's lifeless body, holding his chin. He lets go, and my father's head hangs.

I look around the room and see the shock in some men's eyes. The fear in others. And the rush of pleasure in some. But when Luca turns to look at me, the glint in his eyes shoots me to the core. Excitement is in his eyes. Happiness. Joy. Like he gets a high from murdering my father in front of me. Right in front of me.

A jingle sounds, and Luca pulls out his phone, looking at the screen and smiling sadistically as he reads the message aloud to his fellow comrades.

"Father said, 'Kill him.'" He laughs. "Way ahead of you, Pops." He laughs, and the men around him join in the laughter. But I can only stare at the lifeless body of the man who has never loved me. Even though he hasn't loved me, I have loved him. And his death is shaking me to my very center. I then look at the man that now has blood dripping from his face, his hands, his pants. My father's blood.

He is laughing. Pure joy, even though my father's blood is soaking him. His smile is painfully beautiful. It is just another reminder of how beauty is such a master of disguise. I look back at my father's body and scream. I scream and yank against the cuffs holding my wrists. I scream and scream and scream. Even when Luca is standing in front of me, trying to make me stop, I am still screaming. Even when my throat is beginning to grow raw from the grating, I still scream. I can't stop. So I continue to scream. Even when I feel the sharp prick in my neck, I scream until it dies to a groan.

And then there is nothing.

Chapter 7

Elise

We arrive at the restaurant, and of course, the valet takes the car to park it. The hostess leads us to a dimly lit table toward the back of the restaurant. Today, I have settled for a black lace dress since I am still in mourning. I mean, I only just buried my father earlier this week, and Luca's father doesn't care to give me time to get over it. According to Luca, he *insisted* that I show up with Luca to dinner.

Luca has been cranky around the house, and I know it is because of me. I haven't smiled or spoken in two days. I don't want to. I don't have anything to say. Even when Luca came home with flowers for me, I completely ignored him and the flowers. Instead of taking it out on me, Luca took it out on a member of the kitchen staff.

"Luca! My son and his lovely wife."

Luca's boisterous father greets us as soon as he lays eyes on us across the room. Luca steps up and greets his father, giving him a hug before pulling my chair out for me to be seated. It is obvious Luca and his father get along well. Who wouldn't when you have Luca Pasquino for a son in this line of living?

Luca's face lights up as he speaks to his father. They speak of trivial things, like games, and they speak of the business. But not once does Luca's face fall to that hard exterior I am so used to seeing. For a moment, I feel my heart break. I just want Luca to love me and show that he does. I want love like Ari and her husband's. It is obvious I am not going to get that, though.

I feel a nudge on my arm and look up to see Luca and his father watching me, Luca's face back to the one that I am used to.

"I'm sorry, I seem to have been wrapped up in my own little world over here," I say quietly, not liking the scrutiny I am getting from them.

Luca's father clears his throat. "I said I'm sorry about your father."

I nod to him and express my gratitude, but inside I want to take the fork in front of me and gouge his eyes out.

"It's a shame, really. I thought the plan he proposed was a good plan. To join us together, we would have more strength than the Russians and the Chinese combined. But he just had to be greedy for power."

I look up immediately. Did I hear that right? He is admitting to killing him?

Luca's father is watching me with the same gaze Luca watches me with, calculating my every move. He is waiting for me to show a sign of weakness.

"I really would have preferred if Luca killed you too in that warehouse. Would have been fewer strings to tie up."

My heart slams against my chest at his words.

"Father," Luca starts warningly, but his father continues.

"All I'm saying is, I told Luca to kill you too in that warehouse. But for the first time in his life, he defied me. Told me straight up no and to shove it." He chuckles, as if remembering the moment. "I'm guessing he had a good reason." He laughs to himself.

But I am shaking. He told Luca to kill me? I had no idea.

I feel a warm hand on my thigh underneath the table. I look up to see Luca watching me with an unreadable expression on his face. I turn back to the table and watch the white linen, not knowing what else I can do right now.

After a while, I get up from the table telling Luca I am going to the bathroom. Once I reach the bathroom, I lock the door and let my tears out. My tears of anger and frustration and sadness. I don't know how long I stay in the bathroom, but once my tears stop, I wipe my eyes and exit.

I walk right into someone and stumble backward, caught off guard and balance.

"Whoa, there, miss. Are you okay?"

I nod and look to thank my savior. He is a tall waiter. His hair is a light brown, and his eyes are a piercing blue color. He is very handsome. Not as handsome as Luca, but he is good-looking.

"I'm fine," I lie. I try to walk around him before Luca comes looking for me, but he stops me.

"You don't look fine to me, ma'am." He gives me a small smile. "Looks like you've been crying." He holds out a tissue to me, and I take it gratefully.

"You know, I don't know what's wrong with you, but I know it must have you pretty upset for you to be in such a rush to not be watching where you're going." He is still smiling at me.

"I'm sorry. I just got caught up in my emotions and wasn't paying attention." I look away frantically.

He chuckles lightly. "You shouldn't let things get to you, miss. You are too beautiful to let your light dull in this cruel world." He smiles widely at me. His smile is so contagious that for once in almost two weeks, I smile back.

Everything else happens in a blur.

I don't even see it coming. The waiter is slammed against the wall, hard. He cries out in shock, and I see Luca's hand around his throat. He lifts his hands up out of reaction in surrender, and out of nowhere, Luca plunges a knife into his right hand, nailing it to the wall. The waiter grunts in pain, ready to cry out.

Luca pulls another blade from somewhere, and his voice seeps out like venom when he speaks. Luca looks terrifying, to say the least. His lean body has this man pinned indefinitely to the wall.

"Make a sound, and I will cut your tongue out," he hisses with hate at the waiter.

The poor guy looks shocked and terrified. His eyes are as wide as saucers. I am standing right next to them in shock, with my hands over my mouth. I barely have time to register anything. Luca turns his gaze on me.

"You go to the bathroom and this?"

I open my mouth to say something, but he cuts me off.

"Don't fucking speak. I've been trying to get you to smile for two fucking weeks, and this guy comes along and manages to do it in three seconds?" he hisses.

Wait, he is mad because the waiter made me smile?

He turns his attention back to the waiter. "I suggest you go find a job somewhere else before I kill you." Luca doesn't even take the knife out of the guy's hand; he walks away from him and snatches me by the arm. He doesn't even stop at his father's table. He walks by and speaks as he passes.

"We're leaving."

He doesn't wait for his father's reaction. I look back and see his father leaning back in his seat, a wicked grin on his face and an evil glint in his eye.

Once our car is pulled around, Luca quickly gets in and we take off out of the parking lot. Luca is driving like a crazy person. I look at the speedometer and see we are going over ninety.

"Luca, please slow down." My voice comes out in frantic desperation.

"You don't fucking talk to me! I have tried to be patient with you, and you go and smile at that guy?" He is shouting, and the speed of the car accelerates.

I decide not to speak again, because it will only make him angrier and drive faster.

We reach the house in record time without any police officers stopping us. He gets out of the car, slamming the door, but I stay in, afraid of what awaits me if I get out. Luca stops midstep and looks at me in the passenger seat.

"Get out of the fucking car!" he shouts, but I shake my head no to him.

I am terrified.

He walks over to my side of the car, and I lock the door quickly. If I thought he was mad before, he is angry now. He punches the window, and I scream. He hits it again with his fist, and I scream again.

"Elise, open the fucking door now!"

I don't respond to him, and he pulls out a gun, aiming it at the window. He fires off shots, and I scream, expecting the glass to be broken. But it isn't. That explains it. This car has bulletproof windows. He is shooting at them to make it weak enough to break. He pulls out another gun and fires away at the windshield.

"Elise! I swear to God, open the fucking door now!" he shouts, but I ignore him, only delaying the inevitable.

He begins beating the window, and I can hear the cracks. I close my eyes and put my hands over my ears. Next thing I know, glass is sprinkled all over me and I am being jerked out of the car and dragged into the house. I kick and scream, the cement driveway digging into my skin. But Luca doesn't care.

He drags me through the house, not making a sound. We reach a bedroom I haven't been in before, and he throws me in, locking the door behind him. I almost vomit from the look in his eyes. Pure, unfiltered rage is reflected back at me.

"You want someone else, is that it? You want to belong to someone else? Would you rather go and fuck that waiter than me?" he shouts at me.

I can only whimper in response. He falls to the ground next to me, and I can feel the cool tip of his blade press against my collarbone.

"Would you rather have someone else touch you the way I do, Elise?" His blade presses into my dress, and the tear of the fabric echoes throughout the room as he cuts the front of my dress open.

"Tell me who you're married to, Elise." He looks up and meets my eyes with his gray ones.

"You." My voice comes out in a shaky whisper.

"That's right. Me. No one else. Only I can make you feel like you do." He traces the blade lightly over my stomach. I whimper aloud, biting my lip. My heart is thundering against my chest.

"Luca, please, I'm sorry."

He ignores my pleas and slips a hand in my underwear. My body betrays me, as I begin to feel pleasure from his touch.

"Only I can make you feel this way, Elise." He removes his hand and looks me in the eyes. I don't know what sick thing he has planned for me, but from the glint in his eyes, I know it can't be good.

"Who are you married to?" he asks lazily.

"You," I answer almost immediately.

"No, sweetheart. What's my name?"

"Luca," I answer him again.

"Say it again."

"Luca." I can feel his blade trace my stomach, going toward my ribs.

"Again."

"Luc—ahhh!" I am cut off as agonizing pain rips through my side. Luca is dragging his blade down the side of my body. I can feel the blood trickling down my side. I try to move, but Luca is holding me down.

He finally picks up the blade.

"Who do you belong to?" he asks the question so calmly. while I'm breathing hard, unable to catch my breath.

"L-lu—"

No sooner do the words leave my mouth does Luca begin to drag the blade down my skin once again. I writhe and scream in agony. This time, he doesn't stop; he just keeps going.

The blade leaves my skin, and I am sobbing and crying. I hear Luca's zipper to his pants, and immediately I try to roll over and crawl away. I can feel the blood oozing all over my side, spilling into the carpet.

Luca immediately rolls me over and pins me down. I have barely any energy to fight him. He separates my legs and enters me roughly. I cry out loud. He leans on top of my body, rubbing against the new wounds he has given me on my side. I cry out from the pain, sobbing and groaning. With every thrust, he rubs against my skin, causing me more and more agonizing pain each time.

He grabs my jaw, making me look at him as he fucks me ruthlessly on the floor.

"Who do you belong to?" he says out loud.

I can't think; I can only feel. Even though there is pain where he sliced through me, I can feel pleasure from his earlier ministration. His grip on my jaw tightens.

"Who are you fucking married to?" His voice snaps me out of my trance.

"Y-you," I groan out.

"Say my goddamn name."

"Luca," I gasp as he thrusts deep.

He smiles an evil smile at me.

"That's right. You're married to me. You belong to me. Luca Pasquino. You're mine, Elise, and nobody else's. Don't you ever forget that. Do you understand me?"

The pain mixed with the pleasure is too much, and I feel myself spilling over as my orgasm hits me hard.

"Yes!" I shout out.

"Only I can make you feel this way. Me. Your fucking husband. No one else," he hisses as he ruthlessly fucks me through my orgasm.

I nod and groan, unable to handle the pleasure and the pain. And possibly the blood loss. I black out.

The next time I awake, I'm lying in bed, with Luca's arm wrapped around me, spooning my back side. I can feel his rhythmic breathing against my back. There is a dull throbbing on my side. The tears immediately come. He fucking sliced me open because a waiter made me smile. I shift in the bed and slowly move out of Luca's grasp, heading toward the bathroom.

It seems that he bathed and clothed me while I was passed out, moving me back into our bedroom. I realize I'm wearing one of his shirts. I turn on the bathroom light, squinting from the sudden barrage of light. My eyes slowly adjust as I make my way over to the mirror. I look in the mirror and slowly lift the massive shirt I am wearing. There is a cloth gauze wrapped around my torso. The dull throbbing is getting worse, and I begin to unwrap the gauze, each layer I peel off making me more and more terrified to see what horrible scar will be waiting underneath. As the cloth gets thinner, I can see the pinkish tint seeping through in spaced-out patterns. My breathing speeds up as I get closer to my skin. I let the cloth fall to the floor and gasp at what I see carved into my ribs. Reaching all the way from the underside of my breast to the top of my hip bone:

LUCA

His name is carved into my skin, the angry red lines a reminder that he has used a knife to do so.

I hear shuffling and see Luca's tall figure leaning in the doorway of the bathroom, his steel-colored eyes rooting me to my spot as he leans away from the doorjamb and makes his way toward me. He wraps his arms around my waist and pulls me into him, kissing my neck.

"You're mine, Elise."

I can't stop the sob that escapes my lips.

Chapter 8

Elise

Every day since Luca carved his name into my side, I haven't bothered to run and hide from him. There is no point; he always gets what he wants, and I'll only be making him angry. I just go outside with a blanket, sit on the front lawn, and watch the staff tend to the yard.

Each morning I wake up, I have to rub some antibiotic on the wound. A few days after the incident, the scar began to get infected and scab up, but since Luca took me to the doctor, I was given something to prevent it from getting gross. I also have to change the gauze every day. I've been wearing loose tank tops to keep the shirt from rubbing and trying to keep the pain at a minimum. And now I am sitting outside, trying to air out the wound. Today it began to burn, so I took the gauze off and let the wind caress it slightly.

It is a beautiful day today. I look over to see the gardener tending to the flowers. A beautiful rainbow arrangement covers the front of the house.

"Elise."

I jump as Luca's voice pulls me out of my trance. I look up to see him standing over me and quickly lower my shirt. Every time he sees his name etched into my skin, he gets this look on his face. Like the sight brings him joy. And it scares me.

He moves down on the blanket next to me, propping himself up on his forearm. He cranes his neck to look at me.

"I haven't heard you play in a while," he says, almost as if he were pouting. "I miss hearing your beautiful melodies." His eyes roam down to the hem of my shirt, and he begins playing with it. I don't speak; I only keep my eyes trained on the gardener.

"You know, now that your father is out of the way, the matter of who's going to run the South is very tender. And since you are the only heir he had, well, it'd make sense that your husband take over." He slowly pushes my shirt up so that the *A* and the *C* are visible.

"But I was thinking, maybe we should appoint someone." He is still pushing the shirt up. "But it's just a matter of who." He pauses for a moment, as if thinking, and finally releases a breath before laying his head on my lap.

"I think I want you to play in another recital for me so that the whole world can know how talented my beautiful wife is."

I almost don't register his words.

"What?" I say aloud.

He shifts his head so that he is looking up at me from my lap. And damn, if he doesn't look sexy as hell. His curly dark hair is falling in ringlets away from his face, and his thick lashes are more defined from this angle. He is smiling at me. A smile that radiates joy.

"I knew that would catch your attention. I want to share your talents. You really are a wonderful musician. I actually have an audition set up for you in an hour and a half."

My heart slams in my chest. He what?

He chuckles slightly at my speechlessness.

"But for now, I just want to relax in the sun with my wife." He closes his eyes for a moment, letting the sun wash over his face.

Luca puzzles me completely. I never understand what he is thinking or what he wants. But I think, in his own twisted mind, he has some feelings for me; he just doesn't know how to express them.

As if sensing the direction of my thoughts, he begins speaking.

"You are perfect, Elise. The perfect woman. The perfect wife. I love everything about you. I know you would never want that pathetic waiter. I just wanted to see you smile." He opens his eyes and sits up so that his face is parallel with mine, and he is staring into my soul.

"Can you do that for me, Elise? I want to see you smile." He watches me as if he were staring deep into my soul. So I give him a smile.

"No, I want to see the smile you gave your cousin." His face darkens, and I have to dig deep within myself and give him the smile I had when I saw Ari. He stares at my face for a while, and I have no idea what he is thinking.

"You are so beautiful. Your father was a damn fool to give you away so easily for power. But I'm glad he did." His eyes roam down, and he lifts my shirt so that his name is exposed on my side.

"I love my name on your skin." He traces it lightly with his finger. "Now the world will know you belong to me." He is staring at the jagged scars with a dreamy expression.

"Who do you belong to, Elise?" He doesn't look up; he is still staring at his name etched into my skin.

"You, Luca." My voice is small and frail. Just like me.

I've never had any strong will when coming into this place, and now even more so. I am not going to pretend to be the hard girl in those books that likes to get attitudes and believes she can't be broken. Because this isn't a book; this is real life. And if I ever try to mouth off to Luca, he can lose control and kill me. He is ruthless. And he terrifies me to the bone.

He moves up closer to me on the blanket and places a hand on my face before pulling me in for a kiss. It takes everything in me to kiss him back. I know that if I resist, he will make things worse. He may even kill the gardener just to prove a point to me.

"Go get dressed. It takes about forty-five minutes to get to the city from here, and we need to get to your audition."

I look at him, not knowing what to say, but stand and walk into the house, following his orders.

* * * * *

I zip up the dress I'm wearing to dinner tonight. After the audition, Luca sprung on me that we are having guests for dinner. The audition went great. I earned first chair and actually got a solo in the upcoming tri-city symphony.

Luca's excitement when I told him the news was through the roof.

Luca steps out of the closet, messing with his suit jacket. I watch him from my spot across the room. How can someone so handsome be capable of such cynical things? As if sensing he is being watched, he looks up from the buttons on his suit jacket and takes in my form at the mirror. A smile creeps its way onto his face.

"Damn, if I'm not the luckiest man in the world." He walks over to where I am and leans in to give me a quick kiss on the cheek.

"I wish I could show you how lucky I feel." He winks at me and leans in, giving me a kiss on my exposed neck. My cheeks burn from his innuendo.

He takes a seat on the bed and begins messing with his cufflinks. I turn back to my face in the mirror. I have to wear a loose-fitting dress tonight due to the scars on my ribs. Nothing tight, seeing as it can rub and tear open the healing wounds. I feel a pang of anger toward Luca. How he can walk around here without a care or regret that he used a knife to slice his name into my body, I will never understand.

"Elise, I want you to be on your best behavior tonight." I turn around and meet his eyes in the mirror. He is staring at me with a serious expression. "The guest that we're having is important, and I don't want to do anything rash because you can't control yourself."

Downstairs, I stand at the left-hand side of the table. Luca sits at the head, and I am to sit on his right. That is how it is. The staff is scurrying to set the table and get things in order for the dinner. This is probably the second time I have seen any of them. They steer clear of me, and once their jobs are finished, they leave the house.

Luca comes around the corner, smiling at something his friend said, but there is something off about his smile. The man next to him is barely shorter than Luca, with blond hair and blue eyes to match. He has dimples on his face when he smiles. He looks to be around Luca's age, and I have no idea who he is. Then his date steps in the room, and I see the source of Luca's off smile.

Jessica steps in the room wearing a bright-red dress that clings to her body, showing off every curve she has. Her breasts are falling out of the top, and her stilettos are echoing loudly off the wall with each step she takes. My stomach drops when her eyes meet mine. Her face twists into a smug grin as she looks me up and down, obviously turning her nose up in distaste. She isn't here out of coincidence. And she obviously is going to cause me trouble.

Luca leaves his friend's side and comes next to me to pull my chair out. As I take a seat, he leans in and whispers in my ear, "Don't do anything you'll regret." And as he stands to go to his seat, he pushes a short curl behind my ear, reminding me of how far he will go to make me pay for disobeying him. I shudder and almost begin to cry as I take my seat and see Jessica's scowling face across from me.

"Elise, this is Nicolai. You may or may not recognize him, but he is from the eastern region of the North Mob. I'm looking into his becoming the next head of the South, if we don't integrate it under my rule." In that entire sentence Luca just spoke, a total of three new facts are revealed to me. Who this man is, what he is doing here, and the fact that Luca is considering conjoining us under one rule. His rule.

I bring myself quickly back into reality. "Nice to meet you." I give him the best smile I can muster. He smiles back, both of his dimples being revealed. He has a boyish charm to him. Where Luca is hard and set, he is almost playful.

"Nice to meet you too. Luca has told me so much about you." He smiles at me. I am caught a little off guard. If Luca has told this man about me, then he knows him more than he is letting on.

After a moment of silence, Jessica clears her throat. Nicolai smiles and gestures to her. "Oh, and this is my date, Jessica. We met a few weeks ago."

He obviously doesn't sense the tension between Jessica and everyone at the table. I look at Luca's face, and if looks could kill, Jessica would be dead, dead, dead. Speaking of dead, I seem to recall, the last time Luca said if he sees her, he was going to kill her. Is he going to really kill Nicolai's date?

"Oh, this is a lovely home you have here, Luca." She looks around the room with a smug grin on her face.

I look at Luca to see his reaction, and he doesn't give anything other than a straight face. But I can tell by the muscle working in his jaw that he is irritated. He doesn't even respond to her. Finally, the waitstaff comes out of the kitchen with dinner and begins serving. Some of them look a little shocked once they gaze upon Jessica's face, which only makes her smug grin grow even more.

Luca and Nicolai fall into conversation with each other. They speak of relations, opportunities, and even memories. So it is obvious that this man and Luca are friends. And Jessica somehow knows that, but Nicolai doesn't. Nicolai also doesn't notice when she pipes in with her snide remarks directed toward Luca. I don't know if he is trying to restrain himself from killing her or what, but he is doing a marvelous job.

Finally, the conversations go from an interview to actual conversations that I can listen in on to get more information about my husband. Apparently, he likes to be the one to inflict torture; he can get a clean kill but likes to miss possible shots to make that happen so they can suffer. He is pretty much the man that the stories say he is.

The only normal thing he has revealed about himself is that he is a medical magician. He knows where all the arteries are, the bones, how to stop the bleeding and make it last longer. He has the IQ of a neurosurgeon, and it all leads to killing. Go figure.

He and Nicolai begin laughing boisterously, pulling me from my thoughts. He looks over at me with adoration in his eyes.

"You know, my wife is a musical prodigy. She plays the violin like an angel." Once he speaks the words, Jessica doesn't give Nicolai a chance to respond. She scoffs arrogantly.

"Since when are you into classical music, Luca?" She looks at me through narrowed eyes, probably expecting a response, but I am not about to give her one with Luca sitting less than three feet away from me. If she is going to get killed, I am going to have no part in it.

"Since I heard Elise playing the day of our engagement party," he says, annoyed.

Nicolai is looking at her with a questioning glance, but she ignores him, the adoration Luca is showing me in front of her obviously making her angry.

"Luca, you wouldn't even listen to classical music even if someone held a gun to your head." Her voice is coming out equally annoyed.

"Well, once I heard my beautiful wife here playing it, I instantly fell in love." Luca looks at me and winks.

"You might love her sorry musical abilities, but I know for a fact she can't pleasure you like I used to."

Nicolai looks at her, stunned.

He starts, "Now, wait a se—"

But she cuts him off, standing quickly in her chair, the furniture screeching back on the marble floor. Her eyes land immediately on me, all the hate and rage she is feeling coming at me.

"Tell me, little girl, can you pleasure Luca the way I used to? Can you handle *all* his needs? He's a man, and you're just an inexperienced little cunt that doesn't know who or what she has." I don't even know what to say or how to respond. But I don't have to, since Nicolai speaks up.

"Wait, Jessica, you know Luca?"

She rolls her eyes, as if calling him an idiot. I look over to Luca and see a grin of amusement on his face as he leans back in his chair.

"Of course I know him. I was the one that kept his bed warm before this lowly tr—"

She suddenly stops speaking and holds her stomach, a look of shock on her face. It takes me a moment to register what has just happened. Suddenly, there is a growing dark stain on the front of her red dress. And it doesn't take a genius to put two and two together. I look across the table and see Luca still holding a silencer. It's a gun usually used for silent kills. No one can hear it as the shooter takes a life, and that explains why I didn't hear anything before Jessica was shot.

I gasp and cry out as her dress becomes overly saturated with her blood and begins dripping on the tile. I look at Luca, and he still has an amused glint in his eye. There is the ghost of a smile on his lips.

I run to Jessica and begin putting pressure on the wound, not thinking about the fact that Luca is the one that shot her and she insulted me only moments ago.

Jessica collapses on the ground, breathing hard and looking around frantically.

"Oh god, oh god, oh god," I keep chanting to myself. She can't die. Not here. Not like this.

I quickly jump on the table and grab one of the napkins, pressing it to Jessica's bloodied side. I hear Luca's deep chuckle in the background.

"See, this is why I say I'm so lucky. Even though this woman doesn't deserve it, my wife is still trying to save her life." I hear his footsteps come toward me, but I focus on all the blood that is now coating my hands.

"Luca, help her, please. She's dying!" I shout, but he doesn't respond. I turn to Nicolai, hoping he has some shred of compassion for the woman he unknowingly brought into this mess.

"Nicolai, do something!" I look at him, but he is not even paying attention.

He is watching Luca with a steel expression, as if waiting for his orders. Jessica's body begins spasming, and I shout out in frustration. Why won't anyone help her? My eyes are burning, and I realize I am crying over her body. She can't die here—that is all I keep repeating to myself. She just can't.

I hear Luca's voice but don't register what he says until I feel arms around me, dragging me away from Jessica's body. Luca comes into my line of vision, and I realize Nicolai is pulling me out of the room.

"Luca, wait! Luca, please! Don't do this!" I shout at him, but he ignores me.

He walks toward her body with a new gun by his side. One that isn't a silencer. He looks down at her shaking body, and what I see in his eyes terrifies me. There is nothing. No shred of emotion. No sympathy. Nothing.

He turns and looks at me, his gray eyes meeting mine, and winks.

Nicolai drags me beyond the dining room door, catching it with his foot to swing it closed. But not before I see Luca bring the gun up and aim it. Just as the door blocks him from view, I hear it.

Bang!

Chapter 9

Elise

I have to get out. I can't live like this anymore. I have to escape from Luca. He is insane. Even more so now that he is married. He treats me as if he owns me. I truly believe that Luca needs some kind of help. Each and every time he meets with someone or just has something to do, he will call me into his office to play for him. He also forces me to practice for the upcoming recital.

I never refuse. I never say no. Hell, I never even smile anymore. I just do as I am told. Luca is like a ticking time bomb, and I never know when he is going to blow next.

I walk to his office without my violin today. His trusted right-hand man has come to get me, saying he wishes for my presence, but without my violin. My hands are sweaty, and I am terrified, because I know he possibly has something terrible planned for me.

I step up to the large wooden doors and listen in on the sounds coming from the other side. I can only hear muffled voices, which means he has someone in there. I push open the door and step in slowly. Upon my entrance, Luca's dark eyes meet mine, and a smile lights up his face. My heart drops. I know that smile all too well. It is a smile fueled by cruel intentions. I look beyond Luca's shoulder as he comes near me, and there is a man sitting there. I have never seen him before, but judging by his pale complexion, he is scared too.

"There's my beautiful wife!" Luca makes his way over to me and pulls me in for a passionate kiss. He threads his fingers through my short locks and stares into my face adoringly.

"God, you are beautiful. Isn't she beautiful, Max?" He looks over to the man, and he smiles back at us, agreeing with my deranged husband.

"Come here, baby. I need you as my good-luck charm." He pulls me over to one of the couch seats with him and pulls me down on his lap as he takes a seat. I look at the coffee table in between us and the man he calls Max, and there is a gun sitting on it. Not a normal gun Luca usually uses, but an old-fashioned gun used for …

"We're going to play a game, baby." Luca interrupts my thoughts, rubbing his hands up and down my arms slowly. I look up at the man in front of me and see my fear mirrored back at me through his eyes. What has this man done to incur the wrath of my husband?

"This is Max. He was actually caught a few days ago trying to pull one over on me in one of my clubs. He actually managed to shoot one of my men! He didn't kill him, of course, but he came close. So after some discussion, I've decided to be fair and give him a fighting chance." He picks up the gun and wiggles in the air. He looks at me from his position under me and catches my eye.

"Have you ever heard of this game, baby? It's called Russian roulette."

I can't move. I know this game. I know this game all too well.

He flips open the barrel and shows me the gun as he loads in a bullet.

"How 'bout you, Max? Heard of it?"

Max only trembles in his seat across from us.

"This is a six-shooter, which means it will shoot six times. But only one out of these shots will go off." He sets the gun on the table and slides it over to Max, pulling his own gun out of his gun holster and aiming it at Max.

"Now, Max, if you can fire the gun off three times, then you're free to go. If not …" Luca pauses in his sentence and laughs a little. "Well, you know what will happen."

Luca takes his own gun and aims it at Max. "Don't think about aiming that over here, and don't think about trying to run. I will shoot you before your hand pulls that damn trigger." Luca's voice turns venomously serious.

"Luca, wait, please. I don't want to watch this. I can't …" My voice comes out quietly as I express my fears. I don't want to watch this man possibly blow his head off. I keep my eyes trained on the floor as I plead with Luca. I just hope some part of him will hear my plea and let me leave.

"Now, Elise, what did I tell you about begging?"

I open my eyes and look at Luca with horror etched into my face. He is a monster. He waves his gun at Max and scoots back into the chair, getting more comfortable. "Go ahead."

I turn my head away as Max shakily picks up the gun, his labored breathing the only sound in the massive office Luca has. He picks it up and slowly presses it to his temple. His eyes are wide, and there is a bead of sweat on his lip and brow. I quickly turn my head away, not wanting to watch this insanity.

Luca grabs my chin and forces it in Max's direction.

"No, no, no, I want you to see this." He holds my chin tightly and forces me to watch this man as he takes a deep breath and pulls the trigger.

Click.

I can't help it; I hunch over on the side of the couch and vomit everything I have eaten up to this point, the stress and fear of him pulling the trigger making me tremble. I hear Luca's deep chuckle, as he finds my distress amusing.

"You'll have to excuse my wife. She's not a fan of violence," he says as he pets my hair. I am still keeled over the couch, emptying the contents of my stomach onto his polished wood floor.

"Again, Max," I hear him say. But I don't want to look. I have no choice, though, as Luca jerks my hair up, craning my neck at an uncomfortable angle, making me watch. Max is sweating bullets as he closes his eyes and takes a deep breath, pulling the trigger again.

Click.

I scream, and the tears begin flowing freely as I turn to Luca, sweating myself from this horrible event that is taking place.

"Luca, please stop! I can't take this! Just leave him be!" I grab onto the collar of his shirt and beg and plead, my body uncontrollably shaking. Luca's heartless eyes meet mine. They are filled with joy and amusement at the situation. He pins me to the spot as he stares into my eyes and speaks again.

"Again, Max." He keeps his eyes trained on mine.

"Please, sir, I swear I've learned my lesson." Max is blubbering and crying behind me, begging for his life. Luca's eyes, which have once been filled with amusement, suddenly turn cold and angry.

Pow!

I jump from atop Luca's lap. His gun has gone off. I hear Max cry out in pain and turn to see him clutching his chest. There is blood staining his shirt and saturating it so that it is leaking through his hands. Luca has shot him.

"I hate beggars. Again, Max." Max's cries grow louder as he picks the gun up and puts it to his temple once more.

Click.

I let out a breath I didn't even realize I was holding. He is going to live. He is going to live! He won the game! He—

Bang!

I scream as the unexpected shot fires throughout the room. I didn't even feel Luca move. I slowly look over to Max's now-lifeless body. There is a bullet hole in the middle of his head, his eyes open wide and staring into the ceiling, his mouth still forming a small grin.

"Bull's-eye," I hear Luca mutter underneath me.

I quickly jump up from his lap, trying to get as far away from him as I can. I walk as fast as I can, but I feel his hand on my arm as he yanks me back.

"No, no, no, baby, we're not done playing yet." He yanks me so that I spin around into his chest, and I feel myself fighting him. I push myself away from him.

"How are we not done? He's dead, Luca! You shot him! You lied, you told him he would live if he won, but you lied!"

He is watching me with a dark expression, and the moment something twisted clicks into his head, I see it. My fight-or-flight response jerks into place, and I take off running to the door. I push my legs as hard as they will go, not stopping even when my lungs are burning. I don't know where I am going until the front door comes into view, and I sprint for it.

I almost reach it when, out of nowhere, two men grab me on either side of my arms, stopping my momentum at full force. I am out of breath and going crazy trying to escape them.

"No, don't take me back to him, please!" I scream at them, but they don't listen. "Please don't! Please, I'm begging you!" I scream until my voice is raw.

They take me to another room in this massive place I call home. It looks like another office, except the flooring is carpet and it is much smaller than Luca's office. I see Luca standing behind the desk, watching me with dark eyes. There is no emotion in them. Sitting on the desk in front of him is a revolver.

I begin to struggle again. But they bring me closer, forcing me to sit in the chair in front of Luca. He sits behind his desk and motions for the men to leave the room. I sit there in the chair in front of my husband, trembling like a leaf. I am petrified.

"I wasn't done playing, baby." Luca traces his finger over the gun facedown on the desk. He looks up, and his eyes meet mine. He slides the gun across the desk to me.

"Your turn." He smiles a malicious smile at me, truly reveling in my fear. Didn't he profess his twisted affection for me just the other day? And now he is playing a game of chance with my life.

My hands are shaking violently as I clasp the heavy metal and pick up the gun. I look at Luca, and he is watching me with a grin on his face. All this time, I've wanted an out. All this time, I have been planning. And he just drops the means I need to get out of this in my hands. All I have to do is pull the trigger however many times and hope I can hit him before he retaliates against me. He won't even be expecting it. All the hate and rage I have for this man is boiling up to the surface and driving me to do this. I am going to do this. I am going to kill Luca Pasquino.

He motions to me with his hand. "I said, your turn, Elise. You see how the game goes. You get one try."

I slowly bring the gun up to my temple and take a deep breath. This is for all the abuse I have endured. For all the pain I have suffered at his hands. No more. I am taking control of my life now. I close my eyes and count to three. On the count of three, I open them and take the gun in both hands, aiming it at Luca's skull, and pull the trigger.

Click click click click click click click.

What? I try again, and again, and again, but it is all the same. An empty click. No bullet. I look up from my trembling fingers, clutching the gun so tightly my knuckles are white. When my eyes meet Luca's face, I wish he had loaded the gun so I can kill myself. He is not smiling. All earlier amusement has been wiped clean off his face.

I drop the gun, and it lands on the floor with a thud. I am shaking so badly I'm surprised I haven't passed out. Luca walks around the desk slowly, watching my every move. He doesn't speak; he only stares. He is standing directly in front of me, my eyes level with his chest. I am too afraid to look up. Afraid of what may be there.

I feel his thumb and forefinger underneath my chin as he guides my head up to meet his eyes. If I haven't thrown up earlier, I just may have at this moment.

"You think I'd give you a loaded gun?" His voice comes out calm. And that terrifies me even more. His grip on my chin tightens, and I wince from the pain.

"I'm not an idiot, baby. If you happened to land on the bullet and blow your beautiful face off, then where would I be? Even if I did, you were going to shoot me? *Me.* Your fucking husband?" His hand releases my chin and glides down to my throat, where he squeezes lightly.

"And what were you going to do once I was dead, huh? Run away? They'd shoot you down as soon as you stepped foot out of this door." He stares me down.

I reach up and slap his hand away. "You're a monster! You have killed people in front of me, you've taken things away from me, you've done horrible things to me! Why wouldn't I try to kill you the first chance I got?" I shout at him.

A myriad of emotions flashes across his face. A stinging pain explodes on the side of my face, and I stagger over, about to fall to the floor, but Luca grabs a tight hold of my top and pulls me into him once again. He backs me into the nearest wall and pushes me up against it, hard.

He slaps me across the face once again, and I cry out from the pain. He yanks my hair so that I am facing him and puts his hand around my throat. Rage is burning deep within his gray irises. He rears back and slaps me again, the pain and impact making my consciousness waver. But he is not done yet. Not even close.

I blame it on my anger, pain, and hatred for him in this moment, but I open my mouth and let the next words pour out in a broken whisper.

"Kill me. You'd be doing me a favor."

Luca immediately drops me, and I fall to the floor gasping for breath and coughing. I feel a rough tug on my short locks and meet Luca's steel-gray eyes. He glares into my soul for what seems like forever, until an evil grin crawls onto his face.

"I'm not going to kill you, baby. But when I'm done with you, you'll wish you were dead."

* * * * *

I jolt awake, an ear-splitting scream ripping its way from my mouth as cold water is showered on me, the pain shredding its way through my body. I look around and see Luca standing in front of me. There is blood dripping down my body.

Luca brought me into this room, stripped me, and whipped me into unconsciousness. Luca's aim with a whip is perfect. And he goes to town on my body. My arms are screaming in pain from holding my weight up. He has me chained to the ceiling, my legs dragging the floor barely.

The room is silent except for the sounds of my labored breathing. I shiver as the cold air hits my naked form. I hear Luca's footsteps coming toward me and begin to whimper in fear, the sound of the leather whip dragging along with him making me even more frightened.

His steps halt in front of me, and I can feel the warmth of his body heat radiating off him. I flinch and cry aloud when I feel his touch underneath my chin. He lifts it so I meet his stare. My body shakes in fear. My back is stinging from the angry welts he has ingrained in my skin.

"P-p-p-p-please." My voice is shaking just as badly as my body. Tears are running down my face in large rivulets. Luca pulls my face up to meet his. He doesn't say anything as he releases the chains around my wrists and catches my limp body, cradling me against his warm chest.

I hiss in pain as he rubs my back against him with each step he takes. I drift in and out of consciousness as Luca carries me somewhere within the house. We finally reach a room, and I jerk in shock as he sets me down in warm water. The open scars on my back are stinging, but the warm water feels so good I don't care.

The next time I come to, I am lying in our bed. It is dark outside. The curtains around the room are opened, letting in the moonlight. I try to move but wince from the pain that jolts through my back, the cool press of the sheets making me forget the burning sensation when I first awake. I can feel bandages of some kind on my back. I slowly sit up in the room and look around.

Suddenly, the door to the bathroom opens, and Luca steps out with a towel around his waist, the water from the shower making his hair stick to his forehead. His bare chest and stomach are rippling with muscles. Luca is the epitome of perfection. His face is beautiful, as is his body. But his mind and psyche are not.

He doesn't glance over to the bed as he walks to the closet. He has no expression on his face, and it almost scares me. What can possibly be going on in his head? He reemerges from the closet seconds later wearing boxer briefs and no shirt. He looks at the bed and freezes when his eyes land on me. His face still gives off no emotion. I don't know what he is thinking of. Not even in the slightest.

He walks over to the bed, pulling back the blankets on his side. He still doesn't speak as he gets into bed beside me. After a moment of silence, he reaches out for me, but I flinch away, and my breathing speeds up out of habit. He terrifies me.

I squeeze my eyes shut and can already feel the tears forming.

"Does your back hurt?" he asks in the silence.

"Only when I move," I respond. And it is true. The pain isn't constant or searing. I am guessing it is from some medicine he has given me.

"Come here."

I can't bring my body to move, though. It is utterly terrified of him.

"Elise."

His voice comes out in warning, so I lie back down and move a little closer to him. He puts a hand on my side and rolls me over so I am facing him. I have to bite my cheek to keep from crying.

Luca reaches out, and I close my eyes and flinch once again. I feel his fingers lightly trace my cheek and open my eyes to see him staring at me with all the adoration a queen deserves.

"Elise, I love you."

No, no, no, no, no. No! He can't! If he does, this only seals my fate. He can't love me; his mind can't process love.

"Even though you tried to kill me today, I forgive you. You are the only woman I'll ever love. You are my woman. My wife. I will kill without hesitation anyone that tries to take you from me. *Anyone.*" His gray eyes meet mine, and I am frozen.

"I love you."

With those final words, he leans in and begins kissing my neck slowly. His hand travels down my front to the apex between my thighs. He rolls me over so he is over me as he begins sucking on my neck and getting me ready for his intrusion.

I can only close my eyes and weep.

Chapter 10

Elise

I sit in the practice room, playing anything I can to drown the noise out. The screams. The begging. I've even closed the door, but it has only made the sounds muffled. Luca loves conducting his "business" at home. And now more so than usual, he has a new man to torture each day.

I have no idea which room he is in inside this massive place we live, but he always seems to be close enough for me to hear the screams. Luca's whole attitude and demeanor have been sour lately. He has been on a shorter fuse than usual. He constantly walks around with a scowl on his face and jumps at every little thing. He has even come out of a torture session pissed beyond reason because he "killed the man too fast."

Not only has he been grouchy, but he has also barely spoken to me. He doesn't even look my way. He wakes up before I do and goes to bed after I am already asleep. If he sees me around the house, he only stares for a moment before walking away. I know I should be upset about it, seeing as I am his wife, but I am actually very happy about it. I figure he must still be angry at me for aiming that gun at his head. But if that is all it takes for me to get some space from his insanity, I should have hurt his feelings a long time ago.

I flinch as another wail echoes through the massive halls. It is crazy how much pain Luca knows how to inflict on a person. I remember the conversation he and Nicolai had together when they spoke about how Luca knows everything about the human body. And it's scary realizing I'm married to someone who studies the human body so thoroughly just to know how to inflict pain on it and kill it.

I stand and walk to the door with my instrument in hand. The clock reads 12:30 p.m., which means I have rehearsals in an hour. The thing that sucks about my rehearsals is that they're just me and the director. Luca doesn't want me practicing with the full band until it is absolutely necessary.

I walk to the front door, about to push it open. Usually, I just have someone drive me to the rehearsal, or Luca does it, but he hasn't been in the mood to talk to me lately, so I decide to just go on my own.

"Elise." My name echoes off the walls of the grand entryway, and I freeze. I turn to see Luca standing in the middle of the double-staircase balcony, staring at me. I want to vomit at the sight. Not because of Luca, but because of what is on Luca.

There is blood. On his shirt. On his pants. On his face. Even matted in his hair. He doesn't seem to notice or care.

"Where are you going?" he asks as his gray eyes level me. He's watching me with that calculating expression again, and I can feel myself growing squeamish under his gaze.

"I have rehearsal in an hour," I whisper, trying not to meet his eyes. Or his body, for that matter. I truly wonder how he's able to stand there and speak to me so normally when he's coated in blood.

"Come here, Elise." His voice breaks through the silence, and I feel my heart sink.

This means he isn't ignoring me anymore. I set my violin case down by the door, wanting it nowhere near Luca or his bloodied self. He continues to watch me, and as I get closer to him, I realize there is something off about him. I can't put my finger on it, but something is different. I slowly walk up the stairs and keep my eyes trained on Luca the whole time. I watch him because I am scared he'll do something when I am not looking. But he is watching me with an indescribable expression.

I get close enough to him to see how the blood has dried up on some parts of his body, and some of the blood is still fresh. He watches me like a hawk.

"Luca, are you okay?" I ask him, and my voice is small and shaky. And I do want to know if he really is okay. Something is going on, and I don't know what. But I am too frightened to find out.

He takes ahold of my hand. I let out a small squeal as some of the blood oozes into my palm. He doesn't speak a word, only drags me along the long corridor. I can feel my body starting to tense in fear that he's going to take me back to that awful room that he had me chained up in, but I'm surprised when he drags me into a warm room with steam in it. It's a bathroom. Actually, it's more like a shower room. The whole room is designed just for bathing. There is a massive glass shower in one corner of the room and a pool-size bathtub in the other.

The warm mist is already fogging over the full-body mirrors. Luca seems to have turned on the shower before he came to get me, the steam from the shower already wafting underneath the glass door. He turns to me and begins to peel off his saturated shirt. Even when he takes the shirt off, there is still blood on his bare skin. I don't know how he can stand it.

After a moment of his staring at me, a smirk finds its way onto his face.

"Don't tell me the blood is making you queasy."

I still don't respond to him; he is seriously freaking me out. He only laughs and shakes his head when he realizes I won't respond to him. He completely strips his clothing off and stands in front of me in all his naked glory. I quickly look away from his body, blushing. I hear him laughing under his breath.

He lightly places an arm on my shoulder and turns me around. The sound of the zipper being undone echoes throughout the room, mingling with the shower. He pushes the dress off my shoulders, and it falls at my feet. I can feel myself shaking. Luca traces his fingers over the whelps that are now on my back from his torture. His hands come around. I can feel him tracing his name on my side.

I close my eyes, and I can feel my body vibrating in fear. I don't know what he is about to do to me. I feel a tug on my hand and open my eyes. He is pulling me into the shower. I step over the rise on the floor and into the shower with him. The way the showerheads are is like a constant rain overhead, so once we step in, the water immediately encompasses both of our bodies.

Even though the heat envelops me, I can't help the shivering my body is doing. Luca is watching me closely with those eyes. I just wish I know what he is thinking. People usually say someone's eyes are the windows to the soul, and if that's true, then Luca must not have one.

The water cascades over him, washing the blood off his body. I can see the color as it flows down the drain. He steps closer to me and pulls me into his hard body, looking into my eyes as he speaks.

"Why are you shaking, baby?"

I have to crane my neck to look up at him. I open my mouth to tell him some lie, but he cuts me off.

"It's okay, you don't have to answer." He reaches above me and pushes my hair out of my face. It is clinging to the back of my neck due to the length he has cut it at. He leans in and nuzzles my neck.

"I don't want you practicing today. Stay with me."

"Okay," I whisper. In this moment, I feel like Luca is so close to snapping. And even the smallest thing may send him over the edge.

"Every time I look into those beautiful eyes, I get so heartbroken. You look so innocent. So pure." He pulls back from me, meeting my eyes head-on. "But you're not. You tried to kill me. *Me.* Your husband. The one that spared your life when he was ordered to end it. Not only did I spare it, but I saved it as well. Your father was planning to kill you in cold blood for his own fucked-up gain." He cups the side of my face, making me immobile, unable to move my head. His gray eyes look genuinely curious. Like he has no idea why I've tried to take my freedom.

"Why would you do that to me?"

I don't open my mouth, and he continues.

"I think over and over in my head. If you were anyone else, I would have killed you for thinking you could do something so trivial. But I'd never do that to you." After a moment, he pulls me in for an embrace.

"My father is having a party tonight. You're coming with me. I had a dress bought just for the occasion. I think it'll look lovely on your skin."

He trails his fingers down my ribs, where his name is etched in. I say a silent prayer, hoping he hasn't gotten a dress that reveals this lettering to satisfy his sadistic desires.

"Don't forget who you belong to, baby."

* * * * *

The car is silent. Luca hasn't spoken a word to me since we left the house. He walked in, told me I look beautiful, and led me to the car, not saying anything else. We have been driving for quite a while now.

The dress Luca bought for me is beautiful, to say the least. It's white with one-shoulder that stands out in gold. He picked it stealthily too. It covers up my side and my back, so none of the scars or bruises are visible.

I cut my eyes to see him focused on the road. He looks handsome, as always. Tonight, instead of wearing the usual black, he matches me with a white tux and gold undercoat. I am guessing this is a really formal party his father is throwing; otherwise, he wouldn't have worn white.

We finally arrive at some gates, and Luca pulls up, pressing the four-digit code, and the gates open. He drives up a winding driveway, and I can't believe what I am seeing. This home is huge. Bigger than the home I share with Luca. There are lights at the front and music pouring out of the windows. Luca doesn't at all seem fazed. He pulls up and turns the car off, looking at me.

"Do not do anything stupid."

I only nod.

We enter the house with his hand possessively wrapped around my waist. As soon as we step in, boisterous laughter fills the air. It doesn't take long for Luca's father to spot us.

"Ah! There's my son! And his lovely wife!"

I look up and see his father across the room, shouting at us, with a champagne glass in hand. It's obvious he is happy to see his son.

He makes his way over to us and envelops Luca in a tight hug. "Glad you could make it, *mi figlio!*"[1] He turns and sees me on Luca's arm and greets me as well by taking my hand and placing a kiss on it.

"Glad to be here, Father."

I look up at Luca and see the joy radiating off his face. A smile that isn't sadistic or has some conniving motive behind it, but just a smile that means he is happy for pure reasons. I wish more than anything that he would smile at me that way. I wish that I was lucky enough to have married a man that loves me and wants me to be happy. Not some psychotic man that enforces his will upon me and has no idea what the first thing about love is.

"Come, *figlio,*[2] there are people I want you to meet!" He drags his son away from me, and Luca doesn't even take a glance back as his father drags him deeper into the room. I am left all alone in a group of people I don't know, in a home I am unfamiliar with.

I turn and look around. I see people staring at me. Some women with scowling expressions on their faces, some with disbelief. The men try to sneak glances. They know who I am. They won't be caught looking, or they'll be dead the next moment.

I make my way into an empty corner and stand, just watching the people around me. I envy them. The women look so carefree and happy. Especially the ones that have a man on their arms that adores them. It's moments like this that I wish Ari were here with me. We'd probably make fun of a few people together, or we'd just pretend we were anywhere but here. She always knew how to make me feel better.

"Mrs. Pasquino." I look beside me as a woman startles me out of my thoughts. She's standing uncomfortably close to me and has a not-so-friendly look on her face. She's wearing an unreasonably tight dress, and her chest is pushed up high out of the thing.

---

[1] "My son."

[2] "Son."

"You don't mind if I call you that, right? I mean, you are married to *him*, after all." She says it as if she is being sarcastic.

"No, I don't mind."

She scoffs at me. "Do you know who I am?"

"No," I say, trying to keep my voice even.

"Of course you don't. I know he wouldn't tell you. How does he treat you? I hope like dirt."

I am completely taken aback by her bluntness. "Excuse me?"

"You heard me. The only reason he's with you is that this was a forced arrangement. But don't you worry. I'll have him back in my good graces in no time." She snarls in my face.

I have no idea how to respond. I am hoping that she'll take the hint, seeing as I have no interest in her words but she still doesn't leave.

"He hates you, you know. You should have seen how angry he was when he found out he had to be married to someone." She runs a finger over her hair, as if remembering. "He was a little rough that night."

I gasp, appalled that she is saying all this to me. I turn to leave, not wanting Luca to catch her talking shit to me, but she snatches my arm.

"He's going to ruin you. You can't handle the man he is, the man he is destined to be. You're nothing but a forced burden on him that he can't get rid of. But you'll see. He'll come back to me. And I'll make sure to make your life a living hell when he does. Who knows? Maybe he'll slip up and have a little 'accident.'" She rubs her belly suggestively while smirking at me.

I roughly jerk my arm out of her grasp and stand my ground. I am sick of being pushed around by his whores.

"You know, some other woman came to me, preaching the same thing. And even though I tried as hard as I could to save her, Luca shot her in cold blood on the floor of the dining room. He shot her because she had choice words to say to me. His wife, who he believes in his twisted head that he *loves*. If I could, I would give him to you with open arms. He's cut me open, beat me, and this?" I wave to my short tresses. "This is his doing. So get out of my face and don't tell me how much you want him. Because I don't give a damn."

Her face is pale, and I can feel my confidence growing as I continue.

"So you can try to win him back, I will hope that you do, but you can do so at the risk of your own life. He told me himself he would kill anyone that got in the way of our marriage. And if you know him as well as you say you do, you'll know that he wasn't bluffing."

She looks stunned and doesn't move for a moment. I take that as my cue to leave and turned to walk to another corner when I feel her yanking me by the arm. I whip just in time to see her bringing her hand back, her face red with anger, about to slap me.

Out of nowhere, someone catches her hand, wringing it behind her back, and grabs the back of her head, smashing it into the wall. She cries out in pain, and I cry out in shock. She falls to the floor in a heap, holding the front of her forehead. Luca squats down in front of her.

"If I ever catch you speaking to my wife again, I will kill you."

I hear her gasp, and she flinches away from Luca. He grabs my arm, and we both turn to face the crowd. They are all staring in shock and silence. But as soon as Luca locks eyes with them, they go back to their evening as if nothing happened.

Luca pulls me away from the massive hall and into a study. I keep my eyes trained on the ground, afraid of what I may see if I look up. I hear him slam the door, and his footsteps are pacing hurriedly. I feel Luca snake his hand around my throat and push me back so that my back is flat against the desk. I cry out in shock from the abruptness of it. He immediately leans in and pushes the bottom of my dress up.

"Luca, wait." I try, but he is already yanking my underwear down. I try to sit up, but he tightens his hold around my throat, pinning me to the desk.

"Luca!" I shout, but he is not listening.

He enters me in one swift movement, and I cry out in pain. He leans over the desk so that his body is lying on top of mine as he stays buried and still inside of me.

"You look so sexy in this dress," he whispers. He traces a hand over the side of my face. He slowly begins moving inside of me.

"Do you know who that woman was?" he asks.

I can't speak from the hold he has on my neck, so I only shake my head.

"She was my past. They all are my past. You're my future, Elise. You're the one. They all mean nothing." His thrust speeds up, and his grip tightens. I can feel his large erection inside of me moving back and forth. I open my mouth to let out a cry, but it comes out as a muffled groan.

"You're mine, Elise. I only love you, do you understand that?" He begins literally fucking me against the desk, the loud slaps of our skin colliding echoing off the walls. Pleasure starts to emit from my core from the pace he is going, and I can feel myself reach toward my peak.

He threads his fingers through my hair and pulls my head into his shoulder. "You're all I want. You're all I need. Just say the word, and I'll kill any of those bitches that approach you."

I can't do anything but gasp. Luca doesn't let up at all. I can feel his thick length getting larger inside of me, and at that moment, an orgasm rips through my body. I open my mouth to cry out, but no noise comes out.

"Fuck," I hear Luca ground out, and I can feel him as he spills his release inside of me. Even then, he stays positioned inside of me as we both catch our breathing. He sits up over me, looking me in the eyes.

"None of them will ever be you, Elise. You're the only one." He cups my face in his, locking me in place so that I am forced to look in his eyes. "You're everything."

* * * * *

After we clean ourselves up, we arrive back at the party. No one seems to notice our absence. Either that or they pretend not to notice, seeing as Luca smashed a woman's face into the wall only an hour earlier.

Luca stands beside me, speaking to someone about his thoughts on expanding. I just tune the conversation out. I keep my arm wrapped in the crook of his elbow, because that is proper etiquette, but deep down, I wish I could just go back to my corner in the room. But Luca doesn't want to leave me alone again because he's worried another one of his "conquests" will approach me.

The sound of a glass being tapped with silverware quiets the room. We all look to see a man in a tux standing at the fore.

"Dinner is served!" he announces.

This must be a really special party, because it is now a dinner party. I'm too afraid to ask the occasion. I'm afraid to do anything with Luca, and I hate it. I have been weak all my life. And now even more so due to who my husband is.

We sit at the head of the massive table, Luca's father towards the head and Luca at the right. I sit next to Luca. Dinner is served, and his father never stops talking. He is a boisterous man that is proud of his son's accomplishments. Halfway through, he stands up, catching everyone's attention.

"My friends and my family, thank you for coming tonight. This dinner was in honor of my son's newlywed status. I know it's long overdue, but with everything that's happened lately, well, we haven't exactly had the time. But no one could be prouder than me of my only son. He has proved himself more than worthy to take over as the head of this family when the time comes. He has faced death and danger head-on without hesitation, and he has accomplished so much at such a young age. He has always listened to me and done what I've asked of him." He pauses.

"No one could be prouder than me. And now he gets to start his life anew with a beautiful wife and, hopefully soon, lots of children."

The choice noises that echo across the table make me blush heavily.

"To the perfect soldier and the perfect son, Luca. You have made your family proud." His father lifts his glass, and everyone else follows suit, cheers emitting from every corner of the table. Luca's smile couldn't have been brighter at that moment.

I lift my glass bitterly.

These people are all brainwashed idiots. Congratulating a man for being a murderer. A killer in cold blood. It sickens me how much they make this seem like it is a good thing. And his father sits there promoting it. *Bastard.* It's his fault his son is a sick sadist. And he is proud.

The sound of glass shattering pulls me from my thoughts. I look up and see Luca's father has dropped his glass on the table and is holding his side. Luca immediately tenses up and begins looking around. I gasp as red slowly spreads across his father's suit from underneath his hand. Luca looks immediately to his father, and for the first time in my entire life, I see fear in his eyes.

I immediately jump up from the table, as do the others that are there, as screams of terror fill the room. Luca is quick to spring into action. He pulls out his gun and scans the room. Another shot rings out, whizzing right past Luca, hitting his father again. He staggers and falls to the ground. Luca shouts something and runs to his father's side, his eyes wide and desperate. I watch as he cradles his father's wounded body.

"No, no, no. Papa, no," he is mumbling repeatedly.

He called him Papa. Usually he says Father. But at this moment, when he is vulnerable and open, he is saying Papa. He looks so small and broken sitting there holding on to his dad, begging him not to die. His father's men are already in place, scanning the room, the guests of the party already filing out of the dining room in a panicked frenzy. The room is silent, all except for Luca's incoherent mumbling.

I hear his father take a ragged breath.

"Listen to me, *figlio*."

He reaches slowly and grasps Luca's arm, pulling him down to his level. I can see Luca's eyes widen as his father whispers his dying words in his ear. Then his body falls limp. Luca doesn't seem to grasp that he is gone. He shakes his body, even getting angry and shouting at him to come back. It is heartbreaking. He squeezes his father's lifeless body and throws his head back, letting out a loud cry filled with pain and agony.

I immediately throw my hands over my mouth at the sight. Luca is hurt, almost broken. I take a step toward him.

"Luca," I whisper.

His head immediately shoots up, and he looks directly at me with a murderous expression. He raises his gun quicker than I can register and fires it. I squeal and close my eyes, waiting for the pain to hit me, but am shocked when I hear a loud thud behind me. Before I can turn, someone snatches me and pulls me close into their body. I feel the cold press of steel against my throat.

Luca still has his gun raised, an expression of hatred on his face. The deep voice behind me reverberates through my body.

"I would put that down, unless you want to lose your precious wife here too." Just to show he isn't bluffing, he presses the blade into my throat just enough to draw blood. I whimper in pain.

Luca doesn't waver, though; he still has his gun raised.

Footsteps echo into the massive dining hall, and I can hear Luca's father's men threaten the guy.

"Tell them to back off, or she dies," his voice whips out.

"Abbassate le armi!"[3] Luca begrudgingly growls out.

My heart is thundering so loudly in my chest, and I can hear my panicked breathing as Luca tells them to lower their guard. The man holding me laughs and takes a breath, ready to speak.

"These are the negotiations—"

Everything happens at once. A shot echoes through the room, and excruciating pain explodes through my lower stomach. I look down at my dress and see the red quickly staining the once-white fabric. My knees and the knees of the man behind me buckle, and we both fall to the floor in a heap.

My head feels so heavy it takes all my energy to look to where Luca is standing. I raise my hands slowly and try to press into the wound, my ragged breathing coming out panicked. He shot me. Luca shot me.

Luca's footsteps echo off the dining room walls as he walks closer to where I and the man lie in a wounded heap on the floor. I can see his face in the corner of my eye, and what I see there will haunt me in my dreams forever. Luca looks terrifying. His face is calm, expres-

---

[3] "Lower your weapons."

sionless. Yet it radiates hatred and anger. He walks completely past me to the man, who is trying to catch his breath.

Luca squats directly next to his head.

"There are no negotiations." I don't know if it is from the blood loss or the sound of Luca's voice, but my body runs cold, and I begin to shiver.

"That"—he motions to me with his gun—"is my wife. You are nothing to me. So imagine the fun I have in store for you."

"You're fucking crazy!" the man shouts out.

Luca throws his head back and laughs. He fucking laughs. A chilling laugh that echoes off the walls, piercing me to the bone. I hear footsteps and look to see people dragging the man away. Luca finally comes over to me, and I take what little energy I have trying to crawl away from him.

I cry out and scream and gasp in pain and desperation. I have to get away. I just have to. Luca easily catches me and elevates my head slightly.

"Don't move, baby. You could rupture something if you keep moving."

I take deep, quick breaths. "You … shot … me …"

He looks at me and still has no emotion on his face. I can feel my heavy tears running down the side of my face, over my temples, soaking my hair.

"I only shot through you. I made sure to miss any main arteries. Although I had to get a spot that would knock him on his ass and not let him move, so you'll be feeling weak for a while."

He pulls off his stained red jacket and balls it up, pressing it into the wound. I let out a scream of agony from the pain. It feels like someone is taking a match to my side and burning me but won't take the match away.

Luca did this to me. Like he always does. And I can feel a new emotion festering up deep within me, clawing its way to the surface.

"I … hate … you."

That is the last thing I can get out before my world turns dark.

Chapter 11

Elise

Life is cruel. It is cruel and unfair. I didn't ask to be born. I didn't ask to be married. I didn't ask for any of this. Yet here I am, enduring it.

I lie in bed staring at the ceiling. I can only move the minimum. Even though Luca missed major organs and arteries, the skin is still sore.

Luca's father's funeral is today. Lucky for me, I was shot by none other than my husband, so I have the perfect excuse to skip the funeral. Like I want to go, anyways. Luca and his father disgust me. And I am glad the bastard is dead. But this also means that Luca's position as capo is here. It is his time to take over and be the world's most notorious crime boss. The thought makes me shiver in fear. Luca is probably going to be ten times worse than his father ever was.

I know he heard me when I told him I hated him. And I meant it. I hate him with every fiber of my being. Luca gives no fucks either. To him, I am *his* wife. *His* property. He loves saying that. He loves proving it. He loves every single bit of it.

Luca's mood has been indescribable. He doesn't have personality anymore. He walks in the room with a straight face, will ask the doctor for an update, and leaves. He doesn't even sleep in the same bed as me. And today, he came in, got dressed, and left without a word. I have no idea what his thoughts are. And I know he isn't going to open up to me. Not after what he's done to me and what I've said to him.

I lift my shirt and look at the now-stitched skin. My eyes begin burning as tears begin to fill them up, spilling over.

What am I supposed to do? I have no one. No one but Ari. And I don't get to see her anymore. There is no way I am ever going to see her either more than likely. Not if Luca has anything to say about it. That is when an idea hits me. Ari is just the person I need. I slowly sit up and wince from the pain of the stitches. I ignore it as I roll out of bed and walk to the door. I pull it open with enough room to stick my head through. With it being Luca's father's funeral, only a handful of guards has stayed behind to watch over me. So that means they are posted at the gate and won't be in the house more than likely. My perfect time to make a phone call and not be afraid of getting caught. I slowly make my way out the door and down the stairs to Luca's office.

The giant mahogany door is shut, but with all the strength I can muster, I push it open. There is sweat forming on my brow from all the energy I have to use to get to the office and open the door. I am still weak from the bullet wound. I make my way through his office slowly.

It is strange being in here without him. The room is dim, except for the light coming in through the glass. I make my way to the massive desk that I have been pinned against so many times before. I look at my empty chair in the corner. I can feel the rage boiling up deep within me. How many times have I sat in that chair, playing, as he has spoken, tortured someone, or just done work.

I finally get to the desk and pick up the phone. I dial the number that I have known by heart all these years. It rings a few times but is finally picked up, and Ari's voice comes through.

"Hello?" The tears immediately spring into my eyes from the sound of her voice.

"Hello?" she asks again, her voice getting irritated.

I stifle a sob as I finally find my voice to speak. "Ari?" I breathe out.

"Elise?" she asks, obviously very shocked. "Elise! Oh my god, are you okay?" I can hear the panic in her voice. "I heard what happened to Luca's father. Are you okay? Did you get hurt? Why aren't you at the funeral?" She is firing one question after another, and I can't explain everything to her fast enough.

"Ari, I need your help."

* * * * *

I lie in bed thinking of my future and what it will hold. I am not going to sit back and take this from Luca anymore. The plan Ari and I have come up with will take a while to be put into play, but once it is here, it will work, and I will be free.

I hear the bedroom door open and immediately close my eyes, pretending to be asleep. I can hear footsteps, which I can only assume are Luca's. He is back from the funeral. The steps come closer to where I lie and pause next to me. After a moment, they move away, and I can hear the rustling of clothes.

The bed dips, and instead of him pulling me close like I expect him to, I can feel him laying his head on my stomach, careful not to be near my scar. Then I feel him shaking. I open my eyes and look down to see Luca facing me, but he isn't looking at me. It's almost as if he were looking through me. He is seeing nothing. Like he's not even there. And there are tears falling out of his eyes and onto my exposed stomach.

Luca's tears fall onto my stomach and roll, followed by another, and another. Then the sobs begin. Luca's sobs. Luca is crying. He is crying as he lies on top of me. I don't know what to do. So we lie like that, Luca atop me as he cries.

One Month Later

I sit fidgeting with my dress on the stage. The curtains are drawn. Today is the big day. Well, for me, anyway. Today is the day of the symphonic orchestra's performance. And my solo. On top of that, it is the day I am leaving. And I am nervous as hell.

Life for me has changed dramatically in the past month. What with Luca's big promotion to capo, everything is different. We moved. To a house that is on an estate in the middle of nowhere.

The day after Luca buried his father, it was almost as if he were a new person. He was colder than he had ever been before. As if the last shred of emotion he had died with him the day his father did.

Now he is almost emotionless. Smiles are rare for him. Very rare. He only ever smiles if I walk into the room after not seeing him for a while, and even then, it isn't a full-blown smile. More like an appreciative grin. He barely eats. He wakes up and goes through the motions of life, but it's almost as if he isn't here.

Even at the ceremony they held for him becoming the new capo he wasn't excited in the least. Men in this business are sworn in by blood oath. Once when they are "made a man," and for men like Luca, twice. When they are made a man and when they are made the capo. Luca stood ahead of everyone and swore in blood his promise to the family. He was so shut off, though, it was almost as if he were a different person. But something was wrong with him, because when we got home that night, he was anything but gentle with me. It was like Luca's father's death had really hit home for him.

The sound of the conductor's voice pulls me from my thoughts. He is on the podium next to me, speaking to us all and giving us a motivational speech. He decided to have me standing in front of the band as I play my solo. And Luca was too excited to hear that news. He immediately went out and bought me a brand-new dress. It's one of the other rare times that he has smiled at me in the past month.

The director signals for the band to begin playing, and the curtain is slowly raised. I close my eyes, take a deep breath, and begin playing.

Chapter 12

Luca

Elise stands atop the stage in her red gown, her eyes closed, letting the beautiful melody play out of the instrument she is so talented with. I have listened to her so many times before as she sat in my office, playing for me.

She is stunning. No, *stunning* is an understatement. Her hair has grown in the past months since I cut it, and she has large curls that barely touch her shoulders. I like her hair better short. I can see her face, and she can't hide from me behind those thick locks anymore. The gown I bought her hugs her figure perfectly. Her full lips are slightly parted as she plays, and her eyelashes are fanning her cheeks. She is swaying gently along with the music she is playing, clearly swallowed in her own world as she plays. The melody she is playing is enough to make a grown man cry. And I love her for it.

The day my father told me I was to marry was by far the worst day of my life. I recall it clearly.

"Luca, you know of the Trovoli family, yes?"

I narrow my eyes slightly at him. Why would he be talking about them? Of course I know of them. Everyone does. They are a family of conniving cowards that do whatever it takes to get power. That was how the current capo lost his wife. By being selfish and careless.

"The capo of the South has approached me with a brilliant idea. He wishes for us to grow stronger together, to form a union so we will be better armed against trouble if it arises." The smile on his face grows, and I can only imagine what he is about to say. *"We've decided a union*

between you and his only daughter will be a great way of showing that bond."

I jump up from my chair quickly, anger radiating off my body in waves.

"Marriage? Fucking marriage! That's your brilliant solution to us 'growing strong together'?"

He narrows his eyes at me, but I stand my ground. I am not fucking afraid of him.

"You can just say that you're going to work together, swear it, make an oath! You don't have to drag me into this. You're not about to tie me down with some bitch that's the fucking blood of that coward!"

"Luca, sit down!" my father shouts at me. Anyone else would have shut up and sat down in a second, but I am not anyone else. I am Luca-fucking-Pasquino, and I am not about to be ordered around by anyone. Especially not when it comes to my future.

"No. You can do whatever the fuck you want, but I want no part of this."

"Luca, you will listen to me!" he shouts. I can see the anger growing in his face.

I smile, completely amused. "Or what?" I laugh out loud to show my amusement at how he believes he is in control of this when he is trying to make me marry someone without my consent. "Go fuck yourself," I say as I stand and walk out of the room, my father's voice following me out of the room as he shouts my name.

I skip out on the rounds we were supposed to make collecting the money people pay us for protection. I just go to the bar and get drunk. I know I will have to marry this bitch. If not for my father, then for the good of the family. I always known I would have to marry; I've just never expected for it to be so soon.

I want nothing to do with the girl until then. I don't even bother to seek her out. I don't care to. I send her gifts out of courtesy, but that is about it. The Trovolis are a disgusting group of people. Stabbing their own kind in the back for years. Honestly, I was going to have them all done away with once I became the head. They have done too much to be forgiven for. But with the Russians and the Taiwanese coming farther *into our territory, I can see how coming together will strengthen us. It will give us power across the United States and make us stronger.*

I'll marry her, but I won't give a damn about her. She is just another job, for all I care. I am not going to stop seeing my women, and I am not going to stop living the life I have before her. She isn't going to change me.

The day I finally meet my bride-to-be is a day I will never forget. I am walking through her home, actually, on my way to meet with her father about the negotiations of something. I stopped in my tracks as a sound I have never heard before caresses my ears. The door is cracked to the room, and I push it open slightly.

There is a girl, and she is playing a violin, her long dark locks facing me. The tune has me captured. It is beautiful. She is very talented. She finally ends the melody, and I can't help myself. I start clapping. She tenses in her seat and turns to face me.

Holy fuck! Perfect. She is perfect. I can feel the hardening in my pants as she stares at me with big almond-colored eyes that look back at me. They are wide and full of innocence. Her lips are a lovely shade of pink. Nice and full. Her hair is pitch-black and falls to her waist. She is wearing a light-blue dress that fits her nicely. Not too tight, but tight enough that I can see her lovely figure.

I recognize her from the picture I saw a while back. Except now her face is more developed. And so is her body. She is a woman now.

"So you're my future bride. You're quite the beauty."

She looks away as a bright-red blush crawls its way up her neck. I frown a little. She is hiding from me behind that thick curtain of hair. I don't like that. I want to see her face.

"Thank you," she whispers. Damn, her voice even radiates innocence. I can't wait to hear that beautiful whisper with my name coming off her lips.

After I leave her, my mind is made up. She is mine. All mine. And no one else's. I don't want anyone else. I only want her. I even call that noisy bitch Jessica and tell her I am done with her. Something is festering deep inside of me toward Elise. A strong emotion. And it makes me want her even more than I do just now.

(Even when my father gave me the option of killing her off with her father, I couldn't do it.)

I step into his office. He wants to see me on the information I've found. He is pacing back and forth, obviously pissed that he has almost been had. I've told him not to trust those damn Trovolis.

"Take a seat, Luca." His voice comes out gruff. I sit down and wait for him to calm down before I speak. Even I am pissed with the information I've discovered. When Elise's father went to strike her the night of our wedding, my suspicions grew even further. No man would dare strike another man's wife. Especially mine, if he truly believed this is a union of strength.

I looked into his phone calls, transactions, emails, and I even had Nicolai tail him for me.

"Elise's father has been busy scheming against us." I explain to him everything down to the tracker I discovered is buried in Elise's arm.

He is silent. "Are you sure, son?"

"Absolutely. I told you the Trovolis couldn't be trusted. But you just wanted to be blinded by your clouded beliefs."

My father still hasn't spoken. I can only imagine what he is thinking. I told him not to trust that family, and he goes against his better judgment and plays right into their hands.

"I want them dead," he says while looking at the desk. I'm caught off guard by his choice of words.

"Them?"

"Elise and her father," he says.

Maybe before the marriage, I would have gladly obliged. But everything is different now. I slowly stand and smooth out my shirt. "I will gladly take care of her father. But Elise stays with me."

My father looks up in surprise at my words. "Excuse me?"

I can see the anger beginning to flare. Our thing has always been to kill the betrayer and everyone he loves. Even if he doesn't love them, the family is to be made an example of. But killing Elise doesn't sit well with me. Not now that she is mine.

"I said no, Father. I will kill the father. But not Elise. And this time, I won't budge on that," I say, meeting his glare head-on.

He sits back in his chair and watches me, as if trying to figure out what my goal is. In truth, I have no idea. Usually, I would have done this no problem. But I want Elise. I want her alive. And my father's plan pisses me off.

He chuckles to himself, as if in thought, and waves me toward the door.

"Fine, Luca."

Elise is still playing on the stage. I will never be able to fathom how she is so talented. How she can play these notes and make them sound so beautiful. She is perfection. And she is mine.

She is all I have now. My father is gone because of some bastards from her family. They must have been trying to avenge her father's death. How they found out it wasn't an accident, I still have yet to find out. They snuck into my father's party and killed him. I am so close to just eradicating the world of that filthy bloodline. The only thing that is keeping me from doing that is the woman standing on the stage right now.

My father and I were close, so his death has really been hard on me. And the fact that Elise's family is behind it makes it hard to be around her. I want to destroy her in every little way possible. Make her pay for her family's sins. But I figure the gunshot wound I've given her is enough to sate my anger. Honestly, I felt as though that was the only way I could save her from the man that held her at gunpoint, but once I finished with him and figured out who was behind all this, well, I don't feel so bad about her getting caught in the middle.

It is her tainted bloodline's fault that my father is dead. I want to make them all suffer. As soon as I was sworn in as the capo, my subordinates thought that was what I was going to do. But the feelings I have toward Elise since I've married her are stronger than ever. And killing her is not going to happen.

She finishes the melody, and the applause begins. People even stand to show their appreciation of her talents. I can't help but smile, pride swelling in my chest. I knew they would love her.

After the concert, I stand in the entryway, waiting for her. I watch as others meet and greet their families and friends that have come to watch. All Elise and I have now is each other. I can feel the bitterness in me rising as I think about the bastards that have taken my father from me. I try to stuff the feeling back down. This is Elise's night.

I see her open the doors and walk through, looking even more magnificent up close. She looks around until her eyes meet mine, and makes her way over to me. I can't help the smile that comes over me. This amazing woman is mine.

I pull her warm body into mine in a tight embrace.

"You were wonderful, Elise."

She mumbles a thank-you, and I pull back and study her. Her heart rate has increased. It's faster than usual. And her skin is warm. As if she is nervous about something. She also can't look me in the eye.

"Something wrong, Elise?" I ask her.

She clears her throat and keeps avoiding eye contact with me. "No."

Hmmm. I place my hand on the small of her back and lead her toward the door. A man walks up to us with excitement on his face. He comes up so quickly I, out of instinct, reach for my gun just in case. But he only comes to compliment Elise.

"Wow, that was amazing! Your talent is incredible. I've never heard anything like that before." He is smiling at her. When I look down, she is smiling back. I feel a deep rage boil up within me. I told her that. I smiled at her. And she can't even return the smile. But when this stranger comes out of nowhere, she offers him a smile just like that? Fuck no.

I pull her away in the middle of his talking, not caring about how rude I am being. Once I have Elise in the car, I try to rein in my anger, but it is getting fucking hard.

"Luca?" Her timid voice breaks through my haze. I hate it when she tries to act like she's done nothing wrong. I have told her before, I just want to see her smile. That is all I fucking want.

"What the fuck is wrong with you?" I ask. I am trying to stay calm, but it is getting near impossible. "I do everything for you. Everything! All I want from you is a smile. A goddamn smile!" I squeeze the steering wheel, but my anger is already getting the best of me. I look at her in anger.

"You—"

I am cut off immediately as something happens that I never expected in my life. Elise reaches over and pulls the steering wheel. She catches me off guard completely. The car immediately swerves off the road and slams right into a tree, deploying the airbags. Glass shatters everywhere as the loud thunder of the car being crushed explodes around me. Pain wracks my entire body, and I can feel the blood rushing down my head when it collides with the side of the car. My chest is burning. I immediately look over at Elise, and she has barely any damage. She is breathing hard and frantically moving around. She has a few cuts and bruises, but that's about it. She braced for impact.

My vision is getting blurry, and I am fighting consciousness. Elise opens her violin case quickly. Her hands are shaking, and she is fumbling with stuff. What the fuck? Her violin isn't in the case, but there are different objects I can't make out from the injuries I've sustained. She pulls out handcuffs. And her eyes meet mine.

Her eyes are wide and full of fear, and I see a slight hesitation. Whatever is holding her back, she pushes it from her mind. She immediately reaches for my hands, and I jerk, trying to prevent her from grabbing them. My fucking seat belt is jammed, preventing me from moving away, and my body is wracked with pain. There is the deafening sound of the handcuffs being cuffed around my wrists, and she cuffs me to the steering wheel.

"Elise! What the fuck!"

She completely ignores me and turns, trying to kick open her jammed door. She is weak, too, from her injuries, but she somehow finds the energy to kick it open.

"Elise!" I shout again. Rage is boiling up deep within me from this betrayal. "Elise! Get your fucking ass back here!"

She still ignores me.

I can feel myself barely hang on to the consciousness. A cough makes its way out from my body, and blood comes out. Fuck. I must have internal bleeding from the seat belt crushing my chest. Elise looks back one last time, and I see a look on her face I have never seen before. Hatred. Pure hatred. For me.

"I hope you die." Her words float between us. She gives me one last glance and runs. I can't see where.

"Elise!" I shout.

"Elise!" I try again, but she is really gone.

This is why she was nervous. This was all planned. The fucking bitch knew what she was going to do and did it. And she told me she hopes I die. I smile, and the action brings out another fit of coughing. At this rate, I just may. The car is literally crushing me. I am hanging on to consciousness by a thread, and I had no security follow me tonight because I figured I wouldn't need any outside of the estate. I would be with my wife.

I am certifiably screwed.

Bitterness seeps into me as I recall my words to my father. *Never trust a Trovoli.*

And now I am eating those words, possibly with my life. The fucking bitch.

If I make it out of this alive, she had better pray I don't find her. If I do, God help her.

Chapter 13

Luca

Two months. Two months, and we have no trail. No sign. Nothing. It's almost as if she has disappeared. How does someone like Elise manage to outsmart the Mob? I keep this to a minimum between me, Nicolai, and Romelo. They are the only people I can trust with this delicate situation. If anyone finds out the *ruthless* capo was almost killed by his wife and that she has run away on top of that, they will see it as an opening. And bad things will start to happen. It's been hard enough keeping this a secret, and it's getting even harder with each passing day.

Lucky for me, someone came by and found the wreckage before I lost too much blood and suffocated from the seat belt crushing my chest. Unlucky for me, that means they called the police. Which means hospital visits. And records. Which I don't need right now. The cops are already hot on my tail about a recent incident that some of my people have slipped up in.

I laugh aloud to myself. She's actually done it. She has out-smarted me. And I have no idea how she did it. The only trail we've been able to pick up from her is a rather-large amount of money exchanged at a pawnshop in New Jersey. We went to the shop as a lead, and sure enough, her wedding ring was sitting in the window when we arrived. I almost murdered the man in the shop for even taking it.

We had set up perimeters to show of any uncommon activity in surrounding areas and found none. And with the tension between us and the Southern Mob, keeping this quiet is crucial. If anyone finds out the daughter of their late capo is missing, they will assume the worst and all-out war will break out between us.

I take a seat in my desk, pondering this. Where could she possibly have gone? And how does she keep avoiding us? How is she surviving this long off the radar? There has to be someone helping her, but who? Who would be dumb enough to cross me and help her? I've thought of this before but have come up short. I've kept her isolated. She has never spoken to anyone around the house and rarely goes out. It's not like she has a phone.

A thought pops into my head. I quickly move to the computer and go to the website for my phone. There is no way to pull up the call log on the phone since we've moved and gotten a new one, but I can follow up on my suspicions another way. The online call logs. I scroll and scroll until something pops out at me. That's it. A number I have never seen before is sitting there, staring back at me. I look to the area code, and sure enough, it matches Elise's hometown. I didn't make a phone call to them. And if I did, I would have at least recognized the number. But who? Who from the South would dare defy me as to help my wife?

She has a cousin. I've completely forgotten the girl's name. But she has a fucking cousin that she has always run to when we would visit. The very cousin that she has always dragged away from me when she needed to talk to her. I change the website and book a ticket.

Three hours later, I'm sitting in the car that will take me to Stefano Gudierri's home. That's the name of Elise's cousin's husband. I've done a background check on them. Ari is the daughter of Pietro Trovoli, the brother of Elise's father. He was killed during a raid in a warehouse when Elise's father was younger.

I have brought Nicolai and Romelo along with me. Nicolai is my best friend, and Romelo is my most trusted man. The closer the we get, the more my anger festers as I think of this woman's role in my wife's escape. *These traitorous rats.*

I look around at the scenery that passes me by. So this is the area Elise grew up in. I've never paid attention to it, because each time I've been around it, Elise has been with me, so there's been no need. Even though she almost killed me and told me that she hopes she did it, I don't want to kill her in return, which is surprising to me.

I step out of the car and knock on the door, scanning the yard. They have a very lax security system for their reputation. All the guards are stationed outside the gate. They also live close together. Too close for my taste. I wonder how many times Elise has come to this house to visit her dear cousin.

The door opens, and there she is. Her cousin is standing in the doorway with a large smile on her face, which falls immediately when she sees it's me standing on the other side of the door. I don't bother giving her a smile. If she is the reason my Elise has escaped from me, she better hope some miracle will happen soon.

"Is your husband home?" I ask. I can see the hesitation in her face. She wants to lie to me.

"Yes. I'll go get him," she says.

I can already tell that she is guilty of something. In the past, when she saw me, she would shoot me hateful glares when she thought I wasn't paying attention. Even when I was, she would at least stand her ground and show me she has distaste toward me. But now she can't even look at me. And judging by the tremors in her voice, she is nervous.

She leaves us standing in the entry area as she goes get her husband. I look at Nicolai and Romelo, silently reminding them of the plan we are about to put into play. If this bitch helped my wife escape me, there will be hell to pay. I've had it with these disgusting Trovolis.

Stefano rounds the corner with a smile on his face. He obviously doesn't know the extent to which we are here. But his dear wife does. Poor man. Elise's cousin is a Trovoli also, her father the brother of Elise's father. She has the same despicable blood running through her veins.

"Luca Pasquino, it's an honor to have you here with us in our home! To what do we owe this visit?" He holds his hand out, and we exchange a firm shake. I keep my attention focused on his wife, though. She is standing behind him with her eyes downcast. She is guilty.

"Is there anywhere we can speak in private?" I ask.

His smile falters a bit, and he leads us around the hall to his office, opening the door. He is about to close it, leaving his conniving wife on the other side, when I stop him.

"Actually, I would like it if your wife was to join us."

He pauses a moment, and I can hear her light gasp. He slowly motions for her to come with us into the room.

"What's this all about?" he questions.

As soon as we are in and the door is closed, the plan is put into action. Nicolai turns on Stefano, attacking him so that he is kneeling on the ground and completely immobile. Romelo is standing over him, aiming the gun at the top of his head. Elise's cousin lets out a short scream, and I pull out my gun, aiming it at her. She shuts up real quick.

I motion to one of the sitting chairs with my gun. She slowly sits down, and there are tears brimming in her eyes.

"Do not move, or I will kill him where he kneels."

Her eyes are wide as she nods her understanding. I can feel the adrenaline coursing through my veins as I feed off the terror shining in her eyes. She has no idea what she has gotten herself into.

"What the fuck is this?" Stefano shouts from his place on the ground.

I step to him slowly and aim my gun underneath his chin. "Why don't you ask your beloved wife?"

He looks at her frantically, and she is crying her eyes out from her place across the room.

"Here's how this is going to work. You're going to answer my questions, or I will shoot him. Try to move, and I will shoot you, and then I will shoot him."

She nods violently and keeps her eyes trained on her husband.

"Show me your phone."

She slowly reaches into her pockets and retrieves a small phone, handing it to me with shaking hands. I unlock the screen and go to the call log. There's nothing but random numbers. I'm about to give up when I come across a number that looks familiar. Mine. More than a month ago. I press the number to see the date the call was made. The day I buried my father.

I can feel my rage pooling and grow more and more angry. This fucking bitch. I look up from the screen, and before I know it, the phone is flying across the room and shatters against the wall. I'm up out of my seat, screaming before I can comprehend anything else.

"You fucking helped her escape! You helped her get away from me! What the fuck did you do?" I am shouting at such a close vicinity.

I hear shuffling behind me and turn to see Stefano moving, trying to get to me. I walk close to him, and my foot lashes out, connecting with his face and stomach. I can hear Elise's cousin scream and beg me to stop, but I keep going until he can barely move on the floor beneath me. There is blood pooling beneath him from his nose and split lip. I ought to shove his face in it. Drown him in his own blood.

Then I turn back to the dumb bitch that helped my wife escape.

"Where the fuck is she?" I ask.

She doesn't respond. She is sobbing continuously, and it is irritating the fuck out of me. I yank her hair back and force her to look at her husband. A shot fires through the room, and she screams as Stefano grunts in pain, holding his arm. I motion for Romelo to fire a shot that will harm but not kill the man.

"I don't know!" she shouts. She is lying. I can tell by the frantic movements she is making.

I lift my hand to tell Romelo to fire another shot when she jumps from the seat.

"Wait, wait! Please." She is sobbing in her hands. She falls to the floor on her knees. "She called me from a phone in Colorado a few weeks ago." I can feel my blood boiling beneath my skin. I have to fight so hard to keep my rage suppressed.

"How did she get there?"

"I … I helped her escape. She didn't deserve to be with a monster like you! Elise is kind and loving, and you're killing her! You're breaking her into nothing but a shell of her former self! She can't live like th—"

I press the gun into her shoulder. The space that is right underneath the bone. She gasps aloud and begins whimpering, but it does nothing but fuel my anger. I pull the trigger without hesitation. The fire echoes throughout the chamber, and I can hear Stefano shout a string of curse words. Elise's cousin sits in front of me screaming in agony, and I watch, mesmerized, as the blood soaks her shirt. I take my thumb and push it deeper into the wound.

"I'm a monster?" I laugh, truly finding amusement in her choice of words. "You just awoke the demon sleeping within me. You obviously don't know exactly *who* you are dealing with. And now because of you, she may not live at all."

She is biting her lip in pain. I have had it with these people. I want my wife back. Now.

"I will fucking mutilate your husband and make you watch as I paint the walls with his dead carcass. What else aren't you telling me?"

Her eyes widen in terror as she finally realizes who she has crossed. I don't know why the fuck she even bothered to help Elise out, knowing who her husband is.

"She moves every two weeks to a different location. The next time she moves will be two days from now. I'm sorry. I'm so sorry! P-please!"

Her words have no effect on me. If anything, this little stunt helps set my decision on these filthy people.

"Sir." Romelo's voice pulls me from my thoughts. I look up. Stefano is holding his shoulder in pain, but the look in his eyes shows that he is hurt by his wife's actions and infuriated by the fact that I've shot her. It's just a flesh wound. Nothing that will kill her. I stand and walk away from them both, turning before we exit.

"Do not cross me again. I will kill all of you, including Elise."

I let Nicolai and Romelo exit before I turn and look at Elise's cousin.

"Do not contact her again. It is clear that you can't be trusted with the little bit of freedom you did have." I make sure to slam the door behind me.

We leave the house with a new directive and a fresh, new trail to find that traitorous bitch. Just like her whole family. Something needs to be done about them. All of them.

"Set up a perimeter around Colorado. I want everything nearest any pay phone tracked. I want the phones tapped and wired. I want hotel tickets monitored. Any that's been there or checked in at the beginning of the twelve days from Friday and any after."

No sooner than the words leave my lips do Romelo and Nicolai take action. I hope Elise enjoyed her time away from me, because just like her wishing I were dead, well, when I am done with her, she'll be wishing she were.

Chapter 14

Elise

"I'm leaving for the week, Frank!" I shout across the room. My boss, Frank, looks at me and, with a sad smile, makes his way over.

"Sad to see you go, Elise." He hands me my check and a slip of paper. "This is your referral. You work harder than anyone I've ever had before. You said you were moving to Nevada, right? Well, go to a restaurant called Forks and ask for Robin. Give him this letter, and the job is surely yours." He smiles a smile full of kindness. I will really miss him.

But I can't afford to get attached to anyone. Luca can be on my trail even at this very moment. That is why I can't stay in one place for very long.

When I first ran off, the planning and the waiting were all worth it. Ari wired me the money to keep me afloat, and I've made sure to move every two weeks so I can't get too comfortable. There's no time to stay in one place. If Luca picks up even a fraction of my trail, he'll find me quicker than I can plan an escape.

That's why when I first move to a different area, I scan the area and come up with multiple escape routes just in case. The first week of my runaway was scary. In all honesty, I thought Luca died, because his injuries were so bad. So I had a mini heart attack when I saw him. Luca had come meters from catching me. After I pawned my wedding ring, he came to the pawnshop within minutes. I had been across the street, eating, when I saw him pull up. Lucky for me, he was too angry about the ring being in the window to think to search the area, and I got away.

Me landing this job waitressing was pure luck. Lucky for me the man that owns the joint is kind and doesn't need an explanation as to my strange moving patterns. But somehow, he understands I am in trouble and has helped me out by giving me this job. It keeps my mind busy and helps me earn some extra cash. I need to stop contacting Ari, because pretty soon, the phone calls and money-wiring will add up and Luca will catch the pattern. I hate myself each time I get Ari involved in this mess, but until I am stable enough to keep Luca off my trail, I need her.

I have made sure to keep my moving patterns random so Luca can't detect them. And I think I've done a pretty good job as of late. But it's time for me to go so that Luca doesn't catch me. I need to have a whole day to cover my trail and disappear off the radar from this area before I leave.

I give Frank a hug and grab my coat before leaving the small diner for good. It's hard to believe that I've eluded Luca this long, but it has been heavenly and peaceful. And I love it. Even though I am paranoid, the fact that I don't have to be scared of him being in a bad mood and taking it out on me has done wonders for me. This must be the freedom people talk about. Not living in fear, but pure joy, because you have no psycho killer as a husband.

I walk with my head down, as I always do. I don't know if Luca has people on the lookout for me or not. I don't want to risk it and get caught because I am being careless. But Luca will have to give up eventually on finding me, and I will be free.

I finally reach the hotel room I have rented out, and unlock the door. It's a medium-size room with a small kitchen and bathroom and an area for the bed. It's big enough for me and has enough space so I don't need to crowd anything in. It's not like I have a lot of luggage, anyways. When I escaped from Luca, I ran with nothing more than my violin case and the contents of it. I had taken my violin out the night of the concert and put things I would need for survival. That was my only hope of escape. I had taken a change of clothes and the tools I needed to escape.

I take the little bit of clothing that I do have and stuff them in the empty case. Tomorrow is going to be spent covering my tracks here, and when Friday comes, I will move. This time, I will be going to Nevada. I have a map that I drop a coin onto so I'll just get there randomly and not have a plan. It's the only way I can move around without having a pattern. Even subconsciously.

After I pack everything up, I decide to take a shower. I strip my clothes and stop in front of the mirror, looking at the scar that will be forever inscribed into my skin. I run my fingers over the skin. It is smooth and flat. The scabbing is gone, so now all that remains is lightened skin that spells out *Luca*. Every time I look at it, my hatred for Luca brews even stronger.

I step into the shower and let the warm spray wash away the week's stress.

Living like this isn't healthy. Always looking over my shoulder, afraid that Luca may be there. I am constantly paranoid of someone being too nice to me. Or someone that is angry at me.

I even grow nervous when someone stops me to ask directions. I can't even answer them, because I think I have been caught.

I step back into my room after my shower and lie down in my bed. This has never been the life I envisioned for myself, but it is necessary to get away from that crazy man I have been forced to marry. My life has never been happy until this point that I am at now. My father never showed me the affection I craved, and my whole life has been used for his power and his gain. Eventually, my thoughts run me ragged, and I let sleep take me.

I don't know what it is that wakes me in the middle of the night, but something isn't right. My eyes shoot open, and immediately I try to sit up in bed, but something holds me down. No, not something, *someone*. My heart explodes in my chest as a deep chuckle reverberates throughout the room.

"If you move, I will cut your throat where you lie."

My blood freezes in my veins. Luca is lying behind me in the bed. As if to prove his point, I feel the cold press of the steel against my throat. He is holding me down with one hand, while the other is wrapped around my side, holding the knife. How? How did he find me? I've been so careful. I didn't leave any clues!

His hands roam under my shirt. "I missed your skin."

He leans in so I can feel his warm breath tickle my ear.

"You thought you could run away from me? *Me*. The capo." I can feel his hands thread through my hair, and he jerks roughly on it, yanking me at an uncomfortable angle. I gasp aloud from the pain.

"And you were foolish enough as to drag your naive cousin into it."

My heart jumps as I take in the meaning of his words. "I ... I swear if you touched Ari—"

He cuts me off and begins laughing, as if he really finds my words funny. "What? You're going to kill me? You better be glad I didn't shoot you in your sleep."

I bite my jaw in pain as his grip on my hair tightens. All this time, I thought I was doing good. I thought I really had a chance. But Luca has caught me. Easy.

He yanks me out of the bed, and I cry out in pain. It's time for me to put the training and escape plans into action. I drop my body, the weight catching him off guard.

Both of our bodies drop to the floor, and my hand shoots out, the palm nailing him in the chin. I hear him cry out in pain, and I take off across the room, making sure to grab my case, which I have set by the door. I yank the door open and take off up the hallway, or at least I try. Hands reach out and snatch me before I am good out the door. My violin case clatters to the floor, everything spilling out of it down the hall.

The hands that are holding me on either side of me force to kneel in front of the dark doorway that was once my room. I struggle and cry out in frustration. My eyes are burning from the newly emerging tears as I realize I have been caught. That it is over. These men work for Luca. One I recognize as Nicolai, and the other because I have seen him around the house all the time as if he were Luca's shadow. Luca emerges, looking as scary as he had the day he lost his father.

His cold gray eyes pin me to my spot, making me afraid to move an inch. He's rubbing his chin and watching me with a wicked gleam in his eyes. One that I've never seen before. Luca has always kept his expressions unreadable, but now he doesn't care at all, and I am seeing everything. My heart rate speeds up, as if sensing danger. Luca squats in front of me and reaches out slowly. Out of nowhere, his hand connects with the back of my head, smashing my face into the carpet.

I cry out and lie there in pain, but not before he yanks me back up. I have seen Luca angry before, but the look on his face now is something I never hoped to encounter. I can taste the metallic tang as blood fills my mouth from my now-split lip.

"Let me explain something to you in case you haven't realized the severity of this situation. You almost killed me—"

I can feel the hatred I have brewed up for Luca and smile in his face before interrupting him. "Good." I then emphasize my claim and spit at his feet.

A muscle in his jaw clenches. Before I can register what's going on, my face is being smashed back into the carpet. I don't even have time to get a grip of my surroundings. His hand wraps around my throat, and he squeezes.

"You tried to fucking kill me, you dragged your family into it, and you ran away from me." He squeezes even harder, as if emphasizing his point. I try to struggle, but Luca is too strong for me.

"L-luca …," I try to squeak out.

"Save your fucking begging. You're going to need it."

The last thing I register is my face being forced toward the carpet. Then nothing.

* * * * *

My head is hammering as I slowly regain consciousness. My throat feels dry, and my mouth feels as though cotton balls have been shoved in it. The events of Luca catching me come rushing back to me. I don't bother moving just in case Luca is around. I just move my eyes so I can see the room I am in. My heart jumps as I take in the room.

I've never seen it before. The bed is massive, with a red canopy draped over it, and black mahogany on all four corners holding up the frame. But that isn't what shocks me. The walls are a deep red, and in front of the bed, elevated on four columns, is a cage. A big cage.

I look to the left of the bed, and there is a long table and metal chairs, and on the walls are all kinds of tools I have never seen before. There are even cuffs attached to the wall. I don't wait around for Luca to appear out of nowhere. It's obvious this room is designed for some kind of torture.

I sit up quickly, ignoring the spinning room, and make way for the door, only to be yanked back roughly by my throat. Wait, what? After a coughing fit, I sit up slowly and look to the frame of the bed. There's a chain. The chain leads all the way to the fucking collar strapped around my throat.

Repeated gasps fill the entire chamber as I break into a full-blown panic attack. I immediately wrap my hands around the chain and yank with all the force I can put into it. It doesn't budge.

"You're not going to break that with your dainty hands, baby."

I jump and follow the sound of Luca's voice to see him stepping into the room from a dark door. I look beyond him and see stairs and a dark corridor. Wherever he has me must be underground or something.

I slowly lower my hands and feel my body vibrating. I am shaking in fear. Literally.

Luca's tall frame enters the room, and he looks devastatingly handsome as ever. He isn't wearing a shirt, so all his tattoos are visible. Some have names and dates, others have detailed pictures, and there is a quote under his rib I can't make out in this lighting. His pitch-black hair is untamed on his head in wild curls, and his flawless face is watching me. How much easier life would be if he were at least unattractive. Then I wouldn't be betrayed by my body all the time in his presence.

He walks even closer to me, going as slow as he likes, never taking those steel-colored eyes off me.

"Do you like it?" he says as he gestures to the room around me. "I had it especially renovated for you." He doesn't come to the bed, only walks to the wall filled with all kinds of strange implements.

"Of course, I got brand-new tools for you. Wouldn't want to use the same tools I used for interrogations on my lovely wife." He pauses and comes to the bed.

"You are still my wife, Elise."

He reaches in the back pocket of his jeans and pulls out that damn ring I pawned all those weeks ago. He reaches out and slowly takes ahold of my shaking hand, slowly pushing the ring back into place. His eyes move up, and he reaches out, trailing a finger around the collar latched around my neck.

"Can't have you running off anymore. Do you like your new jewelry?" He loops a finger underneath between the collar and my skin and pulled me closer to him.

"I had it especially made just for you. Real diamonds, baby. You wouldn't imagine how much it cost me." He smiles, but it is not at all kind.

I open my mouth, but nothing comes out. Luca is so calm, so nonchalant right now. And right before he knocked me out, he told me I would need my begging. His attitude is making me even more terrified.

His eyes drop to the choice of clothing he has decided to make me wear. Just a lacy white pair of bra and panties. I can see the moment his pupils dilate the adrenaline of something fueling his system.

"Damn, you are so sexy, baby." He traces his name on my side slowly, as if mesmerized by the skin.

"So tell me, when you ran from me, wrecked my car, told me you hoped I died, did you at all bother to think of the consequences your actions would entail? Or did you think you could actually get away with it?" He is watching me with that calculated gaze.

"Your cousin obviously didn't think of the consequences of defying the capo."

My heart thunders, and either bravery or stupidity brews up deep within me at his implications.

"What the fuck did you do to Ari?" I shout.

That is just the opening Luca is looking for. His eyes flash, and he yanks on the chain connected to the collar around my throat, forcing me backward on the bed. He immediately crawls over me and wraps a hand along my jaw.

"Oooh, baby, seems like you got a little potty mouth in my absence." His malicious smile grows less and less human by the second. "Don't worry, that will be the first thing to go while we're here."

Then he says, "Your cousin isn't dead. Yet. Though I should have killed her the moment she confessed."

All my anger evaporates as I take in the meaning of his words.

"C-confessed?" I whisper.

Luca smirks at me as if I were stupid for even asking the question.

"Yes, baby, *confessed*. She told me *everything*. Including your little movement pattern. It didn't take quite as much pain as I would have liked to get her to tell, but I still got it out of her."

Tears well up in my eyes. He hurt Ari. And she told him everything. I don't know whether to feel angry at the betrayal or shameful for dragging her into this. I've lost. This is a game I should have never gotten involved in. I don't know why I thought I could escape from Luca.

"I originally had this room made for anniversaries, birthdays … you know, special occasions. I was going to show it to you when it was finished, but in your absence, I decided to change it up a bit. You know, for the occasion." His eyes are filled with amusement as he imagines something probably fucked up.

"I can't wait to break the room in with you."

"P-please, Luca, d-don't do this …"

I can barely get the words out as a newfound fear for my husband develops within me. I'm an idiot for thinking this could work. And now he's going to make me pay for this. *Big-time*. Luca's deep chuckle brings me out of my thoughts. He leans in and licks up the tears running down the side of my face.

"You want to know what I love more than your tears?"

Suddenly, he yanks on the chain, and it tightens around my neck like a noose. I immediately jerk and reach up to put my hands around the collar as it cuts off my airflow. Luca leans into my ear as I gasp quietly for air.

"Your screams."

Chapter 15

Elise

Luca sits across the room, reading a book. I don't know what book it is, I don't know how long he has been reading it, but I am glad he is, because it gives me a break from his mood. He's sitting at a desk, with one leg crossed over the other, just reading, his face intently focused on the pages in front of him.

The thing about Luca is that he is very intelligent. Too smart for his own good. But he somehow can't understand the basic knowledge of emotions and feelings. It's scary how he knows so much and has no idea what to properly do with it. His father has raised him to be a killing machine, without a conscience or any sympathy.

I jump as he flips the page, the sound scaring me. Luckily, he still sits there reading the book, his dark hair falling slightly in his face. His head is bent at an angle so that I can see the slight furrow of his brow, his thick lashes touching his cheeks each time he blinks.

How can someone that looks so innocent while reading a book be the complete opposite of what he looks like?

As if sensing he's being watched, Luca's eyes meet mine. I immediately gasp and shrink back away from his emotionless gaze. If there is anything I've learned from him in the past six hours, it's that he's a man to be feared.

He quietly folds the page, marking his place, and closes the book. He rises from his spot and makes his way over to me, making sure to grab a jacket, I assume, he brought with him when he arrived.

I honestly don't know what to do. I'm a sitting duck in the middle of this room. He has me literally latched to the bed. So I'm completely at his mercy.

"You know, each time I look at you, I get angry all over again," he says.

I can see the hate creeping into his gaze, but he does a good job covering it up. His hands are stuffed deep within his pockets. I know all his guns and knives are off him, because he made sure to unload his holsters slowly in front of me, making me fear what is to come. He sits on the edge of the bed, watching me with no emotion in his gaze.

"Did you know the human body has ninety-five to one hundred billion nerve cells in it?" He reaches out and slowly grasps my shaking hand. He looks down at my arm as he speaks.

"But out of those, only three run through your arm." He flips my arm over and trails a pattern, starting at my elbow. "The radial nerve." He flips my arm over again so that my palm is facing the ceiling. "The ulnar and the median nerve." He is tracing a pattern on my arm, as if he knows where the nerves are underneath my skin. He looks truly mesmerized by the sight.

Suddenly, his expression changes. He drops my arm and looks me in the eyes.

"But I don't have to know that to make you feel pain."

I immediately open my mouth to begin begging when an exploding pain sears across my face. Luca slapped me. I cry out in pain and hold my cheek, tears welling up.

"Don't you dare fucking beg." He looks murderously angry. And it terrifies me to no end. I only nod, hoping it will calm him down.

"God, I swear if you were anyone else, I would have shot you down in that hotel room. But for some reason, I don't want to kill you. But I can't help but hate you." He pauses and stares at the ceiling. He moves quickly and comes to the bed, messing with my "collar." He comes back around and has the chain in his hand. He yanks hard enough to jerk me off the bed. I fall off in a heavy heap and hit the ground with a loud thud.

He doesn't give me the chance to set myself upright; he continues to drag onto the chain even when he sees that I'm struggling, his large strides catching me off guard.

"Luca, wait." I try, but he is tugging so hard and fast I don't have equilibrium to stay upright. Suddenly, he's in front of me with an angry glare, jerking me up by the throat until my feet are off the ground. I cry out and spasm from the sudden roughness, but he doesn't care. He seems to be enjoying my struggles, from the sick look in his gray irises.

"Fucking keep up!" he growls into my ear. He drops me on the floor, and I cough, trying to breathe in air that was restricted from me moments ago.

We reach a door that was hidden in the far corner of the room. Luca turns to look at me, and there is no pity, no warmth, nothing in those depths. And now I really do fear for my life. He opens the door, and my heart drops into my stomach.

The room must be below freezing. I can see the air as it is being blown everywhere. My eyes widen in fear, and I immediately back away from the door. I go as quickly as I can until the chain stops my movements. Even then, I continue to pull on it. Luca doesn't even look back as he drags me into the deep freezer. The ground is freezing cold against my bare feet, and the bra and underwear I am in do nothing to help keep me warm.

I cry out as the cold floor stings the underside of my feet. Luca drags me to the center of the room, and I finally see what we are headed for. In the center of the room, hanging from the ceiling, there are cuffs. But they look like gauntlets. They are leather. There is a rough jerk on the chain, and I go tumbling into Luca's arms. He still doesn't speak.

I can feel my body temperature already dropping from being in this cold room. My body is slowly beginning to shiver from the cold.

"L-l-luca, p-p-please ..."

Luca ignores me and roughly grabs my wrist, securing it into the leather cuff. He does the same with the other. He walks across the room and presses a button. Out of nowhere, the cuffs begin rising higher to the ceiling, and my body is now elevated off the floor. My arms are already screaming in pain. My feet dangle above the floor uselessly as I try desperately to get some kind of footing.

"I use rooms like this when I want to derange the mind. Helps all kinds of information to come out. Even information we're not looking for." He looks around the room as if admiring the structure. "Except in the other rooms, we use metal cuffs. But I don't want your skin tearing from freezing to the cuff, so we'll use leather." He grabs a chair from the corner and walks near me, his breath visible in front of him. He sets the chair down and takes a seat.

My breathing is erratic and loud. I can't focus from all the unpleasant feelings that are bombarding me right now.

"Now, we're going to have a little discussion." Luca is eyeing the front of the bra. "Do you want to know what I hate the most in this world?" His eyes slowly travel up, and he meets my tear-filled eyes.

"The Trovolis."

My mind clears just a moment. Long enough for me to process his words. He hates the Trovolis? But I am a Trovoli.

"I told my father this whole thing was stupid when he wanted me to marry you. 'For the sake of our family,' he said." Luca chuckles bitterly. "I told him not to trust you people. And look where it got him. Dead."

I don't quite understand where he is going with this conversation.

"You know, your mother learned the hard way, marrying one of those monsters."

My heart stops. My mother? What is he talking about?

"Your father kept it a secret, you know. The truth behind your mother's death. Using it as a ploy to get his family behind him and into war. But the truth is, he sent her to her death. Purposely."

Immediate anger erupts from me. How dare he say that to me!

"Stop lying!" I scream at him, mustering all the strength I can. He is lying. I know he is!

Amusement twinkles in his eyes as he watches me.

"I'm not. Your father wanted power. And the territory he wanted was overrun. So to get a turf war started and gain control of more land, he had your mother killed and mutilated to trick his own into believing someone else did it. Perfect way to get people's loyalty in your back pocket."

"Shut up, Luca, just shut up! You're a liar!" I scream.

The tears running down my face are stinging from the cold, but I ignore them as a desperate need awakens in me. A need to know that it isn't all a lie. My whole life isn't a sham. Luca seems to be enjoying my disdain. He smiles a bright white smile in pleasure at the horror in my face.

"I'm serious, baby." He stands and walks closer to me and begins fondling with the bra I am wearing. "Wanna know how I know?"

I close my eyes tight and shake my head vigorously. I don't want to know.

"Because your low-down father asked for our help in locating his son. His illegitimate son. Your mother found out about the affair and had the boy sent away, and because of her bravery, she was given the ultimate punishment. I mean, it was the ultimate package deal for your father. Get rid of the wife, gain a son, and get a whole new territory in the process."

He reaches out and pushes my hair back behind my face. I can do nothing but stare at him in horror.

"And guess who we've had under the radar for the past fifteen years."

His smile widens as he watches the understanding cross my face. I have a brother. A half-brother. And Luca knows who and where he is. But the real question is, Why is he telling me this? Why is he destroying my world with only the words coming out of his mouth?

"I've always hated your family. Your whole bloodline. I wanted to eradicate you as soon as possible, but my father believed in a different path for your filthy bloodline. And now, because of your family, he is gone." Silence echoes throughout the chamber. Oh god. My family is behind his father's death. Bile immediately comes rushing up my throat, but I swallow it down immediately.

"I think I've had enough of the Trovolis. You're all a disgusting waste of space that needs to be wiped out. Every single one of you." Luca turns to leave, and I have to dig deep within me to speak. The cold and the pain physically and mentally are taking a toll on me.

"W-w-wait, L-Luca, p-please."

He stops and turns around, slowly facing me. Still, there is no emotion in his eyes. He hates me. He hates my family. He hates the very blood that runs through my veins. But I have to cling to the little piece of hope that is fluttering above my head.

"P-please don't k-kill my brother," I say. "P-please d-don't kill A-ari." I open my mouth to continue to beg for my family, but Luca is standing directly in front of me now. I am literally shivering from the cold and in fear.

"I won't kill you. Because you are mine. And despite everything you've done, I still want you. I won't kill your brother, because I have other plans for him. But Ari is as good as dead."

My stomach churns at his words. "N-n-no! Please! I'm b-b-begging you, Luca!" My voice is cracking as the cold slowly numbs my whole body. This is misery. Luca only smiles at me.

"It was your cousin, you know. The one that told about your father. I guess out of retaliation, they felt the need to kill mine. Which was a big mistake. She should've quit while she was ahead."

No, no, no, no! I am the one that told Ari about my father, and she must've told. And now, because of my weakness, she will surely die.

"L-Luca … I'll do anything, j-just please don't hurt her …" I try one last time, hoping that somewhere in there, Luca has a heart and will listen to it for once.

There is silence, except for the sound of my labored breathing due to the temperature.

I look up when I hear retreating footsteps. Luca is walking toward the door, with his back to me. He is leaving me here. In this freezer-type room. He stops by the door and turns back to me with an expression void of any emotion.

"I'll think about it."

And with that, he turns out the light and leaves me in the freezing dark with nothing more than the heart-wrenching sound of the door creaking shut.

Chapter 16

Elise

The first thing I register as I come to is the warmth. My body is tucked snugly underneath a massive comforter, and warmth is radiating from the blanket, seeping heat into my body. I don't want to open my eyes for fear of something I may regret, but I open them anyway. I'm still in the torture room, except I'm not chained to anything. There's a fire going in the fireplace that's keeping the room comfortably heated. This is heaven compared to being in that ice chamber.

I have no idea how long I was left in that miserable room, but I was more than happy when I lost consciousness. That room is something I never want to experience again. It is dark and cold, and time is nonexistent. My body feels exhausted. Like moving is a hassle for my muscles. I shift and look around the room to see if Luca is anywhere, but it's empty. Thank God.

I finally sit up in the bed, letting the sheets fall around my waist. I am dressed in a T-shirt and underwear, but that's about it. The stupid collar is still latched around my neck and hooked onto the headboard. There is also an electric blanket folded and sitting on the bedside table neatly. It seems that while I was unconscious, Luca has took care of my body. I could scream from the situation I am in. I lie back down, pulling the blanket over me, and stare at the ceiling. It makes me angry to no end, and I don't know what I can do about it. How is any of this fair to me? What have I ever done? I have always been an obedient child and never given my father a reason to hate me other than the fact I was born a girl.

Oh, shit.

I completely forgot. Luca revealed I have a brother. A half-brother that was born a few years after I was. I know I should feel some bitterness about it, but I can't help but feel curiosity. Who is he? Does he know who he is? Does he know who his father is? The thing that upsets me the most was that my father had gotten rid of my mother in behind him. But my brother didn't ask to be born. He didn't ask for that fate. So I can't feel anger toward him.

But one thing is for sure: I need to find him. Luca didn't specify whether he is in this line of work or not, but I hope he isn't. I hope he is good and kind and nothing like my horrible father. Now I have a new purpose to survive, to want to get out of here.

One thing is definitely for sure; Ari and my brother are the only close family I have. And I need to protect them at all costs. The rest of my family ... well, I have no idea what fate awaits them. But the way Luca speaks of them, it can't be good. Luca is crazy. He must have some kind of mental disorder to think that his behavior is, in any form, okay. But I can't really say that because of who he was raised by. In this line of living, to be born without a conscience and a low-tolerance mind-set is to be perfect. And that is what Luca is. He has no tolerance for any inconvenience in his life.

As if sensing the hope in my thoughts, the door to the far side of the room opens, and in strolls Luca. He's looking down at a box in his hand and doesn't seem to notice that I'm awake. So I do what any sane person would do. I close my eyes and fake sleep. I hear his footsteps get closer and do my best to calm my breathing. Luca is a trained killer, so I am pretty sure he'll be able to tell that I'm faking sleep. The edge of the bed dips, and I hear more shuffling. The blanket is slowly pulled back off my body, and I try my best to remain calm.

Instead of feeling Luca's groping hands like I expected, I feel him lift the T-shirt and pull my underwear down a bit. Then something cold is rubbed in a circle near my hip bone. A sharp prick startles me from my focus, and I jolt up with a shout. I immediately rub my burning hip and look at Luca. He has an amused smirk on his face, and his head is tilted to the side as he watches me.

"I knew you were awake, baby." He leans in and gives me a light peck on the lips. "Nice try, though."

I am still trying to rub the sting from my side. Luca gave me a shot of some kind, and I am beginning to freak out. "What did you inject me with?" My voice comes out groggy and rough.

Luca walks back to me with an even larger needle and a smile on his face. My eyes widen in fear. There's no telling what this is all about. I mean, he fucking locked me in a deep freezer for God knows how long before he pulled me out.

"That, my sweet, was a numbing agent. And this …?" He wiggles the needle through the air for emphasis. "Is your new microchip implant."

I am completely taken aback.

"W-what?"

"The little stunt you pulled made me realize something in the months you were gone. I gave you too much freedom. And because of that, I had trouble finding you. So just in case you feel like doing something stupid in the time coming, we're going to keep a GPS on you. You know, for safety measures, of course." He winks at me, and I can feel my anger bubble up.

"Are you crazy? I'm your wife, not your pet! I refuse to have that … *thing* put inside my body!" I shout at him, but his smile grows even wider. The look on his face is almost as if he were daring me. Just waiting for me to do or say something stupid so he can do something in return.

Suddenly, his smile drops and he crawls across the bed, coming closer to me. The look on his face keeps me rooted to the spot, afraid to move. I can't even run if I want to, because he has me bolted to the bed. He gets even closer to me, entering my personal space and keeping his gray eyes locked on mine. His eyes flicker to my lips, and he opens his mouth slightly.

I still can't move. He reaches a hand behind my ear and pulls me in closely before his eyes flicker from mine back to my lips. I can't think straight with him this close. He pulls me in, and I can feel his warm breath fanning on my lips. Then he kisses me. Soft and warm. Not possessive like it usually is. I feel a dull pressure against my hip, the same area that Luca swabbed earlier.

Shit.

I finally get my wits about me and shove him off me. Hard. The syringe is empty, and the chip isn't in the tube. So it's now in my body. Luca distracted me. I look at him in horror, and he's smiling. Pure amusement is written all over his face. He turns away from me and drops the empty syringe on the metal tray.

"You're right, Elise, you are my wife. *My* wife." He walks closer to the bed, and I can see the malice slowly forming in his eyes. Malice toward me. He begins to unbutton his shirt and slowly pulls it off, revealing his gun holster.

"So imagine my utter shock when I find out that it may possibly be my wife's fault my father is dead." He begins to unfasten the holster and drops it to the floor with a loud thud—the gun is obviously loaded. My eyes are wide and filled with fear. I have no idea what he is talking about. I had nothing to do with his father's death.

He crawls in the bed and comes toward me. I don't dare speak. Luca is a ticking time bomb. I know the topic of his father is very tender, so I don't want to say anything that may set him off. He's finally in front of me and pushes me so that I'm lying on my back. He crawls over my body and straddles it and begins playing with my hair.

"It's like every time I think there is no more horrifying news regarding you, I find out more."

My heart rate begins to skyrocket. I have no idea what he is talking about, but whatever it is can't be good. He doesn't speak for a moment, just keeps playing with my hair. Then his hands move down and begin tracing my face. Starting with my cheek and running over my lips.

"The man we interrogated from the shooting told us who was behind it. Your filthy bloodline, of course. But he only recently spilled how he got the information of your father's then-impending doom." He traces his finger from my jawline to my throat. His eyes are roaming over my face slowly. Without warning, his hand tightens around my throat, and he shoves me roughly into the bed.

"Imagine my shock when I find out that Ariana Gudierri is the one that told the information to the fucking attackers." My eyes widen in shock, and I try to pry Luca's iron grip from my throat, but he is not having it. His eyes are filled with such a deep rage.

He drags me up the bed, slamming my body into the headboard, causing me to cry out in pain. Luca is in my face the next instance, shouting at me.

"How could you do this to me? You're supposed to be my wife! You're supposed to be loyal to me! Not any of them! Your last name is Pasquino now, *not* Trovoli! You do as I say! You keep my secrets! You stay loyal to me!"

Luca is so angry I can see a vein popping out of his neck. He jerks me away from the headboard, only to slam me right back into it. My head bounces off the wooden headboard, and stars explode across my vision from the impact. His hand is growing even tighter around my throat, making it even harder for me to breathe.

"This will never be good enough, will it? You will always try to go back to them, be only loyal to them!" He spits the words out as if he were disgusted. I can feel my head begin to pound from the impact and lack of oxygen. I try to open my mouth to say something, but as soon as Luca sees the action, he immediately jerks me off the headboard, only to slam me back up against it again. His face turns murderously angry.

"Don't you dare fucking speak!"

He lets go of my body, and I fall forward, coughing and sputtering, trying to catch my breath. I don't even have time to be in shock. Luca has a hold of the chain and drags me out of the bed. Literally. He jerks hard enough that the collar pulls me off the bed and I hit the ground. I am being dragged across the floor by my throat. I struggle uselessly.

Luca finally stops and looks at me, no emotion in his eyes. The same as last time, when he dragged me into the deep freezer. And I hope to God he isn't about to put me back in there.

* * * * *

Twenty. Twenty and counting. Luca has me chained to some kind of overhead rafter. My arms pulled above my head. This time, though, my legs are touching the ground. But I can barely hold myself up. Luca has been whipping me for I don't even know how long. Not just on my back this time, but all over my body. And not hard enough to draw blood, but hard enough for me to feel pain.

He stands in front of me with a look of rage.

"L-Luca, please. I … I'm sorry." I can barely get my words out from trying to catch my breath. I have been begging, hoping for some form of mercy from him, but I have gotten none. If what Luca said is true and Ari is behind this, then it is all my fault. I was the one who told her about my father. The truth behind his death.

"I didn't know she was going to tell, I swear." I choke on a sob. My body is in pain, it is freezing cold, and I am naked and chained to the ceiling. This is misery in its purest form.

Suddenly, my arms are released and I drop to the floor in a miserable heap, still bawling in a pile. I hear Luca's footsteps come toward me, and he picks me up slowly, cradling my body as he carries me somewhere. I still don't open my eyes, though.

I just want to die. This isn't a life worth living. And I now know I have no one. Ari has betrayed me in more ways than one, even if she didn't know the consequences. She should have thought of what would happen to me if we were found out. But she didn't. And now I'm suffering.

Luca steps into a room that is abnormally warm, and I open my eyes.

We are in the bathroom. There is water in the large tub, with small vials of different colors perched on the side. My body is still burning in pain from Luca's torture. He lowers me slowly into the tub, and the pain grows even more as the heat from the water deepens the pain. Luca takes a seat on the side of the tub. His face is blank. He reaches for one of the vials and pours its contents into the tub. After a moment, the pain subsides.

Luca stands up to leave, but I reach out and grab his arm in desperation. Water from the tub splashes out everywhere, and I look into his steel depths, pleading with my soul for him to hear me.

"Kill me."

The words hang in the air. It's completely silent except for the sound of the water rippling in the tub.

Luca looks as if he doesn't quite comprehend what I'm saying.

"Please. I … I can't live like this." My vision grows blurry, and fat tears roll down my face. "I don't want to live like this. I don't want to live, period. I have nothing, Luca. I have no one. I've never had anyone. Just please …" I take a deep breath. "If you really love me, just kill me now."

Emotion finally graces Luca's face. But only for a moment. Not long enough for me to comprehend what it is. He moves so quickly I don't have time to register what is happening. Somehow, he wrenches his arm from my grip, and the next thing I know, my head is being plunged under the water of the tub. I have no air in my lungs, so suffocation for me begins immediately. My body's instinct for air kicks in, and I begin struggling.

My chest is burning from lack of air. This is it. This is what I asked him for in the first place. And now he is giving it to me. The edges of my vision begin to turn cloudy, and just when I think I am going to lose consciousness, I am yanked above the water by my hair.

As soon as I break the surface, I take in huge gulps of air. I cough up water and gasp for air all at the same time. My chest is still burning from the lack of oxygen in my system, and my throat is raw from all the coughing. I open my eyes, and Luca is standing in the tub right in front of me, his face still blank of emotion.

"Don't ever ask me that again. You are all I have. And I am all you have. I told you before, I will kill anyone, *anyone*, that gets in the way of this. We're married. We belong to each other, with each other. Which is why I can forgive you for your wrongs." He leans in closer to my face and finally lets his blank expression drop. And what I see chills me to the bone, even in this heated bathtub.

"But what I cannot do anymore is forgive the Trovolis. And I swear on my father's grave, I will make every single one of them pay for his death. I've had it with that filthy bloodline. And I refuse to let them live any longer."

He stands up and walks away from me before I can form a coherent thought, slamming the door behind him.

Chapter 17

Luca

Love is a strange thing. It makes you do strange things. In my case, it makes you kill. Everything I have done in my life is because my father told me to do it. And because I loved him, I followed every single one of his orders without hesitation. Pretty soon, my life became my form of normal.

I lived to please him. I lived to keep the family strong. I lived to please myself. But I'm not so sure about that anymore. Protecting the family means killing the Trovolis, but by doing that, I will be hurting the only family I have left. My wife.

I look across the room to where Elise lies. She is on her side, staring at nothing. Small tears are running out of her eyes. Damn, if she doesn't look beautiful. Even when she cries, she is an angel. She sniffles a bit and takes a deep breath, the sound coming out shaky. I don't know what to do when it comes to her. Anyone else would have killed their wife by now. The fact that she has told my business and the leaking of that information has led to not only the capo's but also my father's death ... well, that is a crime fit for worse than death. She just doesn't understand. The world she lives in, the man she is married to, all of it is different now.

Her cousin is a bitch for putting her in a corner like this. She is a conniving Trovoli. She feeds off Elise's naïveté and almost got her cousin killed. And if it wasn't me that Elise is married to, she would be dead. I see the knowledge that lurks behind Ariana's eyes. She knows more than she is letting on, and she purposely keeps information from Elise so her poor cousin can come to her, unknowingly feeding her all kinds of information. She's right about one thing, though: Elise isn't built for this world. She's too soft. Too kind. Nothing like the filthy blood that runs through her veins. She is different.

I look back over across the room and see that she has fallen asleep. Her dark lashes are touching her cheeks lightly. They are so long. I stand and walk over to her to get a better look. Her lips are parted slightly. She has to breathe out of her mouth since her nose is stuffy from all the crying.

I was taken aback when she asked me to kill her. And I almost did on accident. The anger that filled me from the thought of her willingly wanting to die at my hands was enough to force me into a rage. The look on her face, though, when she had spoken those words had been ... heartbreaking. Many women have looked at me with that look—heartbreak, sadness, sorrow—and I have never been fazed by it. But when Elise looked at me with her almond-colored eyes, I saw something that made me stop. Made me, for once in my life, feel pity. But it was only there for a moment, because the rage took over in an instant.

I take a seat on the bed and push her hair back from her face. It has gotten longer, and pretty soon, she'll be able to hide from me once again behind it.

"What am I going to do with you?" I murmur aloud.

I love her. There is no doubt in my mind about that. She is perfect. She is kind and innocent and beautiful. And so damn naive. I almost want to shield her from the horrors of this world. But I don't know how to express that to her. I can't change the way that I am. It's far too late for that. But I can prevent her from making the same mistakes and facing me because of her naïveté.

I stand and immediately text Nicolai. Hopefully, my meeting is already set up, because with my current state of emotions ... this will be perfect.

* * * * *

Ariana Trovoli. Now Gudierri. She is married to Stefano Gudierri by her father to further increase ties in the South. No doubt Elise's father had something to do with it. She was married off when she was eighteen to Stefano, and they have been together "happily" for seven years. Stefano is so lost in his emotions he doesn't even realize how sneaky his wife is. I step into the interrogation room and look beyond the one-sided glass. He's sitting there calmly, probably unaware that his world is about to come tumbling down. I step into the room, and he looks up immediately. He doesn't smile, only nods in respect.

I'm guessing he's still sore from our last encounter. I take a seat in front of him and set the file down on the table between us.

"How are you, Stefano? Did you enjoy the flight?" I ask. I keep my voice level and my eyes trained on him. He's already uneasy, and he doesn't even know what is about to happen.

"I'm good, Capo. Thank you. The flight was fine."

I scoff aloud. "Tell me something, do you know who you're married to?"

This catches his attention, and he looks up at me with an uneasy gaze. "Uh ... excuse me, sir?"

"Your wife, Ariana. Do you truly know who she is?"

"Yes, of course, sir." He speaks as if I were the idiot for asking that question.

I push the file across the table and motion for him to open and read its contents. I wait patiently and watch in pleasure as his whole wall of safety and comfort comes tumbling down as the proof of who his wife truly is dawns on him. I lean forward in my seat on the desk, folding my arms in front of me.

"I have a little pest problem in the South that I would like to get rid of. And with your cooperation, I think I can make that happen."

He is still in shock, staring at the folder. "W-where did you get all this?" His voice is shaky.

"Records. Reports. And I had someone tail her for the past few months. It does help that I have a few contacts in the justice system under my wing."

The folder contains everything Ariana has been involved in within the time she's been married to Stefano. The whole reason behind their marriage is so she can have easy access to unlimited information about all kinds of things and report it to her father, who, in turn, reports back to his brother, the capo of the South. It is a brilliant plan, no doubt. A great way to utilize your daughter. Going for a man's weakness in the comfort of his own home.

The Gudierris are a crime family known for their cunning. The information they gather from having contacts on the inside of every legal department across the United States makes them practically untouchable by the feds. Which is why Elise's father wanted to utilize it. There is proof in Stefano's database that information has been stolen by none other than his wife. Saved to a flash drive.

And now that his wife has betrayed him, caused my father's death, and helped my wife run away, well, Stefano is now completely at my mercy, and this is the perfect opportunity.

"I'm going to make you a proposition. You will be the new head of the South."

He looks up, startled.

"That's right. But you have to help me deal with one little problem."

He narrows his eyes at me, and I continue.

"I want to eradicate the Trovolis from the face of the earth."

His eyes widen for a fraction, and then he wipes his face of emotion. "What do you mean *eradicate*?"

"Dead. All of them. You of all people should know everything they have done and caused us. I want nothing to do with them."

"Including your wife?" he asks.

I have to take a deep breath to keep from strangling him. "No. I want my wife alive. What you choose to do with yours is up to you. I will not interfere there."

"I want her alive as well," he says the words quietly. Poor fool.

"Done. I hope you realize your wife is behind my father's death." Judging from his reaction, he didn't. "The men that shot him were relatives of hers. Sharing the same filthy bloodline. She told them the truth behind Elise's father's death, and she ordered the hit on my father. They were supposed to take me out too, but Elise stepped in the way just in the nick of time."

I clench my fists as memories of that horrible night flash through my mind. I stand and push my chair back from the table, looking Stefano right in his eyes as I speak, hoping he hears me and the force behind my words are enough to sway him.

"If it weren't for Elise, you and your wife would be dead. The only reason I am giving you an option right now is her. Even though your wife deserves to suffer for everything she's put Elise through. You may be the capo of the South now, but you will take your orders from me. Your decisions will be my decisions. And the South now belongs to me. Do you understand?"

He stares at me for a moment before bowing his head in respect. "Yes, Capo."

"Good." I turn to leave but stop in the doorway as I remember something. "I will contact you with the plan to dispose of them all."

* * * * *

I could almost laugh. Almost. Ariana sits in front of me, seething hatred. Her face is set in an angry scowl, and she obviously believes she is on top. I want to break this bitch in half.

"Do you understand how much Elise cares for you?" I ask.

She doesn't answer me. I can't control myself. I reach across the table before she can blink and slam her face into it. She cries out in pain. She meets my eyes with fear. Fucking finally. I can feel the pleasure rushing through my system, but I need to calm down. If I kill her, Elise will be upset. Her gasps fill the chamber.

"Don't you dare ignore me, bitch! You used your own flesh and blood for your selfish gain. You knew how naive Elise was, yet you used her to fish out information."

She looks up at me with hatred in her eyes once more. "I love Elise, but she needs to face the realities of the real world. The only way to instill survival of our own family is to be ahead. Elise didn't understand that. She was too weak!"

I can feel the anger inside of me boiling up at her. How Elise can't see past her fake facade, I have no idea. But there is no way she can fool me.

"If anything, you should be mad at yourself. You shouldn't have exposed her to so much. She's fragile! She doesn't know what the real world is like! And now, because of your idiocy, your own father is dead. All thanks to your lovely Elise." She smiles wickedly at me, and it takes every ounce of my willpower to stay calm. "You don't know what it's like to have something so precious as Elise. You don't deserve her!"

I slam my fist down on the table in anger. "Don't you sit there and act like you care about her! You can cut the shit! I know everything! I have your file! I have your information to a tee! So you better not speak one more word about her, or I will rip your tongue out and make you swallow it whole. The *only* reason you are still alive is that Elise wants it. The only reason after her that you are alive is that your husband, for whatever reason, still wants you even after I gave him that file."

Her eyes grow wide in shock at my words. "You what?"

"I gave him the file. He knows everything. Down to the smallest detail."

I enjoy the defeat as it creeps on her face. I stand to leave the room. The only reason I came here was to see how deep her "love" for her cousin runs. Now I can move forward with no regrets. Everything is falling into place perfectly. Elise's father started all this trying to gain power for himself, but in the end, he has made me the most powerful, and on top of that, I get to keep the most beautiful woman by my side as I take control.

* * * * *

I step into the room and immediately look for Elise. I just want to hold her tonight. I frown as my gaze lands on the bed. It's empty. I didn't put the collar back on her after I puller her from the bath. I didn't the heart to. But the door can only be opened with my authorization, so she's somewhere in here.

"Elise?" I call out but get no reply. I try to remain calm.

"Elise," I try again. Still nothing.

I walk around the corner and see the light to the bathroom on. I calm down a little. She's just taking a bath. I open the door to the bathroom, and for the first time since the night my father was killed, fear explodes in my chest.

Elise is in the bathtub filled with water. The water is tinted red. Her head is tilted back, and her eyes are closed. *Fuck!* I sprint across the floor, vaguely registering the shattered mirror. There are mirror fragments with blood on them scattered around the tub. I reach into the water, immediately grasping for her arms, pulling them from the submerged water.

"Shit!" My voice echoes off the walls. Her wrists are sliced to ribbons. Literally. The flesh is cut in different pieces, some deeper than others, like she closed her eyes and just started stabbing. Her skin is cold and crusted with the blood that has floated to the surface of the water.

I immediately grab her out of the tub and rush her to the bedroom, trying to get whatever I can to stall the wounds. In all the frantic moving and getting her to a stable condition, I don't have the time to check for a pulse. I just pray that when I do, there is one there.

Chapter 18

Elise

Beep beep beep.

The rhythmic sound pulls me from my slumber. I crack my eyes open, and I'm looking at an unfamiliar ceiling. I look over, and my heart jumps when I see Luca sleeping in a chair in the corner. Wait. If I am awake and Luca is there ...

I pull my hands up in front of my face, and sure enough, there is a thick gauze wrapped around my wrists. *No, no, no.* I look over to Luca's sleeping form again. He must've found me in time.

I'd had it. I'd had enough. I didn't want this anymore. This life, this existence. I didn't even know why I was here in the first place. I had no one. And that was enough for me to extinguish my life. I didn't know how, since Luca left nothing in that room for me to improvise with, but I remembered that glass could be used as a weapon. And when I shattered it, the only way to slice deep enough was to stab at it. Or so I thought. The amount of blood I lost in that tub was enough to make me pass out. I thought I was dying. And strangely enough, I was okay with that.

Tears well up in my eyes as the realization of reality dawns on me. Luca has foiled my plans once again. Why? Why does this have to be me?

A loud sob escapes my lips, and to my dismay, Luca jumps up quickly, scanning the room and reaching for his concealed gun. His eyes land on me, and he visibly relaxes. He stands from his seat and steps toward me with concern laced in his eyes. I immediately ignore him and begin tearing at the gauze. Maybe if I can get the gauze off and tear the stitches out fast enough, I can still do this.

My hands are shaking bad, and I can barely focus on what I am doing when a pair of hands gently places themselves over my wrists. I look up, and Luca is so close to me, his gray eyes boring into mine. I immediately recoil.

"Don't touch me!" I jerk away from him. I squeeze my eyes shut, expecting some kind of repercussion for shouting at him, but I am surprised when there is none. I look up in the silent room and see him standing there with a troubled expression on his face.

"Elise, how could you do that to me? Do you realize, if I were five minutes later, you would've been gone?" I narrow my eyes at him.

"Yes. That was what I wanted. That was the plan, to be gone! From all this, from you, from the torture, and from the pain." I cut myself off as tears overwhelm me. "This isn't a life worth living." I look down at my hands, unable to make eye contact with Luca. This isn't worth it. I have nothing to live for.

I hear Luca take a deep breath before his footsteps echo throughout the chamber. He walks to the door and opens it, slamming it loudly and leaving me alone.

It turns out that this room is a bedroom in our new home together. I had yet to see it because I ran away from Luca in the time I would have gotten to know my own home. Dr. Shotwell comes in to check my vitals and begins speaking to me.

"You gave the capo quiet a scare, young lady. You lost three pints of blood. Any more, and you would have died. Good thing he found you when he did." He smiles at me, as if I am lucky to be alive. I want to kick him. He knows what is really going on.

Dr. Shotwell is the family physician for Luca's family. Being a major crime boss means that hospital visits should be kept to a minimum. Hospital visits mean records, and for the type of injuries Luca sustains, police records would be involved. They set the room up with all the machines and equipment of a normal hospital room, so I get the best care and treatment from home.

There's minimal sunlight streaming into the room, so it's very dimly lit, and from all the medication, I eventually lose consciousness.

When I open my eyes again, Luca is back. He is quietly reading a book in the corner. The room is dark, which means I've been asleep long enough for the sun to go down. I look over, and there is a steaming bowl of soup on the tray next to the bed. Luca's eyes flicker over to me, and he closes the book, slowly standing from his spot across the room.

"I see you're awake," he says.

I don't respond. I just eye him with an untrusting look. He holds my gaze before looking away with a small chuckle. He grabs the bowl off the tray and sits next to me on the bed. I try to scoot away as much as I can, not liking the close proximity that he has with me.

"Stop that, Elise!" he growls out at me. I obey immediately, afraid at what may happen if I keep moving. "Dr. Shotwell said you need to rest and keep something in your system. Your body is going to need help in replenishing all that blood you lost." He dips the spoon in the bowl and brings the steaming spoon to my lips. He gets irritated when I don't open my mouth. He lets out a deep breath.

"Elise, I'm not going to play these games with you. Eat."

After a moment of silence, I finally open my mouth and let him feed me. And damn, if that isn't the best soup I have ever eaten. After I finish the soup, Luca sets it aside and comes back to the bed, taking a seat. I keep my eyes downcast until I feel his fingers underneath my chin, bringing me up to meet his cool stare.

"Elise, don't you ever try to take your life again. Do you understand what that made me feel? I thought I'd lost you. I couldn't live if I lost you."

"Don't you realize you almost lost me because of you?" I stare into his eyes as I speak, searching for some kind of understanding from him. When he doesn't respond, I continue with a little more confidence. "You broke me, Luca. You tortured me. You carved your name into my flesh for God's sake. You killed people in front of me. How do you not expect me to want to end my life?"

He stares at me for a long time and doesn't speak. I wish I knew what he was thinking. What could possibly be going on in his head for him to think any of this is okay?

"Your cousin's husband is replacing your father," he says, suddenly pulling me out of my thoughts. I am caught off guard but understand what he's saying.

"What?"

"Stefano. He's the new capo of the South."

I don't understand why he is telling me this. He completely disregards what I just said.

"You want to know something funny, Elise? He told me he would help me with the extermination of the Trovolis."

My heart jumps. "W-what?" That meant my family. My blood, not just the crime family.

"That's right, baby. Wanna know something else? Your cousin would have been thrown right into that mix if Stefano asked for it." He pauses. "You're wondering why I'm telling you this, right?"

He turns and looks at me with a knowing look on his face. He sits on the edge of the bed and squeezes my cheeks in between his hand.

"Your face is so easily read, sweetie." He leans in before I can move away and gives me a light peck on the lips. "Now, I know you're not a heartless person. I mean, you've gone through hell to save even people you don't know."

His tone is whimsical, which scares me.

"So let's make a deal. I'm going to let one more Trovoli live. Your brother." His eyes meet mine, and he loses all jokiness in his tone. "But I swear, if you try to kill yourself again, I will find him. And I won't kill him, but I will make him suffer every day for the rest of his miserable life. Do you understand me, Elise?"

I meet his glare, trying so hard to keep a straight face, but I lose when my lip starts to tremble and tears well up. I shut my eyes tight, and the tears fall miserably down my face. He's won. Even though I don't know him, I can't sentence my brother to unknown torture because of me. And I know Luca will follow up on his promise. He *is* Luca Pasquino.

I feel his hand on my cheek and open my eyes.

"Oh, baby. It's only because I love you."

I immediately bring my hand around to slap his away from my face, but he catches it in midair. He stares at me, and something flickers across his face. He seems to be fighting his emotions. He takes a deep breath and stands from the bed, speaking to me as he walks to the door.

"Remember what I said, Elise. Your brother's life depends on it."

He closes the bedroom door behind him, and I take the pillow I am lying on and chunk it at the door. I fall back in the bed with tears stinging my eyes. Now I have someone else's life to think about besides my own. Now escape isn't an option for me anymore. Luca has me. And he can do whatever he wants all because he is dangling my brother's life in front of me.

I jolt awake as a sound from the door pulls me out of my sleep. I must have nodded off again. It is still dark outside, and the room is only illuminated by the floor lamp. I look to the direction the noise comes from and see none other than Ari standing in the room. She is staring at me with uncertain eyes.

I don't know whether to feel happiness or betrayal. Ari is my best friend and the person I go to about everything. But finding out that she has intentionally set me up on several occasions to fish out information … looking at her is a little hard right now. I immediately look down at my hands, unable to look at her.

"What are you doing here, Ari?" My voice comes out very low.

She still doesn't speak, but I can hear her shuffling and look up to see her taking a seat in the chair across from me. After a moment of silence, she finally speaks.

"He's planning to kill them, Elise. All of us. He wants to exterminate the Trovolis."

I don't respond to her; I already know that. But there is nothing I can do to stop him. He is one of the most powerful men in the world. And Ari's actions of killing his father has put him in that position that much quicker than he should have been.

"You're just going to sit there? Let it happen?"

I can hear the irritation in her voice. I still don't speak. After a moment, I hear her let out a breathy laugh.

"You can't be this weak, Elise. You have to do something. You can't just sit back and let him win! This is our family we're talking about. We have to protect them!"

She is shouting at me now, and I finally lose my cool. I jump up from the bed, immediately regretting the decision, as I am too weak to stand, but I ignore the spinning room, letting my anger fuel me.

"We? We? *We* don't have to do anything. *You* can do what you want, Ari. They may be my blood, but they are *not* my family. Where were they when my mother was being murdered by her own husband, huh?"

Ari gasps and puts her hands over her mouth.

"Yeah, you didn't think I knew about that, did you? You knew all this time! How could you not tell me?" I shout at her.

"I was protecting the family!" she shouts at me.

"Fuck the family!" I scream at the top of my lungs.

"Where was my family when Luca shot through me in cold blood? Oh, that's right, they were standing right behind me, holding a fucking knife to my throat! Bargaining *my* life! As if I didn't matter! I have begged and pleaded for *your* life so many times, and do you know what becomes of me for begging him?" I yank the shirt I have on off, exposing my side. I motion to Luca's name. "This!" I immediately spin and show her the welts on my back from his beatings. "This!" I bring up my unbandaged wrist and show her the faint scar on it from being cuffed to that chair and begging for my father's life.

"This is what I get for trying to protect you! My only family that I thought I had left! That I thought I could trust!" The tears are coming hard and fast, and I can feel my temper rising. I tear off the bandage from my arm and show Ari the stitching done. Some of the stitches are torn, and there is blood oozing from the wound from all my frantic moving. I grab fistfuls of my hair, showing Ari another example of what Luca has done to me.

"This is what I get for trying! For fighting back, for caring about other people's lives! And what do I get in return? A cousin that used me. Used me! That fed on my frailness, on my stupidity, on my fear of my husband! You never told me! You … you killed his father? Can you even begin to imagine the punishment I had to go through because I was the one that gave you that information? Because I thought I was confiding in my cousin, not giving you information to further our precious family's power!"

I feel so weak, but I push through the pain. This needs to be said.

"Our family—no, *your* family is as good as dead. There is nothing I can do that I haven't already tried. I … I'm just Luca's property now. I have no authority. I've tried to run, and thanks to you, I was caught. I tried to kill him myself, and that didn't work, and I tried to end my own life, but as you can see"—I motion to the room around me—"it didn't work."

A violent cough racks its way out of my body, and I begin to shiver. But I ignore the pain and continue to speak my mind. All the hurt and betrayal I am feeling is finally coming to the surface.

"I wasn't lucky like you. I didn't get a husband that adored me and worshipped the ground I walked on. At this very moment, Stefano still loves you even though you betrayed him so bad. He still wants you alive. I got thrown in with Luca."

The room seems to be getting darker, and I can feel my body getting clammy.

"You're just like my father. Using me to further your own gain. Our family may have been great, but we're no match for Luca. Luca's on a whole other level. Luca hates us so much. Now more so because we are the reason his father is dead."

I cough again. What is going on with my body?

"You sealed our family's fate, Ari. And now all I have left is my brother. And I have to protect him."

Ari doesn't even blink when I mention my brother. She probably already knows about that too. Of course she does; she is older than me by seven years. I am sure she is aware.

"Whatever happens to them is on your conscience, Ari. I paid my dues. I took my punishments as long as Luca promised not to touch them. You awoke a sleeping beast. And now your whole family is going to pay the price."

I cough again, even harder, and look at Ari through my cloudy vision. She is staring at me in disbelief and fear. No, not me. I feel a jacket around my naked shoulders and realize Luca is behind me.

"I think you've had enough time to say your goodbyes, Arianna." His voice comes out cold and detached.

Ari doesn't respond; she only stands and quietly leaves the room. I collapse in Luca's arms, not having the strength to push him off me. My body feels like someone has stuck a lot of weight on it, and I can't move. Luca is leaning over me with a worried expression on his face, but I can't comprehend it, as darkness finally overtakes me.

Chapter 19

Luca

It's been two days since Elise passed out. Tearing open her wounds and moving around like she was caused them to get infected, and the infection caused her a high fever. I sit once again by the bed as she breathes quietly, with her lips slightly parted. The doctor gave her some antibiotics to help get rid of the infection, so she should be waking up any day now. But all the shouting she did and overexerting herself has worn her already-weakened body out even more.

I can feel the anger boiling up within me. If I hadn't made a deal with Stefano, I would have already shot Arianna dead. I told her to say goodbye to Elise, but she hcame into my home and tried to turn her cousin against me. And by doing so, she got her riled up and sick.

Someone needs to put Arianna in her place, and that someone is going to be me. Stefano obviously isn't going to. He lets this bitch have her way with whatever. Arianna is too confident in her position, and I don't like that. At all. I smile as a plan already unfolds itself in my head. I know just how to put her in her place.

I pull out my phone and call Stefano. He answers on the first ring.

"We're going to have a little change of plans."

* * * * *

I stand at the top of the massive dining hall, looking down at the grand dinner table. This is going to be fun. We are stationed above the table, and currently, only one person is seated there at the bottom. Arianna. She is unconscious from the sedative. She is locked in a chair, with her hands bolted to the underside of the table. Stefano stands next to me, squirming uneasily.

"Are you sure this is necessary, Capo?"

I frown immediately as Stefano's voice cuts through my pleasure-filled haze. I look at him in irritancy.

"You're not backing out on me now, are you, Stefano?" I ask.

I make sure to keep my tone steady. He obviously is uncomfortable. He can't even look me in the eye. Hmmm. Maybe this capo thing isn't a good idea for him.

"No, sir," he says. But his voice is still wavering.

I quickly pull my gun out from behind me, aiming it right between his pathetic eyes. I have zero tolerance for pussies.

"Let me explain something to you. If you do anything to jeopardize this plan, I will shoot you where you stand and kill your wife slowly and painfully."

He swallows and nods visibly. Coward.

I look away as Nicolai and Romelo step into the room, followed by several other men. I can feel the light tingling on my skin as the anticipation of what is about to happen draws nearer. Nicolai looks at me with a knowing gaze.

"Everything's set, Capo."

I nod in acknowledgment. Below us, Arianna is jolted awake from her drug-induced sleep. She quickly looks around, breathing hard, but unable to really move. All thanks to the little drug we've injected into her bloodstream. It allows her be awake and conscious, but her body is as good as paralyzed. The doors below open, and in file the people that I despise most in this world. The Trovolis. All the disgusting men in this family that have dared plot against me. We used Arianna's phone and sent a message to all the people of the Trovolis that she has regular communication with. By pretending to be her, we managed to set up a meeting at this location.

They all walk in unaware of the situation that is about to occur. Some are laughing. Some are silent. Some are skeptically scanning the room. I laugh softly to myself. *Idiots.* Once they all enter and are seated, the doors close behind them and, unbeknownst to them, are locked.

Arianna is looking with frantic eyes as realization dawns on her about what is about to occur. Smart girl. I grab the mic and clear my throat, ready to speak into it.

"Good evening, Trovolis."

They all immediately jump and scan the room, some even pulling their guns out. Idiots.

"I know you probably all thought you were summoned here by your dear Arianna to come up with another treacherous plot to dethrone the newest capo of the North, Luca Pasquino. You weren't."

Some of them are shouting obscenities and frantically looking around. They won't be able to see us, though. I've spent weeks preparing for this very moment. And that includes modifying the building for one specific purpose. Massacres.

I raise my hand, and my men get their guns ready, aiming them down at all the filthy vermin below.

"You have been summoned here by the man you've been aiming to kill. I know all about your plots and schemes. And quiet honestly, I'm fed up with it. Thanks to your dear Arianna, I know all your business." I can't help the laugh that erupts from deep within me as I look at them all frantically searching and looking. Disgusting people.

"Rot in hell, motherfuckers!"

I lower my arm, and a chorus of gunshots erupts throughout the chamber. I watch in pleasure as they all get shot down. Each of them trapped like the cockroaches they are. A pleasurable feeling seeps into my bones, and I can't help the smile that creeps onto my face as I watch the floor and walls slowly become painted with red. I see Stefano flinch next to me as his dear Ari is almost hit. Cunt. If it were up to me, she'd be shot down with them. But since Stefano wants her alive, I made sure to get the best shooters in the business so she won't be hit by accident. Her punishment is to watch up close as her beloved family is all shot down like the pathetic weaklings they are. Maybe next time she will think before she decides to cross me again.

I turn to Stefano, and he turns to me with a troubled look in his eyes. This is why the Gudierris are always working under someone. All they are good for is information. He is too soft. Too weak.

"I've changed my mind. Nicolai!" I shout. Nicolai comes to me immediately. "You are the new capo of the South until further notice. Stefano will be your second-in-command. He will be working under you."

I see Stefano's face and almost laugh.

"You don't really think I'd leave you as capo, do you? You're too soft. Any man that flinches at the sight of blood isn't a man at all. And definitely isn't fit to be capo. Be glad that I'm still sparing your life. Especially after what your wife did." I look over the balcony and see Arianna with heavy tears streaming down her face. Some people's blood is on her. I can't help but smile. Maybe now she'll know.

"You should be thanking me. Now your wife will be a little more obedient. And you won't have to worry about her getting you into trouble anymore." I smile at him.

My phone vibrates in my pocket, and I pull it out to look at the screen. A message from Dr. Shotwell appears.

She's awake.

I smile. Now it is time for me to go see my beautiful wife. Even though she is tainted with that filthy bloodline, she is still mine. And different from any of them. And now she is awake. I can't wait to see her. I exit the building with the sounds of screams and gunshots echoing behind me and a huge smile on my face. Yes. Today is going to be a good day.

Chapter 20

Elise

He's here when I wake up. He's here when I go to sleep. He's here when I am just sitting there, contemplating my miserable existence. He's always here. Acting like he loves me. Staying by my side. Making sure I eat. Making sure I get enough sleep. And always making sure I'm not about to die.

Wouldn't want his precious toy disappearing from existence, I think bitterly.

He's once again at my bedside. He's been in an abnormally good mood lately. And it's almost creepy. He smiles a lot more, and I catch him on multiple occasions staring at me.

"I want to go outside." My voice cuts through the thick silence that envelops the room.

I haven't been outside since the day before Luca caught me. I miss the fresh air. I'm tired of being stuffed up inside this room. There's sunlight pouring in from the windows, and I am dying to touch it. My fever has dissipated, and the infection is gone. I also have less gauze on my wrist. My body is healing slowly but it is healing nonetheless.

Luca is writing something in a thick notebook as if he didn't hear me.

"Luca, I want to go outside," I try again, my voice louder this time.

He stops writing and looks up at me with a clear expression. "Why?"

I'm a little caught off guard by his question but recover quickly. "I'm tired of being stuffed up inside this house."

He seems to be thinking for a moment before finally answering. He lets out a deep breath and closes his notepad. "Okay. But only the backyard. The front is off-limits today."

I tilt my head in confusion. "Why?"

His expression shifts immediately, and irritation is evident. "Maybe I'll just make you wait till tomorrow, since that's not good enough for you."

I sit up immediately, shaking my head. "No! The backyard's fine. I just wanted to know why ..." I trail off, trying not to dig myself an even deeper whole.

He stands up from his chair. "Get dressed. I'll have the cook make lunch, and I'll join you later. I have some business to attend to."

He walks closer to the bed and pulls my head in, giving me a kiss on my forehead. He then exits the room as if his mind is elsewhere.

I immediately jump out of bed and head straight into the closet. I really wanted to go to the front yard, because that's where all the beautiful flowers and scenery are. But since Luca doesn't want me there, I'll have to settle for the backyard. It's just as nice as the front, but there is more artificial nature. I settle on a tank top and shorts.

After I change, I finally walk out of the room and into the hallway. The sunlight is streaming into the house, brightening my damp mood. There is no sign of Luca, or anyone for that matter. Luckily, there are no screams echoing through the house. I can hear the buzz of a Weedwacker out front. Lawn maintenance must be here. That must be why Luca didn't want me in the front today.

I step out into the backyard, sliding open the door to the pool. I don't want to swim. Not like I can with these stitches, anyway. The yard is beautiful, and the plants and greenery are unlike anything I have ever seen. I step into the sun, reveling in the warm glow. It's been so long since I have seen sunlight. Tears well up in my eyes and spill over. Just this tiny luxury that so many people take for granted is enough to bring tears to my eyes. It feels amazing, the warm rays caressing my skin.

"Why are you crying?"

I almost jump out of my skin as a young voice startles me. I open my eyes and look down to my left. There's a boy definitely younger than me standing next to me, with big green eyes. His hair is pitch-black and curly; it is also wet with sweat and sticking to his head. He has a wheelbarrow filled with colorful plants and mounds of dirt. His face is streaked with dirt, and there are two big garden gloves on his hands. He has to be at least fifteen or sixteen. He is adorable, actually, and there is something familiar about him, but I know I've never met him before.

"Well?" He crosses his arms, looking at me still, and I realize I still haven't answered his question.

"I … uh, just the sun felt so nice. It made me happy." I smile sheepishly. I probably look ridiculous to him. He smiles and begins laughing at me.

"Well, I guess the sun would feel nice if you weren't working in it all day," he says, looking toward the grass.

It is really nagging me where I've seen this kid from before, but I can't put a name to his face.

"What happened to your arm?" he asks, pointing to my wrist with gauze wrapped around it.

He's a blunt thing, isn't he? I decide to answer a question with a question, not wanting to explain to this kid why I have a wrap on my arm.

"What are you doing working here?" I ask him, genuinely curious.

He narrows his eyes at me and reluctantly answers. "Mr. Pasquino came by my house one day, asked if I was interested in a job, and I said heck yeah! He pays me really good, and all I have to do is tend to the flowers and keep the yard looking pretty." He pauses for a moment. "He pays really good. So now I have enough to get my own food." He smiles like he is proud.

"What do you mean your *own* food?" I ask.

"Oh. Well, my mom kinda blows all the money she gets on drugs. We were fine at first, but then my dad died, so we were on our own when the money stopped coming. But it's okay, 'cause Mr.

Pasquino said he'd take really good care of me. But I had to earn it." He motions to the yard. "So here I am."

I can't help but smile at him. Well, at least Luca is doing some good in this kid's life.

"I'm sorry about your father," I say, feeling pity. I know all too well how it feels to have your father taken away from you.

He only shrugs. "It's okay. I never really knew him. He came around rarely and only ever talked about how I was destined for greatness." He bends his head and begins picking at a scab on his arm.

"What are all the different flowers for?" I ask, trying to change the subject to something a little less depressing. His eyes light up at the mention of his work.

"Mr. Pasquino requested them. He said his wife likes all the different-colored flowers." He motions to each of the flowers as he speaks. "I got lilies, azaleas, sunflowers, all the different colors I could find. Mr. Pasquino said his wife was feeling under the weather lately, so he wanted different flowers to cheer her up!"

I can't help but be shocked. Luca actually paid attention to something that isn't for the purpose of inflicting pain on me? He requested that these be planted for my expense?

The boy's smile slowly disappears as he thinks of something.

"Which reminds me ... I should probably get to planting these before she gets up and sees them on accident."

I would laugh if I weren't so shocked at the thoughtfulness of Luca's actions. This kid obviously doesn't know who he is speaking to.

"Can I join you?" I ask.

I know he has work to do, but I don't want to sit around the yard doing nothing, and something about him is comforting.

He looks as though he is thinking it over. "Hmmmmm, I dunno. I mean ... I guess. But you can't slow me down. I have to have these done before noon."

I giggle to myself at the serious face he gets with me. It is adorable.

"Okay. I'm Elise, by the way." I give him a small smile and hold my hand out.

"Matteo." He smiles and shakes my hand with his.

We work on planting the flowers in the backyard. Each time I try to plant them somewhere that isn't right, Matteo stops me in frustration, getting upset when I almost "mess up the order". He keeps fussing about how these have to be perfect. By the end of the day, I'm sweating and have dirt crusted under my fingernails, but I am the happiest I have been in a long time.

Matteo is a funny kid. Turns out he is fifteen. His mom had gotten knocked up, and the guy that got her pregnant had to get rid of her because he was married, but instead, he put her up somewhere, living in luxury. Unfortunately she is a greedy woman, using the money he sent her, blowing it all on drugs and alcohol. And when his father died a few months ago, the money stopped coming, and his mom ran through what was left of it, leaving them to struggle.

There is a light tap on my hand, and I look into Matteo's frustrated green eyes.

"You can't put that one next to the azaleas, for the millionth time, Elise."

I give him a small smile. "Sorry, I wasn't paying attention to what I was doing."

"Well, you should. Mr. Pasquino will be really mad if we mess this up. And he'll definitely get mad at me because I let the maid help do it."

I turn my head away, rolling my eyes in the process. If only he knows.

"How do you know Luc—I mean, Mr. Pasquino, anyways? You sure do talk about him a lot," I ask.

Matteo is digging a hole to plant the next set of flowers before he begins talking.

"Well, Mr. Pasquino actually showed up sometime last year. I thought he was another one of my mom's suitors, but he actually has helped me a lot. He taught me how to shave, how to drive, how to play cards. He said he was getting married soon to someone special and wanted to learn more about being around people, whatever that means." He pauses to wipe some sweat from his brow. "He actually talks about her a lot, which is why these flowers have to be perfect.

He has helped me so much. He even paid our bills sometimes and made sure I had food at night when Mom wasn't around."

He looks up to the leaves of the massive tree above us.

"I asked him once why he was helping us out so much, but he just shrugged and said he was doing it for someone special."

"Matteo! What the hell are you doing back he—"

We both jump and look behind us, where one of the workers stands. He is shouting at Matteo to come but stops immediately when he sees me.

"I … I'm so sorry, missus. He knows better than to be roaming the grounds. He knew the job he's been given." The man looks at Matteo with a stern eye. "We're leaving, Matteo."

Matteo jumps up frantically.

"But we're not finished with the flowers!" He is genuinely upset.

"Look, kid, we told you our shift is over at twelve. You're going to have to explain why the job on your behalf isn't done. Or you can stay here and finish and walk home."

I decide to step in on Matteo's behalf.

"I can take him home. This is really important to him."

"Elise!"

I jump, and even though it is eighty degrees outside, my blood runs cold. I turn and see Luca's icy gaze, pinning me to the spot. He is wearing shorts and a nice short-sleeve button-down shirt. He is walking toward me with an irritated expression on his face.

"Where have you been? I've been looking everywhere for y—"

His gaze shifts and lands on Matteo, and his whole demeanor shifts. He becomes tense. Something that I've never seen him do unless he was anticipating some sort of threat.

"Matteo, I thought I made the rules around here clear." His voice comes out cold and calculated. I look at Matteo, and he looks frozen to the spot.

"I …"

"It was my fault." I cut him off. "He told me he was busy, but I insisted on his company."

Luca's gaze shifts between us, as if he's thinking something.

"Come, Elise, lunch is ready." He turns away from us and walks to the patio. I look at Matteo with an apologetic smile, and he's staring at me in disbelief.

We take a seat at the outdoor table, and Luca wrinkles his nose at me.

"Elise, you're filthy. You have dirt all over you."

"Sorry."

He looks up from his plate and eyes me with curiosity. "Why aren't you eating?"

"It's just … I didn't get Matteo in trouble, did I? He's just a kid."

Luca tilts his head at me. "No, you didn't."

"Okay. Well, I kinda told him you would take him home since I slowed him down on his work."

Luca only grunts in response. His mind seems to be elsewhere right now.

"What did you guys talk about?" Luca asks.

I look up from my plate, and his steel gaze is burning right through me. I don't know what I should keep out of telling him. He's being so serious right now and I honestly don't even know what I did wrong.

"Nothing, really. He mostly yelled at me for putting the plants in the wrong place." I give a nervous laugh.

Luca is still staring at me. I can tell he is deciding on whether to believe me or not.

We eat our lunch in silence, the only talking when Luca asks me questions. When we finish, he stands to go into the house to get his keys so that he can take Matteo home.

I immediately stand up from the table and go find Matteo. I step around and am surprised by the yard. It's beautiful and colorful. It looks like something a professional would do, not a fifteen-year-old. The yard is like a rainbow of flowers. It is obvious he has put a lot of effort into this.

"Do you like it?"

I jump. Matteo is standing right next to me. How on earth does he keep sneaking up on me?

"It's beautiful, Matteo," I tell him. And I truly mean it. This is amazing.

"Why didn't you tell me you were Mr. Pasquino's wife?" he asks.

"I don't know. You didn't seem inclined to ask, and you thought I was the maid, so I didn't feel the need to correct you. Besides, we had fun today, didn't we?"

He shakes his head, his curly hair bouncing in front of his face. "He told me specifically not to make any kind of contact with you. He's going to be so mad at me."

I feel my heart sink into my stomach for him. I once again may have gotten someone into huge trouble because of my stupidity.

"I'm sorry. He said he wasn't mad about it. I just … it was nice talking to someone else for a change."

I turn and look at him, but he is focusing on something else. Who is this kid to Luca? Why is he helping him out so much? And why does he look so damn familiar to me?

"Matteo!" Luca's voice comes across the yard like a whip. Matteo turns to me, holding his hand out.

"It was nice meeting you, Mrs. Pasquino."

He gives me a huge smile. I smile at him and shake his hand. He then takes off across the yard to Luca. I watch as they turn and walk toward the garage. Luca is speaking to him, surprisingly calm. He isn't yelling or anything. They finally disappear from view, and I head into the house to take a bath and wash all this grime off me.

After I wrap my wrist up, I take a seat in the warm water, letting it relax me. My thoughts wander back to Matteo. He's only fifteen and has gonethrough so much. But what connection does Luca have to him that he feels obligated to help this kid out? I've never taken Luca for the caring type. The thing that bothers me the most is the fact that there is a nagging in the back of my mind. But I can't think of where I know him from.

I sit in the water until it starts to get cold. I step out of the tub and into the bedroom freezing in my tracks. Luca is standing in the doorway, eyeing my naked body up and down lustfully. He pushes himself off the doorframe and makes his way over to me.

My heart is thumping heavily against my chest. Luca isn't speaking. His face is blank. I don't know if he is mad or happy or what. He takes my hand and leads me to the doorway. We both step out of the room and into the hallway. We step down the hallway and come to a massive double door. He pushes it open, revealing a massive en suite bedroom. I don't have the time to admire it. Luca pushes me gently up against the wall. He nuzzles my neck and brings his hands down to my butt, pulling me into him. I don't dare fight him. I know what will happen if I do. So I just close my eyes and give in.

"It's been so long since I had you, Elise."

His hands pick me up, and I gasp aloud. He carries me to the bed and drops me on top of the warm sheets. I can feel myself sinking into the soft mattress. He leans over me, straddling my body. His lips meet mine, but they are not possessive and harsh like usual, but soft and warm. I feel his hand drift down between my thighs. A soft moan escapes my lips as he begins moving his fingers to arouse me.

His lips leave mine, and he leans down, capturing my breast in his mouth. I can't help the pleasure that explodes within me. I hate my body in that moment. It always betrays me just because Luca knows what he is doing manipulating it. I can hear shuffling and open my eyes to see Luca shedding his clothing.

He uses his knees to spread my legs apart, and I can feel his hot erection pressing at my entrance. He slowly pushes into me, stretching me to accommodate his large size. I gasp and open my eyes to Luca's lust-filled gaze boring into mine.

He slowly starts thrusting into me, eliciting little sparks of pleasure each time. An involuntary moan escapes my lips. He threads his fingers through my hair and pulls my head to the side, exposing my throat. He leans in and begins sucking hard on my throat. I cry out as he picks up his rhythmic thrusts, pounding deeper and deeper into me each time.

"I missed your body so much, baby," he groans in my ear.

All at once, my orgasm hits me, and I open my mouth to let out my moans of pleasure. Luca captures my mouth with his, swallowing my moans. I can feel him getting even larger inside of me as he finds his release with a pleasured groan. We stay like that for a moment, our labored breathing echoing throughout the room. Luca slowly pulls out of me and picks my limp body up, taking me to the bathroom.

For the first time in a while, Luca lies next to me as I sleep. I decide to put all the negative thoughts out of my mind for once and let my weakened body rest.

Chapter 21

Elise

Luca is a strange person. I have never seen him be kind to anyone except maybe his father. Or Nicolai on rare occasions. But as I sit stretched out on the pool, I watch him as he teaches Matteo how to use garden shears. I honestly don't know what it is about this kid that makes him feel obligated to teach him how to garden.

Luca is calmly explaining to him while showing him the right way to use the massive clippers. Matteo is watching him with careful eyes, focusing on what he is saying very intently. Matteo only works here three days a week, and on those days, Luca makes sure to keep him busy or keep me busy. If it's such a big deal for him not to speak to me, why hire him to work here? Matteo must be someone really special if Luca is putting in all this effort for him. I know he can't be Luca's child, because the age range doesn't add up. He can't be related to me, because Luca hates my entire family—he even threatened me with my brother's life—so why would he bring him here and help him out? That leaves only one option, that he is Luca's sibling. But he must be Luca's half-sibling, because Luca is an only child as far as I know.

I wish I could just ask him, but I know he'll be angry if I do. Every time I say something about Matteo, he tenses up and closes himself off. So I know Matteo is a sensitive topic to him. But the real question is, *Who* is he?

I jump in my seat as I hear something I haven't heard in a long time. Laughter. Luca's laughter. I look up and see him with his head thrown back and a large smile plastered on his face. It is a sunny day, so the sunlight is shining directly on him. Damn. I really wish Luca were at least somewhat unattractive. It would make it easier for my body to be repulsed by him when he touches me.

Luca is a puzzle to be figured out. I don't understand him at all. His moods are up and down like a roller coaster. He's been home very rarely as of late. Today is one of the rare days that he's actually here. I guess he has dealings to do. I honestly don't know what Luca's workday consists of. I just know when he leaves and when he comes home.

He points to something, and Matteo eagerly nods as Luca hands him the clippers. As if sensing being watched, Luca looks at my direction, his gray eyes catching me staring. He gives me a sexy grin, and I immediately blush and study the book that I am reading.

"Elise."

I jump and look up to see Luca standing over me. He moves fast. There is a light sheen of sweat glistening over his skin, and he has a small smile on his face. I hate it when he looks at me like that. He has this look of adoration, as if I were so precious to him. He is about to say something when Romelo comes running out of the house and up to Luca, panting.

"Capo, we have a problem." His eyes are wild and full of fear.

Luca's face shifts, and he pulls Romelo off to the side, out of earshot. I watch them as Luca takes in the news, and his face grows irritated. He says something to Romelo, and he shakes his head vigorously. Luca crosses his arms and runs his hands through his hair. Romelo nods in agreement and walks off the opposite direction.

"I have to leave to take care of something that has come up. I'll be back home later, okay?"

I nod slowly in understanding.

Luca begins to walk away but pauses and looks at me with a serious expression. "Don't bother Matteo."

I nod once again, showing him that I understand. He leans in and gives me a quick kiss on the cheek and steps into the house. I wait a few minutes before I follow his lead, heading into the house to get a glass of water. Luca is already pulling out of the driveway when I reach the kitchen. I pour myself some water and take a small sip, looking out the window over the sink. I can see Matteo in the distance.

He is really focused on trimming the bushes. His brow is slightly furrowed, and he keeps shaking his head to move his hair out of his face. I laugh softly to myself. Maybe he should wear a headband if his hair is getting that long. You'd think he'd learn by now. He pauses, dropping the clippers on the ground and hunching over to take deep breaths. He has to be hot. It's at least eighty degrees out there. I step over to the fridge and grab a cold-water bottle and head back out onto the patio.

I walk up next to him, catching his attention.

"You look like you could use a break." I give him a small smile while handing him the water.

He eyes it untrustingly and looks back at me. "Look, Mrs. Pasquino. Mr. Pasquino said not to talk to you. And he made it pretty clear what my consequences would be if I did."

I can feel my frustration boiling up. "It's just water," I say with an annoyed tone.

He stares at me for a moment longer before reaching out and taking the bottle from my hand. He opens the bottle and takes a long swig before speaking to me again.

"I'm sorry. I know you're just trying to be nice. Thank you." His eyes flicker to my wrist. "You seem to be healing quite nicely," he says.

I involuntarily move my arm behind my back, looking away. The stitches have been taken out, so now all that is left is a light scar. "Well, I don't want to get you in trouble," I mumble and begin to walk away before stopping. I never know if I'm going to get another chance like this. "Are you and Luca related? You know, like brothers or half-brothers or anything?" I ask.

He makes a face at me and laughs to himself softly. "No. I don't have any siblings. And I never met Mr. Pasquino before last year."

I look away in frustration. Then why is Luca so nice to this kid? And why doesn't he want me near him?

"If that's all, Mrs. Pasquino, thank you for the water, but I'm going to get back to my work." He turns away from me and goes back to working on the bushes.

I huff and walk away in frustration.

* * * * *

The sun has gone down, and I am all alone in the estate. Of course, there are Luca's men here to keep me company, but they are just guarding the house. I have no phone, so there is no way I can contact Luca. Or anyone, for that matter. Not that I have anyone. I take a deep breath and exhale it. What am I going to do for the rest of my life?

I step into the living room and turn on the TV. I haven't watched TV in a while. I eventually settle on some cooking channel and snuggle into the soft couch, falling asleep.

There is a tickle on my thigh. It slowly moves its way up, circling a pattern. I twitch and swat at it. There is another tickle on my face, tracing my cheek. I try to swat at it, but it starts back up. I open my eyes to find the source of the feeling and gasp when I find it. Luca is kneeling in front of the couch. The only light in the room comes from the TV, and it is causing him to be silhouetted.

I look at his face and his clothes, and he seems to be drenched in something. Sweat? He is staring at me with an emotionless expression and reaches out to touch my face.

"God, you are beautiful," he murmurs. His hand reaches my face as he cups my cheek, and that is when it hits me. The metallic odor. I let out a small gasp, my heart rate increasing.

"L-Luca?" I reach out with shaky hands to feel the front of his saturated shirt, praying that it is water or sweat. My fingertips brush the front of the shirt, and the sticky residue that comes with it answers my question. Blood.

I immediately jump back from Luca, falling off the other side of the couch and scrambling away from him on the floor. He is still watching me with that frightening expression.

"Oh god!" I gasp aloud. Obviously, none of it is his blood, or he wouldn't even be here right now.

He leans away from the couch on his hands and knees and begins crawling toward me with a sadistic look on his face.

"Luca, what's going on?"

He doesn't speak to me; it's like he's not even there. He grabs on to my leg, and I squeal as the blood running from his arms oozes onto me. I jerk my leg away and try to kick him.

"Come here, baby." His voice is terrifying. He's not himself. There's blood all over the carpet from where he is standing. "I just want to love you," he murmurs while moving closer to me.

"Luca, please, you're not yourself right now," I try to beg and hope that he will resurface, but to no avail.

He yanks on my leg, dragging me toward him so that I am trapped underneath his bloodied body, the blood from his shirt seeping into mine as he lies on top of me. I scream and cry, begging him to get off me, but he doesn't listen. He grabs my face in between his hands and makes me meet his eyes. They are void of any emotion. His dark irises keep moving across my face as he takes in each of my features.

"You're so damn beautiful. I'll protect you, baby. I won't let them get you," he murmurs. He leans in and begins nuzzling my cheek, smearing blood all over my face. I gag from the scent.

"Luca, please," I try again.

"Shhhhhh." He puts his hand over my mouth, and that is all it takes for me to vomit.

He cringes his face in disgust and removes his hand as all the contents of my stomach are emptied. I take the opportunity to jump up from him and take off through the dark house. I sprint for the stairs, trying to take them two at a time, when I feel a hand on my ankle, causing me to fall and face-plant into the stairs. I cry out in pain as he drags me down the steps toward him.

"Luca!" I scream in desperation. Whatever he went to do wasn't pretty at all, and it sent him into some kind of semiconscious state.

He pulls me down the stairs so that I am lying on the hardwood floor. I look up into his eyes and whimper in fear. He is angry.

"Don't you dare run from me! You're my wife!" he shouts.

I close my eyes and cringe. He flips me over on my stomach and shoves my dress up. I immediately begin to struggle in panic.

"Luca, please stop! You're covered in blood. Please don't do this!" I frantically cry out.

He flips me back over so that I am lying on my back. I am crying so hard in fear right now I can feel my breathing come out in quicker pants as a panic attack takes over. Luca moves a little, and I open my eyes. I am looking up the barrel of a gun. He is aiming it directly at my face.

I open my mouth and close it, unable to make any sounds. I don't know what to say or do. The gun moves to the underside of my jaw, and he presses the cold metal against my skin. He leans in slowly and begins kissing the other side of my jaw lightly.

"Don't say a word," he whispers.

He continues to kiss me lightly down the side of my throat, slowly making his way to my collarbone. There is no sound except for my frantic breathing and his kisses. His hands are roaming all over my body. I can only struggle underneath him. I close my eyes tightly as the tears fall freely down my face.

Suddenly, Luca is lifted off me. I open my eyes to see Romelo and Nicolai on either side of him. They are covered in blood as well, but not as much as Luca is. They struggle with him, slamming him into the wall. His eyes are still on me; he has a crazed look in his eye as he watches me.

Nicolai and Romelo are shouting at him, trying to calm him down, but he is not listening; he is just watching me with that terrifying expression.

"Elise!" I look up, and Nicolai is shouting at me. They are having a hard time restraining Luca. He is trying to break free.

"You have to run. Go lock yourself in your room—"

Nicolai is cut off as Luca breaks free of him, elbowing him in the face, splitting his eyebrow. Blood trickles down the side of his face. Luca scrambles toward me, and Romelo tackles him from behind, pinning him to the floor.

"Go!" he shouts.

"Don't you dare, Elise!" Luca growls out.

That is all it takes for me to take off. I sprint up the stairs, down the hall, to the farthest room I can find, and lock the door. I slide down the door, my legs trembling. I hold my hands out in front of me and look at all the blood, someone else's blood that is now on my body. A scream tears its way from my throat. I beat the door with all my might, letting my anger and frustration flow.

I am stuck here. I am stuck in this. I can't do anything about it. Luca is sick. He is more than sick. He is deranged. A person that loves blood and gore, killing and murders. And I am married to him. There is no way I can change this man. He has been this way all his life.

I can hear the struggles of Romelo and Nicolai. If it weren't for them, there is no telling what would have happened to me.

* * * * *

Rain. I can hear it. It isn't light either. It's a heavy and dark rain. I open my eyes to see the dark raincloud covering the sky. Water is soaking everything. I sit up and feel the tightness of my skin. I look at my arms and the front of my dress to see the crusted blood still on me. If I hadn't vomited last night, I would at this moment.

The room I'm in has no bathroom. I walk to the door and slowly open it a crack, looking down the empty hallway. I have to get this stuff off me. I look down the corridor, and Luca is nowhere in sight. I step out into the hallway, looking for the nearest room that has a shower in it. Once I find one, I hurry and strip my clothes off, turning on the steaming water.

As soon as the warm water hits my skin, I begin to cry. I look down at the water flowing down the drain and cry even harder as the water tints. I immediately grab a towel and begin scrubbing my skin. And even when I'm done, I continue to scrub it even harder. I scrub and scrub and scrub until my skin is screaming in pain. My body is red from the heat and all the constant scrubbing I have done. I collapse on the bathroom floor and let my loud sobs echo off the wall. I take the scrubber and continue to scrub my skin, growling in frustration.

A pair of hands encompasses mine, and I look up to see Luca staring at me. A scream tears its way out of my throat, and I back away from Luca as fast as I can, slipping and falling back down as I try to escape. He steps into the shower, still not making a sound. He is wearing clothes, so they get drenched as soon as he steps in.

"Please …" I close my eyes in fear. I don't even know what I'm begging for.

I open my eyes and see Luca reaching above me. He still hasn't said a word. He grabs a large towel and wraps it around my body, turning the shower off. I keep the towel wrapped around me as we both walk down the hall into our bedroom. He still doesn't say a word; he only lays a dress on the bed for me to wear and exits the room quietly. I don't bother putting on the dress. I settle for a sweater shirt and some leggings. I don't want to wear anything he has picked out.

Once I finally leave the room, I head into the kitchen. My stomach is growling, seeing as I haven't eaten since lunch yesterday. I step into the kitchen and freeze. Luca is standing at the counter, with a coffee mug in his hand. His head immediately turns upon my entrance, his gaze meeting mine head-on. I immediately take a step back, ready to leave the kitchen.

"No. I'll go," Luca says softly and exits the room without sparing me so much as a sideways glance. His mind seems to be somewhere else.

I peep around the corner to see where he is going. He has his back to me and seems to be heading toward the direction of his office.

I am sitting in the kitchen, quietly munching on a piece of toast, when Nicolai walks in. I gasp as I take in his face. Where Luca has no scratches or bruises on him, Nicolai has stitches above his eye and a swollen cheek. His eye is also turning black. He meets my gaze and immediately freezes.

"Oh. I'm sorry, I didn't know you were still in here." He tries to duck out of the kitchen.

"Wait!" I call out, and he stops, turning slowly. "Did Luca do that?" I ask.

He looks as though he doesn't want to respond. "Yes. But please don't say anything to him about it. You weren't supposed to see me." He steps closer to where I am on the barstool. "It's not his fault. Sometimes he just loses control. Please don't hold it against him." He looks at me with pleading eyes.

I nod to give him peace of mind. He then hurriedly exits the kitchen.

I look out the window, wishing more than anything that the rain would stop falling. I sigh. I wish Matteo were here. Even though I never get to speak to him, something about him just sets me at ease. It makes me happy to see his innocence and optimism. He won't come back for another two days, and that's only if the rain stops.

A loud rapping on the back door startles me, and I spill my mug of coffee all over the counter. I look up and see none other than Matteo standing on the other side of the door. He is wearing a tank top and some shorts and is getting soaked in the rain. I immediately jump up from the counter and run to the door, pulling it open.

"Oh my gosh, Matteo, are you all right?"

He looks panicked. "I … I'm so sorry for barging in like this, I just don't know anyone else. My mom had no friends, I didn't know who to call, I don't know what to do …" He keeps mumbling in a panicked state, not really making any sense. He looks as though he is in shock from something.

I grab his face in my hands, making him focus on me. "Matteo, calm down. How'd you get here?" Our house is literally in the middle of nowhere, and the nearest bus station is forty-five minutes away.

"I took the bus into town and walked … well, ran," he says.

I take in his frantic form and step around him to close the door. "Come on." I grab his hand and lead him into the living room. The fireplace is going, luckily. I sit him on the couch. "Wait right here."

He doesn't seem to be listening; his eyes are empty, and he looks as though he is in a daze.

I sprint out of the living room and pass Luca's office. The door is closed. Obviously, he didn't hear us, or he would be in the living room by now. I grab a blanket from the cover closet and run back to the living room, sneaking a glance at Luca's office, making sure the door is still closed. When I arrive back into the living room, Matteo is sitting with his head in his hands. I wrap the blanket around him and take a seat next to him, rubbing his back.

"Now, tell me what happened."

"I … I tried to call Mr. Pasquino, but he didn't answer. I didn't know who else to call, so I came here. You guys are the closest thing I have to a family." He pauses and begins to cry even harder. "My mom … she's missing. She won't answer her phone. And she never leaves without leaving a note. I tried the police, but they said they couldn't do anything for twenty-four hours. And they hate her. She's been in trouble with the law quite a few times."

He looks up.

"This isn't like her. She knew how dangerous the world was. She always stressed it to me. She wouldn't just up and disappear like this." There is worry evident in his eyes.

"Okay, how about I go get the keys and I'll take you home, and we'll begin our search there, okay?"

"But what about Mr. Pasquino?"

"He's busy right now," I lie. I don't want to bother with Luca. One, I am terrified to speak to him, and two, there is no telling what he'll do if he finds out Matteo and I are speaking to each other. I grab Matteo's hand in mine, giving it a light squeeze. "We're going to find her, okay? It'll be all right." I give him a light smile.

I head toward the garage. Luca keeps all the cars in there and the keys to each hanging on their own hooks on the wall. We step into the garage and turn on the lights. The garage is underground, like a parking garage, so Luca won't be able to hear us leave, especially with this rain. I grab the first set of keys I lay my eyes on and press the button. The Audi lights up. Perfect.

I don't have a license, but I know how to drive. Hopefully, we won't get pulled over on the way to Matteo's.

* * * * *

I can't help feel pity as I look around. This place is filthy. It is obvious that a drug addict lives here. But it isn't obvious a fifteen-year-old boy lives here. There is trash everywhere, burnt foil, clothes, dirty dishes, and food residue. The place is tiny and grimy. I look at Matteo in disbelief.

"Matteo, you live here?" I ask.

He nods, not speaking to me. In all honesty, this place doesn't look livable.

"I told you my mother blew all the money. This was all we could barely afford."

He walks toward me with an eviction notice in his hand. I feel my heart break for this boy. If all this is happening to him, what could possibly be Luca's connection to him?

A loud noise startles me out of my thoughts. I turn and see Matteo has thrown something across the room in frustration.

"Why are we here? We should be looking for her, not searching where she's not. I already looked here," he growls in frustration.

"Matteo, we need to see if she left any clues of where she might be or anything. Maybe she did leave a note, just not in her usual spot? It never hurts to double-check."

He is staring at me in frustration, and I turn away from him, reaching on the top shelf of the bookcase for any stray paper. My shirt rides up slightly, and I hear a gasp, followed by the yanking of my shirt.

I immediately look down in horror but am met with the same horror. Matteo is staring at me in shock.

"Dear God, did he do that to you?" He motions to my side.

Shit. I was careless. He's seen my side. He's seen Luca's name. I don't answer him.

"Elise, that's his name … and that's not a tattoo. It looks like it's been … carved into your skin," he says in disbelief.

"Matteo, this isn't about me. I'm fine. We need to find your mother." I walk away before he can respond, feeling stupid. How could I have been so careless?

I step into the hallway, and there is a closed door.

"Matteo, whose room is this?" I ask.

He looks at me with irritation before answering my question. "That's my mom's room."

"Why's the door closed? Did you close it before you left?" I ask. His eyes widen in realization. "No."

I make a face and turn back to the door. I slowly turn the knob.

"Well, then, she must've come home while you were gone. She must be in he—"

I am cut off as I open the door to his mother's room. A scream rips its way from my throat, and I back away from the door as quickly as I can. Bile immediately rips its way from my stomach, and I hunch over. Matteo is coming my way quickly with a worried expression. I immediately slam the door shut and brush past him, trying to pull him with me.

"No, Matteo, don't go in there," I plead, with my eyes at him.

"Why?" His face grows panicked as he takes in my tone. He turns his head toward his mother's room and tries to step that way, but I hold his arm steady, shaking my head.

"No, Matteo."

He looks at me and at the door and back to me in a panic.

"We need to get Luca. He'll know what to do ..." I trail off.

I'm an idiot. I should have never come here in the first place without Luca's knowledge. Then it hits me. If someone has been here to kill Matteo's mother since he's been gone, they could still be near. And we could be in danger.

"Matteo, we have to leave now." I begin to grow panicked and paranoid, looking everywhere. I don't even think Matteo knows what Luca is into. Possibly, someone that sees Luca's connection with Matteo is looking to hurt him somehow. But why? Nothing is making any sense.

I am tugging frantically on Matteo's arm, but he is in shock as he stares at his mother's door.

"Matteo, please. Our lives could be in danger."

This catches his attention, and he looks at me questioningly. I don't have time to explain, so I drag him out of the house and into the pouring rain, right into a large body.

Chapter 22

Luca

"The body has been put into place. Everything else has been taken care of," Romelo informs me.

I need a fucking drink. The past twenty-four hours have been hell, to say the least.

After I left the house yesterday, I drove straight into a bloodbath. That bitch Elise's father knocked up found out who I am and wanted revenge for his death. She was nothing but a crack whore that was mad because her money source is dead.

In the past year, I have made myself a normal part of Matteo's life. As soon as I met Elise, I pushed my way into his life. He's a good kid. He and Elise share similar facial features, which makes it easier for me to be nice to him, seeing as he has his father's blood running through his veins. Matteo's mother had almost gotten her son killed on several occasions, and when I met him for the first time, he was starving. She had taken the money sent for his benefit and blew it all on drugs and clothes for herself.

So I took it upon myself to take care of him in the shadows. At first, it was to use him against his father, because I didn't trust the bastard one bit. But when I realized Elise wasn't aware of her half-brother, I knew something more powerful had to be at play here. So I took care of him and taught him what it means to be a man. Even though my views are different from his, I tried to be as normal for his sake as I could. For Elise. She doesn't know I have contact with him.

Hell, she doesn't even know she is looking at her little brother every day. And I want to keep it that way. For how long, I have no idea.

Matteo's mother had orchestrated a very smart plan to take me out. She had one of my clubs raided, killing some of my men and wounding many. It wasn't business hours, so only the people that I put in charge that were there. And when I showed up, she had somehow gotten ahold of men to attack us.

I clench my fists in frustration as I remember her threat.

"I'll kill that wife of yours. Everything she has, my son deserves! I'll kill her slowly and make her suffer."

She never got anything more out of her mouth before my world went dark, all the rage and hatred consuming me. All I remember are bits and pieces. Her screams of agony, her blood, the blood of I don't know how many other men. The pleasure and bloodlust that coursed through my veins was so intense I lost myself. Even in my haze, I could hear Elise's voice, but I hadn't realized I almost hurt her in that state.

I woke up locked to a desk, with blood crusted all over my body and Nicolai and Romelo having bloody bruises and cuts, but not from the club. From me. Once they explained to me everything that happened, I could only imagine the horror Elise felt. And she showed it when she looked at me this morning. She was terrified. I felt nothing but guilt when I found her this morning rubbing her skin raw in that shower. I can't imagine what I almost did to her. But I can only imagine when I awoke and found bloodstains that were everywhere. I had to get the staff to scrub it out before Elise woke up.

My phone goes off, and I pull it out, looking at the screen. I frown. One of my cars has been taken. I have a system that lets me know whenever a car is taken from the garage. But I obviously haven't taken any cars anywhere. I immediately stand from my desk.

"Go find Elise." I bark the command at Romelo and Nicolai.

As they take off out of the room, I pull up my security system to watch the film. No one has broken into the garage, but … Matteo? I watch as he frantically runs around the house before settling on the back door. He stands there for a moment before walking into the house.

Fuck. I pull out my phone and pull up Elise's tracker. Sure enough, she isn't here. But she is moving. Fast. Which means she is the one that has taken the car. And Matteo is probably with her. And they are probably headed to his house, where the fucking body has been dumped.

I jump up from my seat behind my desk, sprinting out of the office.

"Romelo!"

They must still be searching for Elise. Fuck! If I don't get there in time, she will see my handiwork. And worse, she and Matteo are alone together. I sprint out of the house to my car, sending Romelo a text to meet me at Matteo's while I am running. The plan was falling into place perfectly, but Elise's being there is unexpected.

I make it to his house in record time, and sure enough, my Audi is parked out front. I open the door, and the rain plummets down on me. I walk as fast as I can to the front of the house when Elise's frightened face exits the house with Matteo right behind her. Shit. She's found her. Elise is so panicked and frightened she doesn't even see me standing there as she slams right into me full force.

Chapter 23

Luca

"We had been searching the house for about thirty minutes. I ... I didn't hear anything, but when I opened the door, sh—"

Elise cuts off her sentence and begins sobbing again. She turns her face into my chest. I can feel the violent sobs as they shake her entire body. We have been sitting out here for an hour in the pouring rain as the police slowly turns this area into a crime scene.

I rub her back comfortingly. I look over to where Matteo is sitting on the back of an ambulance. He looks as though he is focusing on nothing. The cop is talking to him, but he isn't responding. He is watching as his mother's body is wheeled out of the house under a white sheet. I know that look all too well. Shock. *Damn.* This isn't what was supposed to happen.

The original plan was to stage his mother's death, and seeing as I am the only other important role in Matteo's life, I would have taken him in and sworn him into the family. But when his mother found out who I am and tried to kill me, I lost control and mutilated her body. We were to use that in our favor, telling Matteo the truth behind his father and that someone from a rival Mob must have figured out who he is, pinning the death on someone else so his rage would fester and he would join the family without question, to "avenge" his mother's death.

It would have been the perfect retribution for their blackhearted father and his treacherous family. The only son of the infamous capo of the South, under my rule. Even if he found out the truth behind my motives, there would be nothing he could do about it. He'd be sworn in. No way out. Everyone would have seen the example that has been made of the Trovolis. Completely exterminated, all but who I decide. And even then, under my rule. Controlled by me.

"It's okay, ma'am, we'll get to the bottom of this," the officer says comfortingly to Elise.

She nods slightly. If only she knew that this officer and more than 70 percent of the police department are under my control. I look him in the eye as he puts away his notepad. He returns my gaze with a grim nod. He probably already knows this is my doing, but they will rule this as a random crime and move on.

"What about the boy?" I ask.

The officer looks up. "He'll probably be placed into foster care. We'll be sure to get him in the system."

I nod and lean into Elise, whispering in her ear, "Go wait in the car for me, baby."

She looks at me with watery eyes and nods slightly, walking to the car. Once she is out of earshot, I turn back to the officer, giving him a hard stare.

"You and I both know that boy isn't going into the system. I want him. I want the paperwork in my home tomorrow."

The officer's eyes widen, and he shakes his head slightly. "B-but, sir, there are protocols we have to follow, reports we have to dr—"

"Do you know who the fuck you're talking to?" I interrupt him, giving him a murderous look to get my point across. Whoever this man is doesn't understand who he is dealing with. His eyes grow wide, confusion evident on his face.

"Sir, I think you need to calm your voice down and—"

"No, let me tell you something, you pathetic excuse of a human being. I'm the man that holds your job in the palm of my motherfucking hand. Whatever the fuck I say fucking goes, and I'll be damned if some mall cop has the nerve to tell me about fucking protocol." I take a step closer to him and can feel the fear radiating off him.

"Is there a problem here?" Officer Benson steps in between us.

I know Officer Benson well. He is the man that I trust with my cases. And I add a hefty bonus to his paychecks to keep it that way.

I look back to the cop I've just cussed out. "Is there?" I narrow my eyes at him.

He immediately shakes his head as he takes in the gravity of the situation. I turn to Officer Benson.

"Sorry, Mr. Pasquino. He's only been here a few months."

I ignore him and keep my eyes on the *new* officer. "I want the paperwork tomorrow." I walk away without waiting for a response. Nicolai and Romelo are waiting for me. I speak to Nicolai first.

"Take my car home," I say, gesturing to the one Elise has driven out here without permission. I then turn to Romelo. "Take Matteo to my home once you're finished here."

He nods to me, and I walk away to the car I brought out here, which Elise is now sitting in. I step into the car, and Elise has her head in her hands. I don't know if I should feel angry at her for leaving the grounds, taking my car without permission, and speaking to Matteo or if I should feel pity for her because she has personally seen my handiwork.

I don't speak to her as I sit in the car. Now that all this is behind me, I can feel the anger and resentment boiling up deep within me. She brought this on herself. If she weren't so damn disobedient, she wouldn't have found anything.

I put the car in drive and head home.

We reach the house in record time. Elise still isn't speaking; she is just looking out the window with a blank stare on her face. There are still tears flowing freely out of her eyes. I shut the car off, and the only sound is the rain pelting the car. I open my mouth to speak, but Elise starts before I can get a word out.

"It was you, wasn't it?"

The car is silent. She still isn't looking at me. I can see her lips trembling. For once in my life, I don't know how to respond.

"You disappeared yesterday and came back last night covered in blood." She chokes on a sob. "And the next day, his mother wound up dead." She places her hands over her mouth as violent sobs rack her body.

"He told me he searched the house. Including her room. And when we showed up there, she was suddenly in her bedroom." She finally turns and looks at me with big brown eyes. She is too smart for her own good.

I grow irritated as I feel something once more festering up inside me. Guilt. She is searching my face for any sign that it isn't true, but I keep my expression blank. She sits back against the window and gasps.

"Oh god, Luca … why? What did that boy ever do to you? Why would you treat him so nice, give him a job here, just to mutilate his mother? H-how could you do that to a woman?" She seems to just be talking now.

I reach out for her, and she immediately recoils from me, slapping my hand away.

"Don't touch me! You … you're a monster! You're fucking sick!" She is shouting all kinds of obscenities at me, and I can see that she is forgetting who I am. She is forgetting her place.

"Elise!" I snap at her.

All the anger dissipates from her face as she shuts her mouth, and it is replaced with fear, her training kicking in. Good. She looks back down at her lap and stifles a sob. She bites her lip softly and takes a deep breath as she brings her gaze back to mine.

"I thought you, of all people, would understand the pain of having a murdered parent. How could you consciously bring that pain on someone else? An innocent boy?" She keeps her gaze locked with mine as we both sit in silence.

I don't know what to say. She is right.

She sighs and shakes her head, opening the door and stepping out into the rain, closing it behind her. I watch through the window as she makes her way into the house.

Fuck! I hit the steering wheel with all my might. There is this heavy weight on my chest, a weight that feels unfamiliar to me. That fucking bitch! How dare she make me feel this way! This is all her fucking fault in the first place! No, it is her disgusting father's! Yes! That is why all this is happening—that is the source of our problem!

I hop out of the car quickly, all the rage and anger coming to the surface. I force open the door with all my might. This is all their fault. All her fault for making me love her. She should be dead now, along with her father and the rest of her tainted line. I take the stairs two at a time, searching for her. I am going to put an end to this right now.

I reach for my holster, pulling out my gun. No more games. I walk quickly past each room until I hear it. Something I haven't heard in a very long time. Elise's violin. A beautiful melody is pouring out in a room. I walk to the door to see it wide open. Elise is sitting in a chair, her back to me. She is swaying softly to the music. I step in the room quietly, making sure not to make a sound. I walk closer and closer to her unsuspecting body, each step bringing her fate into play. I am right behind her as I bring the gun up, aiming it to the back of her head. She is still playing that lovely melody, not knowing that I am directly behind her, about to end her life.

I run my finger over the trigger. Just one pull, and it will be over. Completely. I squeeze the trigger. *Lightly.*

I can't do it.

Elise is still playing, immersed deep in the song she is creating, unaware of the danger that is standing behind her.

I slowly back out of the room.

Chapter 24

Elise

I haven't seen Luca since I left him in the car. It's beginning to get dark out. To be honest, I never want to see him again. At the moment, I am scared and confused. I thought Matteo's mother's death was random, but the fact that the officer told me "We'll get to the bottom of this" without asking any further questions when I am the one that found the body, I began to get suspicious. When Luca told me to go to the car, I watched him speaking to the officer, and getting heated from what I could see. I went out on a limb accusing him in the car but when he didn't respond, I knew.

But why? Why would he do this to Matteo?

I hear the front door open and sit up from my seat on the couch. I quickly walk to the entry area, thinking it's Luca, but I am surprised when I see Matteo and Romelo. I slow my pace as Romelo stands there.

"What are you doing here?" I ask.

Matteo is looking at the ground, not acknowledging me.

"Luca said for me to bring him here. I can't seem to find him anywhere, though. Have you seen him around? He's not answering his phone."

I am a little stunned at that.

"No. He never came in the house when we got back. I assumed he had business to do," I tell him.

Romelo looks a little confused but tries to hide it.

"I can take Matteo and put him in a room until Luca gets back," I assure Romelo.

He grows tense as I take a step toward them.

"No. That's all right, we can wait for him."

My irritation and nerves get the better of me, and I stand a little straighter and look Romelo straight in the eye.

"I said he can stay here. This is my home. I will tell Luca when he gets home that Matteo is in a guest room. Matteo doesn't know you and needs to be around people he knows right now, especially with this situation." I give him the best bitch face I can, and he shifts uncomfortably, obviously weighing his consequences in his head. He finally relents, though.

"Yes, Mrs. Pasquino. I apologize for forgetting my place." He turns and exits.

I look at Matteo and immediately give him a hug. He stands there for a moment before the sobs finally come. I can feel his arms slowly wrap around me as he lets out his sorrowful wails for his mother's death. I know the feeling all too well.

* * * * *

"There's a bathroom in there. You can take a warm shower. You'll probably want one after being in the freezing rain all day." I walk over to him, handing him a stack of clothes.

"These are Luca's. They may be a little big, but we'll have to make them work until we figure out what his plans are for you." I cringe a little at the double meaning of what I just said.

Matteo is looking at the floor with a vacant expression. He's sitting on the bed in one of the guest rooms. I put him in the farthest one from our bedroom in fear that Luca may be looking for him when he gets home. Luca killed his mother for some reason, but I don't know that reason. Then he had him sent here to stay with us. Something is going on behind the scenes, and I have no idea what.

"The towels and soap are all in the cupboard in the bathroom, and you can just throw those extra pillows on the floor if you don't want to use them."

Matteo still doesn't respond. I walk over to the bed and take a seat next to him, rubbing his back comfortingly.

"I know how you feel right now. I lost my father also in a horrible way. But things will get better soon, and we're here to help you get through it."

Matteo looks up at me with his large emerald eyes, tears flowing heavily out of them.

"Thank you. I don't know why Mr. Pasquino is doing this for me, but I appreciate you both. All I really have now are you guys." He breaks off into a fit of violent sobs.

I wrap my arms around him comfortingly. After his sobs die down, I stand and walk to the bedroom door. I can feel my heart shattering in my chest as I replay his words. We are all he has, and the man he is appreciative of is the very reason he is here in the first place. I turn back to him and give him a small smile.

"Try to get some sleep."

* * * * *

I step out of the shower in nothing but a towel, my wet hair clinging to my shoulders. As I open the door, my heart jumps in my chest. Luca is sitting in the bedroom. His pupils are dilated, and he has a blank expression on his face.

I freeze in the doorway as he watches me. He doesn't say anything; he only watches me. I walk slowly toward the closet, and his eyes follow me across the room. I turn my back to him to open the door, and suddenly, I am being yanked back by my hair. I cry out in pain and stumble backward. Luca shoves me roughly onto the bed, jerking the towel off my body, exposing me to his gaze. His eyes are so dilated they look black. He runs his eyes up and down my body, still not speaking.

My breathing is rapid as fear swells up within me. Something is wrong with him, and I am here naked and vulnerable to him. He steps back from me and drops the towel on the floor. He comes closer to me and grabs ahold of my leg, yanking me roughly off the bed so that I fall in a heap on the floor. I cry out as the carpet burns my naked butt.

I hear Luca break into a fit of giggles as he stands over me. I look up at him, but he is not smiling at all. He is just laughing, with a deranged look on his face. I don't know what to do in this moment.

He kneels on the floor next to me and begins speaking as he pulls my body in close to his like he is cradling me.

"I want to kill you so badly."

My heart skips a beat as he speaks. He leans in and nuzzles my neck softly, moaning in pleasure. I can feel his erection straining against his pants as he grows aroused. I realize that I can smell something on him. Alcohol. He's drunk. Oh god, Luca is drunk. Luca is insane when he is sober, and I have no idea what kind of drunk he is.

"But I want to fuck you too." He purrs into my ear.

He reaches behind him and pulls out a blade. I immediately begin to struggle. *Please don't let him carve something into my skin again!* His face grows serious as he brings the blade to my throat.

"You move, and I slice your throat and let you bleed out on this carpet. But wait, you wanted to die. Maybe I should go get your brother instead." He chuckles to himself, as if he knows some kind of joke that I'm not in on.

He hauls me up onto the bed and turns me over so that I am on my stomach. He reaches under my belly and hauls me up so that I am on my hands and knees. He slaps my ass hard, and I cry out in pain.

I can feel him rubbing my butt.

"Baby, you're so damn sexy," he groans.

He leans in and kisses each of my butt cheeks. I begin to whimper in fear. I hear the sound of his zipper, and before I can think, he shoves into me roughly from behind. My body is still wet from the shower, so he slides in without having to get me ready for his intrusion.

He begins pounding me roughly, and I cry out in pain. He reaches around me, and I can feel his hand around my throat as he shoves my face into the bed. The sound of our skin colliding echoes throughout the room, and I have to bite my cheek to keep from crying out. Luca threads his fingers through my hair and jerks my body upright so that he is level with my ear.

"I hate all of you," he groans out. I have no idea who he is talking about. I can barely focus from the brute force he is using as he slams into me over and over.

"You're just like your father, manipulating me to your will. I want to kill you, but I fucking can't. I should kill your brother instead to make you suffer, just like I killed his pathetic mother."

I gasp. "What?" I cry out, but Luca places his hand over my mouth, silencing me.

"Yeah, I killed her. Because of you. I was protecting you. And I enjoyed every second of it. I loved the sounds of her screams as she begged me to stop. I'll do the same to your innocent little brother. He deserves it. He's right up the hallway. I know, because I told them to bring him here. And I can end his life just like that."

I begin screaming underneath Luca's hand as realization dawns on me. Matteo is my brother. Matteo is my *fucking* brother. I have been looking at my brother every day for I don't know how long. That's why he looks so familiar. He has my father's features! I hadn't realized it then because I rarely saw my father. But now as I realize it, I feel like an idiot. It all adds up now.

My body is shoved forward into the mattress as Luca's thrusts speed up, and I can feel him getting larger inside of me before he leans over my body, shuddering in pleasure as he finds his release.

He pulls out of me slowly and rolls me over so that I am on my back. His eyes are frightening pools of emptiness as he stares at me.

"Cross me, and I kill him. You've seen what I'm capable of. Don't you dare speak a word of this to him either." His voice is cold and deadly. He places his hand lightly around my throat, giving me a threatening squeeze.

"I have plans for the both of you. Big plans."

He stares at me a moment longer and leans in and begins sucking violently on my throat. I cry out from the pain, and he finally lets go. He stares at my throat in satisfaction. He rolls over and pulls me with him, wrapping me tightly in his arms.

"The whole world will know you're mine. All of you," he murmurs before his breathing evens out.

Chapter 25

Elise

Luca steps out of the shower with nothing but a towel wrapped around his waist. He walks by the bed, only glancing at me momentarily before entering the closet. I don't know if he remembers what he did last night. He has yet to speak to me this morning.

The knowledge that my little brother has been here all along is shocking, to say the least. All this time, I've been looking at him and have been completely unaware of who he truly is. It now makes sense why Luca never wanted me near him. But why does Luca have him here? According to Matteo, Luca has been in his life over a year. I'm guessing, from the time we were married since the time slots add up. But why? Why is Luca interested in my little brother?

Luca steps out of the closet dressed in all black. He is pulling a dark shirt over his head when I call out his name.

"Luca." My voice is small. I am scared. I am definitely risking a lot by doing this, but I need to know. "D-do you remember anything from last night?" I look up at him after a moment of silence as he watches me with those emotionless eyes.

His eyes flicker from my face to my throat, where he left a large hickey on my neck. His brow furrows a moment, as if thinking, before he responds.

"No."

I take a deep breath. What I am about to do is either really smart or really stupid.

"You told me about Matteo … the truth …" I look down at the floor, not wanting to see his reaction, in fear of what may be waiting for me. I look up after I hear footsteps. Luca is walking toward the door.

"Wait!" I shout. He pauses and looks back at me. "Please, I have to know, What do you plan on doing to him?"

His hand drops from the doorknob as he sighs heavily, looking at my direction. "That doesn't concern you."

I can feel my anger immediately flare up. I jump up from the bed with my fists clenched in anger as I stare Luca down.

"Not my concern? That's my little brother! It's every bit of my concern, Luca!"

His eyes narrow at me, and my mind is screaming at me to shut up and sit down, but I can't, not when my little brother's life may very well be on the line.

"I think you're forgetting your place, Elise." His voice comes out like a whip, but I don't budge. This is for Matteo. The only family I have left.

"No. He's my brother, Luca. My blood. It is my business."

He looks at me with a dangerous glare, and I have to swallow my fear. He steps away from the door, coming toward me until he is standing over me at his full height. Intimidating me to the center. His face is blank as he stares me down, until a small smile creeps its way over his lips. He reaches forward and cups my face in his hand, piercing me to the spot with his gaze.

"I plan to swear him in. By blood. I plan to train him and make him just like me. I plan to use him as retribution for my father's death and use him to kill the rest of your bloodline that I couldn't get to."

Something clicks in my head. "The rest?"

His smile grows wider. A small chuckle finds its way from deep within him.

"Oh, did I forget to tell you? Half of your family is finally dead." He says it as if he were revealing some kind of happy surprise to me. But I can only gasp in horror. "And if you don't believe me, you can ask your stupid cousin Ari. She had a front-row seat." His smile grows more and more vicious. "The ones we couldn't bait to come here have gone into hiding once they heard about their relatives getting shot down in cold blood. So I plan to track them all down after your brother is sworn in and use him to end their existence. They all know who he is. He was a part of their plan once you and I were out of the way. A perfect scheme set up by your father will be the downfall of the Trovolis."

I've always known that Luca is evil, but this is beyond that. He's going to use an innocent boy and make him murder his own family? Just to teach them a lesson? Even though I don't know some of my relatives, the fact that Luca has baited them and shot them down in cold blood makes me see him in a whole new light. He isn't just evil; he is evil incarnate. How can one man be capable of such things?

I take a step back, and Luca follows the movement with his eyes, his smile dropping.

"Why are you doing this? To me, to him? Why, Luca? Surely, you can't be that … evil?"

Luca quirks an eyebrow at me, and a small laugh escapes his lips. Followed by a full-blown laugh. This one is nothing like the one he had when he was with Matteo. This one is the same laugh he had when he murdered my father. I can feel the chills as they break out across my skin.

Luca's laugh finally dies down.

"You don't know what I'm capable of. This is what it is to be capo. Instilling fear in the hearts of others so that they don't revolt against you. Taking care of the family, through whatever means necessary. Taking down anyone that dares get in the way. Compared to the things I've done, this is child's play."

My legs grow weak, and I collapse on the ground. Who is this man? What is this man?

"I'll kill him." The room goes silent as Luca takes in my words. I know I sound crazy, but I am grasping at straws, trying to find some way to protect my brother from this cruel fate Luca has planned out for him. "I'll kill him, and I'll kill myself. You won't have him to hold against me anymore. You won't have me to torture and abuse anymore. And you will lose everything."

Luca only smiles wider at me.

"Then I'll keep you separated. I'll lock you up. I'll torture him before you can do anything about it. Don't forget who you're talking to, Elise." His smile disappears, and he kneels on the ground in front of me, placing his fingers under my chin, forcing me to look up.

"Besides, do you really think you could kill your own brother, Elise?" His eyes are filled with amusement as he takes in my predicament.

I can feel the tears welling up in my eyes. My sobs fill the room. "Please…don't do this."

I can't think of anything else. Once I open my eyes again, Luca is heading toward the door, not looking back. He slams the door behind him.

When I finally grow the courage to leave the room, I walk toward the kitchen and pass by Luca's office to see the door slightly open. I slow my pace and peep in the door. Luca is sitting at his desk, with papers in front of him. He is speaking, but I am so far away I can't hear what he is saying. My heart clenches as I see Matteo in front of him. Luca is looking down, but when he looks up, his eyes immediately meet mine. He doesn't falter in his speech when he sees me.

He looks to his left and motions to someone, pointing toward the door. Next thing I see is Romelo coming to the door with a firm face and closing it. I drop my head. I can't believe what is going on.

Chapter 26

Luca

I set the picture down in front of Matteo, watching his reactions carefully. His eyes slightly widen as he takes in the photograph.

"Do you know this man?"

The room is silent as he contemplates how to respond. It's almost strange looking at him all this time. He shares similar features with Elise, but also his good-for-nothing father.

"Yes. That's my father."

I nod. "Eli Trovoli, capo of the South Mob, mostly known for their brutality, betrayals, and lust for power." I pause, gauging his reaction. "Do you know what the capo is, Matteo?"

He slowly shakes his head.

"The capo is the head. The leader. The don. Your father was one of the most powerful men in the United States. He's responsible for countless power crisis in the United States. And he's dead."

I take another picture and set it down in front of him.

"You know who this is," I state matter-of-factly. It's a picture of Elise. It was taken the day of our wedding. She looks beautiful. Sweet and innocent. It's one of the few pictures I have of her.

"Elise. She's my wife. What you don't know is that she is the only child of Eli Trovoli. That is, until her father realized to gain more power, he needed a son." I watch as Matteo's eyes grow wide in understanding.

"So she's my—"

"Half-sister, yes. Don't worry, she was unaware of this fact up until last night." I lean back in my chair, loving how things are playing out.

"So that leaves my role in all this. Of course, you know me as Luca Pasquino. But I am, as of late, the new capo of the North Mob, the most powerful Mob in the United States. I inherited this position sooner than I would have liked due to your family's need for power." I watch his face closely as the news comes down on him.

"I originally planned to kill all the Trovolis. That includes you. But when I married your sister, I had a change of heart toward them. I was going to leave them alone. But they interfered once again for more power. And that was where they fucked up. They killed my father. And they were going to use my wife, their own blood, as a pawn in their hunt for power. And I cannot look past that. The only reason you are alive right now is that I love your sister so much."

His eyes widen. "You love her, huh? Then why would you engrave your name into her flesh?"

Matteo meets my eyes, and his are filled with anger. I can feel amusement and excitement bubbling up inside of me. He thinks that just because he now knows that is his sister, he can talk to me any kind of way. Before he can blink, I am standing in my chair with a gun aimed at his forehead. I see Romelo flinch in the corner, ready to stop me if I go too far with this boy. I can feel the fear radiating off him as he finally realizes who he is dealing with.

"Do not get my attitude in the past with you confused with how you can speak to me. I am your capo now. You will learn in time the way things are around here."

I look at Romelo and motion for him to grab Matteo and take him to begin his initiation. Romelo walks over to him, snatching him out of the chair, and begins dragging him out the door.

I begin to take a seat when I hear something coming from the hallway. Rage immediately boils over. Elise. I push up from my chair and make my way quickly to the hallway to see Elise literally on top of Romelo, trying to jerk her brother from his grasp. I immediately grab her off him, holding her down. She is screaming and crying and continuing to struggle under me.

"Luca, stop! Don't do this! You can't do this to him!"

Matteo is watching her with wide eyes and struggling hard against Romelo. Elise turns her head to look at me, and her eyes are wide and filled with tears. Her face is flushed a beautiful, rosy shade. I can feel myself getting hard. Damn, she is beautiful.

I haul her up and jerk her into my office, slamming the door behind me. She is still struggling and screaming all kinds of obscenities at me, but I'm not even paying attention. I keep watching the way her breasts are moving underneath that tight dress she is wearing. She always wears dresses. I like it when she wears shorter ones, so I can see the curves of her legs as they lead up to her pert little ass.

I set her atop the desk, and she is still struggling and trying to push me away.

"Elise." I calmly say her name, and she stops struggling, staring at me with wide eyes.

That is another thing I love about her—she can be in the biggest rage you have ever seen, but when she hears my voice call her name, she immediately snaps out of it and is silent.

I reach out to push her hair out of her face so that I can see it better. It's now down to her upper back. Much longer than when I originally cut it. Maybe she should start wearing headbands so I can see her face more often. Or I just may cut it again. I smile at the thought. She notices it and visibly flinches.

My eyes drop to the turtleneck she has on. The dress is short, but instead of there being a V-neck collar, she decided to wear one that covers the love bite. I reach out and pull it down, revealing the mark. I don't remember doing it. Hell, I don't even remember telling her about her brother. All I know is that I was so angry yesterday that I'd left and gone to the nearest bar. I needed something to erase my emotions. I always have control of them, but being around her makes them go crazy. Everything is a blur after that.

I woke up this morning before her, and when I was getting dressed, she claimed to know the truth about her sibling. That was dumb of me, but there's no use in dwelling on it now. *What's done is done.*

"What do I get if I leave your brother out of this?" I look up from the hickey and into her eyes. She has the most beautiful eyes I have ever seen. They are a beautiful chocolate brown. The small area around the pupil has a jagged pattern, as if a sandstorm were blowing in those amazing irises.

I gently push her down so that she is lying on her back on top of the desk. I reach my hands underneath the dress and push it up so that her lower body is exposed. She has an amazing body. I slide my hands up her body and over her breasts, resting one palm over her heart. The rapid thundering is enough to excite me even further. My eyes drop to the side of her where my name is. I can feel my erection getting even harder, but I am going to make myself wait. I want to just look at her.

I reach down and grab my knife from the holster in my shoe. She jumps from the desk, but I hold her down.

"You still haven't answered me, Elise. What will I get for leaving your brother out of this? He is a key component in this plan." I bring the knife up and press it against the soft fabric of the dress, enjoying the sight of it being sliced off her body. She gasps.

She is now lying on my desk on nothing more than her bra and panties. And she is wearing all white today. I lean in and press kisses over her stomach. I pull up and stare at the flat surface for a moment. A fleeting thought crosses my mind. She takes a deep breath, causing her stomach to rise and fall with the breath. I step even closer to her in between her legs and lean over her body.

"I'm going to ask you one more time, Elise. What do I get?"

She is looking at me with fear in her eyes. She finally opens her mouth.

"I … I'll give you anything you want."

I chuckle at that. She is so naive. "My sweet, naïve girl, I can already have anything I want." I look at her in pleasure as defeat crosses her features. Hmmm.

I kneel down and pull her underwear down, tossing them on the floor. I take the knife and bring it to the center of her bra, cutting it off and exposing her perky breasts. They are by no means what I am used to. All my life, I've fucked big-breasted women with curvy bodies and big asses. Elise is small and petite, and her breasts fit perfectly in the palms of my hands.

"Luca …"

Her small voice pulls me out of my musings. I love it when she says my name. I kneel so that I am level with her body and gently push her legs apart, exposing her to me. I can feel her slight resistance, but she knows better than to deny me. I wrap my arms around her thighs so that her legs are resting over my shoulders and pull her closer to me. She gasps and immediately tries to sit up.

"Luca, wait," she starts, but I don't give her the chance.

I dip my head in between her thighs, pressing my lips against her folds. I hear her as she gasps above me. I give her a long, slow lick, tasting her sweetness. I shudder in pleasure, and it heads straight to my dick, making it twitch in my pants. I begin giving her pleasure, growing more and more restless as I listen to her moans of pleasure. She loves to pretend she is invincible to me, but I know her body better than she does. And I enjoy drawing pleasure from it. I press my tongue to her clit, and she jumps in pleasure under me.

I can feel her body tensing as she is about to have an orgasm. I latch on to her clit and begin sucking as I insert a finger in her slick wetness. That is enough to send her over the edge, and her loud moans fill the room. I can feel her tightness spasming around my finger as she rides her orgasm. Before she can come down from it, my pants are down, and I guide my cock to her entrance, pushing in all the way to the hilt. She is tight and warm around me, and her inner muscles are still spasming around my hard length. I can hear her as she cries out. I look up, and her eyes are closed, her cheeks are flushed, and her mouth is slightly parted. The sight is sexy as hell. I arch over her and thread my fingers through her soft strands, placing my forehead against hers as I fuck her on the desk.

She is crying out with each thrust, and I can't help but be mesmerized by her. I watch her every move, every sound. I can see the light sheen of sweat forming over her flushed skin and the slight furrow of her brow. I keep my eyes open and watch her as she writhes in pleasure underneath me. I lean in and lightly trace her bottom lip with my tongue. I capture her mouth in mine. Her lips are soft and warm against mine. She opens her mouth in pleasure, moaning into mine.

I pull back and continue to look down at her. I feel a strong need brewing deep within me and speak before I can process anything else.

"Tell me you love me."

Her eyes fly open, and she looks at me in shock. There is a light glaze over her brown eyes as they meet mine. She opens her mouth, only to close it.

"Say it." My voice is louder this time. I can feel the sweat forming on my back. She looks as though she is caught in some inner turmoil.

"Tell me you love me, Elise." I slow down, only to give her a hard thrust, the pleasure exploding on me. I can feel myself getting closer and closer to my release.

"I … I love you."

That is all it takes for me to reach my peak. I can feel the tingle in the base of my spine as I explode inside of her. Her muscles begin uncontrollably squeezing me, and I know she has reached her orgasm too. Her orgasm continues, drawing mine out even longer.

I finally collapse on top of her, both of our bodies slick with sweat. The room is silent except for the sound of our breathing. After a moment, I stand up and pull out of Elise. I look down and am mesmerized at the sight of my seed spilling out of her. I watch until she sits up slowly, avoiding eye contact with me.

"I'll leave your brother out of this." I am speaking before I even realize what I have said.

She looks up in shock, and her breathing picks up as tears well up in her eyes. She hops off the desk and jumps into my arms, her naked body pressing against mine.

"Thank you," she whispers in the crook of my neck.

I slowly bring my arms up and wrap them around her, enjoying the feel of her warm body against mine. This is probably the first time she has shown me any form of physical affection willingly.

* * * * *

I step out of the shower, and Elise is already in bed. She is asleep. I step closer to the bed and take in her features. She looks lovely. She is lying on her side with her arms underneath her head. I reach out and push her stray hairs out of her face. She stirs but doesn't wake up. I take a seat next to her on the bed and push the cover lower from around her waist. She only wore a tank top and underwear to bed. The tank top has ridden up, and her stomach is exposed. I reach out and lightly touch the flat surface. Hmmm.

I stand up and walk out of the room, walking to my office. I open the filing cabinet with Elise's medical records in it and pull out the file. She is currently on the shot. We go in every three months to keep her from getting pregnant. I look at the dates marked and feel a smile coming onto my face. The next time we are to go in is in five days. Hmmm.

I pull out my phone and make a call to Dr. Shotwell. He answers on the first ring.

"Yes, Mr. Pasquino, is it an emergency?"

"No. I have a few questions for you."

Chapter 27

Elise

I'm drinking some coffee when Matteo steps into the room. He looks my direction and pauses, just staring at me. This is the first time we have seen each other since that day. Luca swore to me that he wouldn't hurt him, and he agreed to leave him out of his sick planning. But why haven't I seen him around the house?

I give him a light smile and motion for him to come sit next to me.

"I can make you some breakfast if you want."

He shakes his head no and walks over to the coffee maker, pouring himself a cup. I can't help but stare at him. It's strange. All this time, my brother has been in the same area as me, and I hadn't even realized it. Looking at him now, I can see some of my father's features. But he also has softer features, probably from his mother. And those eyes. They are a bright green. My father didn't have green eyes, so I'm guessing he inherited that from his mother. He walks to the counter, where I am sitting, and sits in the seat across from me, staring down at the coffee.

"So you're my sister." He doesn't look up as he speaks. I can't blame him. This is strange, to say the least.

"And you're my brother," I respond. He blows on his coffee and takes a sip. After he sets the mug down, he speaks.

"Our father was in the Mob?" He finally looks up at me. I nod gingerly.

"Did he really try to kill you?"

I nod again.

"And Mr. Pasq—I mean Luca, he's your husband?"

"Yes."

"And you were both arranged in this marriage."

"Yes."

"And Luca … is the Mob too."

"Yes."

He shakes his head in disbelief. "There's so much I want to ask you. But why did you save me? If what Luca says is true, I'm the reason your mother's dead. So why do you even like me? How can you even tolerate me?" He looks up at me, and he looks genuinely confused.

I reach across the counter, placing my hand over his. "You're the only family I have left. And you're my brother. It's not your fault, everything that's happened. I can't hate you for that. You're all I have left, and I just need to protect you," I say.

And that is the truth.

He is all I have left. Ari and I are enemies now, and the rest of my family is out to kill me. Honestly, if it weren't for Luca, I wouldn't even be here now.

We sit in the kitchen for hours and just talk. I tell him about our father, about our lifestyle, and how I grew up. I tell him about my feelings when I found out about my marriage to Luca and how I even ran away. I tell him of Arianna and our family's crazy obsession for power. I open up to him immediately, and he listens. I can see the pity on his face when he hears of the betrayals and suffering I have had.

He then tells me about his life. About how our father visited him rarely and kept him and his mother afloat. He tells me about how he had to grow up quick and drop out of high school because he needed to take care of his mother. We sit there and slowly bond with each other, trying to catch up on all the years lost.

Matteo suddenly looks behind me, and his whole demeanor turns tense and rigid, his eyes visibly darkening. I turn to see Luca entering the kitchen. He is wearing only a pair of sweatpants that hang low on his waist. He obviously just finished working out. He looks our direction, and his eyes sweep over Matteo and visibly lingers on me. His hair is wet and sticking to his forehead. I wish he weren't so handsome. He doesn't make a sound as he grabs a water bottle. He comes to where we are sitting and kisses the top of my head.

"Good morning."

I give him a small smile. I don't want to do anything to get him riled up. He has been abnormally calm the past few days, and I don't want to be the one to set him off. Especially in front of Matteo. Luca gives me a small smile, and it completely disappears as he looks at Matteo. Matteo doesn't speak to him; he just glares. After a moment, a small laugh escapes Luca's lips, and he walks to exit the kitchen.

"Elise, come with me." His voice carries across the kitchen, and I immediately hop off the table to follow Luca.

Once I exit the kitchen, Luca grabs my hand and pulls me into the nearest room.

"I have made a big sacrifice in not swearing your brother in. So I do expect respect in my home. Make sure he knows that. He will also be attending school from now on, and when he's not busy on the weekends, he'll continue his yard duties. I will not give him a free ride around here. Understand?"

I nod vigorously.

"Romelo will shadow him. Teach him how he's supposed to act around here. I don't want to lose control and end up injuring your brother because of his stupidity. Make sure he knows that."

Luca doesn't blink as he relays all this information to me. I just nod in understanding. Luca cocks his head as he stare at me.

"We're having a party tonight. In honor of your brother's … *arrival.*"

* * * * *

Matteo is working hard on the backyard. I sit on the patio and watch him, unable to keep myself at a distance from him. All I do is watch him. I don't want him to be caught alone with Luca. I have to protect him. This is actually the only time that I have been alone.

Luca has been with me every second of every day. Always watching me.

I have time to be alone with my thoughts. And my feelings are starting to catch up to me. I am exhausted. Scared. Angry. Confused. Sad. And the little bit of happiness that I do have comes from my brother's being here with me.

I am exhausted from always being on guard with Luca. I am scared because he brought my brother into his home. And even though he told me he wouldn't swear him in, I still believe that he has some kind of sick plot waiting for the both of us. I am angry because Matteo and I are the last of our bloodline. As well as Ari. But I have no idea what Luca has in store for her. I am confused because here lately, Luca is anything but his usual self. By that I mean he is sweet. Nice. And he is keeping his word when it comes to Matteo. He is staying away from him.

"Do you want to know something?"

I look up as Luca comes outside. He's behind me. See what I mean? I'm hardly ever alone. He pulls out the chair next to me and sits down facing to where Matteo is. He reaches out across the table, grabbing my hand in his and bringing it to his lips.

"I love you so much. You would not believe the people that have asked me for favors. Even some had something to give me in return for the favor, and I turned them all down. But you ask me for something that deals with my personal plans, and I can't help but give you what you want." He looks away from Matteo, meeting my eyes. "You are my weakness."

I am silent, unable to respond. He breaks my gaze and looks back at Matteo.

"He should be dead. You should be dead. Your cousin should be dead. If I weren't so weak when it came to you, I wouldn't be having the problems I'm having now." He laughs bitterly. "You're all I have left, Elise. My family is dead. All of them. Everyone I have ever loved, they are gone. You're the only family I have. I won't let anyone take that away from me. I'll protect you and your brother."

* * * * *

I step into Matteo's room quietly and see that he is intently focused on the ground. I knock lightly on the doorjamb, and he looks up tensed but visibly relaxes when he sees it's me. I give him a small smile.

"Hey, you ready?"

He gives me a light smile and shakes his head. "I don't know any of these people. And from what Luca has told me, they all hate the blood that runs through my veins."

I frown at that. He is right. Most of these people are of the North Mob. And if not a part of the family, they are important figures in society that the North has in their pockets. And for some reason, Luca is throwing a party to "celebrate" the arrival of another Trovoli after he only recently got rid of virtually all of them. Something isn't right about this.

I take the tie from the dresser and begin to fasten it around his collar.

"Well, tonight is in honor of you. And you have me. I won't let anything happen to you. And neither will Luca."

Matteo grabs my hand and looks me dead in the eyes. "You don't truly believe that, do you?"

I open my mouth to respond, but nothing comes out. I really am speechless. Because once again, he is right.

The party is held in the east wing of the house, meaning one of the ballrooms is in full swing by the time I show up with Matteo on my arm. Luca meets me in the archway with a wickedly handsome smile. He is wearing all black except for his red tie. He looks from me to Matteo with a wicked glint in his eye.

He motions for Romelo to come get Matteo. I take ahold of Matteo's hand as Romelo gets closer. Luca notices the motion.

"Now, Elise, I am the host and you are my wife, so you are to be on my arm tonight."

Romelo finally reaches us, and Matteo looks at me with a small glint of fear in his eye. I look at Luca with pleading eyes.

"Please, just let him stay near us tonight."

Luca studies me for a moment before finally relenting.

We step into the party, and all eyes turn on us. Everyone is looking with mixed gazes. I make sure to keep Matteo in my sight. People also look at him. Some have gazes filled with hatred and disgust, while others are in shock.

Luca spends the first half of the night speaking to everyone while keeping me at his side. He smiles and plays the role of the perfect host. If you were on the outside looking in, you wouldn't even know that he is a psycho. But I know him. And looking at him right now, I can tell something bad is going to happen. His whole demeanor and attitude is off. And not in the way that seems strange. The way that Luca gets before he is about to implement one of his plans. Or kill someone.

I look around me, quickly scanning the room. That's when it hits me. Luca isn't the type to just do something. He likes having a stage. He doesn't like just announcing things. He likes everything falling into place, and you don't realize anything until it is too late. He has intricate, calculated plans. And I have a bad feeling in my stomach.

Luca also never lets me out of his sight. He brings me with him to speak to people and won't let me near Matteo. He keeps Romelo in between us. Whatever he has planned has something to do with Matteo.

"Well, if it isn't the big bad capo himself and his lovely wife."

I look up to see Nicolai walking toward us with a big smile on his face. For the first time tonight, Luca lets go of me to give Nicolai a hug. Nicolai looks at me and takes my hand, giving it a light kiss. He turns back to Luca.

"Can I talk to you for a second?"

Luca looks at me then to Romelo, who gives him a small nod. He leans down, giving me a light peck on the lips. He pulls back and stares into my eyes for a moment. He looks as though he is having an internal battle with himself.

"I love you," he says before pulling me into a tight embrace. He turns away with Nicolai, leaving me stunned.

I turn to Matteo. "How are you feeling?" I ask, concern evident.

He gives a small smile. "I'm good at the moment. Do you guys do stuff like this often?"

"Not a lot. Since Luca's capo, we rarely have the time to make it to anything, because he's always busy ..." I trail off as my eye catches some people in the North family. They are looking at Matteo in disgust. Some people are eyeing both of us. This is a party for the family. Luca said to introduce the newest member. So everyone here is either blood or sworn into the North Mob. Which means majority of them knows it is my family that is behind their capo's death. Which explains the glares.

"Elise?" I feel a tap on my shoulder and look to see Matteo eyeing me with concern. I open my mouth but stop when I see random movements throughout the room. Romelo puts a hand over his ear.

"Got it," he murmurs. Before I can say anything else, he looks at me.

"The capo needs to borrow your brother for a moment." He grabs Matteo by the shoulder and walks through the crowd of people. Matteo looks at me with a confused expression, but we both don't have time to do anything. As soon as I try to step, Nicolai appears in front of me. Wasn't he just with Luca?

He has a big smile on his face.

"So how have you been, Mrs. Pasquino?"

I eye him in confusion. Something isn't right. I try to step around him, but he moves in front of me.

"Excuse me, but I need to get through," I say, my voice sounding a little frantic. Panic is beginning to set into my bones deep. I step around Nicolai, only to feel him grab ahold of my arm firmly. I look back in shock and am frightened. There is sorrow deep in his eyes.

"I'm sorry, Mrs. Pasquino."

The mic turns on, and I look up in horror to see Luca's smiling face onstage. I am all the way at the back of the room, and Luca is all the way at the front. His eyes scan the crowd and immediately land on me. His smile grows wider. I can see the excitement pouring off him. He planned this. All of this.

"Good evening, everyone. I want to start by thanking you all for coming out here tonight. We all know who this night is for, right?" There is a loud applause as Matteo is pushed onto the stage. His eyes are wide and filled with fear. Luca pulls him in closer to him, wrapping an arm around his shoulder.

"How many of you recognize this face?" He pauses as a majority of the guests shouts. Some in anger, some in excitement.

"Yes, we all remember Eli Trovoli, correct?" The crowd erupts in a fit of boos, and Luca's smile grows wide.

"I know, I know. We all knew actually who he was and what he represented. We all know of the trials and scandals he has put us through." He pauses as the crowd erupts in hate-filled comments.

Even a man no less than ten feet away from me shouts, "Fuck the Trovoli family!"

Wow, these people really hate us with a burning passion.

I am frozen to the spot, my mind running a thousand miles a minute, trying to figure out what exactly Luca is doing.

"This is the illegitimate son of Eli Trovoli." Luca takes a step back as the spotlight shines on Matteo. I try to jerk out of Nicolai's grasp, but he holds me firmly.

"Now, we actually had an incident the other day with Matteo's poor mother. She tried to kill me!"

The crowd erupts in a fit of anger, with some people even yelling for Matteo's death. I begin to struggle frantically to get to my brother. I am supposed to protect him.

Luca holds his fingers over his lips. "Shhhhhh, now, calm down. We took care of it. That we did. But! Recent developments show that one person was behind this little plot to kill the capo of the North Mob!"

Slowly the floor opens up, and up through the stage emerges Ari. She is strapped down and bloody.

I gasp in horror. What the fuck!

"I would like to introduce everyone to Arianna Gudierri, whose maiden name is actually Trovoli!"

Boos immediately erupt from the crowd. Realization dawns on me as I take in the situation. I turn and immediately catch Nicolai off guard, pulling my body flush against his. This puts him in shock long enough for me to bring my knee up hard. He collapses on the ground in agony, and I take off toward the stage.

Luca walks to Matteo. "This woman is the cause of my father's death, and she is a rat that loves to steal information for the benefit of the Trovoli family. She is the one that got his mother involved in trying to kill me. She is the reason his mother needlessly died."

People are literally shouting in anger. These people are sick in the head. They are literally screaming for her death. And judging by the look in Luca's eyes, he is going to give that to them.

Understanding dawns on Matteo's face.

"Now, I promised my wife I would not swear her poor little brother into the family, but that doesn't mean I won't give him the chance to become a man. To gain his revenge. And that is why I invited all of you here tonight. To witness the night that Matteo Trovoli becomes a man and takes his first kill."

The crowd erupts in excitement. Someone near me knocks me down, and I fall to the ground hard. But I don't have time to waste. I scramble up from the floor and keep running toward the stage, trying my hardest to get in between people in the crowd.

Luca is smiling from ear to ear, joy radiating off him at the situation. He is like a dark angel upon that stage with evil intent. To lead the world into suffering. My world, at least.

Matteo has tears in his eyes and is looking at Ari with hatred. And Ari is looking at him in shock. Luca walks up to Matteo and pulls out a gun, handing it to him. *Dear God.*

"Go ahead, Matteo. Take what's yours. A life for a life. Prove your loyalty to us."

Matteo is walking toward Ari with all the hatred and rage in the world. He slowly raises the gun.

"Any last words, Arianna?"

She stops her struggles and looks at Luca with mirrored hatred.

"I'm glad I killed your father. And I wish you were dead too. If his mother had been able to pull it off, we would have our revenge." Her gaze meets Matteo's, and it is filled with disgust. "She was nothing more than a burden to the family, just like you. She deserved to die. She was an outsider and a junkie. And you are nothing but a bastard child we accepted because you were supposed to be our liberation and lead us to greatness, and now you're crying over some dumb whore's death?" She laughed in disgust. "Maybe this life isn't cut out for you after all."

That's all it takes for Matteo's resolve to snap. I finally reach the stage and jump on in my small dress, sprinting toward Matteo.

"Matteo, don't!"

I don't reach him, though. Luca snatches me before I can do anything. I try my hardest to struggle against him. I try my hardest to scream anything at Matteo to get him to pay attention to me, to get out of that evil haze Luca has drawn him into.

"Matteo, no! This isn't you!"

But it's too late.

As the North Mob watches in excitement and pride, I can only watch in horror as Matteo pulls the trigger.

Chapter 28

Elise

Excited shouting erupts throughout the room, with everyone following what they hear instead of what they see. But I am up close and personal. And I see Matteo coughing up blood. And Ari is still in her position, completely unscathed. She has a malicious smile on her face as she watches Matteo. Matteo drops to the ground on one knee, clutching his side. I scream in horror as fear envelops me.

I wrench myself from Luca's grasp and sprint to Matteo, falling next to him. I immediately run my hands up his body, trying to find the source of the blood. He's been shot. There's a hole in his tux, and blood is staining his clothes. Tears well up in my eyes as I press the wound.

"Luca!" I shout.

I turn to look at him through teary-eyed vision, and he is looking frantically through the crowd. The crowd finally takes notice that it is Matteo on the ground, covered in blood, and not Ari. Luca's eyes focus in on someone in the crowd, and horror crosses his vision. He doesn't waste a second as he sprints in my direction, jumping right in front of me just as the sound of a gun goes off. He drops to the ground, and a long string of curses erupts from his mouth.

He reaches for his gun and pulls it out, aiming into the crowd. I can't see what he is aiming for because I immediately look back at Matteo, and he is beginning to convulse.

"No, no, no, no! Matteo! Hang in there, stay with me, please!"

His eyes are filled with tears as he stares at the ceiling. He is not focusing on anything I am saying.

Luca's men immediately begin to clear the room, leaving behind Nicolai and Romelo. And Stefano. He is holding a bloody arm as he stares at Luca in hatred. Luca is holding his chest and is breathing heavily, but he keeps his gun raised as Nicolai and Romelo restrict Stefano.

Luca turns to me, breathing heavily as he crawls in my direction. His hand is over his chest, and there is blood spilling heavily from his wound, flowing over his fingers. I keep my hands pressed into Matteo's wounds as Luca comes closer to me. I can only stare with wide eyes as a lazy smile slowly spreads over Luca's face. He reaches out and touches my cheek lightly before his hand runs down my face. He collapses face-first onto the ground in front of me. I don't know what to do.

I frantically search the room.

"Nicolai!" I shout in panic.

He looks up from Stefano in shock as he takes in Luca's slumped form in front of me. He immediately runs toward the stage. He finally reaches me.

"Press his wounds!" My voice is shaky and filled with panic as I speak to Nicolai.

He takes over Matteo's body, and I crawl to Luca, rolling over his body. His eyes are shut, and his chest looks really bad. I immediately reached for his holster, pulling out the knife he always keeps by his ribs. I immediately begin cutting at my dress, wrapping it around Luca's wounds and tying it tight. I can hear my frantic breathing.

With shaky hands, I move back to Matteo and do the same while speaking to Nicolai.

"Check Luca for a pulse." I put my fingers under Matteo's chin, checking for a pulse. I breathe a sigh of relief when I find one. It is very faint, but it is there.

"We need to call an ambulance. This is too much even for Dr. Shotwell."

I am speaking to Nicolai, but when I turn around, I see Romelo on the floor. Two of Luca's men are on top of him, pressing their knees into his back. That's when I realize. They are working for Stefano. A shot goes off, and Nicolai grunts in pain, falling to his knees. I frantically look around in panic, not knowing what to do. Stefano is holding the gun and walks slowly toward Luca, pure hatred in his eyes. He is standing before Luca's body with a look of rage. He aims his gun.

"How's this for weak, *Capo*?"

In the next instant, I don't think. I reach for the gun Matteo is holding, and as soon as it is in my hands, I fire. My shot is obviously not fatal, as Stefano stumbles and looks at me in shock, as if just realizing that I am there. I vaguely register Romelo wrestling the other men for his life and his capo's. They must've let their guard down when I shot Stefano.

He immediately raises his gum, aiming it at me, and I can hear Arianna behind me, encouraging him. Tears well up in my eyes. The last bit of hope I have for Ari dissipates in that moment. I don't think twice as I pull the trigger again. Stefano does at the same time, except Nicolai, in his weakened state, has managed to knock him sideways. My shot hits Stefano in his chest, and his shot hits my arm. I cry out in agonizing pain as the bullet goes skimming, tearing at the flesh atop my arm.

I can hear shouts from everywhere—Romelo shouting as he puts all the force he can to fight off those traitors, Nicolai as he pushes through his bullet wound to knock over Stefano, Stefano as he hits the ground with another bullet wound in his chest, and Arianna behind me, screaming for her husband.

And as if it were a miracle, the doors burst open and reinforcements arrive. They immediately restrain everyone. I look at Matteo's still form. And Luca's. And I look at Ari. She is screaming at me with such hatred and rage. She is calling me names and telling me how much she wishes I were dead just like my parents. I walk even closer to her, drowning out her shouts. My whole body is numb. I slowly raise the gun, aiming it at her, and she immediately grows silent, as does the whole room.

"Elise," I hear Nicolai's uncertain voice say, but I ignore him.

"You ... you killed my mother ... my father ... my brother's mother ..." The tears are rolling fat down my face. "You used me, used us … for the sake of the family. You used your own husband …" The gun begins to shake in my hand. "You lied to me, all these years. I protected you! Look at what you've caused!" I shout.

Arianna was my best friend. My closest family. But all of it has been a ploy for her. And now my brother may be dead. Everything that I've gone through is her fault, because she can't keep her mouth shut.

"Luca was right, you're better off dead." I pull the trigger.

The shot doesn't hit Arianna, though. Someone comes up behind me, grabbing my hand and forcing it toward the ceiling. Arianna is screaming, and she looks at me in shock.

"You don't want to do this. This isn't you, Mrs. Pasquino." I recognize Romelo's voice behind me. He is still holding on to my arm, and I slowly release the gun into his grasp.

Then the sobs come. Louder and louder, until I am screaming in agony.

* * * * *

"Best of wishes to you. We hope the capo recovers soon." I give another weak smile.

One week. That's how long it's been. And neither Matteo nor Luca have regained consciousness. I spend my nights at the hospital. I can't leave in case one of them wakes up. People have been showing up to show their respect, in hopes that my husband will recover, but I know it is all out of fear.

Between the two of them, Luca's wounds are worse. The shrapnel from the bullet has caused not only flesh wounds but also the arterial veins to his heart to be damaged. Any later and he would've been dead. The great and powerful capo of the North almost died. Not by his fault, though. I haven't forgotten. Luca jumped in front of me. Luca took a bullet for me. Which is why it doesn't sit well with me if he dies. Because that should have been me lying on that stage. The fact that Luca was standing where I was kneeling … if he weren't in front of me, I would've been shot in the head. I owe him my life.

Just because Luca's wounds are worse doesn't mean Matteo's aren't almost fatal too. His ribs are broken from the impact of the bullet, one puncturing his lung. They have to keep him on a ventilation system until he is able to breathe on his own.

"You can go home and get a quick shower if you want, Mrs. Pasquino. I can take over here until you get back."

I look up from my thoughts to see Romelo standing in the doorway. I check my watch. I spend an hour in each of their rooms, waiting for them to wake up. And when visiting hours are over, Romelo takes over for me so I can go and change and get some clean clothes to come back and stay the night in.

"I actually brought some clothes this time, Romelo. Thank you, though." I give him a small smile.

Romelo is the one I have always been skeptical about. He follows Luca around and sticks to him like glue and always follows his orders without hesitation. But he saved me from myself and has been watching over us in the hospital.

"I actually think it's my turn to sleep in Luca's room tonight." I always alternate between rooms.

He nods at me. "I can take over here."

I give him a smile and make my way past him to go to Luca's room. Once I enter, the rhythmic beeping assaults my ears again. I make my way over to the windows, pulling them shut. I catch a glimpse of Luca as I pass his bed, and I stop. I walk closer to him so that I am standing over his body.

If I hadn't lived it, I would have never thought Luca was capable of the things he has done to me since our marriage. His usually pushed-back hair is falling in his face, and his lips are slightly parted in his sleep. His face is free of any emotion, which makes him look more human than he usually does, with that constant blank expression he wears. How can someone be so evil? If I wanted to, I could end my suffering and probably that of countless others. I could end his life. Right here. But I know I can't do it.

I walk to the cot the hospital has supplied me with and lie down, waiting for sleep to overcome me.

Chapter 29

Luca

"Luca, listen to me very carefully." I look at my father with wide eyes. He is speaking to me as if he has something very important to say. I live to please my father, and now he is giving me something important to do, and I will not fail him. "Today, I want you to do something very important."

We are sitting in the shadows of the car. A woman walks past us with a little girl that looks to be about four years old. She is yanking the little girl along, causing her to fall and stumble, unable to keep up with her mother's frantic pace.

"We have been given a very special opportunity by our brethren in the South, and I want you to carry out this mission."

I nod, feeling the pride swelling in my chest. Papa has been training me for this all these years, and now he is going to finally let me become a man.

"Now, look, mi figlio. Do you see that woman? She has done something very bad to upset the capo. He wants her dead."

I look at him, confused. "But why, Papa?"

My father slaps me across the face. I can taste the blood welling in my mouth. But I don't dare cry. I just spit the blood out in the car, showing him I feel no pain. I am strong.

"Don't question me, boy."

I make sure to wipe my face of emotion. Papa feeds off fear. If I show him no fear, he won't continue to beat me. I nod.

"I want her disposed of. And you know what to do when it's over." I nod. Dispose of the body. Except the capo has strange instructions for us. I then remember something.

"What about the girl? The little one?"

My father responds immediately, "He wants her back. But not without bruises."

I nod. I don't understand the capo of the South's thinking. He wants his wife dead and his daughter brought back to him? But I am not one to question things. I follow orders. If I pull this off perfectly, I will have Papa's unconditional pride and love.

I hop out of the truck with my gun and knife. The woman is frantically looking around, pulling the little girl with her. The poor little girl is tripping over her own feet, trying to keep up. I don't hesitate. As soon as I am in close-enough range, I aim for the woman's head and fire. I smile to myself.

"Bull's-eye," I murmur aloud.

The woman falls flat on her face, pulling the little girl with her. I hurry over to the little girl because she is screaming now.

"Mommy? Mommy!" She spies me and immediately begins crying to me. "Please, is your mommy or daddy around? Something's wrong with my mommy."

She is staring at me with big almond-colored eyes that are red and puffy from the tears, her dark hair blending in with the night. I don't speak as I step closer to her, taking the butt of my gun and ramming it into the side of her head. She collapses.

I check my watch. I have about four hours until the girl regains consciousness. The mother is bleeding profusely from her skull, tainting the dirt below her. I pick up the little girl by her coat collar, looking at her unconscious face, which causes me to hesitate.

Then my father's words flash in my head. I ball my fist up and swing at her unconscious body.

* * * * *

I am jolted awake in the bed, breathing heavily. That memory always causes me panic. I quickly take in my surroundings. Where the hell am I? There is a monitor next to me, and there are IVs in my arm. I immediately yank them out. I don't like being pumped with anything. I look around and finally figure I am in the hospital. The last thing I can remember is Elise's panicked face, then nothing.

That bastard Stefano went back on his word. He shot Matteo and tried to kill Elise. She would have been dead, too, if I hadn't been there, jumping in front of her.

I quickly survey the room, and to my utter surprise, she is sitting in the chair near my bed, her feet balled up and a hospital blanket draped around her. I smile as I take in her form. She has grown so much from that little girl all those years ago. The thing is, that memory never seemed to bother me up until now. I've had a hand in everything that has happened to Elise. I'm the one that killed her mother and beat her to a pulp when she was four. Of course she doesn't remember any of it, because it was so long ago.

I struggle profusely but eventually get out of the bed, trying not to make a sound. I bite my cheek, trying to focus on something else other than the excruciating pain that is erupting throughout my chest. If Elise is in here, that means Romelo or Nicolai are somewhere outside the door. I try not to make a sound with my weak body as I pass Elise. I step into the hallway and see Romelo standing near the door.

He turns when he hears the door creak a little, and shock appears clearly on his face when he sees me.

"Capo!" He immediately makes his way toward me with joy in his expression. He falters a little as he nears me.

"Are you okay? Do you need something? Has Elise seen you yet?"

I shake my head and open my mouth to speak but immediately cough from the dryness of my throat. Damn, how long have I been asleep?

I point toward the sitting area, wanting to be away from the doorway just in case Elise awakes and tries to come looking for me. We finally reach the sitting room, and Romelo comes toward me with a water bottle. I take it from his hand and drink it down until the bottle is empty.

"What the hell happened?" My voice comes out rough and groggy. Probably from the lack of use. "How long have I been out?"

Romelo looks at me and takes a deep breath before answering. "A week and a few days, Capo."

I tense in my seat. I've been out for almost two weeks? That means I've been in the hospital that long. Which means there is now a file on me. *Damn.*

"What exactly happened? And where the hell is Nicolai?"

Romelo looks a little uncomfortable, and I brace myself for the bad news I am sure is to come. "Elise gave Nicolai leave. He was shot."

I can feel the white-hot rage boiling up inside me as Romelo tells me everything that happened.

He tells me how Stefano shot Matteo and me and how we should have been dead but we are two lucky sons of bitches. He tells me how Nicolai was shot and how Elise tore her dress to staunch both Matteo's and my bleeding. I can feel my heart softening at that. Elise could have let me bleed out in that room, but she didn't. She tried to save me. I am shocked when Romelo tells me that Elise shot Stefano and almost shot her cousin at point-blank range. She didn't kill Stefano, thank God. She would probably hate herself once the anger receded and she realized she killed someone.

She did end up saving us, though. All the traitors were captured and taken downtown to our underground cave. Once I am well enough, I will go and visit all of them. How the hell do I keep getting rats in my family? Something has to be done, and soon.

"Has Matteo awoken yet?" I ask as I stand to go back to my room.

"No. Your wounds were greater, but him being his age and the extent of his wounds … it's a miracle he's alive at all. They're keeping him on a breathing machine until he wakes and is able to breathe on his own."

I cock an eyebrow at him in confusion.

"His ribs were shattered and punctured his lungs."

I nod. *Damn.* "I want to be out of here tomorrow. I hate hospitals."

Romelo nods and helps me walk to my bedroom.

I step in to find Elise still asleep. Good. I quietly get back into the bed and ignore the pain shooting through my chest. I stare at Elise's beautiful form and finally let sleep overtake me.

Chapter 30

Elise

"We cannot recommend that, Mr. Pasquino. We have to keep you at least seventy-two hours after you wake to make sure your vitals are nor—"

"I don't give a damn about what you *recommend*! You can't keep me here if I don't want to stay. And I don't."

My heart jumps, and my eyes fly open to see Luca sitting up in his bed, his face contorted in anger at the nurse. She slowly backs out of the room, mumbling something about paperwork, and leaves us alone. Luca's eyes immediately turn to me when he realizes I'm awake. His anger immediately dissipates from his face. I can only sit there and stare at him. I don't know what emotion to feel. Luca is alive and acting as if he hadn't been shot.

I look down at his bare chest and look at the scars on his chest. Most of them are covered by the most frightening tattoos I have ever seen. I move my eyes farther down to one tattoo I hadn't noticed before, covering the area where his heart is.

Elise

"Elise." I look up in shock and see Luca watching me. "Come here."

I stand slowly and walk toward where he lies on the bed. Once I reach him, he throws his legs over and pulls me in a tight embrace. I slowly wrap my arms around him in return.

215

"When I saw him aiming that gun at your head, God, I thought for sure …" His embrace tightens around me.

I open my mouth to reassure him. "Thank you for saving me, Luca."

He jerks my body away from his and stares me in the eyes.

"You don't ever have to thank me for that, Elise. I am your husband. I will protect you no matter what." He reaches out and cups my face. "Because I love you, Elise." He gives me a soft smile.

I can only stare back into those eyes. Each time he tells me he loves me, it makes me that much angrier. How can you tell someone you love them and do the things he has done? This whole mess is his doing. He wanted to make a spectacle of Ari's death and drag Matteo into it with him.

Luca's smile falters as he takes notice of the tears that are slowly forming in my eyes.

"What is it?" he asks.

I shake my head vigorously, not wanting to make him angry or cause a scene. He opens his mouth to say something else, but the doctor walks in with his paperwork before he can.

* * * * *

It's a whole other week until Matteo finally awakens. His eyes open, and he immediately begins to look around frantically. It brings me joy when his eyes land on me and he relaxes. We fill him in on everything that happened. Personally, I don't want to tell him, but Luca thinks he should know.

Matteo is finally breathing on his own, and so the doctors move him off the breathing machine. When we are in his presence, he is happy. But sometimes I catch him with a hardened expression on his face.

We are finally able to take Matteo home after a few days. Luca is at the front desk, signing him out, and I sit in the room with him to keep him company.

"Elise." Matteo's voice suddenly pulls me from my thoughts. I stand up from my seat across the room and immediately walk to him.

"Are you all right?"

He nods and takes a deep breath. "I wanted to do it, you know. I still want to."

I look at him with a confused expression. Before I can say anything on the subject, Matteo looks at me with his deep-green eyes.

"I want to talk to Luca. Alone, please."

I don't know how to respond; I only stand from the edge of his bed and walk out into the waiting area. Surely, he doesn't mean what I think he means?

I round the corner and pause when I see Luca standing by the wall of brochures. He has one in his hand and is reading it very intently. He turns to the side slightly, and I am shocked to see a pamphlet on babies in his hand. I look back at his face to see if he is just doing some bored scanning, but he is very focused on whatever it is he is reading.

I hope he doesn't want a child. Living with Luca is already torture enough, but trying to raise a child and protect him or her from their father will be too much. It will be a punishment in itself. If there is one thing I know, it is that Luca Pasquino is not ready for kids. I don't think he ever will be.

"Luca." His head shoots up, and he nonchalantly moves the pamphlet behind his back.

"What?"

"Uh … Matteo wanted to see you."

I am having trouble looking at him. The way he is watching me makes me feel squeamish. He doesn't respond to me as he takes a step around me and walks into Matteo's room.

Chapter 31

Luca

I sit in my office, with Matteo seated across from me. Revenge. That's what he wants. And I am more than happy to give it to him. I lean back in my chair and study him closely. His body language says that he wants this, but something small is holding him back. It's been three weeks since we've taken him home from the hospital. His recovery has been going well. As well as my own. I am quickly starting to feel like my old self again. And I love it.

Although I've been injured, that hasn't stopped me from having sex with Elise every day. Even times throughout the day when she happens to be alone, I find her and fill her with my seed. I smile to myself. Her last shot was actually a prenatal drug instead of birth control, which means she's been injected with a substance that will make her fertile. Not only that, but I've been putting those kinds of pills in her food too. For some reason, recently I have been wanting a child. Whether it is from almost dying or my feelings before that event, I can't tell. But I know that if I express that with Elise, she will do everything in her power to make that impossible.

"So they're still alive."

Even though Matteo's voice comes out very quiet, he interrupts my train of thought. He almost reminds me of Elise in this moment, averting his gaze from mine like she always does. They both do that when they are asking about something they have no business in.

"Yes. It is traditional for the capo to decide how those who have risen against him will be punished."

Matteo finally looks up. "And how do you plan on punishing them?"

I sit back in my chair. I haven't really thought about that. Lately, I have been so preoccupied with Elise I haven't even bothered to think about those people. But since I am almost as good as new and Matteo is also, their punishment can very well be carried out.

When Matteo asked me in his room in the hospital that day, he wanted one thing. Revenge on the person that has caused all the pain and suffering to him and Elise. And I am more than happy to give that to him. But we have to delay it due to the fact that we've had to get stronger and heal from our wounds.

Now that we have recovered, it is time for me to fulfill my promise to Matteo.

"You need to know I can't swear you in. I made a promise to your sister."

Matteo looks at me and nods. "I know. I won't ask you to swear me in, but I do want to ask you another request."

I lean back in my seat, waiting for the question I already know he is about to ask.

"I want to be the one to kill Arianna."

The room is silent as his request hangs in the air between us. In all honesty, this has all worked out perfectly. Matteo's killing of those that threaten his capo's life will make him somewhat acceptable into the North family even though I can't swear him in. He will have some form of respect, and a target won't be on his back because of his bloodline.

I open my mouth to respond, but something catches my eye. There is a shadow underneath the door. It's barely there, and if it hadn't moved, I wouldn't have noticed it. I can feel my irritation bubbling up. I stand, and Matteo looks at me with fear on his face. Probably from my abrupt stance. I stalk over to the other side of the room and jerk the door open. Sure enough, Elise is standing on the other side.

She stumbles back, staring at me with wide eyes. If I weren't so furious, I would have smiled. She looks like a little kid that's been caught stealing from the cookie jar.

"Is there something I can help you with?" As I speak to her, I let my irritation seep through.

She continues to look at me, speechless. Her eyes then travel past me into my office, landing on Matteo. She slowly reaches out, and my eyes immediately follow the movement.

Her frail fingers clasp around the sleeve of my jacket, and she slowly tugs me away from the office. Her steps are unsure and fearful. I decide to just follow her and see what it is she wants. When she pulls me far enough away from the door, she finally speaks.

"Luca, you can't let him do this … kill Ari. He's only fifteen, he doesn't know what he's saying! He's just acting out on anger."

If I weren't so entranced by her innocence, I would have slapped her across the face. Instead, I reach out for her face, cradling it in between my thumb and forefinger, forcing her eyes to meet mine.

"Elise, how old was I when I became a man? I'm sure you know." I give her an amused smile, trying my best to hide my anger. She avoids my gaze and looks at the ceiling instead.

"Ten." Her voice comes out in a whisper.

"So I think Matteo's decision is very reasonable, don't you?" I ask.

She still doesn't look at me. She is looking at the floor. My anger immediately flares. I thread my fingers through her hair and shove her with all my force into the ground. She cries out, kneeling.

"You wanna look at the fucking floor? Fine. Take a good look." She just kneels there with her head down, not speaking.

"Luca, if you let him kill them, I will never forgive you." Her voice comes out controlled and strong.

I can feel a laugh bubbling up within my throat. I can't help myself as amusement flares within me, and I laugh. And laugh. And laugh. She can't be serious. I don't give a damn if she doesn't forgive me. And she has no damn business trying to demand me, the fucking capo. It is obvious she has forgotten her damn place since I have been injured as of late, and I am going to have to remind her.

Before she can move again, I yank her up from the floor and carry her quickly up the stairs.

* * * * *

Drip drip drip.

I stand in the middle of the abandoned barn in the middle of nowhere. This is where we do some of our executions. Matteo is standing next to me, a serious expression on his face. It is obvious from his stance he is ready.

The four traitors stand in front of us. Arianna and Stefano and their two men on the inside posing as my men. There is a table of implements next to me, all kinds of different tools on the walls, but as I look at these people, something snaps inside of me. Something primal and evil. Something I've tried to keep down, because once it takes hold, it is hard for me to shake it, and it changes me into a worse person than I already am. But looking at these people makes me blind to being rational.

"You two are in luck," I say, looking at Arianna and Stefano. I let all the malice seep into my voice. Stefano keeps his gaze down, and Arianna is looking at me with fear in her eyes. "I hate you. Both of you. You've put me and my wife at risk too many times. And if not for my wife, you would have been dead a long time ago."

I step away from them and pulled out the gun I keep in my holster, handing it to Matteo.

"He wanted the honor of killing you. And since I don't want anything to go wrong during torture, I want both of you dead now."

I step away from Matteo and up to my two men, looking them deep into their souls. I can see the fear pouring off them, and it heightens my excitement.

"You aren't as lucky." I snap my fingers, and Romelo comes up next to me, ready to take them into the next room. I am going to make their deaths slow and painful. I turn to Matteo.

"You can dispose of them however you wish. Once you're done, you can come watch my handiwork or go wait in the car. It's your decision."

With that, I exit the main part of the barn, heading into one of the rooms with the poor souls that will next die at my hands.

As I sit in the room, getting ready to begin, I hear a beautiful sound that makes the hair on my skin prickle with excitement, adrenaline coursing through my veins.

The gun I gave Matteo goes off.

Chapter 32

Elise

Matteo steps into the room, and as soon as we make eye contact, I stand to leave.

"Wait, Elise," his voice calls out.

I can't even begin to look at him. He's just like Luca. It should have made sense, because Luca has been the only male figure in his life. I should've paid attention more. Ever since Matteo did what he did, I've been avoiding him like crazy. Every time I look at him, I see Luca's conniving face. And Matteo has been following him around like a lost puppy. If Romelo is Matteo's shadow, then Matteo is Luca's new shadow.

"Please stop being mad. I did what I did for the both of us. Arianna has ruined our lives. Because of her, my mother is dead. And so is yours. Because of her, you've had to suffer. She kept information from you and used you. Elise, you should be happy I got rid of her."

I look at him in horror.

"My god, Luca has brainwashed you. You can't really be that naïve, Matteo. *Luca* is the one that killed your mother! Luca killed my father. Luca did this to me, to you! How could you possibly think that Arianna had any part in that?"

Matteo's eyes grow angry as he stares at me. "Luca did those things to protect his family!"

"So did Arianna! What do you even know of family, Matteo? You grew up away from all this! From the Mob, from the family. You're not even sworn in! How can you speak like that?"

Matteo looks away with an irritated expression. He looks back at me with those deep-green eyes. "I meant you. You're his family, Elise. He did everything he's done to protect you …" He trails off, looking in the hallway before continuing. "Luca has saved my life countless times. He has always taken care of me. And he's taught me things. Even though it was unorthodox, he gave me the chance to get my revenge. He gave me the chance to be accepted by this family, because life would have been hard for me because I wasn't sworn in, and especially who I was. And you should know this, Elise. I know he killed our father, but he did it to protect you. He took care of me because it was what you would have wanted. He's been watching out for you this whole time, Elise."

I shake my head. "You can't really be this blind, Matteo. You acted as if you hated him just a few weeks ago!"

"I know. Because I did. He hurt you, and you're my sister. My blood. But when it all comes down to it, Luca is the one that I know better. And last night, Luca gave me the chance that I needed. Whether you want to admit it or not, Luca has been looking out for us." Matteo walks to the door before turning back to me with an expression filled with anger. "All your life you had it easy. Luca's life was hard, as was mine. And I see daily what he deals with. Being capo isn't easy, Elise. The least you can do is be thankful to him for saving you. For saving us."

He walks out of the room, and I can feel anger flaring up within me. I jump from my seat and run out into the hallway, determined to find Matteo, but I run face-first into Luca. I stumble backward in shock, but Luca immediately reaches out to steady me.

I open my mouth to apologize. "I'm sorry."

I look up at Luca, and he is watching me with a curious expression. He takes a step to the side. "You chasing after your brother?" He looks at me expectantly, like he is waiting for me to dash out of the kitchen.

"I was … yes." I look down, not wanting to meet his eyes. I can feel his fingers under my chin as he guides my face up to meet his. He looks into my eyes, making me want to fidget under his piercing gaze.

"Well, aren't you going to go get him, then?" Luca has an amused smirk on his face as he watches me.

"No … it's okay. We both just need to cool off." I try to step around Luca, but he grabs my arm.

"How about you come with me for the rest of the day?" Luca doesn't wait for me to respond; he takes me by the hand and guides me upstairs to our bedroom. Once the door closes behind us, he takes my hand, leading me to the bed. He lays us down, dragging my body close to his.

"Why are you bothering Matteo?" His hand is lightly tracing my stomach. I am honestly afraid to respond.

"I wasn't. He started talking to me first."

Luca lets out a deep chuckle behind me. "I find it amusing that you went through all that trouble to get him and now you won't even speak to him." Luca's amusement at my predicament causes irritation to boil up within me.

"I didn't expect him to be just like you."

Luca stops tracing the pattern. "Me? How so?"

"A killer." I squeeze my eyes, afraid of what Luca is about to do to me.

"A killer, huh?" I feel his chest heave behind me as he takes a deep breath. He jerks away from me and gets out of the bed.

I immediately sit up and watch him as he paces back and forth in front of me, running his fingers roughly through his hair.

"Elise, you act like I chose to be this way." He finally looks over to me, and I am shocked to see the hurt in his eyes. "You act like I was born into a normal family, with normal parents, with normal jobs, and I just chose to grow up and be this way. You act like the world is filled with nothing but love and rainbows." He gives a bitter chuckle before continuing.

"Well, I hate to be the one to bear the bad news, babe, but it's not. We live in a world where such a thing called the Mafia exists, and I was the lucky bastard born into leading it. And you were born into it also. Except you led a nice little life where your biggest problem was your father not paying attention to you. My biggest problem was shooting someone in the neck instead of the head because if I kept them alive, it was my life on the line. My biggest problem was learning to interrogate people, hurt people, kill people because it was my duty to my family. And if I didn't, I was beat and starved by my father."

My eyes grow wide as Luca opens up to me.

"Dammit, Elise! You want to hate me because I let your brother take his revenge? If I didn't, he would be dead within the next six months. Your family betrayed us. Everyone here would question his loyalty and allegiance. He would not have survived! I didn't swear him in, but I still gave him the chance to be accepted by the family when I didn't have to! I could have just sworn him in, completely ignoring your request."

He sighs. "You're so selfish! You paint me to be this horrible man when I've done nothing but provide for you, protect you, and care for you! Because you finally get to see what life is like on this side and you can't take it, I'm the bad guy?" He chuckles.

"I was the one forced to murder children. Fucking children! Because their fathers were too stupid to play it safe and follow my father's orders. You wanna complain and paint me the bad guy because you were forced into this marriage? Well, guess what, baby, so was I. And imagine my shock, my guilt, my rage, when I find out that I have to marry the girl whose mother I shot in cold blood right in front of her! Imagine when I have to look at you every day and look at that small scar on the side of your temple from me! From beating you almost to death! Because if I didn't, guess who would have come after me and my family? Your father!"

Luca is full-blown shouting now. But my eyes are wide and in shock. He has just admitted to being the reason for my mother's death.

"W-what?" My voice comes out in a broken whisper. All the anger immediately dissipates from Luca's face, and shock appears as he realizes what he has just said.

"Oh god, Elise …" He trails off and stares at me. He takes a step toward the bed, and I immediately fall of and scramble away.

We both sit there staring at each other in silence. I slowly reach up with a shaky hand and brush the indentation on my temple. All these years I believed it was a birth mark. Some strange scar I could never explain. But it was from Luca?

I stand and immediately take off out of the room, running any-where. And for once, I don't have Luca chasing me. I run to the guard that always takes me off the estate and immediately ask him to take me away from here.

I turn to look out of the window at the estate and see Luca standing on the porch, watching me leave. He doesn't even make a move to stop me.

* * * * *

"Here you go, ma'am. Enjoy your meal!" The cashier hands me my food with the brightest smile I have ever seen. I wonder if her homelife is happy. I give her a small smile and take the tray, walking to the table where my driver sits.

"I didn't know what you wanted, so I just covered the basics. Cheeseburger and fries." I push the food toward him.

"Thank you, Mrs. Pasquin—"

"Elise. Please just call me Elise."

He eyes me, confused, before finishing his sentence. "Elise … I don't eat on the job, though."

I roll my eyes. "Of course you don't." I take the spoon off my tray and dip it into the soup.

Luca has shown me two sides of himself today. He killed my mother on my father's orders, but he has also shown me how part of him resents doing the things he does. *That is, until he grew to like them, I guess.*

"Are you all right, Elise?" I look up to see my driver looking at me with concern. I feel a wetness on my face and realize I am crying. I hastily wipe my eyes.

"Uh, yeah, I'm sorry."

We are all messed up. This whole thing we call life. And I have been foolish enough to think that I could somehow be excluded from it. All I want is a man to love me at least if I am going to be forced into marriage. My whole life has been a plan. All of it was schemed and mapped out by my father. A mad, power-hungry bastard.

I think back to Matteo's words. Luca has been protecting me, but his other actions say otherwise. He's been driven to insanity by his father. It's not like he had a choice in becoming who he is. He is raised that way, and he has to keep it that way because he was the leader.

I take a deep breath. Am I really selfish? It's not only Luca who said it, but Matteo too. That I have been raised away from everything. My head is pounding from all the stress.

"Elise … uh, Mr. Pasquino is requesting we return home." He looks at me with worry. I can understand why. If he refuses Luca's orders, he'll be in trouble.

I take a deep breath and move to throw my soup away. The last thing I want to do is face Luca. Especially after this revelation. But I don't want this poor man to get maimed because of me.

We step out into the car, and night is already falling. We are driving in silence when, suddenly, a car pulls out in front of us, slamming on their brakes.

"What the fuck!" my driver shouts. He swerves around as another car pulls up close to the bumper, slamming into it.

"Shit!" he shouts and tries to swerve out, but the cars have us blocked. There is another car coming toward us to block us in, but the driver slams on his brakes and swerves right, allowing us to break free.

"Shit, someone's after us!" He immediately presses something in the car and begins talking into his earpiece.

"This is Violli. We're being hit pretty hard. Whoever is after us wants us alive! We're in the downtown district, heading south toward the interstate—ah!"

Bullets fly across the windshield, and I give out a small cry of panic. The windows are luckily bulletproof.

"Yes, she's safe for now!" he shouts.

Suddenly the car is jerked hard to the right, and I am sent flying into the door. The driver reaches into his pocket and fishes out his phone, handing it to me.

"Dial *864. Hurry!" He jerks the car again, causing an array of horns to erupt around us. I dial quickly and hold it to my ear as it rings.

"What?"

I gasp. "Luca?"

"Elise? What the hell are yo—"

I shout, unable to listen to him any further as a car rams us from behind, "Someone's following us! They keep hitting the car—"

The car swerves again, and my stomach lurches as we become airborne. It feels as if everything is in slow motion as the car flips over several times before landing, finally coming to a halt upside down. The seat belt is crushing my chest painfully. I can feel a burning pain on my forehead, and my arms are hurting.

"Elise! Elise! What's happening?" Luca's voice is shouting at me from the phone that is now on the roof.

I grunt in pain and can feel the warm trickle of blood. The darkness envelops me as I hear shouting coming toward the car. I can't make out a word of what is being said. All I know is that I am happy when I finally pass out.

* * * * *

I jump up in bed, gasping aloud as I finally awaken. The movement causes pain to spasm throughout my body. I cry out in pain and fall back on the surprisingly soft bed. I have to constantly blink to force my vision to focus. The room I am in is small. The floor has carpet, though, and there are no windows. It is surprisingly clean. I immediately check my body for permanent damage, such as broken bones, but there are none. I sigh in relief and slump back in the bed.

There are cuts and bruises on my body, and I can feel the thick gauze on my forehead from what, I must assume, is a nasty cut. I can't check because there are no mirrors in here.

The door to the room sounds, and in comes a woman with blond hair. She is carrying a tray with steaming food on it, and bags are draped over her arms. She sets the bags down and drags the mini table over to the side of my bed, setting the food down. She smiles at me.

"I see you're awake."

I study her with clear confusion. Last thing I remember, the car was upside down and there were not-so-friendly people after us. My stomach loudly growls, and she gives a soft chuckle.

"Someone's hungry." She gestures to the plate of food. It's chicken and rice. And it looks delicious.

I don't touch it, though. I don't know if it's poisoned. The woman seems to sense my hesitation and gives an irritated sigh. She grabs my spoon and shovels food into her mouth to prove it isn't poisoned. As soon as she sets the spoon down, I grab it and dig in. I have no idea how long I've been passed out, but it was definitely long enough for my stomach to grow empty.

She reaches for the bags and begins pulling things out.

"We got you some soap and clothes and a toothbrush. Oh, and a brush, some magazines, and some lady products when it's that time of the month." She smiles so big at me, as if I weren't a hostage.

"Why am I here?" I ask.

She stops shuffling with the groceries and looks at me, her smile faltering. Her eyes quickly glance to the corner and back to me.

"Look, you don't need to know why. You just need to know you're not leaving anytime soon, okay? So don't waste your breath asking questions, sweetie. And save your strength." She snatches my plate from me even though I am not finished eating. She then turns back to me. "You're gonna need it."

She then walks out of the room, slamming the door. My heart drops as I hear the lock of the door on the other side.

I stare at my hands for a moment. Suddenly, I remember the way she glanced at the corner behind my head. I slowly look over my shoulder, and sure enough, there is a camera there overlooking the entire room. I have no idea what is happening. What is about to develop. But I do know the familiar feeling brewing deep within me. It is one that I have grown accustomed to since marrying Luca.

Fear.

Chapter 33

Elise

I am jolted awake by the sound of the door unlocking. I don't know how long I've been in here. There are no windows, and there are no clocks. I try to keep up with time by the number of meals they bring me, but from my count, if they bring me three meals a day, I have probably been in here almost a week. A whole week, and no one has come and said anything to me. The pretty blonde comes in and holds conversations with me, but I refuse to respond. And when I ask her why I am here, she just ignores me.

I sit up in the bed and look toward the door to see a man walking in. I have no idea who he is. He is dressed in a nice suit, with dark hair and blue eyes. He has a folder in his hands that has "Pasquino" printed on it. He has a carton with two cups of coffee in it, I am assuming. He takes a seat at the table in the room, placing both objects on the table. He opens the file, flipping through it, still not speaking.

He finally looks up at me and grabs a coffee out of the carton and pushes it across the table toward me.

I stay seated in the bed, not daring to move as I eye him suspiciously. He looks to be about the same age as Luca. Except his face is softer. He must smile a lot.

"Sorry for the delay. I was actually out of the country, finishing up a case, when I got a call that we had Luca Pasquino's wife in custody." His eyes shift to the untouched cup of coffee.

"Not thirsty?" His voice is light and carefree.

I still don't answer him. He only shrugs. Just by this small confrontation, I can tell he is not in the Mafia. The fact that he hasn't slapped me for ignoring him when he is talking to me tells me sure enough. He shrugs at my silence and opens the file.

"Elise Trovoli, now Pasquino since your marriage into the Pasquino family. Twenty years old next month. No occupation, no driver's record, hell, not even a license. No school record, no credit cards, nothing. I can see why Luca kept you under the radar. You are a pretty thing, aren't you?" He looks up, giving me a light smile, but I am still trying to understand his comment.

"Kept me under the radar?"

He looks around, as if trying to come up with the right words to explain.

"Kept you away from the government eye. Quite honestly, we didn't know you existed until the incident with your half-brother. Your whole statement was scratched from the record." He places the file on the table, and I can see articles and pictures of Luca.

I look up at him, still confused.

"Before we get into the logistics of things, I want to first apologize for the way things went in your car. We thought you were your husband." He gives me an embarrassed smile.

I still stare at him. What the hell is going on?

"My name is Agent Jeffries. I work in the top secret division of the US government. That's really all I can give you right about now. If I tell you anything else about us, well, I may have to kill you." He laughs, but immediately stops when he sees I am not laughing. I guess he doesn't understand that kind of thing isn't funny to someone like me.

"Look, miss, bottom line is, we have been trying to bust your husband for years now. But men like him are smart. Too smart. They do things that make it impossible to catch them. Your husband is a threat to us and everyone else, and I think you know what I'm talking about. All I need from you is a statement, and we can have probable cause to search his properties. Maybe even some of the clubs he owns. There are whole halves of the city that are indebted to him because they pay for protection but refuse to give statements for fear of their lives. Do you know how many lives and people can be liberated from him? He is the biggest crime boss in the United States, probably has just as much power, if not more, than the president. He controls so many interconnected networks, and if we can just take him down, then we will have made the largest bust in the history of the United States." He sits back in his seat, smiling at me.

I can only stare at him.

"A statement?" I laugh bitterly aloud. "Luca is not one to be messed with, sir. And for good reason. He would probably kill me if I did something like that."

Agent Jeffries stares at me.

"Quite honestly, I'm surprised he isn't here now. He implanted a fucking tracking device in me."

This catches the agent's attention. He leans back in his chair and pulls a baggie out of his pocket.

"You mean this?" He sets down what is left of my tracker chip on the table. "We had it taken out and destroyed before you even left the car. You probably didn't notice it because the pain blended with your injuries from the wreck."

I can only stare at the chip.

"I really support you guys in this, I really do, but I don't think you understand what you are asking of me. I can't turn against my husband, and not for the reasons you think. I have my own life and my brother's life to think about. I'm sorry, Agent, but you're not getting anything out of me."

He sits back in his chair, frowning. The room is silent for a moment.

"Look, I know you're scared, but if we can just get this from you, we can offer you protection. You're the only option we have. No one else is willing to testify. And your words will definitely get us the court order we need. Once we arrest your husband, we can hide you in protective services."

I continue to shake my head.

"Look, Agent, I told you no. There is no place safe for me if I betray my husband. People won't testify for good reason. They'd be signing a death warrant! You people have rats that work for him already in these top secret divisions. I'm sorry, but you're going to have to find another way to bust him."

His face turns from friendly to angry.

"I see. Then I guess there is nothing we can do for you here." He stands to leave, and upon the door's opening, two men step into the room, grabbing me roughly and dragging me out of the room.

* * * * *

It's completely silent as I ride in the car with a bag over my face. All I can see is the small light streaming in from the little holes. It smells stale. My body rocks as we hit another bump. I have no idea how long we've been driving for. All I know is that it has been a while. Wherever we are going must be somewhere hostile. They zip-tied my hands behind my back uncomfortably tight. My muscles are beginning to ache. I can feel the burning of my wounds coming back. The nice, top secret government facility was giving me pain medicine. But since I am not helping them, I guess they think it's fair to leave me without them. And damn if my hip doesn't hurt where they took the GPS out.

The car suddenly stops, and I am being jerked out of my seat. They are pulling me so fast I don't have the time or strength to catch my footing. For some reason, I haven't shed a tear up to this point. I guess I have Luca to thank for that. If these guys are anything like him, I just may be prepared for whatever they have in store for me.

I can hear the sound of doors opening, and I am hit with cold air. There are people shouting around me. The tops of my feet are stinging from being rubbed raw by the men dragging me across the concrete. I am sat in a seat, and the bag is jerked off my head.

There is a woman in front of me. She is a little on the bigger side and is shouting at the men behind me in Russian. They obviously don't know that I speak Russian. It is something I've picked up in the years of being neglected by my father. I also speak French, German, Spanish, Italian, and Latin, which I barely know, because it is a dead language. So finding lessons on it is hard.

"You bring me this thirty minutes before the auction starts? I don't think so. She can wait until next week."

"We don't have that long. She wasn't taken from some nobody's home. She's the wife of Luca Pasquino. He could be hot on our trail. We need to get rid of her as soon as possible."

I keep my eyes trained down so they don't catch that I can understand them.

"Pasquino? Why the fuck would you bring her here? He finds out she's at this place, we're all as good as dead!"

"No, we'll be fine. The agency gave her to us. They wiped the trail and are leading him on a chase. By the time he finds out what's really going on, she'll be too far gone for him to bother us."

The lady contemplates for a moment before responding. "Fine. Leave us."

The man nods and exits the room. The woman looks at me. She stalks toward me and reaches out to touch my hair, and I immediately slap her hand out of my face.

"Ohh, you're feisty, aren't you, sweetie," she says to me in English. "We'll fix that soon enough." She roughly jerks my left hand, snatching it tightly as she jerks my wedding ring off. "Can't have this where you're going." She sneers at me and walks away, inspecting the ring. It probably costs more than she will see in her lifetime.

Twenty minutes later, I'm sitting in a room, with dark-red lingerie on and an open robe that reveals more than I'd like it to. The woman that scrubbed my skin raw and waxed my entire body has a hard time getting it done. She has giant welts across her skin from my nails to prove it. This is pure madness at its best. For once, I actually wish Luca would come and save me. I don't want to be auctioned off like some piece of meat.

There are two different auctions. There seems to be one for common girls and some private auctions, which is where I and a few other girls are right now. There is a girl next to me that looks as frightened as I feel. She is literally shivering even though she is wearing that heavy fabric over her lingerie. I reach over and place my hand over hers, and her frightened eyes meet mine. I try to give her a small smile of reassurance, but I must not have looked too convincing, because tears fill her eyes and she bursts out into loud sobs.

In total, there are about ten women sitting in this room, and they are all important somehow, because we hold higher value over the general auction. I can remember listening to my father talk about these kinds of things when I was younger. Never did I think I would be the poor soul stuck in one.

"Oh my god, you're Luca Pasquino's wife."

I turn around and see a girl staring at me in shock. I have no idea who she is, but she looks to be older than me by a few years.

"Who are you?"

She looks around before shuffling toward me. "I ... uh, I was ..." Her cheeks burn red as she tries to explain it to me. "I was one of Luca's father's mistresses. You know, when he was alive."

I look at this woman who is sitting in here with me. She looks around my age, maybe older. And she was having sex with Luca's father? Sick bastard.

"He told me about the wedding. Luca's wedding. He showed me pictures. That's how I recognize you. You're very beautiful. Luca is very lucky to have you." She then realizes what she is saying. "How on earth did you get here?"

I take a deep breath before responding, the weight of what is going on triggered by that question. This whole time, I have felt numb, shutting off my emotions and trying to keep it that way. But now the tears I have held back are starting to resurface and threatening to spill over.

"They kidnapped me, and because I wouldn't help them with taking Luca down, they're throwing me in an auction so that he can't find me." A sob breaks out of my throat.

"Oh no," she whispers with her hands over her mouth. Her eyes widen. "They?"

Before I can respond, the girl next to me pipes up. "Please, what are they going to do to us?" she whispers to her.

"They sell us by value. They make the ones that are known for their affairs with the crime bosses go first. Like me." She opens her robe, showing us the lingerie beneath. "They coordinate us by color. See? Girls like me wear gold. The next ones that go are the most valuable, because, well ..." She trails off as she stares at the girl next to me. "They're virgins. They wear white. And they cost a lot. Usually, there's something unique about you, which is why you're in the private auction."

Her eyes meet mine, and they are filled with pity.

"And the ones that go last are the most important. They aren't virgins, but they have a very important significance. They are a major crime boss's daughter, sister, or ... wife. Some form of relation to them. Most of the men that come to these are very important men, so having someone like you is very useful. Which is why you wear red."

I stare at her in horror.

"How do you know all this?"

She looks away, a little embarrassed. "I've done it before. Women like me serve a purpose, and once our boss gets tired of us, he sends us back. But we know what men like them like, which is why we are of some value." She shrugs, as if it were not a big deal, but I feel as if I am going to vomit. I am about to be auctioned off. To the highest bidder.

I look to the girl that is telling us all this with pleading eyes. "Please, whoever you get sold to, you have to find some way to get into contact with Luca. You have to tell him what happened and where I was last," I beg to her with tears in my eyes. I know in the back of my mind that this is stupid of me to want Luca to find me, but human nature is to flee to what you know. And right now, Luca is all I know. And he is my only hope. I am about to be sold to God knows who, and I am terrified.

The door opens, and a man comes in, roughly grabbing the first woman as the auction begins.

* * * * *

I am the last one. The most valuable. My heart is hammering in my chest, and the tears are a never-ending stream as I am led into a dark room with a spotlight being shone on me. The speaker overhead sounds.

"Elise Pasquino, nineteen years old. Not a virgin, but the wife of the North Mob's notorious Luca Pasquino." The robe is ripped off me, and I am stuck sitting in the middle of the room in a pair of sexy bra and underwear.

"Let's start the bidding at $100,000."

* * * * *

The robe is back on me, and I am being rushed, to where, I have no idea. I can hear the sound of the door, and the heat hits me, so I know we are outside. But then I am met with the sound of a door, and I am roughly pushed inside of a car. The towel around my eyes is soaked with my tears, and I strain to hear any kind of noise.

A deep voice comes out of nowhere, causing me to jump.

"My, you are exquisite."

Chapter 34

Elise

I sit in the room with nothing more than a pair of lingerie on and some heels. Alexander. He refuses to give me his last name. Just Alexander, he says. I don't know what organization he works for. I don't know who he is, in all honesty. He injected me with some kind of sedative that put me to sleep, and the next thing I know, I woke up in this large study with him in front of me.

He is sitting across from me, studying me very closely. Slick black hair is pushed back away from his face, and cold blue eyes stare at me. I am shaking in my seat, not just because I am cold, but because I am scared. This man looks like someone you do not mess with.

"Stand up." His voice pulls me out of my thoughts. I immediately stand. He stands with me and walks toward me, his eyes dropping to Luca's name embedded in my flesh. He runs his thumb along the skin, and I immediately take a step back out of instinct, not wanting him touching me. A small smirk appears on his face.

"I see Luca's temper hasn't improved." His voice is dripping with irritation. "We'll have to have that removed. I don't want to be looking at his name each time I want to fuck you."

I immediately gasp and stumble backward, trying to put more and more distance between us. My eyes are filled with tears that spill over.

"Please … don't …" My voice comes out shaky and low.

His eyes flash, and an evil smile I know all too well spreads across his face. "Damn, you are beautiful when you cry. I can see why Luca may have enjoyed seeing your tears. I know I will." He steps closer to me. "And the sound of your voice begging ... damn, if it doesn't make me want to take you now." He steps closer to me again, and I step back.

"L-Luca won't like it if he finds out you've had sex with me." I am literally grasping at straws, saying anything and everything I can to get him to change his mind out of sleeping with me.

Out of nowhere, he grabs me, pushing me into the wall. I cry out in pain as my back collides with the hard wall. He roughly presses his forearm into my throat, and panic blooms immediately in my chest.

"Mention his name again." I can't even if I wanted to. His forearm is pressing roughly into my throat. A smile crosses his face as he watches me uselessly struggle. "I can't hear you. Say it. Say his name."

My vision is blurring, and my throat is burning from the pressure. He leans in so close to me I can feel the heat radiating from him.

"If you ever say that name again, in my home ..." He laughs before continuing. "I will kill you. Luca is no more. He will never find you, as far as I'm concerned. I am the one you belong to now. So you better learn to respect me before you get yourself killed." His face is murderously serious as he watches my frantic struggles.

He lets go, and I greedily suck in air and rub my throat, trying to soothe the burning pain.

"I am a man of ... different tastes. Do as I say, and we'll get along fine. But I can't promise you that you will always enjoy what I say." He walks away from me in my corner, and I close my eyes, counting to ten.

One ... two ... three ... four ... five ... six ... seven ... eight ... nine ... ten ...

I open my eyes and jump up from my spot on the floor, flinging the door open. Lucky for me, this room is the only one in the hallway. Blood is rushing in my ears, and I pump my legs as fast as they will go in the heels. I don't have the time to stop and take them off. I turn left and breathe a silent prayer, as I can see the foyer right in front of me. My heels clatter loudly against the floor as I near the massive oak door. I immediately grab on to it, flinging it open and run into the outside.

My footsteps falter, and my pants are frantic. I can see my breath coming out in front of me. Snow. Everywhere. It is so thick I can see nothing but white surrounding me. Mounds of it. My body immediately breaks into violent shudders. I open my mouth and let out a loud scream. The tears rolling down my face are leaving a burning trail from the temperature.

I am roughly yanked up from the ground, and I can feel warm arms around me. I don't even try to struggle. A deep chuckle reverberates throughout my entire body as Alexander laughs behind me.

"You should not have done that."

I can only cry as he drags me farther and farther into the house.

* * * * *

"I can't hear you, Elise. How many is that?"

I open my mouth, trying my hardest to speak to say anything, but I can't even catch my breath. Each time I breathe in, more pain explodes all over my body. If I thought Luca was cruel, damn, I was so off. Alexander likes to use belts. Not just normal leather ones, but belts that have jewels embedded in them. So that each strike leaves a marring bruise on my skin. And he never lets up either. He starts on my ass and slowly makes his way up my body. My arms are roughly bound above my head, and they are the only things holding me up.

I feel his fingers underneath my chin, and he pulls my face up to meet his.

"Elise, I'm talking to you." He tilts his head slightly as he studies me. "How many is that?"

I still open my mouth again and try to speak, but nothing leaves my lips except a hoarse squeak.

A smile crosses his face, and he laughs at my predicament. His hand moves from my chin to my jaw, and he tilts my head to the side. I don't have the energy to struggle. I squeeze my eyes tightly shut as his lips slowly trace my neck to my collarbone.

He pulls back and stares at me. "Will you ever run again?" He looks at me expectantly, and when I don't answer, he roughly snatches my face in his hands. "I said, Will you run again?"

I frantically shake my head no, loud whimpers accompanying the movement. With Luca, I at least know he has some form of twisted love for me. And he knows when to stop. But this man has nothing to lose. No feelings for me. And I am assuming by the way he speaks that he hates Luca. I am scared more than I have ever been before.

* * * * *

I lie on my stomach on a cushioned bench as Alexander places more ice packs on my back side. Each time it touches my skin, I whimper in pain. There are deep-purple welts on my back side starting at my legs, going up to my midback. Alexander sits right next to my body and traces the welts. I bite my teeth in pain, trying not to make a sound, in fear he might do something.

"I've known Luca a long time. He always had the better things in life. Including you. That's why I wanted you so bad. When I heard who you belonged to, I knew I had to have you. To be able to say that you fucked and broke Luca Pasquino's wife is something any man would be more than happy to say."

He places another pack on my back.

"I won't have sex with you yet until I feel you're ready. You're still too fragile for my taste. I'm going to enjoy breaking you."

He stands and walks to the door. When he opens it, a frightened-looking maid is on the other side. He whispers something to her, and she nods, walking in the room with a suitcase in her hands.

She doesn't look at me once as she unzips the suitcase and starts setting things into place in the room. Everything that she takes out is some form of lingerie. She places them all in drawers and unzips another pouch of products that go in the bathroom. As she steps into the bathroom with shampoo and conditioner in her hand, something catches my eye from the suitcase. There are tampons and pads. I stare long and hard as my heart rate starts to skyrocket. The woman walks out of the bathroom and grabs the products.

"Ma'am, please … what's today's date?" My voice comes out groggy and raw. And if the room weren't silent, I don't think she would have heard me either.

She shakes her head at me and doesn't respond. I am assuming because he has told her not to speak to me. Tears are already forming in my eyes.

"P-please … please, I'm begging you, what's today's date?"

She sighs and looks at me. "It's the nineteenth of February."

My heart slams into my rib cage. *No, no, no, no, no …*

"I can hardly see why it would matter, miss. You're never getting out of this hellhole …"

The woman is still rambling on, but I can't hear her. I'm late. My period. It's late.

Chapter 35

Luca

I can feel the bone smashing under my fist as it connects with this man's face. He staggers back, falling flat on his back, completely knocked out.

"Matteo!" I bark at him. "Finish him off!"

I don't even turn around as Matteo steps over the unconscious man's body, firing several rounds into it. Fuck! I am literally going crazy. Elise is gone. Fucking gone! Right from under my damn nose. I can't eat, I can't sleep, and every time I try to close my eyes, I hear that bone-chilling sound of her screams as the car crashes. That was the last thing I heard before to the phone shut off.

We can't even track her. The chip was last activated at the sight of the crash. And by the time we got there, the police were already tainting it. There is no trail or anything. Her driver was already dead when we arrived on the scene. Which is lucky for him, because I would have killed him myself since Elise is missing.

My resources in the police department can't give me anything on the crash. Each time they try to access it, their access is denied. So I tried asking my contacts in the federal agencies. None of them have gotten back to me. I am such a fool! Why I let Elise leave the estate without me, I don't know. I let my damn emotions get the best of me, and now look where we are.

Someone has her, and whoever it is took her for the hell of it, because I haven't received any threatening calls or ransoms. And that makes me all the more worried. At least with a ransom, I can negotiate her safety and find whoever it is before they hurt her. But with this person … there is no telling what they are doing to her.

"Luca—"

"What!" I shout.

Matteo is standing next to me and cringes at my tone. He's probably the only person that can get near me lately. I know I won't hurt him or kill him on accident because of who he is to Elise. So as of late, he is my right-hand man. Romelo is doing some serious tracking, trying to find Elise, and Nicolai is doing my duties for me.

"It's Romelo," he says, holding the phone out to me.

I yank it from his grasp, walking away toward the car. "What is it?"

"I think I got her trail."

For the first time in weeks, relief floods through me. "Where?"

"There's a pawnshop in the next state over that has her wedding ring."

I immediately feel anger boiling up within me. "She ran away?" I hiss.

"Not likely. I spoke to the shop owner, and he said an older woman came in and pawned it. And get this. She sold it. So she didn't want it back. I tracked the information he gave me to a woman named Sophia Vitale." He pauses, waiting for me to catch on.

"Russian?"

"Yes. I followed her for a few days. She seemed to be working in an old factory, but it turns out the factory is actually an auction house … for women."

"Fuck!" I shout, punching the wall next to me with all my might. The weak plaster gives way, and my whole hand flies through.

"We're coming now. You have my utmost thanks."

"Actually, I just did the heavy lifting. Matteo was the one that found out about the pawnshop. Thank him." He hangs up before I can respond.

I look out the corner of my eyes and see Matteo leaning against a car door. He looks like I feel. Exhausted. In all my rage, I haven't thought about how he feels in all this.

When he found out the news of Elise, he broke down. Apparently, he said some things to her he now wishes wouldn't have been his last words to his newly found sister. He has been working just as hard as everyone else. And I have been screaming at him every day. I walk over to him, trying to rein in my anger. This is what Elise would want.

"Matteo, we think we may have a lead on Elise." I place a hand on his shoulder. "Romelo told me what you did. Thank you. We'll find her."

* * * * *

The next day, we are standing in front of the auction house, waiting. All my men are behind me, waiting for my signal. Without hesitation, I step into the auction house that may be responsible for my wife's abduction, and unleash the bloodbath.

About an hour later, we have everyone rounded up. The women that are to be sold are all in another room. Lucky for us, today isn't an auction day, so we don't run into anyone but the scum that runs this shithole. The Pasquinos don't do sex trafficking. Which explains why they put her here. They knew we wouldn't think to look.

I step over the girls. They are all shivering in fear. The men are all tied up, and some have looks of hatred, while others have fear in their eyes. And for good reason. I keep walking up the hallway in silence until I am standing right in front of the woman I am looking for.

"Sophia Vitale."

Her shivering increases as she slowly looks up at me. I make sure to keep my face blank of any emotion. I squat in front of her and pull the ring out of my back pocket. This is the second time I've had to buy it out of pawn.

"Recognize this?"

Her eyes widen, and she begins sobbing loudly and begging for her life. I can feel excitement bubbling up within me. I love it when people beg. Especially this one. I already have my mind made up with what I am going to do with her life. The fact that she is begging makes that decision all the sweeter.

"Shhhh," I tell her while placing my gun against her lips. "Tell me, what is your job here? You obviously aren't one of the women being auctioned."

She stares at me wide-eyed and begins begging for her life once again. I don't even flinch as I shoot the nearest worker in the head. Her body strains forward against the rope. All the women around me are screaming. I point the gun back at Sophia.

"I won't ask you again."

"I … I … I … get the women p-primped a-and ready f-f-for auction." She sobs. "Please, sir, I am so sorry! I … I didn't know s-she was your w-wife!"

I can tell she's lying. She knew exactly who Elise is. I have no doubt that every person in here knows who she is. The fact that they sold her anyway tells me someone high up must have given her to these people. High up enough that they thought they would be safe. And they just may have been, if not for Sophia pawning that ring.

I bring my attention back to the woman.

"So what you are saying is that you 'primped' my wife for sale?"

I think back to how the girls that are about to be auctioned off are dressed. Skimpy lingerie. And I am betting Elise was a part of the private auction because of who she is.

"You put my wife in barely anything and had her sold to the highest bidder? But before that, you decided to take something as precious as her wedding ring off and sell it for your own personal gain?"

She doesn't respond; she only sobs louder and louder.

"Who bought her?" I ask.

She shakes her head, claiming she doesn't know.

I shoot the nearest girl, and screams erupt. I place my gun under Sophia's chin. "Who fucking bought her?"

Sophia still claims she doesn't know.

A girl near her pipes up, obviously terrified, "We don't know! It was an anonymous bid! Everyone went in anonymous when they figured out who she was! B-but you can look at the surveillance footage outside and see if the car that took her is on it! Please, that's all we know!" She is sobbing frantically.

I stand from the pathetic women in front of me. This is their jobs here. To dress these girls to look nice and sexy for the auction. To be sold. Like meat. I look around until my eyes land on Matteo. His face is filled with anger. And hate.

"Matteo." He looks up at me, and I nod in approval.

He pulls out his gun, and Sophia's cries get louder and louder. Before Matteo can walk past me, I place a hand on his shoulder, stopping him.

"I want their deaths to be slow. And painful. Understand?"

He looks at me and nods, a sadistic gleam in his eye. *Good boy.*

Romelo is standing against the wall, awaiting orders.

"I want them all dead. Castrate them. Shove their dicks down their throats, and then you can kill them."

A smile makes its way on Romelo's face. Russians have dared take my bride, so we will kill them Russian-style.

I walk to the car and pull my bolt cutters out of the trunk. Elise has been sold to the highest bidder. She's been fucking sold. I can only hope that whoever has her doesn't have unprotected sex with her. I've taken her off her birth control, and I was secretly feeding her hormone pills. And there is no way in hell I am going to raise someone else's child. I can already hear the cries of agony as I walk back into the warehouse. They are going to regret the day they dared to defy Luca-fucking-Pasquino.

Chapter 36

Elise

The most degrading thing I have ever witnessed is being "owned" by this man. I have to bring him breakfast, bring him lunch, and eat dinner with him. All the while wearing the most-revealing clothing I have ever had. It doesn't help that I am currently having a heart attack because I still haven't started my period. That is impossible, though. I just got my shot recently. There is no way I can be pregnant. And if I am, why now of all times? How did this even happen? Could Luca have done something?

I feel a jerk around my throat. That's right. He has a fucking collar around my throat and is making me scrub the floor on my hands and knees as he holds the chain to the collar in his hand. He stands from where he is sitting atop his desk, and as soon as he gets closer to me, he smacks my ass. I yelp aloud in shock and pain. The bruises are starting to turn an ugly, greenish shade on my skin, and they still hurt.

I feel his shoe atop my back, and he pushes with all his might, forcing me onto the ground onto my stomach.

"Seeing all these bruises on your flawless skin … damn, I want you so bad." He straddles my body, and I can feel his hard erection pressing against my bare ass. I immediately begin to struggle.

"No, please!"

The collar tightens around my throat, forcing me to arch my back from being pulled. He takes the opportunity to roughly grab my breasts. I can do nothing as I fight for air that is being cut off in this position. My nails are clawing at the floor because of my suffocation.

The pressure of him sitting on me lifts, and I am being dragged out of the room by the collar. I try to stand and catch my footing, but my legs are weak and I keep stumbling and falling.

"Please! Please, somebody help me!" I shout. But it all falls on deaf ears. If there is someone in here, they are ignoring me.

The pressure of the collar lifts, and he yanks on my hair. I scream in agony as he drags me across the house for what seems like forever. We end up in a room, but I don't have the time to make it out. I am thrown onto a table. I immediately try to get up and run, but he slaps me across the face. Hard. Stars explode across my vision. And the room is spinning.

My arms are locked tightly above my head, and my legs are spread and secured so that I am unmovable, but there is enough space for Alexander to step in between them. He has an evil glint in those cold blue depths as he stares my body up and down with a lust-filled gaze.

He slowly begins to undo his shirt, his gaze never leaving my body.

"Please … please, you don't have to do this." I am literally begging him and screaming all in one.

As he takes his shirt off, he steps away from me, going to find a pair of scissors. He slowly cuts the little bit of clothing I am wearing off my skin, exposing me completely to his gaze. He reaches out, grabbing one of my breasts in his hand, and I have to fight the urge to vomit.

He takes his pants off, and his erection springs free. He leans in close to me, sucking on one of my nipples.

"Keep begging. I like hearing that." He leans into my ear. "Say, 'Please, Alexander.'"

I squeeze my eyes shut, and the tears run freely down my face. I refuse to give him what he wants. I gasp in pain as he roughly pinches my nipple.

"Fucking beg me!" He squeezes harder, and I scream.

"Please! Please, Alexander! Please!"

He laughs, licking my tears.

"Good girl."

I can feel his hand rubbing me with a sticky substance. My eyes fly open, and I can see he is rubbing it on his large erection also. He positions himself at my entrance, and I can feel his tip.

"Please, please, please … just don't do this. I'm begging you." My sobs are the only sound. I open my eyes to an evil smirk plastered on his face, his menacing eyes staring at me.

"I know." He pushes, and I can feel him slowly entering my body.

I feel dirty. Disgusting. He is fully sheathed inside of me.

"Fuck, you're tight," he murmurs.

He withdraws, only to roughly shove back inside of me. I cry out in shock from the force. My body is tied down and immobile. There is nothing I can do but cry. He begins to pick up his pace, thrusting harder and harder inside of me, causing me to cry out in pain each time. His hands wrap around my throat, and he begins to squeeze. I tense immediately, but my hands are locked to the table, so I can only sit there helplessly as his hands tighten around my throat.

"From now on, you're mine." He squeezes even tighter, and I open my mouth, trying to breathe in something, anything. He finally lets go of my throat and slaps me across the face. I cry out in pain, but he doesn't stop. He is literally getting off on my pain.

"You do exactly as I say. No ifs, ands, or buts. If you can't follow those rules, I will punish you." He gives his words emphasis as he slaps me again across the face. The pain is unbearable.

"You will answer me immediately when I speak to you. You will come when I call for you." He wraps one hand around my throat again. "You will not lie to me. You will call me sir around the house, and in the bedroom, you will call me Alexander if I give you permission. Understand?"

I can't speak, because he has his hand around my throat, so I meekly nod. A cruel smile crosses his face.

"Good girl." And with that, he shudders in pleasure, and I can feel him as he spills his seed inside of me.

Numb. I feel numb. I am still crying. Sobbing. I can't even cover my body as he pulls out of me. My arms and legs are still locked in an embarrassing position.

Alexander steps back, examining my body. He reaches out, tracing Luca's name, his eyes running up and down as he reads it. A laugh escapes his lips.

"Not anymore," he murmurs.

Chapter 37

Elise

The worst part of my day has become waking up. I barely eat anything. I am never allowed away from Alexander's side. And even if I was, I have no hope of escape. The maid refuses to speak to me, as well as the kitchen staff. And if I did get ahold of a phone, I wouldn't know who to call. I never learned Luca's number.

I can feel the stinging pain as I awaken out of my deep slumber. I stir slowly, immediately flinching from the pain. At least with Luca, he only hurt me out of anger or "punishment." I'm not saying in any way that that is normal, but with Alexander, he is a constant sadist. He enjoys pain. He doesn't even have to have a reason.

Arms tighten around my body as I try to move. "Where do you think you're going?"

I cringe, and immediately, tears spring into my eyes. When I don't answer, he violently shakes me.

"I asked you a fucking question."

"J-just to the bathroom," I barely get out before a sob breaks out.

His arms slowly release me, and I limp to the bathroom, closing the door. I am not allowed to lock it. I look at my body in the mirror, and silent sobs rack my body. I can break the mirror again and slash my wrists. My eyes travel to my stomach. But I have more to worry about than just me now. It has been a whole month, and I still have not started my period. It is safe to assume that I am pregnant. If my math is correct, then it is with Luca's child. And from what I've heard from family members growing up, I have a few weeks until I start to show. I have to get out of here. I have no idea what type of person Alexander is, and there is no way I'll tell that sadist this is Luca's child.

My legs grow weak, and I collapse onto the floor. I am pregnant with Luca's child. This is the last thing I want. I don't need this. I can't do this. I just wish Luca would find me.

The door to the bathroom opens, and in walks Alexander. He sees me on the floor.

"Elise, what are you doing on the floor?" His voice sends shivers up my spine.

"I ... I was just—"

"Crying," he interrupts me. He kneels on the floor in front of me and reaches out to touch my cheek. I immediately flinch away from him. He pauses, studying my face before a small laugh escapes his lip.

"Come." He steps toward the shower, turning it on.

I slowly rise from my spot on the floor and follow him to the shower.

* * * * *

"Elise, you need to eat."

I am literally staring at my plate. All the food makes my stomach churn. I try not to eat in front of him in fear that I will vomit. I also try not to do anything that will make him aroused. Which means keeping movement at a minimum.

"Elise! I said eat." His voice carries across the room like a whip.

I jump in my seat and begin sniffling. Fear of this man has literally eaten me up. I have all but given up on Luca coming to rescue me. I take the food with shaky hands and shovel it into my mouth. I can't even taste it as I force myself to chew and swallow.

And judging from the way I am feeling right now, I will see this food again.

Alexander watches me with those terrifying eyes. I can't help but wonder what happened to him to make him like this. He shifts in his chair, placing his hand under his chin as he stares me down.

"Are you keeping secrets from me, Elise?" A small smile plays at his lips. My heart is trying to beat out of my chest. Surely, he doesn't know. How could he?

"No." My voice is an almost whisper.

He stands from his seat and slowly begins stalking toward me. "Elise, I know you." His gaze travels up and down my body.

I begin shaking in fear.

"I know how you begin to shake when you're scared. I know how you get teary eyes when you believe you've done something wrong, because you know I don't tolerate impudence. And I know how your voice goes to barely a whisper when I'm on the right track. But you know what I know best?"

I feel his fingers under my chin as he pulls my face up to meet his. He has a serious expression on his face, all amusement gone.

"I know that you avoid eye contact with me when you lie." He reaches out and places his hand over my heart. His eyes drop down to where his hand is, and he looks up to meet my fearful gaze.

"Why is your heart racing, Elise?"

Out of nowhere, the maid comes running into the room with wide eyes.

"Sir, you have a visitor."

Alexander's face shifts to one of irritation. "Who comes to my home unannounced?"

She clears her throat. "Uh, Mr. Pasquino, sir."

I breathe a sigh of relief, and tears of joy spring into my eyes. I am saved! I don't think I have ever been so happy to hear Luca is about to step into the room.

I don't even hesitate; I jump up from my seat at the table and sprint to the foyer. Before I can get far, Alexander grabs ahold of my hair, yanking me back roughly. I can feel a few hairs being torn from my scalp. I cry out in pain. Now I really wish my hair was still short.

Alexander puts his hand around my throat. I can feel my feet being lifted off the floor, and I am being slammed into the table. I try to cry out, but I can't from the pressure around my throat. Alexander is in my face. He grabs a knife from the table and holds it over my stomach. My heart stops.

"Listen to me, you think I'm a fool and don't know what's going on under my own roof? You try not to eat in front of me. My maid has heard you retching in your bathroom. And when I went to look, you haven't touched any of your feminine products. I know, Elise."

Oh god, no.

"And currently, I like the idea of having a child with you. But if you make a sound, I will kill that child." Judging from his choice of words, he thinks it is his. I try to use that against him, building up all the strength I can.

"Y-you would kill your own child?"

He laughs. Literally laughs. "I like this bravery. How about we make a deal, huh?" He smiles wickedly at me. Fear crawls its way up my spine. He turns his head and speaks to the maid.

"Let him in and keep him busy until I say otherwise."

Alexander is by far the strangest person I have ever known. Everything in this house that looks normal isn't. His office floor has a trapdoor in it. There is a stairway, and he has me shackled to the columns.

"This is a soundproof ceiling. Which means that we above can't hear a thing. It's simple for you. Make enough noise for him to hear you, and you'll go free. I mean, I'll be dead, anyway, because he'll kill me once he finds out. So good luck." He smiles evilly at me, walking up the stairs and closing the hatch.

I sprint to the stairs as soon as he is gone and begin reaching to bang on the floor. With the way he has my arm chained, only the tips of my fingers can brush it. I pull as hard as I can against the metal, feeling it bite into my skin.

I hear heavy footsteps overhead and look up through the tiny crack and see Luca. He is standing directly above me.

"Luca! Help me!"

He doesn't even flinch. He can't hear me. Alexander was right—the floor, or ceiling for me, is soundproof. I cry out in frustration. If I could only get something to at least beat against it.

Then I realize the stairs beneath me are wooden. Like wooden planks. But they are thick. I push all the doubt and negativity from my mind and begin punching at the wood, ignoring the pain shooting through my fist. Luca is standing no less than two feet above me. I am going to make him hear me.

Chapter 38

Luca

"This way, sir." Alexander's maid is leading me through the dark halls of his home. *Miserable* doesn't even begin to describe how I feel. And walking through this guy's home makes it even worse. I have never met someone that lacks such … personality.

Alexander and I grew up together, and we hate each other—that's a fact. He isn't a part of the Mafia, but he does play a huge part in all our wars. He is a dirty bastard that likes to see people fall. Including my family. He has been behind countless schemes that have had to do with us being set back.

We checked the surveillance footage and found nothing, but we did get a list of people that were at that auction, and Alexander is one of them. I pray he doesn't have Elise. He is known for brutality. Not just to people, but to the women he owns. He is merciless. More often than not sending them to the hospital. I have to calm my breathing. Just thinking of him laying a finger on her makes my blood boil.

As I make my way to his office, I look around me to see if there is anything out of place. Any indication that she is here.

The door to his office is cracked, and I step in. He is waiting for me, standing in front of his desk. A smile that doesn't reach his eyes appears on his face.

"Hello, Mr. Pasquino. I see you still haven't acquired any manners."

I roll my eyes at his tone.

"To what do I owe the pleasure of this visit?"

"I'm sure you've heard. My wife has been kidnapped." I watch his reaction. He doesn't even flinch. He clicks his tongue at me.

"You should be more cautious with your wife, Luca. You know this is a dangerous world we live in." He has a look of amusement on his face. I want to punch him so bad.

"She was in that auction you were at about two months ago. Did you happen to see her? Or anyone that bought her?"

He cocks his eyebrow as if in thought. "No."

I can feel my anger flaring at his blatant lie. I have to calm myself down. If I blow it, then Elise's whereabouts will slip right through my fingers. I decide to bluff.

"Really? Well, we know you were one of the contenders of the private auction."

He shrugs his shoulders. "So? Why don't you go ask the other contenders? I wasn't the only one there."

I bite my jaw in irritation. "We are. I have my men at the others' homes as we speak."

He leans on the desk, crossing his arms. "Are you sure you can trust your family, Luca? I mean, it was your family that helped that traitor Stefano almost kill you. Can't say I'm not disappointed." He smiles at me. If there was ever a time I needed to keep my temper in check, now would be it. I have to keep reminding myself that this is for Elise. He gets a look in his eye as he senses my irritation.

"You know, now that I think of it, I did see your wife." His smile grows wider as he speaks. "You should have seen her there. With that dark-red lingerie on. She did look good enough to fuck. I did try to buy her, but someone else paid a heavier price. Seems they wanted her even with your god-awful name carved into her milky flesh."

He laughs, pushing himself off the table.

"Too bad I couldn't get ahold of her. I would have enjoyed beating her within an inch of her life."

I don't even think; I am flying toward him. I love the feeling of my fist smashing into the side of his face. As he stumbles, I press my forearm into his throat and pull my gun out, pressing the steel against his forehead, the rage I have been fighting so hard to keep contained blowing up.

"If I fucking find out you had anything to do with her being taken away from me, I will fucking find you and kill you in the worst way possible."

His eyes flash beyond my shoulder toward the ground and back up to mine, a cruel smile creeping onto his face. "Well, let's hope you find her before anything bad happens."

There is blood coming out of his mouth, and I can see a bruise already forming on his cheek where I punched him. I glare at him one more second before pushing off him roughly and walking to exit the room. I keep looking for any signs or clues, but nothing stands out.

I yank the door, and it slams behind me as I leave the office. Then I hear a banging. Just three hard hits that come from within the office. They sound muffled through the door. I turn around and stare at the door. He must be angry from me attacking him and hit his desk or wall out of frustration. As quickly as it starts, the sound stops. I walk past the dining room, remembering my way out. I glance in there as I see a body moving. It's the maid. She is clearing the plates from the table. As in *two* plates. Hmmm.

I open the door, stepping out into the cold. The fucking bastard lives up in the mountains, away from everyone. So if there is something he is hiding, he is in the perfect place for it. I step into my car, driving away. I have a feeling he is hiding something. Pretty soon I will have to leave this search to my men, because I have to resume my duties as capo. That is the last thing I want to do. I have to find Elise.

Chapter 39

Elise

Bang bang bang.

"Luca, please!" I am shouting in desperation and pain.

My hand is bloodied and filled with splinters. It is also throbbing in unbearable pain. I am pretty sure the bone is chipped or something. I slam the wood against the ceiling above my head. I can only pray that Luca can hear me. The hatch to the trapdoor opens quickly, and I breathe a sigh of relief. Which immediately turns into fear. Alexander opens the hatch. He looks at the missing step and at me in irritation. I then notice there is a bruise forming on his cheek.

"You almost had him." He smiles at me. He steps down into the room, and when he gets close to me, he yanks the plank out of my hand. He looks ready to throw it, but then he pauses as he looks at it and gets an idea. His gaze travels down my body to my hand.

"Wow, you went through a lot of trouble to get this done, didn't you?" He laughs at my predicament.

Tears of frustration fill my eyes, and I look back at him with hate in my gaze.

"Luca is going to find out you kept me hidden here, and he's going to kill you slowly, and painfully."

He looks at me for a moment before rubbing his jaw.

"Funny, your husband said the same thing." His eyes travel to the shackle around my wrist, which is now burning and seeping blood. A slow smile spreads its way across his face.

"How about we make good use of that shackle?"

* * * * *

Alexander likes to keep me literally near him at all hours of the day. When he conducts business in his office, when he showers, when he eats. Even if he is just reading a book, he makes me sit near him. He always watches me. He even forces me to eat. I lost all hope when Luca left. He didn't hear me. If I had been a second earlier, he would have been in the room and I would have been saved when he heard me banging against the ceiling. Now that he's come here, I have no hope of him coming back through.

I stand in the bathroom, looking at myself in the mirror. I have gotten smaller. I look sick. There are hideous welts and bruises all over my skin. There are bandages around my hand from beating it bloody, trying to break that plank to hit against the ceiling. I drop my gaze to my stomach. There is a tiny bulge there. If I didn't know what is going on, I would think it is a fat bulge from eating, but it isn't. It's a baby. My baby. I slowly bring a hand to my stomach, rubbing over the small life that is now growing inside of me.

Not only do I have myself to worry about, but my unborn child as well. I have no idea how I am going to protect him or her when I can barely protect myself.

I jump, as there is a loud bang on the door.

"Elise, you've been in there long enough." Alexander's voice comes through. I quickly open the door, and he is standing right in the doorway.

"Can I please have some actual clothes to wear? I'm starting to show," I ask. I keep my eyes trained on the floor; I don't want to look into his evil face. I am tired of walking around half-naked. I tried once to wear one of his shirts, and that is a big no-no.

I feel his fingers under my chin, and he roughly jerks my face up to meet his gaze.

"Don't look away when speaking to me. I thought we already went over that."

A shiver runs up my spine. We have. And just thinking about that punishment makes me want to vomit. He grabs me by the arm, walking me into his bedroom. He closes the door behind him, engulfing us in darkness.

"Wait, Alexander, I'm sorry. I shouldn't have asked. Please don't hurt me." I am quaking in fear.

He doesn't make a sound. I suddenly feel him behind me, running his hands down my body. He pushes my hair out of the way and drops kisses on my throat.

"You want clothes? You're going to have to earn them."

I feel pressure on my shoulder and slowly begin to kneel as he pushes me to the ground. My eyes widen as I realize what it is he wants. I immediately jump up from the floor.

"No!" No sooner have the words left my lips than I feel his hand around my throat.

"What did you fucking say to me?"

I struggle as hard as I can to get the words out. "I … said … no …" I feel the rush of air and land hard on the bed. Before I can move, he is crawling on top of me.

As I lie in bed that night with the pain of new bruises, I feel anger boiling up inside of me. Alexander has his arms wrapped around me, keeping me pulled into his front. All this because I asked for a pair of clothes. It was a reasonable question. All the men in this world are the same. Crazy, lust-driven monsters. I will be damned if I let my child be born and raised in this house. I am going to get out of here. No matter what. For the sake of my unborn child.

* * * * *

Survival—It's something I've never had to do really. I've just existed. I would just beg and try to stay out of the way. But now is the time for me to be brave and stop depending on other people. I never speak; I just listen and do what Alexander says. I can't put my child at risk by angering him. The thing is that he never leaves the house. He is always here. And he doesn't trust me enough to roam around by myself. Even when I go to the bathroom, he shows up, telling me I am taking too long.

So on the rare occasions he lets me stay in my own room, I sacrifice sleep to scope out this place. I only need to find the cars, the keys, and the things I can use as a weapon. He has no guards, and only two people work here. The maid and the cook. I never see the cook. And the maid tries to steer clear of me all the time. Even if I can get something of his, I will have to hide it in a room, because he only lets me wear lingerie. I can't hide it anywhere on my body.

I also start to take notes of Alexander's habits. He works on things some days, and some days he just relaxes. He never does anything on the same schedule. The only time he ever lets his guard down is when he is asleep next to me. Killing him is going to be the hardest thing I will ever have to do. Nearly impossible. But if I want to get out of here, I will have to make it work.

Chapter 40

Elise

Three. He keeps three guns in his bedroom. Under the bedside table, under the bed, and in his clothes drawer. The dining room always has a knife. Just one. A knife and a fork. Set out for me to eat with. His office has four guns in it. One underneath the desk, one inside the bookcase, one under the windowsill, and one he keeps on him. The bathroom has no weapons. These are the only rooms in the house I am in consistently. And the only one that he ever lets his guard down in with me is the bedroom.

As for keys to the car, they are located in his office, in the third drawer in the desk. If I am to escape, I will have to kill him then take the keys. Not only that, but I will have to ransack his closet for warm clothes. There is no way I am escaping in lingerie when it is snowing outside. This is by far the craziest plan I have ever implemented. But to protect the life now growing inside of me, I will have to grow up and make things happen on my own.

"Elise, you look so focused."

I look up, and Alexander is standing in front of me with a look of amusement on his face. I have been so focused on my thoughts I hadn't heard him enter the room. He is leaning against the doorframe, watching me intently.

"You're not planning to kill me, are you?" he says jokingly. He walks past me and into his closet, not waiting for a response. *If only he knew.*

He steps out of the closet in nothing more than a pair of shorts and no shirt. He crawls into bed closer to me, never breaking his gaze.

"Elise, you know I like it when you sleep naked," he says, his gaze moving down my body.

I almost cringe in disgust, but if there is something I've learned living with him, it's that showing my true emotions is *not* a good idea.

He traces a pattern on my arm, reaching around to undo the clasp of my bra. He reaches out to touch my breast, but I immediately flinch back.

"Please, Alexander. I'm really tired." I keep my gaze down so he can't see the true emotion in my eyes. He is silent as he studies me closely. I feel his fingers trace from my throat to my heart and back.

"Are you nervous about something, Elise?" His fingers guide my face up to meet his. "You're avoiding my gaze." He looks at me knowingly.

It is men like this that scare me to death. They can read emotions like it is nothing. Even when I do my best to hide them. I have gone over this plan in my head several times, but as we get closer and closer to it being time, I am having second thoughts. All the times I disobeyed Luca and made him angry flash in my head. The punishments, the torture I endured, and then living with this man. These are the types of men that if you are going to do something to escape, you have to implement it perfectly. Because if you screw up even a little bit, they will make you pay. I have the scars and bruises to prove it.

I meet Alexander's gaze head-on.

"I'm just tired."

A smirk crosses his lips as he turns off the lamp, plunging the room into darkness. I feel his hands on me, and he begins to whisper in my ear.

"Well, I'm not."

* * * * *

It takes everything in me to stay awake. Alexander never gets tired. I haven't even the slightest idea what time it is. He doesn't care when I beg him to stop. He doesn't care when I cry in pain. He loves it, and it drives him more. Even if I try to stay silent, he will do everything in his power to make me scream. His breathing evened out a long time ago, and I stay still to make sure he is in an even deeper sleep. I can feel the dried tears on my face from him being so rough. This is what fuels me out of my fear.

I slowly move out of the bed, careful not to disturb him. Men in this business are light sleepers. So even the tiniest thing can wake him up. Which is why I need to act fast. Once I am out of the bed, I immediately begin to feel under the bedside table. But the gun isn't there. Only the clip that usually holds it into place. I try not to panic as I move to feel under the bed. I breathe in relief when I feel the gun.

I press it to make sure the safety is off. I stand and aim the gun at Alexander's sleeping form. As soon as I can, I squeeze the trigger.

Click.

Oh god.

Click click click.

Tears of frustration begin to well up in my eyes. The same deafening sound I heard when I aimed that gun at Luca's head, I am hearing it now. Over and over.

A deep chuckle sounds in the darkness. I gasp and take a step back. Alexander sits up in the bed and turns on the lamp, illuminating the room. My heart pounds at a thousand miles an hour as he aims a gun at me.

I step back wide-eyed and frightened as hell.

"You never fail to amuse me. You think I don't know what's going on? Elise, you are like an open book. When you're planning something, I can see it. I know what's happening, and I gave you the chance. I moved the gun under the table so that you would realize the error of your ways. But it's obvious that you wanted to kill me."

He cocks the gun in his hand.

"At least I got one last fuck out of you. I can't wait to see the look on Luca's face when he finds your impregnated body floating in the river."

The gears in my head are turning a mile a minute, the plan I had in my head all going to shit. I hadn't thought this through well enough. Then an idea comes to me. Before he can pull the trigger, I throw the gun in my hand with all my might at his head. I don't even stay to see if it hits him; I sprint into the bathroom just as I hear the sound of his gun going off and slam the door behind me, locking it.

A split second later, he is banging on the door, screaming at me. I could just pull my hair out. I am such an idiot! Why the fuck did I run into the fucking bathroom? I should have taken off out the door! There are absolutely no weapons in here. I frantically look around as he charges into the door once again, causing it to rattle. Shower curtain, toothbrushes, hair products. But there is nothing in here to defend myself with!

"Dammit!" I shout, punching the wall.

That's it. I go to the mirror and glance at my battered, bloodied, and bruised body. Using all the strength I can muster, I smash my fist into the mirror, ignoring the pain of the skin around my knuckles being shredded from the impact of the glass. Shards fall everywhere, and I pick up the sharpest-looking ones, ignoring the pain of the glass cutting through the skin of my palms. I stand ready at the door as Alexander continues to beat on it. I close my eyes, taking a deep breath.

The door splinters open, and in comes Alexander with crazed eyes. I don't hesitate; I charge at him with the glass in hand, letting all the anger and pain I have been feeling fuel me. I cut at his wrists and chest and legs. I hear the clatter of the gun as I slice through his flesh. I stab him deep in his gut, dragging the glass across the bottom of his stomach. Blood is spilling and splattering on me like a waterfall. When Alexander collapses in pain, I grab the gun off the floor and sprint to the closet. I find an oversize shirt and roll up a pair of his pants about five times as fast as I can. I peep out of the closet, and he is still on the floor, trying to hold his intestines in place. I grab his large coat off the hanger and place it over my body. I am sweating now, but once I step outside, I will be cold. I quickly tiptoe over his body toward the door but pause and look back at him. He sounds as if he is suffocating.

I stand over his body with the gun in hand, and he opens his eyes, staring at me in agony. His breathing is shallow. I slowly raise the gun, aiming it at him. There is blood seeping from my hands where the glass has cut me from holding it too tight. It's dripping over the gun and into the floor.

"You know what? I want to hear you beg." I cock the gun at him. "Beg me, Alexander."

He narrows his eyes at me, and I take that as his not wanting to say anything to me. I squat down next to him and place the gun right next to his temple.

"I said, fucking beg!" I don't feel an ounce of pity as I stand over him. His breathing is coming out in uneven pants. He opens his mouth.

"F-fuck you." His words come out muffled.

I give him the sweetest smile I can muster. "That's not begging."

I am about to pull the trigger when I experience a sharp pain. I recognize the pain instantly. Alexander must have shot me when I ran into the bathroom. But it feels like a graze. I have to get out of here before I lose too much blood. I look back at him.

"A quick death would be too merciful for you."

I tuck the gun away in the pocket of the massive coat and sprint out of the room to find the keys.

* * * * *

I jump into the car that the key I've grabbed onto is for. It is a big SUV. My breathing is hard, and I can barely see. Probably from all the blood loss. And now that the adrenaline is no longer pumping through my veins, the pain I am feeling is excruciating. I need to get to a hospital fast. I start the engine and speed out of the garage to my freedom. I am so glad Alexander doesn't keep people guarding his home.

The fight to stay awake is so hard. I am losing so much blood that I can feel it soaking the clothes. The snow outside is thick, and I can't drive as fast as I want to. I have to think about the safety of my child. I crank up the heat because I am growing so cold. I don't know how long I have been driving for, but my eyes are getting more and more heavier by the second. As hard as I try, my eyes eventually close on their own accord.

A violent shaking wracks me from my sleep. I am jolted awake, and I can feel even more pain exploding over my body. I look up, and the front of the car is smashed into a tree. I passed out and wrecked the car. I've wrecked my only chance at escaping! The glass around me is shattered, and I can feel blood trickling down my forehead. I open the door and look around me. Snow. There is snow everywhere.

I jump back in the car, but it won't start. Dammit! I hit the steering wheel in frustration. I have to survive. I have to get out of here for not just me but my baby as well. But I am losing more and more blood by the second. My struggle to stay awake is a stark reminder of that.

I have to get somewhere. I trudge through the knee-deep snow, making sure to get off the road just in case anything happens. I don't know how long I have been walking, but my breathing is becoming a struggle. The snow behind me is tinted pink from all the blood I am losing. So this is it, then. This is how I am going to die. Walking through the snow in some bastard's clothing, trying to protect my child when I can't even protect myself. I can feel the tears of frustration begin to well up, but I blink rapidly, trying to push them back. I have to be strong. The world around me is swaying bad. Not only that, but it is also becoming blurry. Before I can think of anything else, I fall face-first into the thick snow, passing out.

* * * * *

There is a fire. I can smell the wood burning. I slowly open my eyes, and an excruciating headache begins pounding at my skull. My head feels so heavy.

I look around the room I am in. It is small and cozy. There is carpet on the floor, and directly in front of the bed is the fireplace with a TV mounted on the wall. The windows are open, and I can see the snow falling outside, which means I am still somewhere in the mountains. I look at my arms and hands to see them engulfed in bandages. I reach up and touch my forehead, and there is a bandage over the scar I received from wrecking the car. I am still in the same clothes, but my jacket is gone, which means so is the gun.

The door to the room is cracked open. Where the hell am I? What is going on? I look around the room for the coat because it has my only weapon in it. I slowly get out of bed and walk to the cracked door. I pull it open slowly and walk up the hallway.

The smell of bacon wafts to me. And I am starving. I step out of the hallway, which reveals a nice little living room that overlooks the kitchen. And in the kitchen is a man. He is turned around, focusing on cooking. He has light-brown hair, and that is all I can see from here. But he does have a nice build. He turns quickly, as if sensing my presence, and pauses when he sees me.

I stare him down untrustingly. He slowly raises his hands in the air.

"I mean you no harm. I was just out going for a walk when my dog picked up your scent." He is looking at me with wide eyes that I notice are a dark blue. Like the ocean.

I open my mouth to speak, but the headache is too much and I sway on my feet.

He rushes over to me, helping me take a seat on the couch.

"Whoah, there. You shouldn't be up with your injuries."

I jerk away from his touch, and he flinches back at my abruptness. "Who are you? Where am I?"

"My name is Eli. You're in the mountains in my cabin."

I jump in fear at the mention of being in the mountains still.

"I'm still in the mountains? Oh god, I have to get out of here."

I am pretty sure I look like a crazy person whispering to myself. I have no idea if Alexander is dead or alive. If I am still in the mountains, he can come after me at any moment. I have to get out of here. I look frantically at Eli. I can feel myself beginning to hyperventilate, and I begin frantically running my hands through my hair in fear.

"Wait, miss, just calm down," Eli begins, but I can't hear him.

Fear has enveloped me completely. I feel hands over mine and am pulled out of my panic as I stare into a pair of deep-blue eyes. He is speaking to me, but I can't hear him. It is like my head has been submerged underwater.

"Just breathe …" His voice breaks through, and he slowly breathes in with me, trying to get me to calm down. Tears are welling up in my eyes and falling down my face. I have risked so much. I've come too far to be caught.

"Look, I found you outside barely alive. Judging by the scars and bruises you had, I figured you were running from someone. And knowing who lives up the mountain, I'd say I made a pretty good decision by saving you. I was going to call the police, but they won't be able to make it up the mountain in this weather—"

"No! No police," I interrupt him. If there's one thing I know, it's that the police can't be trusted. It's the justice system that got me into this mess in the first place.

He raises his hands again as if in surrender. "Okay, okay, no police." He watches me with careful eyes, but I don't say anything at all. I just need to think.

"Where's my coat?" I ask quickly.

He points toward the door, and there is a rack with coats on it. "Right there," he says. "Look, why don't you just go take a shower? I have some clothes around here somewhere that you could fit, and when you're done, I'll change your bandages and we'll get you some food. Okay?"

I eye him skeptically. "How do I know I can trust you?" I ask him wearily.

He gives me a confused smile. "Ma'am, if I was trying to kill you, I would have done it a long time ago. Where I'm from, if somebody is in need, you help them out." He stands from his seat and offers me his hand. I lightly take it, and he leads me up the hallway to the bathroom.

"You can go ahead and shower. I'll leave you something to wear on the toilet." He then exits the bathroom.

I turn on the shower, letting the steam waft in the bathroom as I take each of the bandages off. I strip my clothing and stare at my body in the mirror. Hideous bruises litter my skin, as well as cuts. I look at my palms, and they look as if they need stitching. They sting in pain as I take the bandage off, because the gauze has crusted to the wounds. I slowly peel back all the bloodied bandages, cringing in pain each time one is dried to my scabs. I check the sweatpants for any blood or signs that I've lost the baby and smile in joy when there is nothing there. I slowly rub my hands over the area that is now elevated with the life growing inside of me. Tears of joy fill my eyes and spill over.

"Yes!" I squeal in happiness. I jump up and down and do a little happy dance naked in the middle of the bathroom. I am just glad I am free. Free at last. On my own accord. I've saved myself. I've saved my child. I've done it all on my own. I've fucking done it.

"Yes, yes, yes!"

I push all my hair back away from my face as I step under the hot spray. Even though it is stinging all my open cuts and sores, I am happy. Beyond that. I don't have to worry about anyone coming in the bathroom unwelcomed to have sex with me. I eventually just sit in the shower and let the steaming spray wash all the dirt off. Due to the fact that my hands are sliced open, I can't put any soap or shampoo in them.

I turn off the water and step out, grabbing the towel that is waiting for me on the sink. After I put on my clothes, I step out into the hallway, making my way back to the kitchen. Just as I enter, Eli is stepping toward the table with a plate of pancakes and eggs. He smiles when he sees me. But it isn't that possessive smile that Luca has or that sadistic smile that Alexander has. It is a genuine smile. That he is glad I am in the room.

"Nice to see you. I was beginning to think you fainted in the shower," he jokes with me. He walks to the counter, pulling out a metal box and sitting down at the table, pulling a chair out in front of him. He pats the top of the chair.

"Come."

I slowly walk toward him, brushing off the uneasiness I feel from him giving that command. He takes out a needle, and I can see that he is going to stitch me up. I sit in front of him.

"So your hands were pretty bad. I couldn't stitch them earlier because they were dirty and you needed to clean them. A shower is just what you needed." He gives me a warm smile, but I don't return it. Why is he being so nice to me?

I hold out my hands to him, and he begins the stitching. I hiss in pain as he does it.

"I'm sorry, miss. If I had any sedatives here, trust me, I'd let you have one."

"Elise," I say.

He looks up, startled at me speaking. "Excuse me?" he asks in confusion.

"My name is Elise."

A warm smile slowly spreads its way onto his face. "Nice to be of service, Elise."

We eat the food in silence, but it isn't a fearful silence. It is comfortable. And I am starving. I eat about five pancakes and drink several glasses of milk. Eli watches me carefully the whole time.

"So what's a girl like you doing all the way out here? Looking the way you do, no less?" he asks, genuinely curious.

I slowly set my fork down as an uneasiness washes over me. "I was sold. To the highest bidder," I whisper quietly. "I finally worked up the nerve to escape on my own, and almost did, but I lost too much blood. Which is how I wrecked and passed out." A lump forms in my throat.

"I'm so sorry," Eli's voice comes through. "Look, I really appreciate your hospitality, but I've got to get going. I need to get out of here."

"I swear I'm not trying to keep you here, but we're expecting a storm coming in. It's actually, in a way, a good thing that you stumbled upon me, because if you kept driving, you might not have ended up in a good place. The drive to get down the mountain takes a while, so the storm would have caught you." He is watching me with genuine concern in his eyes. "I can tell you've been through something big. But my cabin is all but remote. No one can find it, and that's the way I like it. You're safe here. So you can stay here as long as you like. I'm always willing to help someone in need. Once the storm passes, I can take you into town." He smiles at me.

I slowly nod. "Why are you doing this for me? You don't even know me," I ask, genuinely confused by his hospitality.

"Like I said, where I come from, it's a sin not to help those in need." He stands from the table and grabs my plate along with his, clearing it. "You can go get some rest. I know you're probably exhausted."

I stand and nod wearily. Just before I head to my room, though, I step to the door, grabbing my jacket. I look in the pocket, and my heart jumps when the gun isn't there.

I look at him accusingly, and he is watching me intently with a look of focus.

"Looking for the gun?" he asks.

I nod frantically as I watch him through narrowed eyes. A small smile plays at his lips as he walks to the living room and opens one of the drawers, revealing my gun. He takes it out.

"You don't have to tell me now, or ever, for that matter. But I know you've been through something big. Especially since you were bloodied in the snow with this." He holds the gun out to me, and I take it immediately, checking the bullet chamber. I relax when I see the bullets in there. I look up and see Eli looking at me in amusement.

"You can sleep with it if it'll make you feel better. Just please don't try to kill me in my sleep," he says, walking away.

I quickly head to my room, closing the door behind me and locking it. I crawl into the soft, plush bed, pulling the covers up to my chin and setting the gun underneath the pillow next to me.

I don't know why this stranger is being so nice to me, but I will have to accept his hospitality for the time being. He is literally all I have right now. I stare at the fire crackling in the fireplace, and eventually, my eyes grow heavy. I finally let a peaceful sleep overcome me.

Chapter 41

Luca

"How could none of you find her? She's one fucking person!" I shout, throwing the papers across the room. My office is messy. The desk is overturned, computer smashed, papers askew everywhere.

People are standing around me in fear. Fucking good. It's as if she disappeared off the face of the Earth. We can't fucking find her! I pull out my gun, walking to the nearest person and pressing it to their temple.

"Know what I think? I think we could use some goddamn motivation!" I shout.

"Luca!" I pause as Matteo steps into the room. He has just saved this man's life. Matteo holds the phone out to me. "It's for you," he says.

I growl out loud in irritation, "Tell them I don't want to fucking talk!"

Matteo steps farther into the room. "I think you may want to take this one." I notice the tone of his voice and look up at him. His face looks as if he has seen a ghost.

I yank the phone from his grasp.

"Everyone get out!" I bark at everyone in the room. They immediately take off out of the room. Even Matteo tries to leave, but I grab him by the collar, forcing him to stay.

"What?" I say into the phone.

"Uh, Luca …?" There is a woman's timid voice on the other end. I swear, if Matteo interrupted me for a washed-up whore's attentions, I am going to be very upset.

"Yeah, and who the fuck is this?" I say, irritated.

"This is Lucinda, your father's last, uh, mistress before his passing," she says, as if I'm supposed to know her. I don't know half the whores my father has screwed.

"Okay, what the fuck do you want?"

"It's about your wife, Elise. I was with her in the auction."

My irritation evaporates as pure anxiety and fear rush through me. She doesn't wait for a response before she continues.

"I'm so sorry for waiting this long to contact you, but the last man that had me didn't allow phone calls, so this is the first time I've been able to get one."

She is whispering, so I am guessing she is doing this against someone's orders.

"I saw who took Elise. She was sold last in the auction, but I caught a glimpse of the man that bought her before he went to his car." She is cut off as a man's voice comes in the background. "Yes, sir, I'll be just a moment!" she shouts, probably to her new owner.

"I gotta go. It was Alexander Croff who took her. I really hope you find her, Luca. She was really scared before she was bought. And she told me to call you when I got the chance. Good luck! I hope you're not too late," she hastily whispers before she hangs up the phone.

I stand in the middle of the room in shock, not knowing how to feel. Alexander has her. He had her this whole time, and he smugly lied to my damn face. He had her, and I was there. She was in the same house as me, and I hadn't even known it.

I can feel my rage boiling up to the surface. I turn to Matteo.

"Ready my room in the catacombs!" I growl to Matteo.

I hastily step out of the room. Romelo is right on my heels, as well as Nicolai. The catacombs are where I do all my killings. Where I torture and drain the life from my enemies and victims. And Alexander is going to be my next victim. The smug bastard has had my wife the whole time.

There is no telling how much abuse Elise has endured at his hands. A horrible feeling makes me sick to my stomach just thinking about it. Elise. *I hope I'm not too late.*

"Luca, what's going on?" Romelo asks behind me.

I don't even turn around to respond.

"Alexander has her. He had her the whole time."

Romelo is silent. He doesn't have to say anything more. He knows what I am thinking. I have to get to Elise. And I am going to murder that bastard. In the worst way I know how. And I am going to fucking love every single second of it.

Chapter 42

Elise

"Rocco, get down!" I look up as Eli shouts at his dog for what seems like the thousandth time now. Rocco is a golden Lab with the most energy I have ever seen in a dog.

The storm has been going on for three days. I met Eli's dog the next morning of my being here, and he absolutely loves being near me. I think it's because he can sense the hormone levels in my body and that there's currently a baby brewing inside of me. He even comes to my room and sleeps on the end of my bed.

"It's okay, he just wants some love." I smile at Eli.

Eli has been nothing short of a gentleman since I've been here, and I actually believe him when he says he wants nothing but to help me. I sometimes catch him watching me, but not in a lustful way. There is pity in his eyes. He's the one that tends to my scars and bruises, and each time he does that, I can see the pity lurking beneath his eyes. I don't want his pity.

I want this storm to stop so I can get off this mountain. I need to see a doctor as soon as possible to check for any problems I may have due to my time with Alexander.

Rocco finally settles comfortably at my feet and lays his head down. Eli sits next to me, smiling apologetically.

"Sorry, he's never really been a people person until you."

I smile back at him. "I guess I just have a way with dogs."

He rolls his eyes as he sits next to me on the couch. The room falls silent as I continue to pet Rocco, but then Eli breaks the silence after a moment.

"You know, how you said you were sold … to the highest bidder …?"

I stop my petting and look at him. "Yes."

"I … I was just wondering, were you being serious?"

I look up at him and see the curiosity lurking within his eyes. "Yes."

He sits back on the couch in disbelief. "How did you even get in that situation?" he asks.

I give a bitter laugh.

"My husband is a very powerful man, and many people would love to have even the slightest opportunity to see him fall."

"Oh. So you're married?"

I look at Eli, realizing I let something like that slip. He regards me with careful eyes.

"Yes."

"Then why not just call your husband and tell him you're okay?"

I sit in silence as I try to think of a way to answer his question. I can feel the anger brewing up within me. He's speaking as if I'm choosing to sit in this cabin and not let anyone know that I am okay.

"You know, my father's name was Eli."

Eli looks confused with the sudden change in conversation. "Oh, really? Well, where is he now?"

I let out another bitter laugh. "Dead. My husband killed him." I look at Eli and see the shock evident on his face. I give him a sarcastic smile.

"That's why I won't call him. Because if he came here and saw you, you would be dead before I had the chance to explain your role in my being here."

The room is silent once again. I then realize what I just said to the man that's been going above and beyond to help me out these past few days. I look over at him, reaching out to place a hand on his shoulder.

"Oh my gosh, Eli, I'm so sorry. That came out so wrong."

He shakes his head in disbelief.

"No, it's okay. That's my fault for prying."

He gets up, walking toward the door without looking back toward me. Rocco perks his head up and stands to run to his owner. The door slams shut behind them, leaving me alone in the cabin.

I step out of the hot shower, wrapping a towel around me. Eli still isn't back. Either he got lost in the storm or he left the cabin in fear of his life. Either way, I blame myself for causing him to go. I shouldn't have said what I said to him. All the bitter anger I have towards Luca and his line of work has boiled to the surface, causing me to lash out at Eli for no good reason. Maybe it's because he suggested I call my husband and it angered me that he wants me to when my husband is borderline psychotic.

I step into the bedroom I have been staying in, pushing the door to crack open. I put on a pair of shorts, and as I am pulling my top on, I hear a loud gasp in the doorway.

"Oh god."

I yank my shirt down as fast as I can and look in shock as I see Eli standing in the doorway with his hand around Rocco's collar. But his eyes are trained on me. They are wide with shock.

"I … I'm so sorry. Rocco saw the cracked door and pushed his way in. I'm so sorry." He is looking everywhere but at me.

I walk angrily to the door, slamming it shut. Hard.

When I finally decide to emerge from the room, Eli is in the kitchen, making what I assume is dinner. Rocco's ears perk up as he hears me enter. A whine leaves his lips, and Eli turns around, his gaze falling on me, and he immediately turns away.

"I just made some soup tonight." His voice has lost all buoyancy that it used to have. I don't respond as I take a seat in the chair. Minutes later, he sets a bowl in front of me and sits down across from me.

We sit in silence, only the clank of our silverware making noise. I decide to break my silence.

"What did you see?" I ask.

He looks up from his soup. "Well, let's just say I know you're eating for two and someone named Luca decided to use your flesh as a drawing board," he says.

I give a small laugh at his sarcasm.

"Who could possibly do that to you? I mean, to an innocent woman?"

I poke at the vegetables floating in my soup. "My husband," I say.

"Your husband did that to you?? Why would he do something so ... brutal?" he asks in disbelief.

"My husband is the most powerful man in the United States. Maybe even the world. He's the capo. The don. He's the head of the northern half of the Mob in the Unites States." I keep my eyes trained down, afraid at what I may see when I look at Eli. "That was why I said what I did earlier. That's why I have to leave as soon as I can."

I look up at Eli, placing my hand over his.

"You are a breath of fresh air in the world I come from. I would hate to see you snatched from this world because of my husband. He will do it without hesitation."

Eli watches me with wide eyes.

"In the world we are born in, killing is just as common as walking. They do it every day. They train their sons to be killers so they can gain power and protect the family. My husband just doesn't understand the borderline of violence. He doesn't know where it ends."

"Why would you marry someone like that? You must've known what type of person he was."

I nod in agreement. "You're right. I did. But I had no choice. Our marriage was arranged. To form a stronger bond between families. He's grown some kind of unhealthy attachment to me. He loves me in his own sick way."

"Wait, if you were sold to the highest bidder ..." His eyes trail down to my stomach.

"No. This is his child. I was pregnant before that man up the mountain touched me. I've been trapped there for so long ..." I trail off. "I don't know why I'm telling you all this. You've known me for, what, three days? And here I am, pouring my heart out to you." I laugh nervously. But when I look at Eli, he isn't smiling. He looks troubled.

"What are you going to do once you leave here?"

I shrug my shoulders. "Find the nearest hospital."

He rolls his eyes.

"This is serious, Elise. I mean, if the man you married did that to your body, what's stopping him from hurting you and your unborn child? We have to get the police involved at least so you can have some kind of protection from him."

I shake my head vigorously.

"No. Luca owns half the police force. There's no way I would put my child's life in danger as to do something that would make Luca mad."

Eli opens his mouth to say something more, but I cut him off.

"Look, I appreciate what you've done for me, I really do, but Luca is someone you just can't win against. He has the whole world in the palm of his hands. Including this screwed-up justice system. I mean, how do you think I even got in this situation? There's no hiding from him. Besides, the whole world is out to get me. They want something that will make him weak. And that something is me. Especially now. So I'll be safer in his control, able to protect my child more than I would be on my own."

Eli's face shows that he clearly disagrees with me, but he says nothing more. And quite honestly, I don't care if he disagrees with me.

In the past, I may have agreed with him, but I have more than myself to look out for now. I have to think about the safety of my unborn child. If I just go anywhere, someone will recognize my face and try to use me and my child as leverage. The safest place for us is to be with Luca. I have no idea how he will act about me being pregnant, and quite honestly, I haven't thought about it since I've been here. But I know that I am going out on a limb here, and I am hoping he won't be batshit crazy once he finds out.

Chapter 43

Luca

If there ever is a time when I feel helpless, it is now. We have been at the bottom of this mountain for three days, waiting for this storm to pass. Even when the storm ends, we will have to wait for the snow-plows to clear the road before we can get up there. Everyone is steering clear of me, and I don't blame them. I hate the fact that Elise is up there at the mercy of Alexander.

"You know, no matter how long you stare at the window, the snow isn't going to let up." I tense as I hear Nicolai behind me. I turn to see him stepping into the room with an amused look on his face.

"Yeah, well, sitting and waiting doesn't seem to work too well for me," I say.

Nicolai chuckles softly and takes a seat.

"You know, I don't think I've ever seen you this nervous before. Not even a little bit."

I turn back to the window before I slap that smug grin off his face.

"The sooner this damn blizzard lets up, the better I'll feel."

The room is quiet for a moment before I feel myself break down. My thoughts are beginning to get to me. I walk over toward the liquor fridge, grabbing a small bottle of vodka out. I take a seat next to Nicolai, pulling the cap off and taking a small swig.

I welcome the burn as the liquid runs down my throat and calms my frazzled nerves. I look at Nicolai to see him watching me in confusion.

"I have never been frightened before, but right now, I am terrified. I'm terrified at what I might find when we head up that mountain. If Elise is even alive. Or if Alexander has something horrible waiting for me." I look at Nicolai, for once letting my emotions out from behind the door they are always locked behind.

"I, for once, am at the mercy of someone else."

Nicolai is silent, so I continue.

"The longer we're down here, the worse things might be for her. I know I've done some pretty bad things to her, but I never pretended to be someone I wasn't. I never said I was a good man. I never tried to be someone that I'm not. I never lied to her about who I was."

I look out the window again. As soon as I lay eyes on the snow, my irritation sets in again. Why did that woman have to wait so long before telling me about Elise? I bring the bottle to my lips, tipping back another shot.

"Whoa, slow down. You don't want to be wasted when we finally go rescue your wife," Nicolai says. I look at him, and he has a light smile on his face. "Look, I know you're scared, but we're close. We know where she is, and as soon as the storm lets up, we can go get her." He tries to reassure me.

"You don't understand …" I roughly yank my fingers through my hair, feeling a deep fear coiling up within me. "The last time I saw Elise, I told her about my hand in her mother's death." I hold my head in my hands, remembering the look of horror etched onto her face. The fear and need to get away from me. Far away from me. I don't think I have ever regretted anything in my life more than I do taking her mother away from her.

I never thought I would see her again. It was just a job. A test to show my father I am capable. I do my job and, in return, earn my father's respect. But fifteen years later, when I stepped into my father's office and he told me who he had chosen for me to marry, anger was the least of my feelings.

"You should have heard the fear in her voice on the phone before that car crashed. It's been giving me nightmares. If Alexander broke the little bit of life left in Elise, I don't know what I'm going to do." I tense as I feel Nicolai's hand on my shoulder.

"Luca, we were born to do one thing. Protect the family. And you have done a marvelous job at that. You protected not only the family but your family as well. Elise and Matteo. You spared them and saved their lives on several occasions. Elise may not understand it, because she lived a sheltered life from this world, but you must know deep down that even though you may not be a good man, you have done good things to protect her."

I look at him, not understanding where he is going with this.

"What I'm trying to say is, no matter what state Elise is in, I know you will do whatever it takes to make her feel safe. I honestly hadn't realized how serious you were about her until that crazy ex of yours showed up as my date to dinner." He gives a soft chuckle, remembering the event. I had some words for him after the fiasco, but he claimed he didn't know who the girl was.

"I remember you even referring to her as 'just another job,' but it's different now. And I know you're crazy about her. I know you have strong feelings for her. Otherwise, we wouldn't even be here."

"Sir." I look up to see Matteo in the doorway. "The storm has let up. They are sending snowplows, and we'll be able to go up by tomorrow."

I nod. He leaves the room. The last thing on my mind is sleep. I need to get up the mountain as soon as possible.

"This is my last chance, Nicolai. I've been neglecting my duties as capo, trying to find Elise myself. If I don't find her this time, it's over. I have to go back to my duties."

"We'll find her, Luca," he says. And I hope he is right.

* * * * *

We are driving up the mountain with the snow falling softly. Everyone is deathly quiet. They know that if Elise isn't up this mountain, there will be hell to pay. Nicolai is in the car with me, and Romelo and Matteo are in the car behind us along with the others. The closer we get to the top, the more rattled my nerves become. The drive to get there is about forty-five minutes. So I have to sit in the car and twiddle my thumbs.

"Can't you make this thing go faster?" I snap at Nicolai.

He gives a soft chuckle. "No. Unless you want me to drive us off the cliff."

I growl at his response. I know I am being unreasonable, but I don't care. That's why Nicolai decided to drive instead of me. If it were me driving, I would have caused us to wreck due to my impatience.

I am looking through my email when I hear Nicolai.

"Shit," he mumbles under his breath, and the car slows to a stop.

I raise my head to look out the windshield and see an expensive SUV crashed into the tree. There is snow piled up within it, and the only thing sticking out of the snow is the nose of the car. Whoever wrecked this did it before the blizzard. The windshield looks smashed from this angle.

I radio Romelo.

"You guys stay here and check the wreckage. We're going to head on up."

I don't wait for Romelo to respond, but I see his vehicle pull over in the snow. I can also see Matteo's irritation as he gets out of the car. As Nicolai tries to pull off, I stop him.

"Wait." I roll down the window and call out to Matteo.

"Matteo! Come on!" His head perks up, and he sprints to the vehicle. I look at Benji in the back seat. "You stay. Matteo's taking your spot." He doesn't hesitate as he steps out and lets Matteo hop in. As soon as he closes the door, we head up the rest of the way.

After what seems like forever, we finally reach the home of Alexander Croff. It makes me angry that the last time I was here, so was Elise. Damn. I should have been more thorough. I just thought he wouldn't be the fool to take her since he knows who I am. But my arrogance has caused her to slip through my fingers.

Nicolai shuts off the engine, and we all jump out of the car, guns ready.

I step to the door and knock, waiting for someone to open it. There is no way I can kick this massive oak door down. We'll have to get some heavy ammo to blow it down. After a moment, I knock again. I'm beginning to get irritated. The snow is biting at my face, causing it to sting in pain from the dramatic drop in temperature. Who chooses to live on a fucking mountain where there's snow everywhere?

The door slowly creaks open, and I see the old maid that let me in the last time. No wonder she looked so terrified the last time I was here. She knew good and damn well why I was here in the first place. And the fact that she helped in keeping my wife hidden … let's just say I don't have any plans on her living past sundown. As soon as she peeps her head out far enough, I bring my gun to her head. She immediately gasps.

"Open the door. If you warn him, I will tear off your legs and make you drag your pathetic body down the mountain."

She nods vigorously, opening the door. As soon as we step in, I bring my gun down, knocking her unconscious. She collapses in the entry area. I push the door open and motion for everyone to follow me inside.

"Fan out. If you find Alexander, do not kill him. Restrain him and get me. Your main objective is Elise."

Everyone nods in understanding and fans out in different directions.

Nicolai and Matteo stay by my side. I would rather have had Matteo stay down the mountain with the others and that wrecked car, but he is just as eager as I am to find his sister. His lack of experience makes him a liability, though, in this situation. Hopefully, Nicolai will cover him good if something happens.

We walk to the office that I was in when I met with Alexander the last time. I push the door open with my gun at ready and am disappointed when he's not in here. I turn to Matteo and Nicolai.

"Look around."

I walk toward the desk, pulling open drawers, finding no indication of Elise.

"Elise!" I shout.

Matteo and Nicolai jump and look at me in shock. *Never announce your presence to the enemy.* And I just shouted, letting him know where our location is if he is secretly watching us.

"Luca, I know you're frantic right now, but you need to just calm down. We'll find her, okay?" Nicolai is speaking to me as if I am a child. I am trying my best to not punch his face in.

Out of nowhere, I hear Matteo hunch over and vomit on the floor.

"What the fuck?" I say out loud but hurry over to where he is seated. At the desk with the computer screen on. I quickly round the corner to see what has him throwing up his lunch.

"Fuck." My words are the only sound in the room.

Elise is being beat with a belt that has jeweled indentations on it. I can see chunks of skin being literally beaten off her body from the belt. She is tied up and crying. I quickly press the next arrow, hoping it will just be security footage, but it isn't. Elise is tied up, and Alexander is choking her. I press the arrow, and there is more. She is bound in almost all of them. She is crying in all of them. She is being tortured in all of them. He is whipping her in some, and he is fucking raping her in all of them.

I can feel my anger boiling over. Gunshots echo throughout the room, and I am looking at the computer screen that now has holes in it. That's when I realize the gun I am holding is aimed at the computer screen. I shot the screen up in my rage.

"Boss."

"What!" I look up from the screen in rage at one of my men speaking to me in the doorway. He flinches as I shout at him, but I don't fucking care.

"We found him ..." He trails off.

I immediately walk from behind the computer toward the man, grabbing him by his collar and yanking him so close to me I can feel his hair tickling my forehead.

"Then fucking take me to him." My voice is deadpan and cold as I grit out my words to him. I let go, and he stumbles away from me with wide eyes.

"I want that desktop brought back with us," I say to no one in particular. But I know Matteo and Nicolai heard me. I follow my guy out of the room as he leads me to Alexander.

"Have you found Elise?" My voice echoes off the empty walls. I can tell by his posture and the way he tenses that he hasn't.

"No, sir."

He leads me down the hall and to a living room. I can see all my men circled around him, with guns aimed at him. I slowly walk around the couch he is seated on and am shocked, to say the very least, at what I see.

He looks like shit. Actually, he looks like fucking Frankenstein with all the stitches that cover his body. His eyes narrow at me. I stand in front of him, trying my hardest to filter the rage and hatred I have for this man. If I kill him now, I won't be able to make him pay for everything he has done to Elise.

I motion to everyone in the room. "Leave us. Your top priority is Elise." As they file out, I grab one by his arm. "Once Matteo gets here, I want you to send him in. Other than that, no one enters this room. Got it?" He nods with wide eyes.

They all close the door behind them, leaving me alone with the bastard that took my wife. I feel nothing but hate as I stare this man down. I want to kill him right now.

"Where is she?" I ask. The room is silent for a moment before a small chuckle escapes his lips.

"That's the question of the century."

I clench and unclench my fist, trying to calm myself. If I kill him now, I will never know where Elise is. I take the knife out of my back pocket, flipping it open.

"You don't look like you're in good-enough shape to fight me back, so I suggest you tell me where she is," I say again. He stares at me in silence, and I can feel my irritation getting the best of me.

"I knew you would come for me sooner or later. I just planned on having her dead body waiting for you when you arrived. Or we'd be long gone by the time you caught on. But she was as stubborn as a mule." He laughs, as if remembering something. He looks up at me with a sick glint in his eyes. "That's why I had her tied every time I fucked her."

I can't control myself. I lunge at him, about to plunge the knife right in his heart when someone grabs ahold of me. I struggle, but both Nicolai and Romelo are holding me down. Matteo is standing on the other side of me. They arrived just in time.

"This is what he wants. He wants you to kill him quickly, and then you'll have no lead on Elise. Calm down, Luca." It's Romelo's voice of reason that calms me out of my haze.

"I'm fine!" I jerk. They sit me in the chair, and Romelo walks closer to Alexander. "How'd you get those stitches?"

He studies them closely, not waiting for a response. He obviously already knows.

"They look fresh. Very thick scarring also. Like someone did that frantically. Not calculated, but in a panic."

I study the stitching. He's right. The stitches look horrid. Like something a two-year-old would scribble on a paper. The scabs underneath the stitches are dragged as well. As if someone was frantic. He didn't get those wounds from a professional.

"We found these in that car down the road." Romelo pulls out a set of keys, dangling them in the air. He points to a button. "Along with some blood in the seat."

"This works the garage. I'm assuming these are your keys." He tosses them at Alexander, who is watching him with anger behind his gaze. We got him.

"Elise isn't here, is she?"

Alexander doesn't budge; he still glares at Romelo with all the hate he can muster. I hear shuffling behind me and Matteo's irritated voice.

"I don't have time for this." Matteo stands in front of Alexander, taking a knife and ripping through the stitching across his chest, dragging open the wounds. Alexander cries out in pain and grabs Matteo's hand, twisting it, and a sickening snap echoes throughout the room. And now Matteo is crying out in pain.

"Fuck!" I jump up, as do Nicolai and Romelo.

Matteo is crying out in pain, and Nicolai grabs him back from Alexander. Romelo immediately goes to look at Matteo's wrist. I wrap my hand around Alexander's throat and squeeze as hard as I can, shoving him deeper into the couch he is sitting on. my intention was to restrain him, but as he claws at my hand, I don't let go, the darkness enveloping me. I squeeze even harder, thinking about all the things I saw him do to Elise on that video. How he tortured her.

His struggling becomes weaker and weaker. I can feel his pulse underneath my fingers becoming weaker and weaker. Suddenly, my body is jerked backward, and I watch in disappointment as Alexander hunches forward, coughing violently and holding his reopened wounds. He looks at me with hate.

"You know where she is? Dead. She's fucking dead. I killed her, slowly and painfully, and I made sure to leave nothing behind." He smiles at me, and I can feel my heart sinking. He has to be lying.

"I will never forget the sound of her screams as she begged me to spare her. Her cries as I ripped her apart slowly and painfully."

I can't move. I can't bring myself to do anything. He is lying. I won't believe it. I refuse to.

"You should have seen the fear in her eyes. It's something that will keep me smiling in my dreams for a long time." And he laughs. He fucking laughs.

Out of nowhere, Romelo's fist collides with Alexander's face, knocking him instantly into unconsciousness.

Everyone is quiet. No one dares make a sound. She is not dead. She is not. She can't be. He is lying. He has to be.

"Luca, don't listen to him. He's just trying to get you riled up because he knows she's alive somewhere. She must have escaped. We're going to test the blood in the car to see if it's hers," he says.

"Go get the maid," I say. "We're going to interrogate her until she wishes she were dead."

They exit the room. I see Matteo still in the corner, cradling his broken wrist. We have to get that set before it starts healing.

I walk toward him in silence, standing over him. He looks up at me, and I stare back. I bring my hand out quickly, striking him across his face. He cries out in pain, and before he can think, I grab his shirt, pulling him close to me.

"If you ever pull some shit like that again, I will send you away to boarding school. You are not a professional, you are not even in this profession. He could have killed you and taken your weapon. You could have killed him before we got information, and you set off a chain of events that could've ended badly." I let go of his shirt, and he stumbles backward.

"We need to get your wrist set." I step out of the room, not waiting for a response.

I'm not entirely convinced if Elise is alive or not, but I hope more than anything that she is.

I step into the hallway and see Nicolai messing with the desktop of the computer.

"I'm going to find another screen to connect this to. There could be more film on Elise. Maybe we'll find a clue about her whereabouts on film."

I nod. In my anger, I shot the screen. Luckily, I didn't shoot the desktop, because we would have been screwed if I did.

I nod as everyone begins setting up shop. We aren't leaving here until we have some kind of lead on where my wife is.

Chapter 44

Luca

I look at the woman in front of me. She's older, obviously. I can't believe this woman sat there as my wife was tortured and beaten. And she didn't say or do anything to prevent it. According to her, so far, she treated Elise's wounds. She knew who Elise was, yet she did nothing to contact me.

"So what exactly happened?" I repeat to her.

She is shaking in the seat and keeps looking back and forth between me and Romelo.

"Don't look at him. I'm the one you need to worry about right now. Elise is *my* wife." I speak to her with cold words, and she flinches at my tone.

"Now, tell me what happened."

"I … I don't know. I just found Master Croff in the hallway with blood everywhere. He told me she attacked him with shards from the mirror."

I stand up, getting in her face. "Then where the fuck is she?" I shout. This bitch is wasting my time, and it is driving me crazy.

"We don't know, sir, we swear! There was no time to go out and search for her because I had to tend to Master Croff's wounds! And then the storm rolled in! That's all I know, I swear!"

I growl in irritation and leave the room, Romelo following closely behind me. After a moment of us walking, I hear a small chuckle from behind me. I immediately stop and turn, looking at Romelo.

"What the fuck is so funny?"

He immediately regains his composure. "I'm sorry, sir, it's just that she said Elise cut Alexander open like that using shards from the mirror."

After a moment of silence, a chuckle escapes my lips. I was so angry in there I didn't even register it. But Elise has did that damage to Alexander. My Elise. My timid and frightened Elise. It is shocking, to say the least, that such a small girl could do so much damage. But what's more shocking to me is that it was Elise that did that in the first place.

The same girl that threw up when we played Russian roulette and begged me not to do certain things to men I have tortured in front of her. The girl that freezes at the first sight of blood has nearly cut Alexander's organs out of his body.

I turn back and begin my descent to the room that Nicolai is set up in. I open the door, and he is sitting behind the desk with a focused look on his face. He looks up upon my entrance, standing.

"What have you got for me?"

"There were cameras in the bedroom …" He trails off. "I'm still sorting through the footage to see if I can find any clues as to what happened."

I nod in understanding. He is uncomfortable, so obviously, the videos mostly consist of him fucking my wife. There is no way in hell I am going to watch those videos. So I am going to have to wait until Nicolai comes across something.

My phone begins vibrating in my pocket, and I look at the call log to see Dr. Shotwell calling me. This means he has done the bloodwork. Now it is time to see whose blood is in that car.

"Yeah," I answer.

He is silent for a moment, as if hesitating. "Sir, the blood is a match."

My heart begins speeding up. I don't say anything.

"That's not all, sir. The blood sample you sent me … well, it seems that … Elise is pregnant."

"Fuck!" I shout. At the same time, Nicolai jumps away from the screen with wide eyes.

"Oh, fuck," he whispers. His eyes are darting back and forth frantically between me and the screen.

"Sir, are you still there?"

I ignore Dr. Shotwell as I walk to the computer screen to see what Nicolai is looking at. I look at the screen and see why he is so nervous. Alexander made Elise wear nothing but lingerie while she has been here. So in the video, clear as day, is a small bump beginning to form around her stomach. She is obviously pregnant.

"Fuck!" I shout, hurling my phone at the wall. It shatters to pieces.

"Everyone fucking out!" I shout.

Everyone doesn't hesitate as they quickly try to file out. Romelo and Nicolai are among them, trying to leave.

"Not you two!"

They stop right by the door and slowly turn to me. I must look severely pissed off right now, because even they look hesitant to speak to me.

"Fuck, fuck, fuck, fuck!" I shout in anger. I speed around the room, attacking anything and everything in sight. She is fucking pregnant. That bastard fucking knocked up my fucking wife. I don't even have the slightest idea of what to do next. This is all my fucking fault.

"Don't breathe a word of this to *anyone!*" I shout at them. They flinch at my tone. "I'm going to fucking kill that bastard. I'm going to fucking kill him!" I can feel the rage boiling up beneath my skin. How dare he fucking touch my wife when he knows who the fuck I am! Dammit!

If I ever find Elise, I have to deal with her wanting to keep his child. I will be stuck with forcing her to get rid of it or raising his offspring for the rest of my life. Fuck! How could this fucking happen? Is she even alive? Dr. Shotwell said that it's her blood in that car. Meaning, she wrecked it. So where the hell could she have gone from there?

"I want this whole mountain scanned by air. Get me a chopper, and I want the nearest houses to that wreck."

I don't wait for their response as I walk out of the room, slamming the door behind me. I quickly head up the hallway to the room where we hold that fucking cunt. As soon as I am near the door, I pull my gun out, swinging the door open. I don't even give her time to comprehend what is going on. I unload my gun in her body.

I turn around, leaving the room and walking toward the front of the house. I run into Romelo.

"I want this place burned to the goddamn ground." I don't wait for his response once again.

We don't leave the house until three hours later. I look behind us as the place goes up in flames. I've had Alexander shipped to the catacombs already, so he isn't in there even though I really want him to be.

I sent everyone else home besides Romelo and Nicolai. I sent Matteo home also. He is of no use with a broken wrist. He will only be in the way. And if there is any more danger lurking, he will be the first one the enemy will aim for. It is now time for us to search the surrounding area for Elise.

Lucky for us, the sun is still up, so we have plenty of time to search. The chopper above us is scanning the area. The voice comes through the coms.

"There's a cabin about fifteen miles from your current location, but you can't get there by car. You got to go by foot."

We follow the chopper's directions and end up pulling off the road. We stop once we get close to the cabin. Everyone files out of the car, getting their gear on.

We silently trudge near the cabin, the only sound is our boots crunching the thick snow. I am nervous as hell. Even though it is negative degrees outside, I am sweating. Seeing Elise on camera is one thing, but seeing her in person—and her stomach is probably bigger now—I honestly don't know how I am going to react to that.

I can see the smoke from the chimney over the trees. I look at Romelo and Nicolai, motioning for them to cover my rear.

We finally exit the trees, and the cabin comes into view. The lights are on, but the curtains are drawn, so I can't see anything inside. We will just have to play it by ear. If we barge in and Elise isn't here, we are screwed, but if she is, then barging in may be the thing that will save her.

I take a deep breath, trying to calm my nerves. Whatever is beyond this door may change me. I am terrified of what I may find. I haven't seen Elise since she left me because I told her about her mother. And now she is pregnant. After she was captured and auctioned off.

I kick in the door and take it all in at once. There is a dog growling at me, with his teeth bared. There is a man with a knife in hand, standing defensively. And dear God, there is Elise behind him. My Elise. My wife. She looks so beautiful as she stares at me in shock. He hair is in long waves down her back, and her skin has a healthy glow to it. I look at her arms and see hideous bruises sported across it. There are bandages on each of her hands, gauze wrapped around them. She is wearing baggy clothing.

Romelo and Nicolai are right next to me as we all stare one another down. Her eyes slowly fill with tears, and she steps from around the man. He grabs her arm, and rage immediately flashes to the surface as I take in the sight. Who the fuck is this man? I step forward with my gun at ready. The dog's growls grow louder, and I am about to put the miserable mutt out of its misery then.

Elise seems to sense the directions of my thoughts, because she murmurs something to the man and pats the dog's head lightly, getting its attention. Its growls grow quiet as it watches her approach me.

I take in her face and feel so much happiness within me. She is alive. She is alive, and she is safe. I reach out, about to grab her, when I pause. Now that she isn't hiding behind that man, I can see her more clearly. Including her stomach, which is protruding a little too far from her shirt. I have to wipe my face of emotion. I want to stare at her in disgust, but then I want to kiss her. An inner battle is waging war deep within me.

I reach out to cup her face but immediately let my arm fall at my side. I have never felt so conflicted in my life. To finally have her back. Be with her. But at the same time, I can't shake the thought that she is pregnant with someone else's child.

She takes a timid step toward me, her face twisted in confusion, and I immediately step back. I feel sick.

I can feel the stares Nicolai and Romelo are boring into my back. I don't know how long I have been staring at her. These feelings are overwhelming, and for once in my life, I have no idea what I am supposed to do next. Then my gaze focuses over Elise's shoulder, and I take notice of the man on the other side of her. I take a step forward, pushing her behind me.

"Who the fuck are you?" I don't like him already. His gaze shifts to Elise, and I feel my irritation rising even higher. "Don't fucking look at her! She's not the one holding a fucking gun. I said, Who the fuck are you?"

He looks at me and slowly raises his hands.

"I'm Eli. I meant your … wife no harm. We found her passed out in the snow and couldn't just leave her there with all those injuries."

I narrow my eyes at him. There has to be more to this than just helping her. This man is trained in some area. His stance when we walked in is one of a man that knows combat.

I step closer to him, and the dog's growls grow louder.

"Shut that thing up before I put a bullet in its head."

He clicks his tongue at the dog, and it immediately relaxes a little. He watches me with careful eyes, observing me like I am observing him.

"Who the fuck are you?" I say again.

"I'm Eli."

"And I'm fucking Luca. Who the fuck are you?" I say again. I don't like how he is avoiding the meaning of my question.

"I'm no one. I just found your wife and—"

He stops midsentence as I cock my gun so close to his face. A smug grin passes his face.

"I don't think your wife would appreciate you shooting me, *Luca*," he says. He puts emphasis on my name. And I currently am not in the mood for mind games. I fire my gun, and I hear Elise shout behind me. Eli hunches over, a new hole in his thigh.

"I don't think my wife appreciated that either. Doesn't mean a fucking thing to me." I turn away, looking at Romelo and Nicolai.

"Let's go."

Chapter 45

Elise

I don't know whether to feel relief or fear now that Luca has shown up. Initially, he shocked me when he walked through that door. But Rocco had picked up on his scent and began growling, causing Eli to immediately jump into action. Whoever he is, he acted just like Luca at the first sign of danger.

I look behind me frantically at Eli on the ground in pain. I hate that Luca shot him, but I am glad he shot him in his leg instead of killing him. Eli looks up at me with pain in his eyes.

"I'm sorry," I mouth to him, not wanting to set Luca off.

He looks between me and Luca and shakes his head.

We trudge through the snow for I don't know how long, the cold air seeping through the sweater I am wearing. Luca hasn't even said two words to me. As soon as he laid eyes on me, his whole demeanor faltered.

I knew the moment he spotted my stomach. Right now, he's calm and collected. I'm scared to death he is going to mistake this child for Alexander's. I have to tell him the child is his.

"Luca …," I say.

He doesn't respond to me; he is just walking with his back to me.

"Luca," I try again. But he still doesn't say anything.

I reach out to grab his sleeve. As soon as my skin makes contact with his, he jerks away from me. The movement is so sudden and unexpected I fall flat into the snow. Romelo and Nicolai, even though they are ahead, falter in their footsteps, looking at me in concern. But Luca keeps walking. Not acknowledging me at all. I open my mouth, but in all honesty, I haven't the slightest idea what to say.

My emotions are all out of normalcy, so I can feel tears welling up in my eyes from his blatant neglect. He barely even looked at me when he found me. Nothing but confusion was on his face once he stepped in that door and saw me. No happiness. I saw a flicker of disgust before he hid it.

The snow is beginning to seep into my palms, chilling me to the bone. It also is seeping into the pants.

Nicolai and Romelo exchange looks. They stopped, but Luca continues walking.

"Luca!" I try again, louder.

He still doesn't respond.

The tears begin rolling down my face, and I can feel the sting they leave behind from the icy air. I drop my head and let the tears flow freely. He won't even look at me. Won't even acknowledge me. He tops the hill and disappears. Romelo whispers something to Nicolai, and he nods, taking steps toward me.

He bends over and helps me up from the ground, pulling his jacket off and wrapping it around my shivering shoulders. We trudge through the snow in silence. Romelo has now disappeared from our view too. I can't get the way Luca looked at me out of my head. He has only ever looked at me in adoration and need. But for once, he actually looked like he hates me. Like I disgust him.

As we walk in silence, something dawns upon me. Everything. Every pain-filled moment I have gone through is because of Luca. Everything was calculated in his mind. But with every pain-filled moment came a moment where he revealed something to me about himself. That he would always protect me. The only person I have to fear in this world is him. Because if anyone else even tries, he would do whatever is necessary to see that I come out alive.

He proved that when he saved me from my father, when he jumped in front of a bullet for me, when he protected my brother and took him in for my sake. When he warned me about Ari.

Everything that he has put me through, I should hate him for it. I *do* hate him for it. But now as I walk in the silence, I realize how much I depend on him. How much in his own twisted head he cares for me. And how much he believes he is doing right. He is fucked up. And that is the fault of this family we have both been born into. It is his job to be fucked up. Being the capo, you can't be soft and sane. You have to be hard and maniacal. Being with Alexander, I've seen firsthand the type of people he deals with. Luca was protecting me from people like that. I know he was way overboard with me for no justifiable reason, but with everything that I have been through, just the thought of being near him, near safety, makes me feel comfort.

As I walk in the silent, snow-filled forest with Nicolai by my side, I realize something. As much as I hate him, the pain I am feeling from his neglect, from his disgust is too much. I stop in my tracks as it hits me. How could I possibly be feeling this way after everything? Everything he did to me and my family, to innocent people. How could I feel this way after he had tortured me and destroyed any hope I have? After he abused me and everyone around him. After he manipulated me. What the hell is wrong with me?

I love him.

* * * * *

"Tests came back negative, so you're all in the clear." The nurse smiles at me as she sets the envelope with my results down on the counter. The first thing Luca made me do is come to the hospital to be tested. I try to return her bright smile, but I just can't. After he left me in the snow, Luca didn't even bother to ride in the same car as me. Nicolai just got a call and said we have to go to the hospital. For me.

The nurse senses my attitude and gets up to leave.

As she opens the door, I catch a glimpse of Nicolai on his phone. He looks stressed. He sees me watching him and says something into the receiver, walking toward the room. He steps in, looking around, and spots the envelope on the counter. He grabs it and is about to leave.

"The nurse said everything came back negative," I say.

He pauses in the doorway. He is silent for a moment before letting out a deep sigh and turning to me. "Luca asked me to bring him the results."

I narrow my eyes at him, not knowing what to say. He is only following his boss's orders, but that doesn't lessen the sting.

I stand up, walking toward Nicolai. He is watching me with wide eyes. Probably nervous. I yank the envelope from him, catching him off guard, and tear it up until it is in shreds at our feet. I use all my force to shove him out of the room and slam the door in his face.

Chapter 46

Luca

I sit in my office, thrumming my fingers on my desk in annoyance. Nicolai is on speakerphone, and Romelo is standing in front of me with a stupid grin on his face. I take a deep breath.

"She did what?"

"Uh ... she snatched the envelope and tore it up."

I growl in irritation. "And you let her?"

"I honestly had no idea she was about to do it."

"Dammit, what the hell am I trusting you with her life for if you can't even prevent her from snatching an envelope?"

"Sorry, boss," he grumbles.

"When can you get another one with the information?"

"They said it's gonna take a few days. They already closed her file, and it'll take a while to get all that information back in one file without an appointment."

I take a deep breath and run my fingers through my hair. "Okay, just bring her home. And try not to fuck anything up." I hang up the phone before he can respond. "What the fuck are you laughing at?" I snap at Romelo. He's been very brave lately.

"It's just that Elise seems to have taken on a whole new persona in her time with Alexander. I never would have expected her to openly defy you like that."

I roll my eyes and turn away from him, looking out the window.

"You seem stressed. Shouldn't you be happy? I mean, you finally got her back after ... how long?"

"Three months," I respond absentmindedly.

"Three months! That's a long time to be missing a wife. Especially the way you heard her disappear. Aren't you, in some way, glad she's back?"

I want to smash my head onto the desk. He is right. He is. But …

"She's fucking pregnant, Romelo. With someone else's child. And not just anyone, Alexander's. How am I supposed to deal with that? How am I supposed to handle raising his child?"

He shrugs his shoulders. "Just make her abort it. If you're worried about her fighting you, just drug her and do it while she's asleep. Or you can sneak something in her food. Like shark. That'll definitely do the trick."

I look at him. "Unless you want to keep your tongue, I suggest you think about what you're going to say next."

A smile breaks its way across his face. He slowly raises his hands in surrender. "Look, Capo, all I'm saying is, if just getting rid of the child is such an issue, why let the fact that it isn't yours get in the way of your happiness?"

The room is silent as I take in his words. He looks at his watch and chuckles, turning to leave.

"Where are you going?" I ask in irritation.

"I have a date." He walks out of the room, closing the door behind him, leaving me confused about both things he just said.

* * * * *

It's not until twenty minutes later that I hear the front door, which means Elise is home. I stand and step outside of my office to see her walking toward the stairs.

"Elise."

She freezes and looks at me with sad eyes. I motion for her to come into my office. I turn and don't wait for a response. I take a seat behind my desk just in time to see her stepping into the room. Her hair is wet at the ends, courtesy of the hospital letting her shower. Nicolai must've bought her a change of clothes.

I take in her appearance. Her arms are wrapped in bandages, all the way down to her palms, which had to be restitched. There are purple bruises on her arms. There is a new bandage on her forehead, and even her legs are wrapped up in gauze. Every inch of her body is marked up horribly. I have to close my eyes to calm myself down.

"Why do you feel the right to tear up those records?" I ask. I wanted physical proof that nothing is wrong. I need to know how long she's been pregnant. I wanted the tangible proof.

I'm surprised when she glares at me head-on. "You should be able to listen to me when I tell you what the doctor said."

I tilt my head, studying this woman now standing in front of me. She is feisty. Brave. Not the timid girl I married. And I don't like it.

"You're not even home yet, and you're already defying me."

She scoffs and looks at me in irritation. "Defy you? You're not my father, Luca."

I narrow my eyes at her. "You're right. He's dead."

She looks taken aback but quickly recovers. "And who's responsible for that?" she counters.

"He is," I state matter-of-factly.

"No. You are! You put those bullets in his body!" she shouts at me.

"Because he betrayed us!"

She laughs, but there is no humor in it.

"You think this is funny?"

She narrows her eyes at me. I glare at her as long as I can. I can't hurt her. I can't make her understand.

"Ahhh!" I shout, punching the wall. The room is silent. "Get out."

She starts, "Luca—"

But I interrupt her, unable to hear her voice right now. I turn around, facing her, and am unable to even look at her face. All I can see is her stomach. The life she is now nurturing inside of her that is Alexander's.

"I said get the fuck out! I can't fucking look at you with that ... inside of you!" I almost regret what I say. The look of hurt that flashes across her face is quick to make me rethink my words.

She takes a step toward me.

"Luca, if you'd just listen to me—"

"I don't want to listen!" I slam my hand down on the desk, and she jumps. "Get the fuck out of my fucking office!"

I watch, torn, as she stares at me with wide eyes. Her bottom lip begins trembling, and she pulls it between her teeth just as tears begin to fall down her face. She takes a step back before running out of my office, slamming the door behind her.

Fuck.

I don't even know where she went in the house. I stay in my office late, working on things I've let get behind searching for her. That's when the screaming starts. it's bone-chilling and causes my blood to run cold. The first thing I think is that Elise is in trouble. I jump up from my desk out into the foyer. The screams are echoing off the walls of the house.

I sprint up the stairs, pulling my gun out as I take two at a time. Her screams continue. Now that I am getting closer, I can hear her begging.

"Please, please don't!"

My heart is pounding in my chest as I pump my legs faster to get to her. How the fuck could someone have gotten past security to get into this house and attack her? The screams are coming from our bedroom, and I kick the door open with all my force, aiming my gun at the assailant.

Chapter 47

Elise

I am back in Alexander's cellar, tied to the table he loves to use. He is over my body, squeezing the life out of me with his bare hands as he assaults my body. I scream and beg him to stop, the tears coming fast and my air supply being cut off. He pulls out a knife, aiming it right over my stomach.

"Please, please don't!" I shout.

"Elise! Elise!" I am jolted awake, a cold sweat drenching my body. Gray. Steel-gray eyes are staring at me with worry. He is holding on to me.

There is silence as we stare at each other. My breathing comes out in pants as I get choked up.

"Oh god, Luca!" I shout without even realizing what I am doing. I wrap my arms around him, pulling him close to me. "It was so real … I was there … I was back with him …"

I sob into his chest, and he slowly wraps his arms around me, rubbing my back in comfort.

"H-he was killing me … while I was tied up …"

"Shhhh. You're here with me, Elise. I won't let anything happen to you, I swear. You're mine to protect. I will protect you. No harm will come to you … or that child. I swear it."

His words make me feel so much better. He's going to protect me. He said he is.

We sit like that for a while, and I sob into Luca's arms and he comforts me. He tells me how I am safe and he'll protect me.

After I quiet down, he stands up to leave, and I immediately freak out. I reach out and grab his arm with my bandaged hand.

"Please don't leave me." My voice comes out in a whisper.

Being in this dark room alone terrifies me to no end. I feel like someone is going to come and take me at any moment. I drift into these nightmares and imagine Alexander with me again, and that is terrifying.

Luca watches me with concern and slowly sits back onto the bed, looking at me with worry.

"I'm going to go take a shower, then I'll come right back and lie with you, okay?" He is speaking to me as if I were a child. I nod slowly, and he stands to head into the shower.

"C-can I come with you? I don't want to be alone." I look at the ground as I speak, not wanting to see his face. Every time Luca looks at me, I can see the disgust that lurks beneath his gaze.

I feel a hand over mine and stop shaking. I hadn't even realized I am still shivering in fear.

Luca's hand slowly wraps around mine, and he pulls me from the bed toward the bathroom. I sit on the chair as he draws a warm bath, the steam fogging up the mirror. He sits on the edge of the tub, testing the warmth of the water. He still doesn't look at me, though. And quite honestly, I am okay with that. As long as I can be in the same room as him, I feel safe. Luca always means what he says, so if he tells me I will be safe, I feel I can believe that of him.

Luca stands and slowly begins to shed his clothing. He keeps his back to me as he does so. Once he is completely naked, he turns to me, holding his hand out to me. I stand slowly and walk toward him. Once I reach his arms, he pulls my shirt over my head and begins to remove my underwear. We stand for a moment as he takes in my naked form. His eyes trail down to my stomach. He reaches out, slowly unraveling the gauze from around my arms, revealing the cuts and bruises that lurk underneath. He reaches around me and puts some gloves on my hands since I have stitches in the palms and they can't get wet. He stares at the marks along my body and slowly pulls me in for a hug, and we stand like that in the middle of the bathroom, naked, in each other's arms.

He pulls away from me, walking toward the water and sinking himself in. He still doesn't say a word; he just looks at me, and for the first time since my rescue, he smiles at me. He brings his hand out of the water, holding it out to me. I walk toward him and lower myself into the tub with him. He lies on his back and pulls me in between his legs. His hands rest over my stomach. I can feel his chin resting atop my head.

"He told me that you were dead. That he killed you." He brings his hands up and begins playing with my hair. "I don't think I've ever felt so lost in my life. I thought I'd really lost you."

I just listen to his voice, letting it soothe my crazed nerves.

"Actually, I have felt like that before. When you called me. Right before that wreck. Hearing the terror in your voice, your screams, and the sound of the car crashing ... that terrified me."

He sighs.

"I'm a terrible person. I know that. I was made to kill your mother, right in front of you, and you don't even remember it. Your father even wanted us to send you back to him bloodied and bruised so that he could stage a war. And I was the one that was chosen for the task. All I wanted was to protect you. I tried. But I also ended up hurting you. That's just the kind of man I am."

He gives a deep chuckle.

"But dammit if I won't protect you with every breath in my body. You have nothing to fear, Elise. He won't be coming back for you."

We sit in the tub until we both turn pruny. Luca takes care of me every step of the way. I don't even have the energy to wonder why he is being so kind to me after his explosion in his office, and I don't care. That nightmare was so realistic. And the fact that it really happened at one point makes me realize something. Luca is the one that is going to protect me no matter what. He kept me protected until the one time he let me out of his sight. Now I see why he makes me stay with him all the time.

I can feel myself drifting off to sleep, and I can feel Luca's arms around me. Protecting me. My eyelids grow heavy, and I close them. I hear Luca give a muffled laugh.

"I told myself I couldn't raise Alexander's child, but if taking it away means hurting you even more, I don't think I can do it," Luca whispers. His voice sounds as if he is in disbelief.

I open my mouth.

"This isn't Alexander's child, Luca. The baby is yours."

I don't have the energy to listen to his response as sleep overtakes me in the comfort of his arms.

Chapter 48

Luca

My life ended the day I met Elise. By pulling that trigger, I changed hers. By marrying her, I changed mine. I stare at her sleeping form. She looks so peaceful in her sleep. Like nothing can bother her. She said that the baby is mine. I want to believe her more than anything, but I just can't. How is it possible that in the time she was with Alexander, she hadn't gotten pregnant? That would mean she was pregnant before her abduction.

I quietly leave the room, heading to my office to get things done.

Once I enter the kitchen, I see Matteo. He takes one look at me and tries to leave.

"Matteo."

He pauses and looks at me warily. There is a light-blue cast around his arm where Alexander snapped his wrist.

"Elise is back."

His eyes grow wide in surprise.

"What? When? I have to go see her!" He takes off out of the kitchen, but I grab him before he can.

"No!"

He looks at me like I am crazy. "No?"

"You can't see her yet. She can't know what you've been doing with me the past few months. And you can't continue this anymore."

His face slowly morphs into one of anger. "Why?"

"I made a promise to her that I wouldn't swear you in—"

"But I'm not sworn in!"

"But you are behaving like someone who is. She doesn't want you involved in this at all."

He looks at me for a moment.

"I'm not forbidding you from speaking to your sister, but our endeavors these past months are not to be told to her, do you understand? As of today, you are no longer involved."

His gaze goes from surprised to angry in an instant. He jerks away from me and storms out of the kitchen.

I shake my head in disbelief. If it weren't for Elise, I would have broken his arm for jerking away from me like that. But there is Elise. And with her, there always seems to be some kind of exception.

I walk into my office and take a seat, just enjoying the temporary peace. Elise is home. And she is safe. I have her back, and she isn't going anywhere without me. I have Alexander in captivity. I am rid of that crazy, backstabbing bitch Ari and her weak-willed husband, and the entire South is in my control. All that is left is to ask Elise about what happened that led to her kidnapping.

Speak of the devil.

Elise steps timidly into my office. She looks at me through that thick curtain of hair that she loves to hide behind. I've always known Elise is beautiful. I've always acknowledged that fact. The way she walks so timidly as she approaches me is so sensual. She is sex walking and doesn't even know it. Her tongue peeks out as she wets her lips nervously, and I follow the movement with my eyes. Three months since I have seen her. Kissed her.

"Good morning," she whispers, pulling me out of my thoughts.

Looking at the bruises that mar her skin makes me boil with anger. The fact that Alexander had the nerve to touch what is mine outright makes me angry, and I am counting the days until I go to visit him. I give her a reassuring smile.

"Good morning, Elise. Did you sleep well?"

She nods timidly.

"Yes, thank you." She takes a look around my office, and her eyes land on the corner, where her violin is. She stares at it.

I clear my throat to get her attention.

"I put it there. It kept me comfort while you were away."

She nods before taking a seat in front of me. She keeps looking around, avoiding eye contact with me. Which, for Elise, means either she is about to lie to me about something or she is nervous.

"Where is Matteo?" she asks.

"He's around here somewhere. I assumed he went to go find you," I say. And I am really shocked to hear that he hasn't gone to find her. She shakes her head.

"D-does he know ... about ..."

"No. I haven't told him. I felt it better that you tell him since he's your brother."

She looks at me in shock. I give her a small smile. I walk around the desk until I am standing in front of her. I pull her wedding ring out of my pocket, and a small gasp escapes her lips.

"I managed to save it," I say, pushing it back into its rightful place on her finger.

She gives a small smile as she stares at it. I don't think I have ever seen her pleased to wear that ring. Something is different.

"I need to find out as much as I can about your abduction, Elise. Can you remember anything that might be helpful?"

She immediately looks down again and begins messing with her hands.

"Elise."

She looks at me with wide eyes.

"Don't lie to me," I say, letting her know I am serious.

Her eyes widen slightly.

"After the wreck, I woke up in a room. A man came in. He said his name was Agent Jeffries. He was asking me to give a statement so that he could have a reason to put you away. When I refused, he said there was nothing he could do for me, and then I was transported to that auction house ..."

She continues to speak, but I can't hear her anymore. Agent-fucking-Jeffries. That bastard has been trying to take me and my father down for years. I can feel my blood rushing through my body as I get more and more furious. That bastard put my wife in a fucking auction house and caused all this because she wouldn't fucking snitch. Because of him, she is possibly pregnant by someone else.

I immediately stand from my seat, and she gasps, fear filling her eyes.

"I need to make a call," I say.

She nods and immediately scurries out of the room. I pull out my phone, immediately calling Romelo. He answers on the first ring.

"Yes?"

"We have an issue."

Plans are made. Big plans. If I pull this off, I will be untouchable in the underworld. If I fuck this up in any form or fashion, then I will be screwed. I will be worse than screwed. Killing a federal agent is the hardest thing to do. They have the brains, security, technology, and connections. If I don't do everything perfectly, then they will find me and they will lock me away forever until it is my turn to have the death penalty. But he has crossed me for the last time. There is a place in this world for the good guys. The ones that want to bring down the villains and make a difference. But my life isn't one of them.

He is a fool to ever think he could pull this off without consequence. Without me finding out and finding him. I guess he thought my wife would be buried in the underworld, never to be found. But she has, which means bad news for him.

Right now, though, I have the bastard behind it all to make suffer.

I turn out the light in my office, walking toward the door. I haven't seen Elise since she left my office today. A part of me feels bad for shutting her out like that, but another part of me doesn't. I know that's fucked up, but that's just me. I grab my keys and head for the garage.

"Where are you going?"

I stop and turn around to see Elise watching me with those innocent eyes. I hadn't even heard her behind me. She walks so featherlight.

"Out," I say, not wanting to tell her where I am really going.

"Can I come with you?" she asks.

I open my mouth to tell her no, but then I remember something important. She hates being alone. Damn, I am an asshole for forgetting something that important. I can't just leave her like I used to. She needs my presence to feel safe. I let out a deep sigh.

"Uh, Elise, I don't think you want to go where I'm going."

"Where are you going?" she asks.

Normally, I would have already punished her for questioning me so much, but with everything she has been through at the hands of another, the fear that wracks her voice makes me unable to do such a thing.

"To take care of business."

"Please, can I go with you?" she says. Her voice is almost a whisper.

"I can have Romelo or Nicolai stay with you if you're that scared, Elise."

She shakes her head violently. "No. I want to be with you."

"Elise, I'm going to do something that I don't think you can stomach right now. Especially in your condition," I say.

She finally looks up.

"Luca, I don't care. I just want to be with you."

That is all it takes for my resolve to come crashing down. I let out a defeated sigh.

"Okay."

Maybe I am dumb for letting her come along, but the smile that lights up her face is enough to make my heart flutter.

I decide to take the Mercedes since it is a bigger vehicle. The ride to the catacombs is silent. Elise is looking out the window, watching the setting sun.

"How are you feeling?" I ask.

She continues to look out the window when she answers me, "Fine."

I frown, not liking her short response.

"Did you eat today? You need to take in as much nutrition as you can. You need the strength."

She still doesn't look away from the window. A small laugh escapes her lips. "I ate. The doctor gave me some prenatals to take to help with development."

I nod even though she isn't watching me.

"I'm going to the catacombs," I say, hoping that she'll change her mind. She doesn't. "To see Alexander."

This catches her attention, and she finally looks at me.

"He's alive …?" Her eyes widen, and true terror fills her depths. I nod slowly.

She reaches up, grabbing her hair as tears fill her eyes. I reach over with one hand, grabbing hers and slowly bringing it to my lips.

"Shhh. Elise, I won't let anything happen to you. We're going to get rid of him, okay?"

She looks at me, sniffling, and nods. I am going to kill that bastard, slowly and painfully, once I get there, for making my wife feel this way.

We finally reach the catacombs, and Romelo is there to meet me at the entrance. He nods to me, and his eyes widen slightly when he spots Elise. He looks at me in confusion.

"Enjoyed your date?" I ask him.

He gives me a coy smile. "Yes, I did."

I roll my eyes.

"I see you decided to choose happiness," he says as he eyes Elise walking toward us. "Are you sure it's a good idea to bring her here, though?"

I look at him.

"I'm not sure, quite honestly, but she can't be alone right now."

He nods in understanding, and we all walk into the hellhole called the catacombs.

The catacombs are where I keep people that are going to die. It is like death row for my enemies. Except it is a slow and painful death. We walk through the hallways, hearing screams of agony and torture. I can feel my adrenaline spiking as excitement courses through my veins. I sneak a peek at Elise, and she looks as though she is about to vomit. Her eyes are wide.

We step into the room with one-way glass. The lights are dimmed. I pull out a chair for Elise to sit in. She isn't looking at me. She is beginning to hyperventilate as she looks beyond the glass at Alexander.

"Elise. Elise, look at me." She looks at me in a panic.

I seat her slowly in the chair and begin breathing slowly with her, showing her how she needs to slow her breathing.

"It's okay, baby, it's okay. Just breathe, okay?" I try to reassure her. There are large tears falling down her face, and I use my thumbs to wipe them. "You have to be strong, Elise. Be strong for the baby."

This seems to catch her attention, and she frantically nods at me, trying to catch her breathing.

"Good. Good," I murmur to her.

"I'm going to make him pay. You'll be able to see and hear everything. If you don't want to, just ask Romelo and he'll turn off the audio and visual, okay?"

She nods to me again. I give her a reassuring smile and kiss her on the forehead before stepping into the room. Alexander looks up upon my arrival, a cocky smile spreading itself across his face.

"I was wondering when you were coming to carry out my death sentence." His arms are latched above his head, his naked body at its full height. He is secured and at my mercy.

I don't speak as I head over to my table filled with tools. The hairs on my arms are beginning to stand as I get chills. This is always my favorite part. I run my fingers over each of the tools, deciding how I should begin this.

How do I begin my torture? How do I envision my masterpiece?

A smile automatically plasters itself on my face. I settle for the prune cutters. I walk toward him with slow ease. He watches me with steady eyes, already accepting his fate.

"You know what I think?" I bring the prune cutter up to his fingers. "I think you sealed your fate the moment you bid on ..." I place his finger in between the blades.

"Buying."

Snip.

"My."

Snip.
"*Wife.*"
Snip.

Three fingers now lie on the ground at my feet. He is doing a good job of keeping silent. He is biting his jaw in pain. I grab the blowtorch from the table, burning the ends of his fingers to staunch the bleeding. Now I get a groan from him.

"Wouldn't want you bleeding out, would we?" I say. This is going to be fun.

Ten fingers. One eye. Six teeth. Twenty-seven slashes. A shattered knee. Broken arm. Open cuts. And I am not even halfway through.

Alexander is breathing hard. I walk toward him.

"Tell me, was it worth it?" I ask, genuinely curious.

Alexander looks at me with one eye, and small laughs escape his lips.

"You … know … what's … worth all this …? I got to fuck … your wife. I got to beat her … and bruise her. Tell me, can she sleep at night? I have engrained myself … permanently … in her brain. Why don't you try feeding her an apple? See how she responds to that."

He lets out another laugh and takes a deep breath, trying to bear with the pain.

"Why don't you … show her the book … *Pride and Prejudice* … and see how she screams? And best of all, she's fucking pregnant. With *my* child. So you're going to have to decide to get rid of it and make her hate you or keep it and hate her for it." He tries to muster a smile.

The door to the room opens, and in walks Elise. I stare at her in shock. Alexander takes in her pregnant form and laughs.

"I guess the big and bad capo … will be raising someone else's child." He laughs like a crazed man.

But I am not listening. I am watching Elise in confusion. She grabs the large garden shears off the table and walks toward us. Alexander is still shouting at me about raising his child, but I can't help but stare at Elise. Her expression is blank. No emotion. Nothing. She stands in front of Alexander.

"I was pregnant the moment I was auctioned off. This child is Luca's. Not yours."

Alexander doesn't even get the chance to respond. She places the garden shears over his penis and, in one swift movement, pushes the blades close, severing the organ.

Alexander's cries of agony echo off the walls as his manhood is cut from him. Blood is everywhere, new blood from the wound. I stare at Elise in horror. She is still watching him. Her head is tilted slightly to the side, and I swear I can see the ghost of a smile cross her lips as she watches the bastard writhe in pain.

What. The. Fuck.

* * * * *

The sun is out. Elise is sitting at the edge of the pool with her feet dipped, Matteo is in the water in front of her with a smile on his face. They are chatting about God knows what. I study Elise very closely. She has changed drastically. I overlooked it completely when I rescued her. But she has. She is stronger now. I can't get the image of her smiling face as she watched Alexander bleed out of my head. It is *disturbing*.

I have always known her to be *innocent*. But watching her that night ... she is anything but. This is the same woman that vomited on my floor when we played Russian roulette. But as she watched Alexander, she didn't bat an eyelash. She's stayed glued to my side, her nightmares coming and going. Some nights are worse than others. The other night, she actually hit me in the face with her writhing.

The doctor says the hormones from her pregnancy are causing her dreams to be amplified. The doctor also says her term is four months, which means that the chances of the baby being mine are higher. I still am skeptical, though. When I asked about a prenatal DNA test, the doctor said the risk of miscarriage would be higher, so I opted out of it. I'll just have to wait until the baby is born. For Elise, I can do that.

I watch her as she smiles at something Matteo says. She kicks her feet lightly, splashing water. She looks so ... innocent. But her behavior sometimes says otherwise. It is almost as if she is losing herself. Sometimes she seems like a different person. Like she can conquer anything. And others, she is her usual self. Terrified of everything. Today is one of her better days. She is smiling and happy.

I try to look at things from her perspective. She went through a rough time in that house with Alexander. This is her way of coping. I had to push back the plan with Agent Jeffries because she never lets me out of her sight.

We have an appointment today to figure the sex of the baby. Maybe that's what's linked to her good mood. Sometimes when I find her alone, she'll be looking at nothing with a blank expression. Just spaced out. I don't know what to do. When she speaks to me, she sometimes seems like she isn't all there.

She seems to sense my gaze and turns to look at me. She looks stunning as she sits on the edge of the pool, the sun's rays reflecting off her delicate skin. The bruises are beginning to fade, leaving her skin that lovely tone I love.

I stand and make my way toward her.

"It's about time for us to go," I say, carefully watching her reaction. She gives me a beaming smile and stands to head into the house. I watch her retreating figure. Hmmm.

* * * * *

The nurse is smiling at us as she presses the scope on Elise's stomach. I hold her hand in mine. Today is a big day for the both of us. For Elise, she will be finding out the sex of her child. For me, I will be finding out the sex of what could possibly be my child. I know she has told me several times, and the records indicate how far along she is, but I am still skeptical. I try to push that thought aside as the nurse stares at the screen.

I let out a breath I hadn't realized I'd been holding as I look at the baby. I can see it. There, in black-and-white, on the screen. The life that is growing inside of Elise. The nurse pauses and stops moving the scope. She looks at us, smiling.

"Are you ready to know what you're having?"

We both nod in unison.

"It's a healthy baby boy." She smiles at us.

I let out an exasperated laugh. A boy. I am having a boy. I am going to be a father. To a son. I look at Elise to see her smiling at me with a look of adoration. Something that I have longed for the two years we have been married. Tears are rolling down her cheeks.

"We're having a boy." She laughs in joy.

I smile back at her, bringing her hand to my lips and giving her a light kiss. I nod at her.

"Yeah, we are. A healthy baby boy," I say.

"Would you like to hear the heartbeat?" the nurse asks.

"Yes," we both say.

She flips a switch, and the sound of our son's heart beating fills the room. A strong heartbeat. I can't help the smile on my face as it grows bigger. I look at Elise, and she is smiling as she stares at the monitor.

I look at the monitor in joy as a new feeling comes over me. I am having a boy. No matter the results of the DNA, he is mine. Mine to protect and mine to love. My son.

Chapter 49

Luca

Watching Elise lately has been like a slow downhill spiral to insanity. I have tried to rein in my attitude to help her, but she is like a ticking time bomb. Yesterday I caught her out in the middle of the yard just staring at the sky. She had this psychotic look on her face. And the day before that, she was in the bathroom, just staring at her face in the mirror.

There are dark rings beginning to form around her eyes from lack of sleep, and quite honestly, I wouldn't be surprised if I caught her talking to herself. She seems as if she isn't all there. Like her mind is drifting. Wandering.

I have been standing in the doorway of our bedroom for about two minutes, and she has been staring at the wall behind me. I can't even read her. There is no emotion behind her gaze. The only time she ever shows any kind of emotion is when she is with me. Which should make me happy. But in a deep sense, it is disturbing. She is constantly glued to my side. Afraid at every turn. I literally have to give her a pep talk for three minutes just so she'll let me use the bathroom. She hates being alone, and she trusts no one but me.

"Elise." She looks up at her name, and when she spots me, a small smile flits onto her face. I have to admit, though, seeing her smile is uplifting because it is very rare these days.

I step farther into the room, and she watches my every move. I take a seat next to her on the bed.

"Are you feeling all right, Elise?" I ask. She only nods, scooting closer to my side. "If anything is bothering you, you can tell me, you know," I say, trying to reassure her.

"I know" is all I get as a response. "How do you think our lives would be if our fathers weren't so … crazy?" she asks.

I have to control my anger at her words about my father.

"I don't know," I say.

She begins tracing random patterns on my chest lazily.

"Don't you ever want to know what else you could've done with your life? Don't you ever wonder if there was more destined for you than carnage and death?" she says.

I have to really think about her words. When I was younger maybe. But even then, I never had the time to be anything other than what my father wanted me to be. A killer.

"Do you remember your mother?" she asks.

I literally don't know how to respond to her. She doesn't wait for my response, though.

"I don't remember mine. I can't even remember her face. Is that awful of me?"

I open my mouth to respond, but she cuts me off.

"Did you see her face? You know, when you …" She trails off. I clear my throat.

"Elise, this isn't something we should be discussing," I say.

"Hmmm." She grunts, rolling away from me. I close my eyes, trying to rein in my emotions.

After a moment, she speaks.

"Do I look like her?" she says.

"I don't remember much about her, Elise," I say honestly. "She was just a target. Another job."

She rolls over, facing me head-on.

"Do you remember what your mother looked like?" she asks.

I nod slowly. She smiles softly at me.

"Do you have any pictures of her?"

I slowly get out of bed and walk over to my top drawer, pulling out the photo underneath my clothes. I walk back to the bed, handing it to her. I haven't looked at that picture in years. And now that I look, I can feel strong emotions coming back. I watch as Elise holds my mother's picture in her hands, tracing her soft features.

A small smile is curved on her face. "You look just like her."

I actually smile at that.

"Luca, will our son know me?" Her question catches me completely off guard.

"What on earth are you talking about?" I say.

"It's just that, in this line of living, our mothers don't live for very long. And sons rarely know their mothers. We've barely been married for two years, and people are already out to kill me. I just want you to promise me that if something happens to me, you will tell him about me." She looks up at me with a sad smile.

I reach out, pushing her loose strands away from her face. I look her straight in the eyes.

"Elise, I love you. No matter what, I will protect you. Nothing will happen to you, I promise."

Her smile drops.

"Luca, I almost died. I almost died. The whole time I was trapped in that house, I just knew you were going to come save me, to protect me and not let anything bad happen to me. But I was wrong."

She could've jammed a knife through my heart and it would have hurt less than her words. Her body jumps, and I know she is crying.

"He locked me in a room right under your feet, and he chained me to the column. I had to break the stair with my bare fist to beat it against the ceiling, but by the time I got it, you were gone."

I feel my heart sink in my chest. That was her. Those three hard knocks. They were her. And I was so caught up in my anger that I didn't bother to check it out. I assumed it was Alexander.

"He said the room was soundproof. You couldn't hear me screaming your name, and when you left, he didn't unchain me from the column. He raped me against it."

Her voice chokes, and she looks at me with true heartbreak in her eyes.

"I know you'll do everything in your power to protect me. You made that clear when you took a bullet for me. But sometimes it's going to be out of your power, and there will be nothing you can do about it. So I want you to promise me that our son will know me. Even when I'm gone. And please, Luca, don't let him forget my face."

I just watch her. I can feel my eyes stinging, and then I can feel the water as the tears roll down my face. She is right. And I hate it. Women in this line of important heads of families don't live very long. It happened with her mother, and it happened with mine.

She smiles at me, and a small laugh escapes her lips. She reaches out to wipe the tears that roll down my face.

"The big bad capo crying about his wife's fate?" she all but whispers to me.

I grab her hand, bringing it to my face to caress. She is looking at me in confusion.

"I think I'm losing my mind, Luca," she whispers. "Every time I close my eyes, I'm back there … back with him."

"He's gone, Elise. He's never coming back."

"Tell that to my brain," she says. "There are other men out there just like him. They put me in a room, and they were selling me. You should have heard the bids. All because I was your wife." She rolls on her back, staring at the ceiling.

"Elise, look at me," I say.

She rolls over, looking me dead-on. I grab her palm and put it under my shirt over my heart. We sit in silence as she gets used to the rhythm.

"You feel that? As long as it's beating, nothing will happen to you. I will protect you with every breath I have in my body. You are everything. I love you more than my own life. Our son will know you and be raised by you. He will, I promise."

She gives me a small smile and looks as though she is about to say something, but she pauses, a light gasp escaping her lip.

"I think he agrees with you. He just kicked."

I can't help the excitement that flashes on my face. She reaches out, grabbing my hand. She lifts her shirt, exposing her swollen belly, and places my hand on a spot. After a moment, I feel it. A tiny thump. And it drags across my palm. I let out a laugh of disbelief.

My phone vibrates on the nightstand, ruining the small moment we have. I have to roll away from her to answer it.

"Yeah?"

"Boss, it's now or never. Everything is in order. It's your decision now." Romelo's voice comes through the line.

I look over to Elise, who is watching me with wide eyes. I've been putting off getting that agent because she can't be alone for very long. But today, I have made some arrangements.

"Yeah, okay, I'll see you in twenty minutes," I say, hanging up the phone.

I look at Elise, and she has a worried expression on her face. I give her a comforting smile and hold my hand out to her.

"Come," I say.

She tenses as she hears those words but reluctantly walks toward me. We head down the stairs, where Nicolai is waiting. He smiles at Elise, giving her a nod.

"Go wait for me on the patio, okay?" I say.

She gives me a weak nod and heads outside. I walk toward Nicolai.

"We're getting this done tonight. I've made for some people to come over to keep Elise company. High security is staying here while Romelo, and I go ahead alone."

Nicolai looks as though he doesn't like the idea, but he doesn't say anything.

"I want you to be near Elise at all times. Do not leave her under any circumstances. I also want you to make sure Matteo doesn't cause any trouble trying to act like a guard."

Nicolai nods at me in understanding. What I am doing is very risky. I am going to murder an agent of the government for my own personal gain, and the only backup I am bringing is Romelo. I want everyone here guarding Elise so that nothing will happen to her or our unborn child.

There is a knock on the door, and one of my men emerges seconds later with our valued guest. The man I shot in the mountain and his dog. He is walking with crutches due to his leg injury. Which I am not sorry for. And I can't believe I am trusting him in my home with my wife. But from what Elise has told me, I assume his presence will make her forget that I am even gone. He narrows his eyes distastefully at me as he approaches.

"Welcome to my home," I say.

He still doesn't respond, which causes my contained anger to finally erupt. I step forward, kicking his crutch out from underneath him, causing him to lose balance and stumble on his hurt leg, collapsing. The dog growls at me, but I don't listen. It is obviously a trained dog that will only attack on this man's command.

"Do not disrespect me in my own home. I said welcome," I growl out.

"Thank you," he mutters back from the floor.

"Your job is to make my wife feel safe. The way she talks about you, your presence seems to calm her down. That is your role. Nothing else." I study him closely as I speak, and he studies me too. "Do you understand?" I say out loud. He only nods in return to me.

I walk to the patio and see Elise once again looking at nothing. I stand in the doorway, studying her. She doesn't seem to be just looking because she is bored; she is zoned out. She always does that.

"Elise." She turns at the sound of my voice. I walk to her, taking a seat in front of her. I grab her chair, pulling her closer to mine so that my legs are in between hers.

"I have to go for a while. To take care of some business."

Her eyes immediately widen, and pure terror blooms. "What? No, no, please don't leave me."

"Nicolai will be here to guard you, along with everyone else. No one is coming through that gate." Her eyes turn angry, and she grabs my collar, yanking me close to her.

"Do not leave me … please." Her eyes look crazed, and her voice is shaking uncontrollably.

I slowly put my hands around hers, and they are shaking as well as the rest of her body. I clasp both of her hands in mine and take a deep breath, looking her in the eyes.

"Elise, I have to go. I won't say it again." I let my authority seep into my voice. I have been lenient with her as of late, but she is beginning to forget who I am. Either that or she is just that scared out of her mind.

Her bottom lip begins to tremble, and I can feel my heart beginning to melt. But I have to fight it. This is important. I let out a deep sigh, placing her hands between mine.

"Elise, I will be back before you know it, okay? I promise. Nothing is going to happen to you. I brought you a friend." I motion for Eli to step outside. Before he can really step, the dog is running out of the house toward Elise, and her face lights up.

"Rocco? Eli?" she says, watching them. Her reaction almost makes me want to change my mind and shoot the man and the dog.

"You can have your afternoon with your friend, and by the time you eat, shower, and go to sleep, I'll be home. Okay?"

She looks back at me and timidly nods.

I lean forward, giving her a kiss on her forehead. "I'll see you later. I love you."

I stand to leave and walk away from her but falter midstep when I hear the faintest whisper. It almost sounds as if she said she loves me. But when I turn around, her attention is already focused on the dog. I must have imagined it.

* * * * *

The easy part about these things is getting the target and making them pay. The hardest part is infiltrating the target's home, workspace, or just anywhere you can get the target without being noticed. Getting in this guy's house was easy. Unlocking the house code was simple, and once we were in, we had to tamper with the video cameras the guy had set up. Nothing can be out of place.

And now here the bastard is. Tied to a chair, mouth duct-taped, naked, and ready for death. His eyes slowly flutter open, and once he sees me, he jumps in his seat and begins struggling.

"I think you may want to save your struggling for later."

He stops and stares at me with a hateful gaze. I step forward, placing my hand on the tape covering his mouth.

"Now I'm going to remove the tape. And if you make a sound, I will kill you." I wait for him to take in the meaning of my words. Then I rip the tape off.

"HELP!" He begins to shout and scream and cry and plead, and I sit there and wait.

When his throat finally turns raw, he looks at me with wide eyes. I smile back, and a hysterical laugh escapes my throat. This is truly amusing to me. He thinks there is someone around that can help him. I would be an idiot to bring him somewhere people can hear his cries.

"You are really something, Agent Jeffries. You must really take me for a fool. Like I'd bring you somewhere people could hear your screams."

His eyes widen at the revelation I purposely let out. I walk to the table, picking up the handheld power drill. His breathing speeds up when I move even closer to him.

"Now, I want to know why you put my wife in a fucking auction house."

He wipes his face of emotion and spits at me. It almost lands on my fucking face. I push the drill into the thick muscle of his thigh until it is fully sheathed, and even then, I keep the drill on high. Jeffries screams out in agony, and I stop the drill, keeping it fully sheathed in his thigh.

"You do realize that because of you, when I finally found her, she was pregnant?" I motion for Romelo to hand me the hammer and some nails. I place a nail on top of his thigh and aim the hammer.

"She claims she was pregnant before Alexander touched her. But you know, I'm still a little skeptical about that. So imagine what I have to go through, not knowing for certain whether or not that's my child." With that, I hammer the nails in a line down his thigh. He is crying out, but still not cracking.

I look at Romelo. "Get me the jumper cables." I look at Agent Jeffries. "That chair you're sitting in is all metal."

At that moment, Romelo sets down the cables that are attached to a car battery.

"Let's see how quiet you are when you have this current running through your body."

Two and a half hours later, I have my answers. And I do not like them one bit. I am shaking in a rage. Anger is clouding my better judgment.

"Boss."

Romelo's hesitant voice tells me everything I already know. I am not stable right now. There is something much bigger than me at play here. Everyone is against me. Outside of the North family, they are trying to bring me down. Someone has stationed a snitch among my contacts in the government.

They are trying to get rid of me. That's why Elise was chased down in that crash. They thought she was me. They are trying to kill me. And by sending Elise to an auction house, where other leaders are, they know that by buying her, a war is sure to erupt. If that woman hadn't called me about Elise, I would have gone off the deep end and started a war, assuming one of those bastards had Elise. And that is what I almost did.

That is also why my father was shot down and why Matteo and I were almost killed by the disgusting traitors at that party. This goes deeper than the Trovolis. They have other traitors with them as well helping with their affairs.

It is time for me to go underground until I can get everything in order. Until I can weed out the traitors and snitches and make everyone fear me once again and think twice about betraying me.

I look at my watch. Tomorrow. We need to pack everything up and be gone before the day after tomorrow. I turn to Romelo.

"Can you get Jeffries's contacts, in the government address, that snitched on us?" I ask.

He nods. I turn to look at the dead agent's body.

"I want you to send his body in pieces to the man. And tell him he's next. I've had it with traitors."

Romelo moves to grab the ax off the wall and begins dismembering Agent Jeffries. But I stop him. This is fucking personal. I grab the ax myself and go to work.

Chapter 50

Elise

Never in a million years would I have thought I would want Luca's presence, but here I am, watching the door, hoping he'll walk through any second. But he doesn't. Nicolai tries to give me a reassuring smile every time I look toward the door, but it doesn't help. I feel like someone is going to get me unless Luca is here with me.

"So this is where you live?"

Eli's voice pulls me out of my thoughts. He is looking around at my home in fascination. Rocco is sitting at my feet, with his tongue lolling out of his head. He really seems to be happy about seeing me.

"You know, I remember you saying your husband was important, but damn …" He is still talking about the house.

"How'd you end up here?" I ask.

He looks at me with a raised eyebrow. "Your husband said you could use some company. He said you spoke highly of us."

I eye him skeptically. That isn't all he told him. Eli is acting different. I look back toward where Nicolai is standing, and he gives me another reassuring smile. I motion for him to come over, and he hurries to my direction.

"Have you gotten a call from Luca?" I say.

He shakes his head, and I feel my stomach drop. I have been so dependent on him. I need him. I only recently got to the point where I can function without him being in the room. But I have to know which room he is in at least. And how long he'll be gone.

The nightmares have gotten worse. Every time I close my eyes, I am in a horrible situation. The nightmares with Alexander have thinned out. Now it is just with someone that I don't know. Not even a face, but a dark figure that is torturing me. And instead of me being able to escape, there is no way out. Sometimes the dreams end in my child being ripped away from me. And Luca doesn't rescue us.

I am having a hard time adjusting to his absence currently. I feel so paranoid about everything. Every time I round the corner, if I am just standing in the kitchen, I feel like someone is watching me, about to snatch me up to get to Luca. Or worse, the life growing inside of me. I am more than excited that we are having this baby and Luca is growing to accept him, but as the term drags on, more and more doubt wells up inside of me.

If the world finds out about our bundle of joy, enemies left and right will come and try to end him. And what better time to get to him than when he is still growing inside his mother's womb? Not only that, but since it is a boy, that means he is going to one day inherit this empire. Which means when he is born, Luca will begin grooming him once he is old enough. Of course, that isn't what I want for my son, but I don't really have a choice in the matter.

I am shocked out of my thoughts as Eli snaps his fingers in front of my face.

"Hello? Anybody home? Gosh, girl, you seem out of it."

I feel my face burning and let out a sheepish laugh. "Sorry. My mind is just somewhere else right now," I say.

He looks like he is still concerned. "So what have you been doing in the time you've been home? Anything particular?" he says.

"Not really. I've just been trying to adjust. How'd you get out here?" I ask.

"Well, your husband is a very convincing man, and we just couldn't refuse the invitation. Besides, he paid for airfare and everything, so ..." He shrugs, as if it were nothing, but I know Luca. I'm sure he didn't politely ask him out here.

"How's your leg?" I ask.

He motions to his leg. "Well, I have to say that I've never been on crutches before, so it's been a little difficult, but I'll make it."

"And you didn't go to the police?" I ask, really hoping he didn't. If Luca finds out, he'll have him taken care of.

He shakes his head. "No. I remember what you said about your husband, so I figured it wouldn't be the smartest move. I watch the movies." He gives me a smile, and I can't help a small giggle that escapes my lips.

"Yeah, well, this life is nothing like the movies. If anything, the movies downplay it," I say honestly.

He shrugs his shoulders. "So your husband … he's not really a people person, is he?" he says.

I know that tone. "What did he do?"

He gives an off laugh. "Oh, nothing too bad, just kicked my crutches out from under me because I didn't say hello. I mean, honestly, I thought I had every right to not say hello, seeing as he put me on these things in the first place," he says.

"I'm sorry, he's just used to things going his way," I say.

"Yeah, obviously." He points to my stomach. "So you guys know what you're having?"

"A boy."

He leans back in his chair. "Great, a mini version of your husband." He says it jokingly, not knowing how spot-on he is. Once this baby is old enough, Luca is going to train him to be just like him.

"You okay? You seem different."

"Yeah, I'm fine, just a little shaken. I can't help but feel like something bad is going to happen. I'm going to be stuck with someone as bad as that man was and I'll never be saved."

I feel his hand over mine and immediately jerk back, looking around. Nicolai is watching us from the doorway. "You can't touch me like that," I say.

He raises his hands. "Okay, okay, sorry. I'm just really sorry that whatever happened to you happened. I can tell it must have been horrible. You look like you haven't slept in days, and I see the way you keep looking around."

I let out a deep breath.

"It sounds like you may have PTSD. The paranoia, the nightmares … you seemed fine when you were with me, but even then,

I could tell you were a little bothered by something. And it's gotten worse since then."

I look away.

We continue to talk as the sun sets and nightfall begins to take over. I look over, and Nicolai is still standing in the doorway, fully alert.

"Well, I think it's time for me to turn in and go to sleep. I'm exhausted," I say.

Eli smiles at me understandingly. "Yeah, you need all the sleep you can get before that little guy gets here."

I laugh at his response. He gives me a hug, and I pet Rocco one last time before one of Luca's men walks him out.

I walk toward Nicolai, and he looks at me knowing what I am about to ask.

"Have you heard from Luca?"

He looks as though he is about to lie to me but thinks better of it. "No."

I can feel my eyes widening as fear creeps up my spine. Why hasn't he called? Could something have happened? I can feel a full-blown panic attack forming in my chest.

Nicolai places his hands on my shoulders, looking me in the eyes. "I'm sure everything is fine, Elise. He had important business to take care of tonight, and he probably is just too busy to call. You're completely safe here, okay?"

I nod, but his words fall on deaf ears. If Luca isn't here, I am not safe.

I push past Nicolai into the house, walking to the kitchen for a drink of water. I step in to see Matteo picking at some food on his plate. He looks up when he sees me.

"Are you okay? You look a little pale."

I nod vigorously, heading to the fridge and grabbing a bottle of water. I hate how frightened I am. The anxiety I have is building by the second. I feel like I am going to explode into a fit of screams any minute now. I jump as I feel something on my shoulder, a loud scream escaping my lips.

Matteo is right behind me and looks shocked. He takes a step back.

"I was just trying to talk to you," he says.

I nod. "I know, I'm sorry." I don't wait for him to respond as I run out of the kitchen to find Nicolai. The clock reads 11:47. I see Nicolai standing in the foyer.

"Nicolai." His shoulders tense, and he turns around to face me. I can already tell by the expression on his face the answer to my unasked question.

"Please tell me Luca is on his way home."

He lets out a deep sigh, shaking his head. I can feel the tears welling up in my eyes as pure fear begins coursing through my veins. My arms feel tingly, as if someone is watching me, and the paranoia is beginning to set in.

"Call him," I say.

Nicolai looks shocked. "Uh, ma'am?"

"I said, call him. Now." I try to emphasize the urgency.

He slowly pulls his phone out, dialing Luca and handing it to me. It only rings once before Luca picks up.

"This better be fucking important," he growls into the phone.

I flinch from his tone, memories flashing into my head. "I … I …"

"Elise?" His whole tone completely changes. "Are you okay? What's going on? Are you hurt? Is it the baby?" He starts asking me one question after another.

"No, no, everything's fine. I just wanted to know when you'd be home," I say.

He lets out a long breath. "Elise, I want you to go shower. Get Nicolai once you're dressed and tell him to search the room while you're there. Once he's done, get in bed. Close all the windows and lock them and close the bedroom door. He will be standing guard outside your room along with my most trusted men, okay?" He once again is speaking to me as if I am a five-year-old. I guess with my behavior, I am acting like one. I am like a child afraid of the dark.

"Elise," his voice comes through the phone once again, and I realize I haven't responded to him.

"When will you be home?" I ask again. There is a pause on the other end.

"I promise I'll be home by the time you wake up, beautiful." His voice comes out like silk, and I know he is trying to sweet-talk me. "I love you, okay?" he says into the phone.

My heart is pounding in my chest. Earlier, I hadn't thought about it when I responded to him, and it was so quiet he hadn't even heard me when I said it. But now, on the phone, I have every chance to say it back. But am I sure of my feelings? Am I only feeling this way because I am scared?

"Hand the phone to Nicolai," he says.

I frown, a little disappointed, but give in, giving the phone to Nicolai and heading upstairs.

Later, I am standing by the doorway as Nicolai does a thorough search of the room. He walks toward me with a soft smile on his face.

"Looks like the boogeyman won't be getting you tonight, Mrs. Pasquino." He heads to the door, pulling it close behind him. "I'll be right outside. Luca will be home any minute now, okay? Sweet dreams." The door closes, leaving me in the bedroom alone.

I slowly walk to the bed, getting under the plush covers. As soon as I close my eyes, I feel a pressure in my stomach. He is kicking again.

"You always decide to act up when I'm going to sleep," I mumble. I can't help the small smile that creeps on my face. I place my hand over my stomach and feel where he is kicking. In a few months, I am going to be a mother, and Luca a father.

I am excited but, at the same time, terrified. Once he is the right age, Luca is going to take my baby boy and train him to be a cold-blooded killer. And that is the last thing I wanted for my son. I want him to be kind and gentle. I want him to have a chance at life and to love and be loved. I know there is no choice for him in the matter, though. Luca's father and mine are a clear example of what I don't want to happen to him.

I know what he is meant to do, but I want him to know the difference between duty and family. I want him to know what love is. Maybe I can make some kind of arrangement with Luca. Maybe I can talk him out of turning our son cruel.

I let out a loud laugh. As if that is possible. Born in blood—that is what we are. This is a part of us. There are no exceptions, no escape. Just accepting what is.

I rub my stomach as a new thought comes over me. With everything that is going on, Luca and I have hardly had a chance to come up with what he will be named. I will have to discuss it with him as soon as he gets home and things settle down.

Chapter 51

Luca

My watch reads 3:30 a.m. We are just now getting back. We had to dispose of the body, cover every possible track, and make it seem like we were never there. It was a lot of work, but it will all be worth it in the end.

I look at Romelo, and I can see he is just as tired as I am.

"I want my office packed. Leave nothing behind. Wake Matteo, and whatever he wants to bring, tell him to bring it. I want all the important files packed away. Do not wake Elise until the very last second, when it's time to leave. We need to do this quickly and quietly. Tell no one of our plan. As soon as we are gone, take your loved ones and go into hiding as well. I'll give Nicolai the same orders. You two will also be targets because you're my right-hand guys."

He nods, and we go to work.

It takes us about three hours to get everything packed up and situated. Once the cars are loaded and the men are aware of the situation, I call a meeting. While everyone is gathering, I walk up the stairs to my bedroom. Nicolai is standing at the ready once I arrive.

"How many nightmares?" I ask, knowing that she has had some.

"Three total. The last one was the worst. I don't know if she went back to sleep from it or if she's still awake."

I nod and enter the room. Elise is asleep on her side, with pillows in between her legs. I make a mental note to get her a body pillow. I gently shake her, and her eyes open immediately, laced with fear. Once she realizes it is me, the fear is replaced by joy, and I can't help the smile that comes onto my face.

"Hey, baby."

"Hey." Her voice comes out in a small whisper, and she blushes, looking away.

"I don't want you to get scared, but I need you to get dressed and meet me downstairs in fifteen minutes, okay?"

She looks confused and reads the time on the clock.

"I know it's early. I just need you to do what I asked, okay? I'll explain everything later."

She nods and stretches out on the bed. I was planning on turning to leave, but I am so mesmerized by the action. Her hair is messy from sleep, and it looks sexy as hell. And she has worn a tank top and underwear to bed. She looks beautiful. Before I realize what I am doing, I am caressing her cheek with my hand and then cupping her face, leaning in. Her eyes are wide while she watches me. I capture her soft lips in mine. She immediately kisses me back. I can feel my dick getting hard in my pants at the contact. It has been so long since I've felt her lips against mine. And my body obviously missed it.

By the time I finally pull back, we are both panting. I don't know what to say. I lean in, giving her a quick peck on the lips and turn to leave.

* * * * *

I look at all the men in the room. Men I have trained with, grown up with. Some I am related to, and some sworn in. But I trust these men with my life.

"This isn't easy for me to say, and it honestly makes me angry. It's time for us to disperse. There are things going on outside of the North family. Until I can figure out specifically what, our being together and in the open isn't safe anymore. Take your families and go underground. Keep an ear out because I will be in contact with all of you. I am not disclosing my location to anyone. And neither should you. Tell no one of where you're going. And if you do, do so at your own risk. This is much bigger than us. And until we can figure out a way to get out of this, we need to lie low. For how long, I cannot tell you. But stay ready. This is not a vacation. This is a preparation. At any moment, I can call you with the plan. We are the most powerful family in the North—hell, maybe even the world—so we will be back. And we will have our vengeance."

Nicolai and Romelo begin passing out thick envelopes.

"In these envelopes are specific instructions made for each individual in this room. Do not open them until you are in your safe zone. And follow them. If you don't, or anything is suspicious, we will assume the worst."

I look around at all the faces in the room.

"We will meet again, and when we do, we will take back what is ours and get rid of the swine that dared cross the North Mafia."

Cries of agreement echo throughout the room. These men are just as angry as I am.

I step out of the room, and Elise is in the foyer like I asked. Romelo and Nicolai are by my side.

"Luca, what's going on?" she asks, eyeing the men exiting the room.

"I'll explain everything in the car." I grab ahold of her hand and walk her toward the garage with me. Sure enough, the car is running. I can see Matteo sitting in the back seat.

"Go get in the car."

Elise looks at me warily but walks around to the passenger seat, closing the door behind her.

I turn to Romelo and Nicolai.

"Are you sure you don't want us to go with you, boss?" Romelo is the first to speak up.

I shake my head. "Yes." I can tell by his reaction Nicolai doesn't appreciate my answer. "You two are my most trusted men. Not only that, but you are my best friends. Keep in touch. Remember what I told you."

They nod in unison. With that, I get in the car, closing the door. Matteo is asleep in the back seat, but Elise is awake.

"Luca, what is going on?" Her voice is panicked, and I can see her body shaking in fear. I should have explained to her earlier, but I have been so focused on getting out of here and explaining the situation that I forgot she is paranoid. Gosh, I am an asshole.

I grab her hand in mine as we pull out into the road. I bring her hand to my mouth, giving her a gentle kiss. "We're getting off the grid for a while. Something's come up, and it's just a little precaution. I promised you I'd protect you and your brother, Elise, as well as our son, and this is me keeping that promise, okay?"

She nods slowly.

We ride in silence for a little while, and I notice Elise has finally fallen asleep. I want to sleep myself, but I don't have the time. The sooner we get off the grid, the better. I am going to protect my family, no matter what. And I will kill anyone that gets in the way.

Chapter 52

Elise

When Luca said he would explain everything to me, I thought he was really going to do just that, but he proved me wrong, because explaining is the last thing he does. He drives us to the airport and puts us on a plane without so much of an explanation. The flight takes us about nine hours, and even then, he refuses to tell us where we are going.

"The less you know, the better."

That is what he keeps telling us every time we ask.

Since the plane landed, we've been driving for about three hours. I am exhausted and cranky, but I try my best not to show it. Whatever is going on is serious, because Luca is tense and very vague when answering questions.

Wherever we are has to be another country, because the sun is coming up. Matteo is sound asleep in the back, and I can feel my eyes getting heavy, but I can't go to sleep.

"You can go to sleep if you want to, Elise. You look tired."

I sit up in my seat and look over at him. He still has a hard face, as if he's trying to hide his emotions from me. "Are you okay, Luca?"

Now he looks at me. "Why would you ask that?"

"Well, you kind of came home in a hurry … and you just packed us up in the middle of the night and made us leave, and you won't even tell me where." I am a little afraid to admit it, but I feel like I can talk to Luca more now than ever.

He lets out a deep sigh. "There are just things going on right now, and we just need to move out of the open for a little bit."

My heart jumps at his words, and I feel myself beginning to panic. I hate how afraid I am of everything.

I feel a hand over mine. Luca clasps my hand in his. "Elise, I won't let anything happen to you. Where we're going, no one can hurt you, I promise."

After I catch my breath, I respond to him, "And where are we going, Luca?"

"A little cottage I bought on my own a few years back. No one knows about this place, not even Romelo or Nicolai."

I look at him in confusion. If anything, Luca is the last person I expected to buy a cottage, of all things. He strikes me as more of the flashy kind of guy. Which explains why our homes are so large and his cars are so extravagant.

As if sensing the direction of my thoughts, a smile flits over his lips.

"When I was younger, my mother brought me out here on a mini vacation, to get away from the daily hell I was born into." His smile grows larger, as if he is remembering the exact moment. "She hated having guards. So one day, she just took me and we went riding. I was about thirteen at that time. We got completely lost in a foreign country, and we came upon this cottage. It was beautiful, and she absolutely loved it. She said she wanted it to be our secret spot. That no one would know about it. Not even my father. But with her being the wife of the capo, no purchases she made would be private. So when I turned eighteen, I bought it for her. Had it renovated and everything. She used to come out here all the time."

He grows silent, and his smile slowly drops.

"I haven't been here since she died."

"When did she die?" My voice is an almost whisper.

I have always been curious as to how Luca's mother died. No one ever had a clear story of how she died, or even when. But everyone knows she did. She stopped showing up to events, and Luca's father became an unpleasant person to be around. And Luca ... well, it was hard to tell if he was raised that way or if he was acting out because of what happened to his mother.

"When I turned twenty. We were going to an event. The three of us. It was a party at a friend's house. And by *friend* I mean business partner. My father took off with my mother, talking to people and being his usual self. The night was going well until the gunfire started."

I watch Luca closely. I can feel the anger and despair he feels while reliving this nightmare.

"They caught her. They tortured her and did horrible things to her. And when we thought we had her back, they let her walk out of that car across the street to us and they shot her just as she was near. They shot her no less than five feet away from me. I had to watch her die, because we trusted them. We trusted their word. We thought if we did what was asked of us, they would return her to us. But they didn't. They lied."

His hands tighten around the steering wheel. The ride is silent except for Matteo's soft snoring in the back seat.

I can't imagine what Luca feels. He knew his mother. He grew up with her, and he spent a lot of time with her. Judging from the way he speaks of her, he really loved his mother. And she was killed in front of him when he was about to save her. All because he trusted what people said. Now I can see why trust is such a huge issue for him.

"I didn't know who you were when I did what I did to your mother. I knew you were too young to remember it, though, or understand what was going on. I had no idea they were going to make me marry you years later. And I am sorry for that, Elise. But I almost had her. She was right there, right in front of me. And they shot her in the back."

He sighs.

"I loved my father, I did, but my mother was everything to me. A part of me died with her. A part that I never thought I'd get back. That is, until I met you. The moment you said 'I do,' I could feel it. You healed a part of me I never thought I'd get back."

His eyes meet mine, and he looks shocked. There are tears running out of my eyes. My heart is bleeding for Luca. I have never seen him so open before about something so personal.

"Don't cry for me, Elise. I'm not a good man. I've done some things that I can never take back, and some things I don't even regret. I couldn't save my mother because we were weak. We trusted when we should have taken. I won't ever let that happen again."

His eyes drift back to the road. I look down to my stomach, which is now carrying a life. When he is born, will he end up like Luca? Can I save him from that fate?

The thing I fear most is that my son may never know me like I never knew my mother. Or if he does, he'll end up like Luca once I am gone. Luca says he'll protect me, but in the back of my mind, I know that is an impossible thing to promise.

Luca isn't a good man, that I know, but he has good tendencies. He has moments when he makes me forget all the horrible things. And he has moments when I forget he even loves me. But I know the good tendencies must be something his mother instilled in him. He is a mix of both of his parents, and he's been with his father the majority of his life. But now that his father is gone, he has moments when he looks at me with so much love that I almost forget the hell that he dragged me through. *Almost.* And I have his mother to thank for that.

"What was her name?" I ask.

He looks over at me, and a small smile pulls at his mouth. "Lucia. Her name was Lucia Pasquino."

I smile at him, rubbing my stomach subconsciously. *Lucia.*

We arrive at the cottage an hour later. It is in the middle of a forest, but the land around it is cleared out, with a security gate around the property. And there is a large pond behind it. It is a beautiful home. And it looks very warm and inviting. Luca pulls up the driveway, parking the car outside and turning it off. Once he helps me out of the car, we walk inside the front door. He turns, speaking to Matteo.

"You can go and pick which room is yours."

Matteo doesn't hesitate to take off up the stairs. There has to be at least five bedrooms in this place, and it still looks clean, as if someone upkeeps it.

"I have people come in and clean it every two weeks," Luca says, as if sensing my thoughts.

He grabs ahold of my hand, leading me through the large foyer. I can feel the heat from his hand seeping into mine. It is comforting, the grip he has. As if he doesn't want to let go.

"We're going to take the master bedroom downstairs. I don't want you walking back and forth, up and down the stairs in your condition." He smiles at me, opening the door to a beautiful room with coral walls.

The sun is shining through the large windows, and I can see down the path to the lake. There is a large bed in the middle of the room, with a fireplace and two walk-in closets.

"Luca, this place is really beautiful," I whisper.

He and his mother renovated this place and it really turned out beautiful. He gives me a quick kiss on my temple.

"Thank you. I want you to get some rest. I know you're probably tired. If you need anything at all, my office is down the hall to the left." I nod, and he threads his fingers through my hair, giving me a searing kiss.

"You can leave the door open if you want to. I love you." He walks out of the room before I can respond.

Chapter 53

Luca

I sit in my office and set up the security feed. Nicolai and Romelo have already checked in, and everyone else is good to go. Now that we are all out of the spotlight, we need to take down the bastards that are after us.

Apparently, there is a government agency that wants us gone. A group that even the president knows nothing about. Like he could do something if he did. All I know is that that means things will go better for us. Who would miss something that they never even knew is there? So we can kill off every single one of them without having to worry about a big cleanup or any media pressure. This operation can take months to plan and pull off, but I want every possible threat out of the way before my son is born.

I hate it every time Elise speaks of me having to raise him by myself. She thinks that no matter what, she is going to die and not get to raise him. Everything I am doing now is to ensure that she will get that luxury. I won't let her end up like my mother. My father was too trusting. He made mistakes that could have been avoided. And he drove a wedge in their marriage. I am nothing like him.

The thing about dropping off the map is that everything is ensured to you. You have no backup or anything; it is just you making the decisions or having to protect yourself.

After I get done, I walk past the room to check on Elise, and she is sound asleep. I walk around, ensuring that the escape routes are all still working and the security is in check before the sun goes down completely. I am not going to take any chances with Elise and Matteo being here.

I go in search of Matteo and find him fast asleep as well in the bedroom he chose. They must both be tired from the trip. I walk back down the stairs and into our bedroom to find Elise sitting up in bed. Her hair is wet, so she must have taken a shower in the time I've been gone checking the perimeter. She's only in a bra and some shorts, her bare stomach out, and she is smiling while she rubs it. She is murmuring something to him.

She is so entranced with what she is doing that she doesn't even notice me in the doorway. The sun is setting, and the bedside lamp is on, engulfing her in an orange glow. Damn, she is beautiful. She is so damn beautiful. I can't help but admire her.

Women are a peculiar thing. They can nurture life within them, and once that life is born, they continue to nurture that life until the day they die.

The bulge of her stomach proves that there is a life growing inside of her. Something that we've together created. I shouldn't have done what I did behind her back, but at this moment, as I watch her lovingly caress her stomach, I don't regret it.

"I love you so much, my little Luciano," she murmurs.

I let out a surprised breath, and she jumps, looking at me with wide eyes.

"Luca, you scared me! How long have you been—"

I cut her off as I make my way across the room, kicking the door close behind me and kissing her. I kiss her with everything I have in me. And I don't even realize until the cool air hits my cheeks that there are tears running down my face. I pull back from her, looking into the brown depths of her eyes. When I look at her, true happiness radiates from my very core. I love her. I love her with all I have. Everything in me. I love this woman.

I don't even give her a chance to say anything; I press another kiss to her lips, enjoying the soft feel of hers against mine.

"I love you, Elise. I love you so much," I murmur.

I lean down, pressing kisses along her neck and collarbone, and take my hands to push down her underwear. I come back up and continue to kiss her with everything I have in me. And I show her. I show her how much I love her.

* * * * *

We both lie in bed naked and sated. Elise is on her side, curled up to me, fast asleep, her soft breathing keeping me calm. Occasionally, she will flinch and cry out in her sleep, but she hasn't begun to scream yet.

My father always told me that no one woman will ever be enough. He told me I would get tired of the same thing and eventually move on to find mistresses. But for me, that will never be the case. I will never grow tired of Elise, and I will never let anything bad happen to her.

She told me she was thinking about it since we never had the discussion of names. I was always busy, and up until recently, she knew the subject is one that shouldn't be broached. But when I heard her name choice, every wall I had came crashing down. She wants to name him after my mother. *Lucia.* How can one woman come into my life and change me so much?

I place my hand lightly over her stomach. I can feel the small movements he is making. I can't hold back the smile that appears on my face.

Luciano. It is perfect. Just like my wife.

Chapter 54

Luca

Things, for the most part, have been running smoothly. Elise is getting better and better each day, and we have been growing closer. She opens up to me more and isn't afraid to tell me things. With that being said, her fear of being alone hasn't been deterred at all. So I haven't been able to go into town for business or anything, because the last time I tried, she had a really bad panic attack. So I just have the maids that come to clean the house bring me the things I need.

I watch Elise now in the doorway. She is fast asleep, and it is the middle of the day. She is exhausted all the time; the baby keeps her up sometimes, and sometimes her nightmares keep her up. I have considered getting her a psychiatrist but decided against it because too much will be at stake if they figure out who she is.

I walk over to the desk, writing her a little note and putting it on my pillow. One time, I left the room without telling her where I was going, and when she woke up, she was on a rampage. She was screaming and crying, and quite honestly, I thought she was going to pass out from how frightened she was. So now I just put a note in the room if she is asleep, letting her know where I will be. I make a mental note to take her shopping for the nursery. The baby will be here any week now, and we need to be ready whether it is here or back home.

I move to my office and pull out the floor plans for the building our enemy is occupying. I have been studying these for two weeks now. The deadline is coming up fast. I have video calls with all my men and even more conference calls with Nicolai and Romelo. To do this, we will literally have to be perfect.

"Luca."

I look up to find Matteo in the doorway. He's been stalking around upset and angry because I am trying to make him normal for the sake of his sister. But he doesn't want that. He wants to be a part of my world.

I motion for him to take a seat and go back to studying the plans.

"I assume you're here to convince me to let you join me again," I say, not even bothering to look at him.

He lets out a deep breath. "Luca, you've already exposed me to everything possible. I don't see why you're trying to make me settle down now of all times."

"Because your sister is home and safe and she wants you to have nothing to do with this."

"She's my sister, not my mother. Which I don't have anymore, thanks to—"

Before he can finish his sentence, I slam the prints on the table and look at him, letting all the anger I am feeling flourish.

"You're right. It is thanks to me that conniving bitch is dead. And I would gladly do it again if I had the chance. But it is also thanks to me that you are alive. And as long as Elise wishes it, you will stay out of the business. Understand?" I glare down at him.

He nods slowly with wide eyes.

"If that's all, you can go now." I slowly take my seat. He stands to slowly leave my office. "If you want to do something, get stronger for your sister so you can help protect her if a problem arises."

Matteo stops and turns to look at me.

"Then why won't you at least let me train with you? Please, Luca, you don't even have to take me with you when you go do business. Just train me, and when I turn eighteen, let me make that decision for myself."

I study him for a moment. He has come a long way from who he used to be. He has matured. And he is in bloodlust. I can see it in his eyes. He wants conflict. He wants bloodshed.

"Let me ask you a question, Matteo. Do you know the difference between *family* and *business*?"

He looks at me in confusion and chooses not to answer.

"There is no difference. The family is the business. You do what you must to protect your family, which is the business. You should go and check on the only family that you have left. Go talk to her. My answer will stay the same until hers changes. You are not my blood to control. You are hers."

I go back to studying the blueprints, ending the discussion. And Matteo knows it too, because he leaves my office without another word.

By the time I finish with the blueprints, my phone rings just as I set them aside.

"Yeah."

"Sixteen."

"What?"

"There are sixteen agents total. Eighteen if you count the two that run it."

For the first time in a long time, some good news is coming out of this.

"The two that run it are hardly at the office. There are eight there at a time, and eight out on cases. It will be easy to infiltrate, but getting the rest of them once the job is done is going to be the problem."

I sit back in my seat and think long and hard about the plan that is now developing in my head.

"We're going to infiltrate it."

"We?"

"You, me, and Nicolai. Once we get in, we need to tell the others the current location of each of the agents. Send them in twos to take them out. And we will go to finish off the leaders." I say it as if it were easy, but I know once we put the plan in motion, it is going to be a bitch to execute. Not only that, but planning for this will take a while, and time is a luxury I currently don't have since Elise is going to have the baby in less than a month.

Romelo and I stay on the phone discussing the plan for another hour and a half when Elise steps in my office. She is wearing a long dress that hugs her body but grows loose at the bottom, showing off her lovely figure. She gives me a small smile and takes a seat at one of the chairs in front of me.

"Something just came up. I'll call you back later, okay?" I hang up the phone before he can respond, and I stare at Elise. After a moment, a blush crawls its way up her neck, and she looks away sheepishly.

"You didn't have to get off the phone," she all but mumbles.

I can't help the laugh that escapes my lips. She is so adorable. "For you, yes, I did."

She finally looks back up at me, a small smile pulling at her lips.

"How are you feeling?" I ask. It is a routine thing I do every time I see her. Her health mentally and physically is very important to me.

"I'm fine."

My smile drops from my face as I pick up her patterns of movement. She is avoiding my gaze. There must be something she wants to say to me.

"Elise, if there's something you need to say, say it."

She seems to realize what she is doing and finally looks at me.

"Did you let Matteo tag along when I was missing?"

I let out an annoyed breath, leaning back in my chair. *You've got to be kidding me.* The punk went and snitched on me to his sister?

"Did he say something to you?" I ask, trying not to let anything on.

"No, it's just that … he's different now. He's quiet, and he won't talk to me, barely. And he has this … look in his eyes. Like he's seen something he shouldn't have."

I cock my head to the side, trying to convince her that I don't understand what she is talking about. But I know exactly what she sees. And now I am faced with the choice of lying to her or telling her the truth.

I've never had a problem in the past with lying to her, but now, for some reason, it is literally tearing me apart.

"Damn," I mumble aloud. And I know she hears me, because she sits back in her seat with wide eyes and looks as though she is about to cry.

"Luca, you didn't …," she whispers. And it breaks my heart.

"I just couldn't leave him alone. He was a nervous wreck! And he wanted to help in finding you!" I sound like an eight-year-old trying to defend myself.

She throws her hands in the air. "God, Luca, you could have just let him tag along, not let him participate in the killing! I asked you to keep him away from this, and you promised me you wouldn't get him involved. You promised!" Tears are spilling over, and she is looking at me with such disappointment. She drops her face in her hands.

"Elise—"

"Just don't!" Her tears stop immediately, and she looks at me in anger. I am actually shocked at her. She growls aloud and stands, forcing her chair to scrape loudly against the floor.

"I trusted you!"

I open my mouth to say something else, but she interrupts me yet again.

"No! You lied to me, you—"

"Elise!" I shout.

She immediately shuts up, and that damn bottom lip begins to tremble before she takes off running out of the room. Damn. I have never felt so guilty before.

After I finish everything, I head to our room, but she isn't in there.

I find Elise later in the living room, watching TV. Her legs are propped up on the ottoman, and there are the strangest food combinations around her. Peanut butter, pickles, mustard, bread, chocolate syrup, chips, baked chicken from the other night. And in her hands currently is ice cream. Which she is mixing with salt.

I step into the room silently, and as I get closer, I see she is crying. But when I look at the TV, *The Smurfs* is playing in French.

"Elise …"

She jumps but doesn't acknowledge my presence. I let out a deep breath, trying very hard to fight the urges that are currently building up within me. I take a seat next to her, and she fidgets away from me. After a moment of silence and taking in *The Smurfs*, I look at her.

"Elise, do you even know what they're saying?"

She doesn't even spare me a glance. "Oui." She turns her head and looks at me with an angry glare. "Vous pouves aller loin maintenant menteur." *You can go away now, liar.*

I have to hide my shock. I had no idea she could speak French. Then I have to rein in my anger because of her choice of words.

"Look, Elise, I'm sorry, okay? But your being gone was a dark time for me, and I wasn't thinking straight. He said he wanted to help and he wanted vengeance, so I gave it to him. I know how I felt when I was his age, so who am I to deny him that?"

She still doesn't look at me. She reaches out and grabs the jar of peanut butter, dipping a pickle in it and shoving it in her mouth without even flinching. I turn my nose up in disgust. I guess it is the pregnancy hormones. I read something about cravings in a pamphlet.

"Elise, can you please come to bed?"

She still doesn't respond to me, and my irritation is boiling up, about to spill over. She grabs a piece of chicken and is bringing it to her mouth, but I stop her, looking into her eyes.

"Elise, I am sorry. Please come to bed."

She slowly brings the chicken down and stands from the couch, not responding to me, and heads toward the bedroom. Once she is out of the room, I pull out my knife and throw it at the wall, listening to the satisfying thud as it sticks. I have to rid myself of this anger somehow. Elise is playing with fire, and she doesn't even realize it.

I take a deep breath and stand up to go to our bedroom.

It is the middle of the night when an earsplitting scream wakes me from my slumber. My eyes fly open, and I jump up, only to be punched in the nose, hard. I immediately reach for my gun and search for the threat when I realize it is Elise. She is still screaming and flailing her arms like a crazy person. I grab each of her wrists, trying to calm her.

"Elise! Elise, wake up! Wake up, baby, it's just a dream!"

Tears are running freely down her face, and even though her eyes flutter open, she is frantically looking around, like I'm not even here.

"Elise!" I shout, but it is no use. Her screams only grow louder, and her movements more frantic. Even her legs are joining the party. Her breathing has become frantic pants, and she won't listen to me, so I slap her across the face. Her screams stop, but her breathing is still frantic as she looks at me with wide eyes.

"Elise, I'm here. I'm right here." I try to comfort her.

She reaches out and touches my face, her hands moving down to my torso. I can feel myself immediately getting aroused but try to push that aside because Elise needs comfort right now.

"Hey, hey, I'm right here, baby. I'm right here."

Her eyes are still wide, and she nods frantically. I slowly pull her into me, and she sobs into my chest.

"Do you want to talk about it?" I can feel her head shaking no in my chest.

Dammit, if Alexander weren't already dead, I'd kill him. I can't imagine the torture Elise went through for her nightmares to have lasted this long. And her fears. She is still whimpering in my arms, and we both lie back in the bed, the light from the moon illuminating us.

I slowly push out of bed, and Elise cries out, grabbing onto me frantically.

"I'm just going to shut the curtains, okay?"

She nods slowly, and I walk over to the windows, closing the curtains and engulfing the room in darkness. I make my way back over to the bed and pull Elise close to me.

"Do you like it out here?" I try to start any kind of conversation so she can focus on something other than her fear.

"Y-yes." Her voice is shaken and very light.

"Well, you haven't been around much. How do you know if you like it?"

"As long as I'm with you, I'll like it." Her voice is still a small whisper.

I let out a soft chuckle. We have really come a long way from when we first got married. There was a point when she couldn't stand being in the same room as me. You would never guess a time like that existed with the way she is now.

"Luca?" Her voice pulls me out of my thoughts.

"Hmmm?"

"Does Luciano have to be sworn in?"

The room is deadly silent.

I don't know how to respond to her in the state that she is in. "Yes."

"But why?" she responds almost immediately.

I let out a deep breath. "He has to be, Elise. He's a Pasquino."

"But I don't want him to be," she all but whispers.

"There is nothing I can do about that, Elise, you know that. You know how things work with us."

Her sob pulls at my heartstrings.

"You're going to take my baby and train him to be a monster." She sobs into my chest.

I decide not to respond. Even if she wasn't in the state that she is in, we both knew that one day we would have to have an heir. If it's a boy, he is sworn in by blood. He is born into it. If it is a girl, she will be married off to someone of status, or since I am the capo, another capo, giving us more status. That is how we keep the crime families strong. That is how things always will be.

I can't help it that Elise will see him as a monster. I will see him as a successor, just like my father, and his father. To train him to be strong and fearless is to groom him to be capo when it is time for me to retire. I became capo at a very young age because my father was murdered. But I was ready, because my father made sure I would be. And I will do the same with Luciano. It doesn't mean I don't love him; I am doing it because I love him. And Elise doesn't understand that.

Her cries pull at my heartstrings. She sounds so sad and broken. But nothing I can say will be of any comfort, so I just let her cry on me until exhaustion takes over. She rolls away from me on her side, and I hear her mumble.

"You took my father, my mother, and my brother away from me, and now you're going to take my son."

* * * * *

"I like the yellow." Elise points to a yellow quilt that is made of a very soft material. I point to it, and the employees grab it off the shelf and take it to the front. I have decided to take Elise shopping for the nursery today. She has been down lately and needs something to take her mind off things.

After her meltdown, she gave Matteo her permission to resume his work with me. She knew he wasn't happy being normal. She said she was doing what was best for him, what will make him happy, but I could see her heart breaking the moment she told him the news. So I keep him on small things and haven't let him in on our plans. He may be her brother, but he needs all kinds of training before he goes with us into the actual field.

So here I am in the nearest town, taking my wife shopping for the nursery. Matteo is even here with us, helping pick out some things for his nephew. If you watch us from far away, we look like a happy little family excited about a new arrival. But up close, we are a family of issues.

"What do you think, Luca?" Elise asks me, catching me completely off guard.

"I'm sorry, what?"

She rolls her eyes at me, showing her irritation at my not paying attention. "I said, which do you prefer? Baby blue or navy blue?"

Shit. I am not even paying attention to what she is saying, so I have no idea what she is talking about.

"Baby blue," I say.

She watches me before finally turning away. As we walk to the next aisle, she starts talking to me.

"Luca, can you at least pretend to pay attention?"

I try, I really do, but I get distracted from the way those jeans are hugging her ass. She's been wearing a lot of dresses lately, and today she is wearing "pregnancy pants," so I can see every luscious curve.

"Luca!" she shouts, and I look at her, startled. Tears well up in her eyes. "You don't even care."

If she weren't so upset right now, I might've laughed. Lately, Elise has been crying about every little thing. The other day, there was a dog food commercial on, and she was literally crying while it was on. Just a random stream of tears when she saw the food.

Not only that, but she grows very angry over the strangest things. She was watching some soap opera, and the doctor ended up kissing his patient, and she threw popcorn at the TV, shouting all kinds of obscenities. She has been a very interesting person to be around, quite honestly, and I wonder how much of that is going to change once Luciano gets here.

Sometimes I catch her talking to him and apologizing about how she can't save him or how she won't be able to raise him. It really hurts me to see her so vulnerable. Not only that, but we have had two false alarms in the past three weeks. So I am literally on edge with everything. I have to execute this plan this week, or I will be screwed.

Once news hits that I have a boy, they will be all over us and we won't stand a chance. There are just a few setbacks with the plan. If I am out of the country and Elise has the baby, I won't be here. There are so many different things against me right now, but I need to get this done before he gets here so that while I raise him, there is no chance of him getting carelessly hurt.

Right on cue, my phone rings, and I look at the caller ID. Sure enough, Romelo is calling me. I give Elise an apologetic smile and step away from her to answer the phone.

"Yeah."

"It's now or never."

"What?"

"It's now or never, boss. When's the soonest you can leave?" he asks.

I look over at Elise, and she is now looking at cribs. "The soonest I can leave would be tonight."

"You gotta leave sooner than that. How long's the flight?" he asks.

"Fuck. It'll take me four hours to get to the nearest airport. And on top of that, the flight will take about nine hours."

"Damn, when you said go into hiding, you weren't bluffing. You need to leave now, or we won't be able to pull this off."

"Yeah, I got that. Just let me get Elise and Matteo home, and I'll be heading out as soon as I can."

"Okay, boss. Hurry."

I hang up the phone, walking toward Elise. I hate to do what I am about to do to her, but this is for her safety. I touch her lightly on her back, so as not to startle her.

"Elise, baby, we got to go."

She notices the look in my eyes and nods, not even bothering to argue with me. I look for Matteo and motion for him to come on. The drive to get home is an hour. Once I get there, I immediately begin putting the cottage in lockdown.

I've already explained everything to Matteo, so he begins to gather the necessary items and heads down to the bunker I have underground.

I walk Elise down into the bunker, and she doesn't make a sound. It is spacious and has room for eight people. There are bedrooms, a kitchen, bathrooms, and a living room, all for the comfortably wealthy to live in, well, comfortably. I take Elise to the room we have shared and set her on the bed. Her face is blank of any emotion. She has barely spoken a word to me since we left the town. I check my watch. I don't have much time.

"Elise."

She looks up at me, and her expression is filled with sadness. I take a deep breath because I know what is coming next.

"I have to leave for a few days." Her breathing catches in her throat as she watches me and slowly begins to shake her head. "Listen to me, okay?"

I grab her head in between my hands and look at her dead-on.

"You will be safe here, okay? Matteo knows the codes in case of an emergency. No one is getting inside of this place unless it is me. Okay?"

Her eyes fill with tears, and she shakes her head no. "No, Luca, you're supposed to stay here. You're supposed to protect us." Her voice comes out filled with pain.

"Elise, this is what I have to do. To protect you, our son, our family. I have to do this. Matteo will protect you while I'm gone."

I don't give her time to respond; I pull her in for a long, hard kiss. I wish more than anything I could have more time with her to prepare. But this may very well be the last time I will be with her. What I am about to do could very well kill me. These people are highly trained agents. And one slipup, I will be done for. They aren't trained to take prisoners; they are trained to kill on sight.

I pull away from the kiss, and Elise's cheeks have a rosy blush on them. I take in each and every one of her features. Her perky nose, her flawless skin, her full lips, and her wide brown eyes. I lift her shirt and look at my son. I can see my name stretched across her skin from the bulge of her stomach. I trace it lightly and place my palm over her whole stomach. I can't help the smile that crosses my face. I am a lucky man.

I trace my fingers over every inch of her skin, remembering the soft texture. I pull her in for one last kiss, reveling in the feel of her soft lips against mine.

"I love you," I murmur. I place my hand on her stomach. "Both of you."

"I love you too."

My eyes shoot open, and I look at Elise in shock. She said she loves me. She just said it.

She reaches out, grabbing my arm. "Please, Luca, I love you too. Don't leave me. Don't leave us."

What I do next is something I'll never forgive myself for. I lean into her, pressing my lips against hers. And I take my hand and the small needle and bring it to her arm, injecting her with the fluid. She lets out a small cry before she falls limp in my arms. I lay her down on the bed and take in her sleeping form. She is so beautiful.

I walk out of the room, closing the door behind me, and walk to Matteo, who is waiting by the door. I hand him the keys to one of the cars.

"You know the code. You are only to leave if she goes into labor. Protect her, comfort her, be there for her," I say seriously to him. "She's going to be upset when she awakens. If I'm not back in a week and you haven't heard from me, assume the worst. Call me *only* if it's an emergency."

Matteo takes in every one of my commands and nods. I place my hand on his shoulder and nod at him.

I head up the stairs and away from my future. I close the secret door and lock it, typing in the code and concealing the keypad. Once I am in the car, I take in everything that has just happened.

This will be at the top of my list for most dangerous things ever done in my life. We will literally have to be perfect to pull this off. If we aren't, I may never get to see Elise or my son.

* * * * *

Two days later, we are sitting in front of their headquarters. The plan is foolproof, and everyone is in position. We've gone over it, had run-throughs, played out worst scenarios, and now we are ready. Romelo, Nicolai, and I will take down the eight agents inside. Everyone else is on standby to find the other eight once we figure their locations and end them. Then we will find the leaders of this organization and take them out too. All of us are ready to die for our families. If we fail at this, no one that is a part of the North Mafia will be safe.

I look over at Nicolai on my left, then to Romelo at my right. They both nod, signaling to me that they are ready.

Pure adrenaline is coursing through my veins, and I can feel chills running through my body as I anticipate what is to come. I take a deep, calming breath, clearing my mind of everything. Now is the time for the distractions to come to a halt. I take a step forward, and they follow close behind me.

I have left the beast caged up deep within me to control myself with Elise. And now he is clawing to get out. A smile comes onto my face in anticipation of the night ahead of me. This is going to be fucking fun.

Chapter 55

Luca

Imagine something that you are passionate about. Something that you love to do without hesitation. Once you begin with this passion, imagine the way you lose yourself. You immerse yourself deep into this action that you love. And you love it so much you do it so damn well. That is how I currently feel.

I can't help but smile as the man in front of me screams in agony. The smell of blood, sweat, and urine permeates the air. Puddles of blood are beneath my feet. There are five dead and three currently tied up for interrogation. One of them managed to lock the system before we could get to them, so we have no idea where the other agents are located. And we won't figure it out until someone tells us the code. This is a major setback, and if we don't do something soon, things for us are going to go straight to shit.

We made sure to leave two of the men alive and only one woman. It is a psychological form of torture. She is the one we are watching to crack. But honestly, with the way things are going, the man that is next looks like he is going to crack before I even make it to him.

"You know, I could sit here all night. I enjoy this, I really do." I smile at the man in front of me. I really am enjoying myself. This is the most fun I have had in a long time.

I pull the knife out of my holster and plunge it into this thigh. He screams, but I don't stop there. I drag the knife, watching, mesmerized, as the skin separates and blood wells to the surface.

"I just want the password," I say.

He looks at me through tear-filled eyes, his breathing ragged. "Go … to … hell …"

My smile grows even larger, and I shove my hand into the now-open wound on his leg. The warmth from his body is engulfing my palm, and I form a fist to force the skin to stretch even farther. He cries out in agony, and I cut him off by putting my hand around his throat. I can hear the woman behind me crying as she anticipates her fate. I can feel the man struggling to breathe and enjoy the look of panic in his eyes. His hands are jumping as he tries to pull at the ties, keeping them bound behind him.

I slowly pull my hand from the now-gaping wound in his thigh. He hunches over, spasming beneath my fingertips, and suddenly I am wrenched backward from the man. Romelo is holding me down, and Nicolai goes to check the pulse.

"Dammit, Luca, you were supposed to scare him, not kill him! He may have had the information we needed!"

I slowly try to pull myself down from this high that I am feeling from killing the man. I can't help it. I laugh. I hear the two agents left cussing behind me in fear. I slowly move, and Romelo lets me go. I stand up, dusting myself off. There is thick blood dripping off my hands, and I take notice that the female agent is literally shaking in fear. I pause in what I am doing and take slow, deliberate steps toward her. Her whimpers grow even louder the closer I get.

I squat in front of her and grab her face in my palm, forcing her to look at me. She squeals even louder as the blood from my fingers meshes where our skin meets. I study her face closely. She is attractive. But nothing compared to Elise. Her face is round. She also has freckles dusting her skin. The only thing about her that remotely reminds me of Elise is the way she is staring at me. Pure fear. I cock my head to the side to study her more closely, and she squeezes her eyes shut in fear.

"You won't get anything out of us. We have been trained for this kind of thing. No matter what you bottom-feeders do." The man that is still alive begins speaking.

I stand and look at him. He is staring at me with hatred. Loud, boisterous laughter fills the room, and I realize it is coming from me. I am laughing so hard my stomach is beginning to hurt.

"Bottom-feeders?" I am still laughing and can barely get the sentence out. I walk closer to him until I am standing over his tied-up body. He has to crane his neck to look at me.

"Please, I would love to know what you mean by *bottom-feeders*."

His breathing is slowly speeding up, and I can see the exact moment he realizes the mistake he has made. The room is silent when he refuses to answer me. Out of nowhere, an idea pops into my head. I walk back over to the girl. She begins whimpering loudly. The sound brings more excitement to my body. I stare at her dead-on as I speak to the man behind me.

"You know, how about we play a game?"

She closes her eyes, and more tears spill over as she shakes her head no. "Please, please, please no," she whimpers. If only she knew how much I fucking hate begging.

"I have people awaiting my orders and not a lot of time." I walk over to the black bag, pulling out a pair of pruning shears, and her cries grow louder. Romelo and Nicolai remain silent and waiting by the computer. As soon as I get these answers, it is time to move.

"I'm going to ask you a question." I motion to the man in the corner. I step closer to the woman, grabbing her hand, and she cries out. "Each time you don't answer me, well, that's a finger." I place the shears over her finger for emphasis. She tries to jerk away from me, but she is nowhere near strong enough.

"Here's the catch." I motion to the woman. "You can't answer me. Only he can. So whether or not your fingers stay intact is up to him."

I look at him, and his eyes are wide with shock as he stares at the woman and takes in her predicament.

"Let's get started, shall we?" I pull her forefinger in the shears. She starts screaming and begging, and I turn on her, giving her the most malicious glare I can muster.

"If you don't shut the fuck up, I won't be able to hear him. And if I can't hear him, I will assume he didn't answer." She immediately pulls her lips into her mouth, trying to stifle her sobs, and nods furiously.

"So …" I turn to the man. "What's your name?" I look at the man. He looks between me and the woman, and when he doesn't respond, I begin to press on the clippers. She screams as the blade barely punctures the thin layer of skin.

"Dylan! It's Dylan!" he shouts at me.

I stop what I am doing and watch as the blood begins to trickle down her finger. I wave the shears at him in a scolding fashion.

"You may want to answer a little sooner next time, Dylan."

The girl is behind me, sobbing like a crazy person.

"And tell me, Dylan, what is her name?"

He responds immediately this time. "Lissette."

I give him a sarcastic smile and nod. "Now, understand this, Dylan. Lissette. I have a wife at home. A lovely wife. And she's pregnant. With a son. I believe he's my son. She says she was pregnant *before* she was sold as a fucking sex slave by your superiors. I want my son and my wife to be safe. Which is why I need that password. So, Dylan, what's the password?"

He stares at me with wide eyes and closes his mouth.

Snip.

Lissette screams at the top of her lungs as her finger falls to the floor. The sickening snap of her bone being severed echoes throughout the room. She is still screaming, and the chills on my arms are growing into more excitement as I take in her cries.

"Password, Dylan."

He still doesn't make a motion to speak. I barely register Lissette in the background screaming and begging him to tell. Damn, this guy is an asshole.

Snip.

Lissette is screaming at the top of her lungs. Dylan looks torn, but he still doesn't step up. I move to chop off another finger when Lissette screams the password.

"Porthouse44! Please, it's Porthouse44. We change the password every hour. We just changed it. Just please, please stop!"

I register Nicolai and Romelo putting things in the computer and getting the information. Now that we are in the system and getting what we need, I can have a little more fun. I look at Lissette, giving her a scolding look.

"Thank you, Lissette, but it was Dylan I asked. Remember?"

Snip.

She is screaming again at the top of her lungs, and the sound is sending vibrations throughout my body. I shudder in pleasure at the agony that leaves her lips. I pull out my knife and hold it to her throat, ready to slice it open. She is trembling in fear, and her pants grow darker as she loses control of her bladder.

"Luca."

I stop immediately and look over at Romelo, who has an amused smile on his face. He motions toward Nicolai with his eyes. I arch my eyebrow at them. Nicolai won't meet my gaze. And when he does, I can see a red tint across his cheeks. Then realization dawns on me. I laugh out loud.

"Holy shit!"

I slowly stand and, without warning, throw my knife, loving the sound it makes as it penetrates Dylan's chest. He cries out in shock and looks at me with wide eyes. I step closer to him and pull it out, only to plunge it back in. I move lower and make sure to puncture his lung. When I finally pull it out, he is staring at me in shock, making a choking sound.

"You will not die quickly. You will suffer."

I grab the bucket of blood from the corner, where we've drained his fellow agents' bodies, dropping it in front of him. Before he can think, I kick the chair forward and plunged his head in the thick liquid. I hold his neck down as his body jumps and struggles. Eventually, it stops, and I leave him like that.

"Bring me some ice." A second later, Romelo is setting a bowl of ice in my hands. Lissette is sobbing in the corner. I place her fingers on ice in the bowl, kneeling in front of her, grabbing her face in between my fingers and forcing her to look at me.

"The only reason I am letting you live is that he wants you. If it were up to me, you'd be dead. Pull anything on him and I will drown you in your own blood. Just like Dylan here." I roughly push her face away from me and stand to look at Nicolai, putting on the most serious face I can muster.

"Do you have the address we need?"

He nods.

"Stay here, survey cleanup, make sure this place is destroyed. Leave no trace of us being here." I motion to Lissette. "She's all yours. If she escapes and we get caught, I will kill you before the cops can."

He nods in complete understanding. When I am sure he understands, I let my amusement shine through at the situation.

"Enjoy." I can't help but laugh as I walk away with Romelo to fulfill the rest of this plan.

"Luca!" I stop and turn around to face Nicolai. He has a serious look on his face as well. "Be careful. We don't need Elise becoming a widow now." He gives me a small smile, and I nod.

We all know we are far from in the clear. We have no idea if the leaders already know about our infiltration or not. Romelo and I just know the addresses where they reside and spend most of their time. We are literally going in blind. We have no time to do recon and no time to pick up on patterns, security, etc.

"You too," I say.

Nicolai is in just as much danger as we are. He has to get rid of this place and the evidence before anyone shows up. If there are reinforcements, we have no idea if they are headed this way. Romelo and I exit the building to fulfill the demands of the rest of the night.

Romelo and I are standing together, getting all our weapons loaded and placed in the right places on our bodies. We are silent. The only sound is coming from the reloading of our guns. Once we are ready, we finally face each other. Two leaders. We are both about to split up on our own and take them down. If we fail, we die. If only one of us succeeds, we die. We both have to succeed.

Romelo looks at me with a calm demeanor. He reaches out and clasps my shoulder. "No matter what happens, I'm glad to have been sworn in under you, Luca."

"Thank you, Romelo. I couldn't ask for a better man to be at my right side."

He nods in understanding. From the moment we were born, we have been inseparable. Romelo and I actually grew up together, whereas I met Nicolai years later because of complications with his family. All three of us are very close and would take a bullet for one another. So this is almost like saying goodbye. Until that phone call comes in that we have all done our part, we are not in the clear.

We both move to our cars and depart on our separate ways into the unknown.

* * * * *

Jared Mitchum. Head of the secret agency called A-417. Skilled in hand-to-hand combat, weaponry, torture, etc. Lives in the middle of nowhere. He has been itching to take us down for years. And he almost did. If I hadn't found Elise and gotten things in order, they were going to hit us hard. Kill every last one of us. Elise is my weakness. And in the time she was gone I neglected things I shouldn't have. And they were going to have the perfect opening. But I found her. And I doubled up my security. They were responsible for all the rats in the family. They were the ones that were working with Arianna and the other Trovoli's to take down the northern mob and give the Trovoli's immunity.

It was all a part of Eli Trovoli's plan from the start. Marry his daughter off and kill us using her. But when she proved to be useless, he planned on pitting her against me. Which is where Arianna came in. Getting information from Elise in her emotionally unstable state, which they then fed back to their capo, who in turn feeds it to the feds. Trying so hard to claw his way to the top. To power. To have us out of the way. There would be no one left to stand in his way. But what he didn't take into account was that I didn't trust them. And I foiled his plans. But now that Eli has given them their opening to rid the world of the Italian Mafia of the North, well, they are taking every chance they can.

Judging by the loud music I can hear playing and the lowlights he has currently pouring out of his upstairs window, I am guessing he currently is getting ready for something or about to go to bed. If he is going somewhere, I am screwed. My mind inadvertently wanders to Elise. I wonder how she's doing. I hate the way I left things, and I can't imagine what she is like right now. She is more than likely hysterical that I am not there. She probably won't even look at me when I get back, since I drugged her.

I let out a deep, frustrated breath. Damn. I should be focusing on how to get in the house instead of on Elise. It's distractions like these that will get me killed. I reach in my pocket and pull out my phone, unlocking it and scrolling to Elise's picture. The night of our wedding, the photographer emailed me all the photos from the wedding. Among them are a few individual shots of Elise. She looks so beautiful. So innocent.

I scroll to the photos we took the night of her recital. In that deep-red dress she wore. She looked absolutely stunning. Sexy as hell. There is a small smile on her face, and her violin is in her hands in front of her. She always has that small smile on her lips. Like she is shy. I just stare at the picture, memorizing every little detail. My love, my life, my wife, my Elise. This may be it for me. I really hope it isn't, though. I want to be there when she gives birth. I want to hold her hand and witness the first few moments of our son's life together.

Even if she goes into labor while I am away, I want to be able to go to her and see her once again and meet my son for the first time.

The lights in the window turn out, and I wait another ten minutes before I move. If this goes well, I will be there. For Elise and for my son. And if not, Elise will be free of me. And the Mob. No one knows where she is. She can start a new life and raise our son outside of this life.

I take a deep breath and move from my hiding spot. It is time to execute the plan.

I walk toward the door of the house of the man that has fucked up everything for me. Using my tools, I open the box on the side of the house, from the blueprints, and cut the wires to the security system. After, I bolt the lock back so that if push comes to shove, no one will be able to turn it back on without breaking off the lock.

I step toward the door and begin working on the lock. It opens within fifteen seconds of me messing with it. I slowly ease the door open and close it behind me, grabbing my gun from my holster and heading up the stairs. If my memory serves me correctly, the blueprints read that the master bedroom is up the stairs and to the left.

I carefully tread up the stairs, and to the left, the bedroom door is cracked. I am about to push it open when I register a shadow moving in the corner of my eye. I turn with my hands on the defense just in time for a Louisville slugger to connect with my forearms. My gun falls out of my hands, and I don't have time to dwell on the pain shooting through my arms. I immediately grab the bat with my free hand, absorbing the hit and bringing my leg out to kick my assailant hard. He lands on his ass and lets out a loud grunt of pain. He doesn't give me time to pick up my gun and comes at me again.

He swings at my face several times, not landing a blow. He swings past my face, and I grab his arm, yanking him close to me and smashing my head into his. He stumbles back, obviously caught off guard, and I don't give him time to recover. I immediately start swinging at his face, my fist connecting with bone. He stumbles back, and I can feel the excitement coursing through my veins. It's been a while since I've fought hand-to-hand combat. And this guy is good.

He regains his posture and comes at me swinging again after he takes his stance. I pull my hands up to block my face, and a searing pain flashes across my flesh.

"Fuck!" I cry out.

He has a fucking knife, and it connects with my skin, tearing through the fabric. He lunges at me, and I have to use all my strength as we both go crashing to the floor to dodge the knife. We roll backward, and I eventually kick him off me. Both of us are panting hard.

"Luca … fucking … Pasquino. I knew you'd show up at my door sooner or later. Tell me, how's your wife? Pregnant with another man's baby?" He laughs, as if it's funny. "I'm no expert on how you filthy crime bosses work, but isn't that not good for you—"

He doesn't have time to finish his sentence. I lunge at him, making sure my fist connects once again with his face. Before he can stand again, my leg shoots out, nailing him across the face. I can't get distracted by his taunting.

"You're right, I did fucking come for you, and I'm going to kill you." I pant.

He laughs. Fucking laughs.

"How's your dad these days? Last I checked, you had some traitors in your midst. How'd that go?" He chuckles again. The fucking bastard is trying to get under my skin.

He slowly moves backward toward the archway to leave, but before he can move, I throw another knife I have in my holster, pinning his hand down on the wall. I flip the switch and look at him. I immediately tense. Something in here isn't right. He is smiling. As if he won the lottery.

"You wanna know something about me? I'm a prideful man." He is speaking in riddles.

I only pull out my second gun and aim it for him. Out of nowhere, he pulls some kind of rectangular object with a button on it. His smile drops from his face.

"I'll be damned if I let someone like you be the one to finish me off."

His words cause a switch to flip within me, and I realize why he was so calm about getting his ass kicked, and kept running away toward a certain spot in the house. I immediately take off toward the door. I can hear his words as they follow me.

"Fuck you, Pasquino! Burn in hell!"

With that, the explosion goes off. The house around me is engulfed in a blazing inferno. I try my best to reach the door, a window, anything. The aftershock from the explosion blows my body forward. I feel as though a thousand needles are sticking to my skin. My body feels like it is broken in a thousand places. I open my mouth to cry out in pain, but nothing escapes my lips.

Then there is nothing. Only darkness.

She is smiling at me with such love and compassion, as if I can do no wrong. She is speaking to me, but I can't hear her. There is no sound. She reaches out to me, but when I reach for her, a white light flashes, and I am looking at her. The moment we met. She is sitting in her chair in her practice room, her back to me. And when she turns around, I know my life will never be the same. The scenery changes, and I am watching her walk up the aisle. She looks beautiful. Her eyes are wide and uncertain before me. She touches my hand once she reaches the altar, and the scene changes again.

She is underneath me in the shower on our wedding night. Her face is flushed pink. Her eyes are tightly shut, and her mouth is open as moans of pleasure escape her lips. The water from the overhead shower is cascading down her body, causing her long hair to stick to her body.

The scene shifts, and her hair is short. I can see her face more clearly now. She can't hide behind that thick curtain of hair. I am watching her from a distance. It's the day she decided to check out the library in our home. A small smile brushes its way onto her lips.

Next, I am watching her from behind as she stares in the mirror at my name now scrawled on her side. Tears well up within her big brown eyes.

As I reach around her to pull her in my embrace, the scene shifts, and I am watching her in the front yard. She has her face turned toward the sun, a small smile of appreciation on her face. I see her chained to the chair, screaming at me and pulling at her bonds. Her face is red from exertion.

I see her standing in that beautiful dress when my father was murdered, the look of fear plastered on her face.

Next, I am looking at her onstage. I admire how beautiful she is in red, the confidence she sports when she plays her violin. How she sways with the music and tends to smile at the most beautiful part of her melodies.

Everything dissipates, and I am watching her stare at me with hatred outside of my car. She mouths something inaudible and slams the door, running away from me. My world tilts, and I see her look of horror as she runs away from me out of the house and the look of hurt when I rescue her. The relief and happiness that radiate from her in my office when I tell her I won't touch her brother.

I see the flush of her cheeks when she gets aroused and the way she licks her lips. The way she looks at me as if I were a puzzle she is trying to figure out. I can see the adoration she has for me once we find out that we are going to have a boy.

The love and care that pours out of her. I see the need for me seared deep within her. The love when she touches her belly. And suddenly, I am looking at her. She reaches out and touches my face with her soft fingers. I can't help but close my eyes in comfort. I open them and stare into her lovely brown eyes. She opens her mouth as a smile crosses her face.

"I love you."

People say that when you die, your whole life flashes before your eyes. My life did. My love, my wife, my life. Elise.

Chapter 56

Elise

People tell you the pain is excruciating when you give birth. But even then, they don't describe it enough. They don't warn you enough.

I feel as though my body is being torn in half, like I will split open at any minute. The past few days have been rough for me. Luca fucking drugged me when he left, so when I woke up, he was gone.

I was in full-blown panic mode until Matteo took charge and calmed me down. We sat by the phone each day, waiting for Luca's call, but we never got it. And finally, two weeks later, while we were just sitting at the table, eating, my water broke. Matteo was calm and collected and had a plan. Arranged by Luca, no doubt. We left the bunker and went to the hospital, where my doctor was waiting.

I have been in labor for about nine hours now, and each contraction gets worse and worse. I squeeze my eyes shut in pain as another contraction rocks my body. I need someone here. I need Luca. But he is nowhere to be found. He should be here with me, ensuring that everything goes well. The nurse walks in, and I turn my gaze to her.

"We're going to check your dilation since your contractions are so close together." She smiles at me. It is a sweet smile.

Matteo is sitting in the corner of the room, and he looks as though he is going to be sick. But I have to give it to him; he is doing great being here for me.

The nurse places her hands between my legs, and her eyes widen. "Honey, this baby is ready to come out now," she states.

I can't respond, as another contraction quakes my entire body and I scream in pain. I told them I didn't want anything to numb the pain. The last thing I want in my system is a drug. I've had enough.

The doctor and a few more nurses swarm in the room. They are all talking to me and telling me to calm down, but I can't listen to them. The pain is too much. I feel a hand close on mine and look up to see my brother. My baby brother is standing over me, holding my hand. Even though he looks like he is going to be sick, he gives me a confident squeeze and a smile of reassurance. He stands back only next to me. I can't focus on anything other than the pain.

The doctors are all speaking at once, and Matteo is also.

"You can do this, Elise. You're strong." His voice is calm and steady even though he looks like he is going to pass out at any second.

I don't know how long has passed. Seconds. Minutes. Hours. But eventually, I hear it. The sweet cry of my baby boy. The doctor is smiling at me now, handing him to me.

Tears well up in my eyes and spill over as I cry. He is so tiny, so soft, and pink. His cry is so small. I take in his features. He is beautiful. I wish more than anything that Luca was here. I wish he were the one that was in here to witness this. To meet his son. But he isn't. And we have no idea where he is or what is going on.

I hold Luciano on my chest and cry. I cry along with my son.

Six Months Later

People always use strength out of context. They say it's what pure power is. They say it's what force is. They say it's when people do the hardest things they can. I think it's more than that. Hell, even I can't give an explanation for what it truly is.

I am sitting in the backyard of the cottage. There is a large blanket out, and Luciano is sitting up, smiling at me as he holds some of his blocks in his hands, swinging them around and tossing them on accident. I can't help but smile back. He is so precious. And so loving.

He looks a little like Luca but has gotten my features, giving him a soft look. His hair is dark as night, and he has Luca's eyes. Those gray irises that will forever haunt me in my sleep. Matteo and I are in the dark. Honestly, we have no idea what happened. But Matteo told me that before Luca left, he told him to assume the worst if he didn't contact us within the week. And he never did.

I'll never forget the way I felt. With just having the baby, and this revelation, I literally broke down and cried. I cried so hard, I felt as though my chest was breaking. I remember shouting at nothing in particular. He told me he would always be here. To protect me and Luciano.

I made Matteo enroll in school. Luca told us no one knows of this location or that we are here. We never got a call from Nicolai or Romelo as well, and I remember him saying they didn't know about it either. So with the life of the Mafia behind us, Matteo needs an education. The bills for the house are automatically drafted from Luca's account, and Luca left us four safes filled with cash and a packet of letters that he told Matteo will let me claim everything.

I don't want to, though. I don't want to accept that he is gone. Even in the hospital, the doctors offered to fix the scars that spell out Luca's name, but I refused. I didn't want him to be angry with me when he got back. And when we realized he wasn't coming back, I still couldn't do it. Call me sick, or twisted, but it is proof that Luca was here at one point.

I am fine during the day, but at night, when I lie in that room all alone, I cry myself to sleep, only to wake back up from nightmares. They are starting to grow a little less frequent, but they are still there, and I hate it.

I look at my watch, at the time. Matteo should be home in about three hours. I lay my head back and bask in the sunlight. It is a beautiful day today. Luciano laughs, and I open my eyes to find him drooling on one of his toys.

I smile and stand to grab him from the blanket, carrying him onto the back patio and placing him in an enclosed fence so that he can't go anywhere. I open the glass sliding door and step inside the kitchen to grab some water. That is when I hear Luciano laughing like crazy. I freeze when I hear a deep voice.

"I'm here now. I will protect you, *mi figlio.*"

I turn around, and the glass I am holding slips out of my hands, shattering on the floor.

There is a man with his back to me holding Luciano. Luciano is smiling at him with all the adoration in the world. My heart hammers in my chest, and my palms grow sweaty. My mouth immediately dries. Tears blur my vision as the man turns around, and I am met with a familiar set of steel eyes.

Luca. He glares me down, taking in my body like a man would a glass of water in the desert. He walks inside the kitchen, placing Luciano in his crib, which I keep in here. He's here. He's alive. He's fucking alive. His hair is shorter, and there is a scar above his eyebrow leading to the top of his cheek. It's faint, but I can see it. But he is here. He is alive, and he is breathing.

He stalks closer to me and places his hands firmly around my face. I reach out and place my fingers on his, making sure he really is here.

I choke on the sob breaking through my lips. We don't speak; we just stay like that, taking in each other's forms. He dips his head and captures my lips between his. I wrap my arms around his neck and squeeze my legs around his waist with everything I have in me. He is here. He is fucking here.

He carries me to the kitchen table, and I can feel the cooling flat surface against my back. Luca's hands run up and down my body, and moans of pleasure leave my lips. He rips my clothes off me, and I gasp from the suddenness, then his hands are back on me. He runs them up and down my body, squeezing my breast, and I gasp as a familiar heat pools between my legs. He pauses his ministrations, and I open my eyes to see him staring at his name across my side. He lightly traces it with his fingers and meets my gaze. He softly places kisses down each letter, and sparks of excitement travel down my body. I don't have time to register anything else.

His lips are back on mine, and his fingers are between my legs. He gives a groan of approval to find me wet and inviting. I don't even remember when, but his clothes are off, and I can feel his hard cock prodding at my soft entrance. I moan as he runs his thick head over my folds and finally pushes in me maddeningly slowly. I moan out loud as he stretches me with his heated length.

I gaze up at him, taking in his features. Features that I thought I would never see again. His eyes are filled with lust and adoration as he takes in mine as well. Once he is fully sheathed, he leans down, pressing soft kisses on my forehead, my cheeks, my eyes, my nose, and finally, my lips. He begins to move slowly inside of me. Then he thrusts hard, causing pleasurable sensations to spiral up my body. I cry out in pleasure, and Luca's lips are on mine as he swallows my moans.

His hands slide slowly up my body until he stretches my arms over my head and clasps my hand in his. His other hand snakes down my thigh, and he brings it up so that it is latched around his waist, and he penetrates me even deeper. I feel a cool breeze on my cheeks and realize that I am crying. I feel Luca's thumb wiping my tears.

"I'm so sorry, baby."

I can see the sorrow and regret filling his steel-gray irises. Before I can say anything, my climax comes out of nowhere, my inner muscles clamping down on his thick length as he plunges in and out of me. His thrusts become more urgent, and he stiffens above me. I can feel his cock pulsing inside of me as he finds his release. He collapses on top of me but doesn't pull out. He picks me off the table, and we slide down on the floor.

As I catch my breathing, I place my ear on his chest and close my eyes. His heart is beating strong underneath me. I remember his words.

"As long as it's beating, I will protect you."

I can feel him kissing the top of my head.

"I fucked up. You were mine to protect, and I fucked up. I'm so sorry. I'm sorry I left you alone. I'm sorry I wasn't there for you."

I look up at him, placing my hand on his face once again. I reach up and run my finger over the scar. "I thought you were dead," I whisper. "I thought … you died."

He grabs my palm and kisses it. "I almost did."

More tears fall down my face. "What happened?" I whisper.

"Everything had been taken care of. All that was left was for me and Romelo to fill out our duties. The bastard was a coward. He had rigged his whole house to blow. And he did it with me in it. The force of the explosion almost killed me, propelling me into the wall that fell and crushed me. I had a cracked skull and multiple broken bones."

That must be the reason his hair is shorter now.

"Lucky for me, Nicolai's cleanup didn't last as long as we'd anticipated, and after checking to see if Romelo needed backup, he showed up just in time to find me in the rubble. I've been in a medically induced coma up until a few weeks ago."

My breathing hitches. Luca almost died. He really was almost gone from me, forever. I roll over so that my naked body is straddling his hips. His eyes visibly darken as he watches me. I grab ahold of his face in mine and kiss him. Really kiss him.

* * * * *

I stand in my bedroom, getting dressed. Luca said he would watch Luciano while I clean myself up. I am about to walk back in the room when I pause in the archway. Luca is standing with his back to me, holding Luciano in his arms.

"I almost missed you. I almost didn't get to watch you grow up. I almost messed up my promise to protect you." He leans down and kisses Luciano on his forehead. "I love you. No matter what, I will be a better father than mine ever was to me. There will be times when you hate me, and I'm okay with that, as long as you know how much I love you, *mi figlio*. I love you so much."

Luca turns around and gives me a small smile, holding one arm out for me to come to him. I immediately walk into his embrace, and we stand like that in the middle of the living room, Luca holding our son in one arm, and me in the other. The two parts that make up his world.

"I love you," he says with all the tenderness and care in the world as he looks at me.

"I love you too," I say. And I mean it. With every fiber of my being, I mean it.

We don't have that tender, timid, lovey-dovey kind of love. Our love is a compulsion. A need. A dark and twisted obsession between us that no one can understand but us. I know someone from the outside looking in will think we are crazy, but they aren't the one married to Luca Pasquino, capo dei capi of the North Mafia. I am.

Epilogue

Five Years Later
Luca

"Mommy, look what I can do!" I watch as Luciano grabs a soccer ball and punts it hard across the yard.

Elise and I are sitting in the love seat on the patio. She is snuggled up to me, with her hand in mine.

After everything died down, we moved once again, but back to the United States. I wanted us to have a new start, so we moved out into the country.

I watch Elise as she beams at him in pride.

"That was amazing, baby!" she shouts.

His face lights up in joy. He lives to please his mother. He loves her with every bone in his body. And that is okay with me. Who wouldn't love Elise? Luciano loves both of us, but it is obvious who his favorite is. He looks just like her. I can already tell that when he grows older, he will be a heartbreaker with that face. The only thing he got from me are my eyes.

Luciano is a sweet boy. With all the love and compassion you can ever ask for in a child. In the past, I would have tried to rid him of that, but after Elise and I argued about it and she cried, I changed my mind. We will try a new style of training with him.

He takes off running across the yard to grab the ball with his little hands. Once he takes ahold of it, he sprints toward us. I swear this kid never gets tired. We had to resort to locking our room door on the nights we have sex because he walked in our room at two in the morning complaining about how he wasn't tired, right in the middle of us doing things. I still chuckle at the look of horror on his face because he thought I was "attacking" her.

He is a curious kid that explores the world around him with wonder and confidence.

When I woke up in that hospital years ago, I was so scared. I was scared of how much time had passed and if I missed Elise and Luciano. If I was out for years or not. I got lucky. I got so damn lucky. I should have died. The area he planted the bomb, should have killed me. But the debris that smashed my body also protected it.

Nicolai and Romelo were both by my side when I awoke. They were freaking out because they had no idea where Elise was located. Once I told them they calmed down and did some watching on her for me. I was shocked when they brought me back pictures of her with our son. Romelo actually brought back more than just pictures. He brought back a DNA test that proved Luciano was mine.

After that, everything was touch-and-go. I had to go through rehab and a whole lot of pain. The bruising and cuts eventually faded except for the scar over my eye. Elise likes to joke about it, saying it proves I am human. I am lucky I wore a thick layer of clothing. If I hadn't, my skin might've burned off.

"Mommy, can I sit next to you? Dad's had you all day."

I am startled out of my thoughts, and Luciano's pouting face is right in front of me. He gets irritated at the attention I give his mother sometimes, even going as far as to claim that I am "hogging her."

Elise slowly peels her hand away from mine and moves down to pick up Luciano, setting him down on her lap. She brushes his thick black locks from his face and gives him a light kiss on the cheek. He looks at me with eyes that can pierce a soul and sticks his tongue out. He then laughs and laughs and laughs. And I can't help but laugh with him. He is so competitive. Even competing with me for his mother's affection. That is a trait I can admire.

Elise begins humming something to him as she rocks slowly with him on her lap. I can't help the swell of love I feel blooming in my chest. She is a great mother. Patient, kind, understanding, loving.

She is everything my mother was and more, because when it comes to me, she stands up for what she believes in. My mother never said a word when it came to my training. She would turn away and, once my father was out of sight, would make me comfort myself. Once she realized my father wouldn't be upset with her for it, then she would acknowledge my existence. But Elise makes me see other sides of raising Luciano.

She knows that grooming him is inevitable, but we did come to an agreement about it. Even though she still doesn't want him trained to be the next heir, she has no choice. And today she is extra loving toward him, because she knows what today is. It is the marker where we up his training, meaning, it will get harder.

I plan on making him a man by the age of eight. In this world, being "made a man" means killing someone. When you can take a life, you are ready. I know it is harsh, but that is how things are. But we both agreed that I will not snuff the emotion out of him. I will not make him into an emotionless killing machine. I will not make him like I used to be—like I still am sometimes when I can't control it. He will be different. He is the exception.

Elise checks her watch.

"I should get going. Matteo is coming in town and said we could meet for lunch." She gives me a sad smile, knowing that once she leaves, we will begin his training once again.

Out of respect for her, I never train him around her. But if I am too hard on him, I never leave him alone or beat him like my father did to me. Surprisingly, it makes Luciano work harder and do everything it takes to please me. This method Elise talked me into is doing better than my father's method.

"I wanna go with you!" Luciano shout. He drops the ball and makes his way to Elise.

She kneels down in front of him. "Not today, sweetie. Today you'll be spending time with Daddy." She smiles at him, running her thumb along his face. He turns his nose up and makes a face.

"Oh, all right."

"Now, give Mommy a kiss." She smiles at him, and he smiles back, giving her a kiss on the cheek. "I love you." She smiles.

"I love you too, Mommy!" he says back. He turns to me with a mischievous grin, whispering to me, which is not much of a whisper at all, "I love you too, Daddy, but don't tell Mommy. I don't want her to get jealous."

I snicker at his words, pulling Elise in for an embrace. She hugs me back and cranes her neck to look me in the eye, her whole demeanor turning serious.

"Don't break him, Luca. I will never forgive you if you do."

I nod. She always says that to me. It took her a while to adjust to Matteo being a part of this life on the regular, and I'll never forget the hell we went through while she battled her emotions. I don't want that again. So this time, I will keep my promise. I slowly grab her hand, placing her palm over my heart. She looks mesmerized by the rhythm. She has done that ever since I came back to her that day after being presumed dead.

"I won't," I reassure her.

She nods and stands on her tiptoes to kiss me. She waves by to both of us, leaving the house.

It is just me and Luciano now. I take a deep breath.

"Luciano, I want you to go get your birthday present I gave you, okay?"

He nods vigorously and takes off into the house. He comes running back outside with a huge grin on his face. I walk down to the range we have, and he follows me, never once faltering. Like I said, this kid has a lot of energy. I take a seat on the edge of the patio, and he comes to stand next to me. We open the box together to reveal his gun. His first gun. I gave it to him when he was four and taught him how to use it. I didn't put real bullets in it until he turned five. Across the handle, "LUCIANO" is inscribed in silver.

I pick it up, handing it to him, and his whole demeanor changes. He is serious, just like I've trained him to be.

"What does that say?" I motion to his name on his gun.

"Luciano," he responds immediately.

"And who is Luciano?"

"I am."

"And who are you, son?"

"Luciano Pasquino, firstborn to Luca and Elise Pasquino."

"And who will you be?"

"I will be the next capo in line to the northern portion of the Mafia, the strongest and most powerful crime family in the United States."

"And if anyone says otherwise?" I ask.

He holds the gun up and shoots at the five targets lined across the range, hitting all of them dead center, except for the last one; he hit it too far to the left, and it spins and falls off the pedestal.

"Sorry, Dad. I didn't think about the weight lightening after I fired the first four shots. I'll be more careful next time." He smiles at me apologetically.

Have I mentioned my kid is a fucking genius?

He takes a seat next to me, letting out a flustered breath.

"I won't let you down again, Dad."

I look at him in shock and ruffle his hair with a smile on my face. If it were my father, he would have taken the gun and beat me with it for missing my target until the fear of missing had me pissing my pants. But like I promised Elise, I will be different.

"You could never let me down, *mi figlio*."

He looks at me, and relief floods his face. I stand up, smoothing out my clothing.

"Come on, we have about four hours until your mom gets back, and you know she'll be upset if we're not washed up and cleaned for dinner."

His face lights up again, and he jumps up, excited about whatever I am about to throw his way. No matter what I throw at this kid, he is excited to please me and make me happy. He wants to succeed and be the best at everything I put him up to. I remember when I forced him to face his fears. Elise wouldn't talk to me for a whole week because I made him face his fears. But he didn't even realize he was facing them.

When he walked in the house with dirt smudged on his face, the first thing he asked me was, "How'd I do?"

I stand there watching my son. If someone told me that I would marry a woman and fall in love with her, I would laugh in their face.

But I did marry her. And I fell in love with her. I had a child with her, and I would do anything and everything possible for her and for my son. Because they are my life. And I'll be damned if I let anyone take that away from me.

The End

Bonus Chapter

"Wake up! Wake up! Wake up!"

I groan in irritation, rolling over, trying to ignore the small body currently jumping up and down on my bed. As soon as I feel the body lift into the air, I reach out, snagging the small legs and yanking them hard. I hear Luciano grunt and begin laughing like crazy.

Elise rolls over next to me, grinning as well. She hasn't been feeling well lately, and I can't figure out why. So I took the day off to take care of her, and in the middle of our trying to sleep in, Luciano and all his energy comes bursting through the door.

I roll out of bed, dragging him by the leg with me, his body dangling upside down. He is still in a giggling fit as I walk out of the room and into the hallway with him. I flip him right side up, sending him down on the ground, and kneel down to his height.

"Luciano, you understand your mother is sick, right, *figlio*? So you can't be jumping on our bed at seven in the morning," I say, looking him in the eye.

He glares back at me, mirroring my eyes. "But it's snowing, and you promised we could play today," he whines.

I look at him in confusion, not at all remembering having that conversation with him. Then I remember last night, I was preoccupied with Elise while he kept asking me questions. So I just agreed to whatever he was yammering about.

I scrub my hand over my face in irritation. I stand up, walking slowly back to the bedroom.

"Just give me a minute," I murmur.

I hear his little footsteps behind me, and before he can get closer, I slam the bedroom door.

"Hey!" I hear Luciano's small voice on the other side of the door.

I chuckle to myself. He knows the rule. When the door is open, he can come in, and when it is closed, he can't enter. He learned his lesson about barging in a long time ago.

I walk to the bed, where Elise is still lying, crawling over her body.

I pull her into my arms, her snug body bringing me immediate comfort. She groans a little and rolls over, smiling lazily at me. After all this time, she still takes my breath away every moment I see her. I lean in, kissing her gently on the forehead.

"Your son is awake and ready to play," I mumble.

She chuckles lightly under me and reaches up to push hair out of my face.

"He's your son too, you know."

I lean in closer to her, inhaling her scent and placing a light kiss on her throat.

"Yeah, but he gets the enthusiasm from you," I mumble.

She lets out a sigh. "But he gets his stubbornness from you."

I chuckle, not caring to finish our little banter. I just want to be inside of her.

I kiss her softly, running my hands up her stomach inside of her nightgown, and she moans lightly.

"You said give you a minute! It's been a minute!" Luciano's loud knocks sound against the door. "Hello!" he shouts.

I let out an irritated growl, dropping my head against Elise's chest. I can feel the vibrations as she laughs. She begins petting my hair softly, making me just want to go back to sleep. Luciano has been absolutely restless these past few weeks; he has way too much energy for a kid his age.

"Why don't you go ahead and decorate the house with him?" Elise's soft voice tickles my ears. "You promised you would, remember?" she adds.

Apparently, I've been making a lot of promises I don't even recall making.

I prop myself up on my elbows, looking at her. "Would that make you feel better?" I ask.

A small smile appears on her face, followed by a blush as she breaks my gaze. She still can't keep eye contact with me. I eye her thick hair. If it were up to me, I'd cut it. But it isn't anymore. I've been learning to love her like a normal man can. It has been hard—don't get me wrong. There's so much that people take into account for others that I never even think twice about. But it makes her happy. And that makes me happy.

"You can't hide in there forever!" Luciano's voice comes through the door again, and Elise laughs.

I sit up taller. "I better go, before he breaks down the door," I say. I lean in, giving her a quick kiss on the lips, and head into the closet to find something warm to wear.

* * * * *

"I thought we were playing!" Luciano whines from the ground.

I look down at him. He is bundled up and warm, holding lights in his hands. I am currently in the tree, trying to wrap the lights around the branches. I should have just hired someone to do this, but when Elise bats her eyes at me, I am the first to do whatever she says.

"Well, your mother wants us to put up the lights. And it makes her happy to see the lights. So that's what we're doing," I say back to him.

He groans very loudly and falls back in the soft blanket of snow.

I go back to what I am doing when I hear a soft giggle. I look down, and Elise is standing in the snow below, bundled up, with a mug of steaming liquid in her hands. Luciano already has his in his hands, taking big sips. She is looking at me with a smile on her face.

I can't help but admire her beauty. She is so graceful and gentle. She is wearing a light-pink coat and brown boots and a hat and scarf. I frown a little, though, when I notice how pale she looks. I make my way down off the branch of the tree, walking over to her and gently taking the mug out of her hand, placing a long kiss on her lips.

"Thank you." I smile. She gives me a weak smile back. "What are you doing out here in the cold? You look like you're about to pass out. Have you been eating lately?" I ask.

She nods slightly, swatting at my hand when I try to feel her forehead. "I'm fine, Luca. Just a little tired," she says.

I look at Luciano. "See? That's your fault," I say.

His gray eyes grow wide, and he looks at Elise in shock. "I'm so sorry, Mommy! I'm so sorry!" he begins apologizing frantically, and I am about to laugh when Elise gives me a scolding look.

"Don't tease him!" she growls.

If there is one thing I love about her, it is her overprotective nature to her son. I can rarely shout at Luciano without her running in out of nowhere to scold me. That is in everyday life, though. She knows that when it is time for him to train, she isn't to be around.

Elise is kneeling, trying to reassure Luciano, and I begin to study her form. She really is sick. Her skin is pale, she is always tired, and she is getting smaller. I've tried taking her to the doctor, but she insists that it is just a small cold and she should be fine. That was last week.

"Come on, let's go inside," I say, trying to get her out of this freezing weather.

She stands and sways a little on her feet, and I immediately wrap my arms around her, trying to steady her. She opens her mouth to say something smart, I am sure, but before she can, I pick her feet out from under her, carrying her into the house, all the way hearing Luciano behind me screaming at me to wait for him.

* * * * *

"I told you I was not to be bothered today," I growl into the phone.

I look up from my place in the hallway, and Elise is at the piano with Luciano, trying to teach him the chords. She looks in my direction worriedly, and I give her a reassuring smile that everything is fine. She turns back to what she is doing at the piano.

"I need to take care of Elise. I can't be dealing with this right now. Can't it wait a day?" I growl in frustration.

"I'm sorry, Capo. This is the only time he will be in town. And relations with them are dwindling. We really need this," one of my men says back to me on the phone. I have given Romelo and Nicolai vacation time as well, so there is no calling them. I will have to go to this meeting on my own. When I don't even want to.

I let out an irritated sigh, pinching the bridge of my nose. "Fine. Tell him we can meet at ten. I'll be there by then."

"Yes, Capo." The phone hangs up.

Damn. I guess when you're the boss, there never really is an off day.

Since Christmas is coming up soon, there are opportunities to be made in the underground. Everyone is lax during this time, which means it is the perfect time for me not to be. To stay one step ahead of everyone.

"Daddy, listen!"

I look up from my brooding. Luciano is beaming at me in excitement. I push off the wall, walking toward them, and take notice of Elise. She has a small frown on her face. She opens her mouth to ask me about it, but I hold my hand up to stop her. Not in front of Luciano. He is too young to learn the trade yet. Right now is all about building his strength and training him for this position.

I turn my head at Luciano, and he grins back at me and begins playing the piano. He isn't amazing. Yet. He is still learning. So standing through about five minutes of him messing up and playing wrong notes is really testing my patience as a father. It is moments like this that I practice being patient. It is something Elise is so good at. I watch her through all the wrong notes, and she keeps a smile on her face, her eyes lighting up when he plays the right phrase.

Luciano finally finishes, and we both clap for him, showering him in praises. You can't hold a candle to his smile as he listens to us.

"Go upstairs and get ready for bed," I say sternly.

He crosses his arms, about to pout when I narrow my eyes at him. He immediately takes notice and nods, turning and running out of the room up the stairs.

I take a seat on the plush couch, pulling Elise atop my lap.

"Alone at last," I mumble.

She giggles at me, the sound sending blood straight to my dick. I pull her in closer to me, and she lays her head against my chest. I sit still for her because I know what she is doing. She is listening for my heartbeat. It is something she has done every day since she thought I died. And now it's become a habit for her.

"Who was on the phone?" Her voice comes out soft. She is hesitant to ask.

"Just business," I say. I begin playing with her hair, and she lifts her head, looking me sternly in the eye.

"Luca, you don't have to hide anything from me. I'm not that fragile little girl anymore."

I raise a brow at her, sitting up straighter and meeting her gaze. "Oh, really, now?" I say. I hold her gaze, saying nothing else. She tries to stare me down but immediately fails, looking down. I place my finger under her chin, raising it to meet my eyes.

"It's not that I think you're fragile, Elise. There are just some things I need to handle alone," I say, trying to reassure her.

A smile slowly breaks out across her face, and it brings me joy. It has taken me a while to get to this point. The point that I can interact with Elise like a loving husband should. It is hard as hell too, but I am almost there.

I pull her face into mine, giving her a soft kiss.

As much as I want to fuck her right now, that will have to wait. I have to get going. I slowly rise from my seat in the chair, and concern is written on her face. She hates it when I leave.

"Are you going to tell Luciano good night?" she asks.

I shake my head. "Not tonight. I've got to get going. Give him a kiss for me," I say.

I hate that sometimes I can't be there for my son. Like now. But duty calls, and I can't neglect it.

* * * * *

"I apologize to have to call you out here so close to Christmas, but this couldn't wait."

I stare at Don Reno.

"All the mess with the FBI and police has everyone on edge, and I think it's time we come together and show the world that we are united as one. That we are untouchable."

I narrow my eyes, slightly confused as to why he wants a face-to-face meeting for this.

"I agree. But what exactly is it you're trying to propose here? I'm pretty sure a phone call would have sufficed if you were just interested in us joining together."

He laughs aloud, and it pisses me off. He thinks this is funny?

"I am no fool, Capo. We both know that joining together will put me under your thumb. And I do not wish to be controlled by the North's capo, especially with you being as young as you are in this position. You lack experience that only age can bring."

Now it is my turn to laugh. It starts out as a light chuckle, but then it gets louder, until I am actually laughing at how fucking funny this guy sounds.

"I guess you haven't read my record, Reno. I think I've done more than a man even in your 'age' can only dream of," I say in irritation.

I notice his smile immediately drop, and I know he is angry. I don't give a fuck, though. Who the fuck does he think he is telling me I am not qualified.

I stand to leave.

"Thanks for the chat, but this was a complete waste of fucking time." I head toward the door, but his men continue standing in front of it.

"You misunderstand, Capo. I don't want to take your job. I want to help you."

I slowly turn, facing the fat bastard that dared to piss me off. I want to slice his fucking throat. But I don't have time for more war when things have just settled. Especially with me trying to raise my son. So I listen to his proposition.

He motions to the men behind me, and they nod, opening the door. A minute later, a small girl emerges. A child around Luciano's age. I immediately know where this conversation is going.

"This is my daughter Victoria." She walks in with her head down. She has bright-blue eyes.

I cross my arms. I don't know how to feel about this.

"Everyone knows the story of you and your wife. The marriage that made you the most powerful man in the United States. Maybe even the world. You gained power over the North *and* the South. We would like to be a part of that power. Of the family. Standing alongside you as equals."

He wants an arranged marriage. He wants my son to marry his daughter. Like Elise and me. This is the last thing I expected to hear. Do I want that for my son? Do I want to force him into a marriage with someone he doesn't even know? Like me? I recall the feelings I had for my father when he told me the news. I despised him in that moment. But I still loved my father, even after the fact. I knew that it was my duty. And I know it would make us stronger. I know my father was doing it with good cause. And I knew that just because I was married to her didn't mean I had to stay faithful to her. But there is no telling what Luciano will feel.

This could be a big opportunity for us. More power, more security. It's perfect. I realize I am thinking about the good of the family instead of the good of my son. And Elise. How would she feel about this?

"I'm guessing you want this when she's eighteen," I say.

He nods, and I turn my gaze to Victoria.

"Victoria," I say. She looks up at me. "Do you know who I am?" She nods timidly. "You're Luca Pasquino."

I sit back in my chair. "That's correct. You know my son?" I ask.

She shakes her head. So this man claims he wants a power move, yet he hasn't told his daughter why she is here.

"Are you planning on telling her?" I ask.

He nods. "I will, when she's ready," he says.

I nod in understanding. "Well, I want her to meet my son. I don't want them to think they're going to marry a stranger."

His eyes widen.

"You are going to tell him?" he asks.

I shake my head. "Not until he's ready."

* * * * *

I step into the house, about to head up to our bedroom when I hear music coming from the living room. Christmas music. I round the corner, and Elise is sitting in front of the fireplace, wrapping a small box. I smile at her small form. Her hair is falling over her shoulders in large waves. I walk up to her, taking a seat next to her.

"Oh, Luca, you scared me. I didn't even hear you come in." She giggles as she looks at me with those large almond-colored eyes. She frowns when she notices my mood.

"Is everything okay?" she asks, giving me a small smile.

I am about to shatter her happiness with eight words. I grab her hand in mine, looking at her ring finger and slowly rub my thumb over the soft skin.

"I've agreed to an arranged marriage for Luciano."

Her smile drops immediately. The room is silent. She shakes her head, slowly, not wanting to believe me. She jerks her hand out of my grasp.

"No ... no, Luca ... you wouldn't ..."

"Elise, you know that there are some things that can't be helped," I say, trying to calm her down.

But she is not having it. "No! Luca, no! You are not forcing him into some marriage just for your illustrious obsession with power!" she screams.

"Elise—"

"No!" she screams. She is getting hysterical. "You aren't forcing my baby to marry someone he doesn't even know. You're not tying him down for the sake of your own gain!" she shouts. "I won't let you!"

"Elise!" I yell.

Her eyes widen, and she immediately shuts up. She drops her gaze. I expect her to start crying, but she does the exact opposite. She jumps up from her spot on the floor and takes off toward the shelf that holds our family pictures. She takes every single one of them, one by one, and begins throwing them down, the glass shattering everywhere. I am shocked, to say the least.

"Elise, what the hell—"

"No! We don't need these. You don't give a fuck about any of us! You only care about you!" she screams.

She goes on a rampage, grabbing expensive vases, portraits, decorations—throwing everything that she can and breaking it.

I jump up, moving quickly, and snatch the vase out of her hand, restraining her.

"Elise, stop it!" I shout. I have no idea where this sudden burst of energy came from.

She jerks away from me, and her hand comes out to slap me. I catch her hand and stare at her in a mixture of shock and anger. And for once, she is staring at me with anger. She doesn't look away. She meets my gaze. I tighten my grip on her wrist, not liking her new-found courage. She flinches from the pain.

"I don't know what's gotten into you, but I'm going to warn you once. Stop it," I growl. I can feel my rage boiling up inside of me. I try my hardest to keep myself calm, but at this rate, I am losing miserably.

Elise's angry gaze slowly melts, and she begins crying. Fat tears rolling down her cheeks. And her bottom lip begins to tremble. She jerks her wrist out of my grasp and stares at me in disappointment before taking off out of the room.

I hadn't expected that at all. Not from Elise. I haven't seen that side of her in a long time. I let out a frustrated growl and flop on the couch. I wonder if my father went through this with my mother. Probably not. She never expressed her feelings for me to him. She was too afraid.

It takes me a while to clean up. I need to do something to calm myself down. That's when I notice Elise's gift lying in the corner. I pick it up, about to set it under the tree when I notice the label.

^{To} Luca ♡

Damn. I bet the last thing she wants now is to give me this. I set it down under the tree and head up to our bedroom. I push open the door, expecting Elise to be in bed, but she isn't.

I turn around and head to Luciano's room, and sure enough, she is in his bed, with her arms wrapped around his body. I gaze at them. Luciano and Elise look so much alike. If there is something I admire about her, it is her strong spirit. Her need to protect her son. She loves him so much, I can see why she is so angry about my decision. I kneel in front of them, pushing Luciano's hair out of his face and pressing a soft kiss to his forehead. My eyes move to Elise's sleeping form. There are tear streaks on her cheeks. I caused that.

"I'm sorry, Elise," I whisper.

I stand to leave the room. If either of them catches me in here, there will be hell to pay. Luciano is just as protective of his mother as she is of him. Once, he even tried to fight me for the sake of his mother's honor because I didn't like the cookies she made. I chuckle at the memory. She had burned them, for Pete's sake. They were inedible, but Luciano forced himself to eat them and told his mother that he loved them. And when I dared utter the words "They're burned," I was rushed out of that kitchen faster than you could say cookie. By my son.

I stand in the doorway, taking in their sleeping form once more. It looks like I will be sleeping alone for a little while. I look at Luciano and feel a small smile tug at my lips.

"Traitor," I murmur before stepping out of the room and going to mine. Alone.

* * * * *

"Shouldn't we be with Mom today?" Luciano complains next to me.

It's Christmas Day, and we *should* be with Elise. But it's the only time Don Reno can meet with us while his daughter is with him.

"We should, but we're going to meet some friends today."

399

I look down at Luciano, and he is frowning. Elise has been ignoring me all week. She is really angry about my decision. Even more so when she realized we are meeting them. I asked her to come with me today, but she refused.

"I don't want any part in that," she snaps at me.

I would have done something to her for her attitude, but her physique has been getting much, much worse, especially after the news. After the holiday, I am going to take her to the hospital, whether she wants to or not.

She wouldn't even look at me this morning. She hugged and kissed Luciano, but she refused to see me off.

We reach the front door, and I give a knock. I turn to look at Luciano. He is still so innocent. And the day that innocence is to be taken away is rapidly approaching.

"Remember, Luciano, be nice," I say.

He doesn't respond either. I think he is mad at me as well, but for the fact that he picked up on Elise's mood change toward me. And he knows it is because of me she is feeling that way.

The door opens, and a servant leads us into the house. "Right this way," he says. He reaches for the gift in Luciano's hands, but Luciano jerks away from him.

"No. I'm supposed to give this to Victoria," he snaps.

The butler gives an apologetic smile. "My apologies."

We walk into the large living room, and the don and his wife are sitting in their chairs as Victoria plays with her gifts. Reno looks my way and gives me a big smile.

"Glad you could make it, Capo!" he shouts, standing to greet me. A small frown appears on his face as he looks around me.

"Where is your wife?" he asks.

"She's feeling under the weather. I didn't want her to have to travel in this weather," I say.

He nods in understanding. "Well, I hope she feels better."

"Thank you," I say.

His eyes roam to Luciano. "Ah! This must be Luciano. It's nice to meet you, son." He smiles.

Luciano doesn't smile back, and usually, he is friendly even to strangers.

"You too, sir" is all he says, shaking Reno's hand.

"Well, Victoria's right over there." He motions, and Luciano nods, walking toward the girl. I move to take a seat on the chair and notice that his wife has disappeared. Reno notices my gaze and speaks up.

"She knows it's not her place to be here when no other woman is present."

I have to refrain from rolling my eyes. Great. So my son is going to have a docile wife, judging from Reno's treatment of his wife.

"Here." Luciano's gaze is as flat as his voice. Victoria is watching him with wide eyes as he hands her the gift. "I hope you like it. We skipped Christmas with Mom to give it to you," he growls at her.

She doesn't respond; she only nods. But I am shocked at Luciano's blatant dislike for this girl. She opens the gift, revealing the dress that he picked out. She smiles, looking at Luciano.

"Thank you," she whispers.

He only grunts in response.

"How about we leave the kids to get better acquainted and head into my office to talk business?" Reno says.

I nod, walking out of the room with Reno, leaving my son with his future bride.

* * * * *

We spend the day talking about business and upcoming opportunities. The day is boring, and I would have rather been home with Elise than here. I feel guilt eating away at me. She is right. I am being selfish by doing this. I am looking for more power. I could have skipped today and spent time with her and my son, but I am here.

A loud scream pulls me from my thoughts. We both immediately stand and head out of the room, looking to find Luciano and Victoria. Luciano is standing over her body, and he looks angry. As angry as I have ever seen him. Victoria is on the ground, with her curly pigtail on the ground next to her.

"What the fuck happened?" her father roars.

She immediately looks up with fear in her eyes, but I take in Luciano. He is vibrating with anger. He is so upset.

After a moment of silence, Victoria finally speaks up.

"I ... I wanted to show Luciano I was brave, that I could cut my hair, that it wasn't that important to me ... and I accidentally cut my hair too much," she utters.

Silence envelops us, and her father begins laughing next to me. He claps me hard on the back.

"Children are something else these days, huh?" he says.

I'm not listening, though. I am watching my son. He is looking at her with a vivid hatred in his gaze.

"I think it's time we head out. We still haven't had our time with Elise yet, and I really need to check on her," I say, smiling apologetically.

Don smiles at me and gives me a firm shake. "It was a pleasure having you, Capo. I think things are going to be fantastic for our future as well as theirs!" He smiles.

I smile back and call for Luciano, who comes immediately, not even stopping to say bye to Victoria.

* * * * *

The car ride is silent. Luciano is sitting next to me with his arms crossed over his chest.

"Do you want to tell me what really happened?" I say. I could see right through Victoria's little lie.

"I don't like her," he growls.

"Why not?" I ask.

"She's a spoiled brat that doesn't know when to shut her mouth," he says.

"Luciano, what did you do?"

"I cut her pigtail out," he says.

I look at him in shock. "You did what?" I ask.

He looks at me with a serious gaze and pulls the knife I got him out of his pocket.

"She thinks she's better than me. And she said mean things about Mom. So I made her shut up. And I told her if she ever said something like that again, then I would cut out more than her pony-tail next time."

I look at him in confusion. Where is all this aggression coming from? Luciano never acts that way. And it is very rare when we are training. Now he is acting that way toward the girl he is set to marry, of all people.

"I don't like her, Papa," he says.

"Luciano, why didn't she tell on you?" I ask.

"What she said was something her dad wouldn't like."

I open my mouth to ask him more, but we are pulling in the driveway and Elise is waiting for us in the doorway of the house. Luciano's eyes light up, and he jumps out of the car, sprinting the rest of the way to his mother, turning back to that happy-go-lucky child I am so accustomed to. I can't help but wonder if that is something I should keep an eye on.

* * * * *

"She was mean and ugly, Mama. You should have seen her." Luciano is sitting next to Elise, telling her all about Victoria. And he has yet to say anything nice about her.

Elise nods, listening, and occasionally looks at me in anger.

"Well, Luciano, you should give her a chance. You may like her," she tries to reassure him, but he scrunches his nose and shakes his head vigorously.

"No, no, no, Mama. She's annoying. I don't ever want to see her again!" he says.

She rubs his shoulders lightly. "Why don't you go open your presents?" Elise says.

As Luciano runs toward the tree, Elise's eyes fall on me. She stands, walking toward me, and when she stands over my body, she speaks.

"I hope you can live with yourself. You sentenced our son to a life with a woman he hates," she hisses.

I grab her arm, pulling her down, and she squeals as she falls on my lap. I press a long, hard kiss to her lips. "I don't want to fight you, at least. I'm sorry. I was wrong."

Her eyes widen at my admission. I place my palm against her cheek. She is so cold and pale.

"I love you," I say. "I didn't know I was going to feel that way when I first was told I had to marry. But it happened. Maybe we did get lucky falling in love, and I'm sorry I compared Luciano to myself when I found out the news. I wasn't thinking. But I can't change anything now. So please don't stay mad at me. I just want to love you and be near you today."

She stares at me and slowly smiles, leaning into me. I kiss her forehead, enjoying the closeness of her body. I miss it.

Luciano comes running over to us with a box in his hand.

"This one's for you, Daddy!"

He hands me the box. It is the one Elise was up wrapping late that night. I feel Elise tense atop me.

"Maybe now isn't the best time to open it," she murmurs.

I look at her in confusion. "Now is the perfect time," I say.

I slowly tear the wrapping paper off and pull the top off the box to reveal pregnancy tests. Three, to be exact. My heart stops and my eyes widen. I reach in, grabbing one and looking at the results. Positive. I look up at her with a shocked expression.

"Really?" I whisper.

She smiles at me, nodding, tears beginning to form in her eyes. I feel my eyes burn from tears beginning to well up. Excitement burns deep inside of me. She isn't sick; she is pregnant. We are going to have a baby. Another one. That explains her constant mood swings and lack of eating.

I place my palm on her stomach, which will soon grow from the child now inside of her. I laugh out loud, feeling so happy. I pull her closer to me, kissing her again. And again. And again.

* * * * *

Luciano sits in his bed, looking at us in confusion. Elise and I are in his bedroom, ready to tell him the big news.

"Luciano, we have something to tell you. Some really big news," I say.

Now it is Elise's turn to speak. "We're having a baby! You're going to be a big brother." She smiles.

Luciano's eyes grow as wide as saucers, and he jumps up on his bed.

"Really?" he shouts. "I'm going to be a big brother?" He starts running around the room in excitement.

Elise laughs and smiles at him.

Two Months Later

The nurse is placing the ultrasound on Elise's belly. She is holding my hand as we look at the screen. The nurse turns to us, smiling.

"Is this your first baby?" she asks.

Elise shakes her head. "No, we have a son already," she says.

Luciano isn't with us today, though. He is with Romelo, preparing.

"Oh, so I bet you guys can't wait to see what baby number 2 is, huh?" The nurse smiles at us, turning her head back to the screen. The room is silent.

"Are you guys ready to know what you'll be having?"

We both nod in excitement.

She turned to us, smiling. "Well, it looks like you two will be having a beautiful baby ..."

About the Author

Haley Stuart was born and raised in the small town of Liberty City, Texas. She graduated from the University of North Texas in 2018 and now resides in Dallas with her dog Hazel. Haley fell in love with books at a young age and turned that love into writing. If she isn't writing she is reading, dancing, or binge-watching anime. Haley is also the author of the "Pet" series, "The Blood King" series, and more that can be found on Wattpad, Inkitt, And Radish.

For more information and updates on Haley's works!
Instagram: @haleyinez_
Wattpad: @haleystuart2
Inkitt: @haleystuart2
Radish: @haleystuart2

Lightning Source UK Ltd.
Milton Keynes UK
UKHW010747030222
398149UK00001B/7